About t

Jane Porter loves central ⌐⌐⌐⌐⌐⌐⌐ ⌐⌐⌐⌐⌐ ₁oothills and miles of farmland, rich with the sweet and heady fragrance of orange blossoms. Her parents fed her imagination by taking Jane to Europe for a year where she became passionate about Italy and those gorgeous Italian men! Jane never minds a rainy day – that's when she sits at her desk and writes stories about far-away places, fascinating people, and most important of all, love. Visit her website at: janeporter.com

Michelle Smart is a *Publishers Weekly* bestselling author with a slight-to-severe coffee addiction. A bookworm since birth, Michelle can usually be found hiding behind a paperback, or if it's an author she really loves, a hardback. Michelle lives in rural Northamptonshire in England with her husband and two young Smarties. When not reading or pretending to do the housework she loves nothing more than creating worlds of her own. Preferably with lots of coffee on tap. Visit her website: michellesmart.co.uk

USA Today bestselling, *RITA*®-nominated, and critically acclaimed author **Caitlin Crews** has written more than 130 books and counting. She has a Master's and Ph.D. in English Literature, thinks everyone should read more category romance, and is always available to discuss her beloved alpha heroes. Just ask. She lives in the Pacific Northwest with her comic book artist husband, is always planning her next trip, and will never, ever, read all the books in her to-be-read pile. Thank goodness.

The Crown

Trading
the Crown

JANE PORTER

MICHELLE SMART

CAITLIN CREWS

MILLS & BOON

First Published in Great Britain 2023
by Mills & Boon, an imprint of HarperCollins*Publishers* Ltd,
1 London Bridge Street, London, SE1 9GF

www.harpercollins.co.uk

HarperCollins*Publishers*
Macken House, 39/40 Mayor Street Upper,
Dublin 1, D01 C9W8, Ireland

Trading the Crown © 2023 Harlequin Enterprises ULC.

Not Fit for a King © 2011 Jane Porter
Helios Crowns His Mistress © 2016 Michelle Smart
The Billionaire's Secret Princess © 2017 Caitlin Crews

ISBN: 978-0-263-31960-6

NOT FIT
FOR A KING

JANE PORTER

For Tessa Shapcott, who bought my first book in January 2000 and changed my life forever!

PROLOGUE

Palm Beach, Florida

"You *do* look like me." Princess Emmeline d'Arcy's voice was hushed as she slowly circled Hannah, her arched eyebrows pulling over deep blue eyes. "Same face, same height, same age…if our hair color was the same…we could pass for twins. Incredible."

"Not exactly twins. You're half my size, Your Highness," Hannah said, suddenly self-conscious next to the very slim Princess Emmeline. "Itty-bitty, as we say in America."

Princess Emmeline didn't appear to hear her, too busy examining Hannah from head to toe. "Do you color your hair? Or is that natural? Either way, it's gorgeous—such a rich, warm shade of brown."

"It's from a box. It's several shades darker than my natural color, and I do it myself," Hannah stammered.

"Can you buy your color here in Palm Beach?"

Hannah couldn't believe that the stunning golden-blond princess would be interested in her shade of brown hair dye. "I'm sure you can—it's sold everywhere."

"I meant, could *you* buy it for me?"

Hannah hesitated. "I could. But why would you want it, Your Highness? You're stunning, so beautiful as you are."

Princess Emmeline's full lips curved and yet her expression looked bleak. "I thought maybe for a day I could be you."

"What?"

The princess walked away from Hannah, moving to stand at one of the tall windows of her lavish hotel suite where she gazed out over the hotel's elegant, tropical Florida garden.

"I've made a terrible mess of things," Princess Emmeline said softly, hands lifting to press against the glass as if she were a captive instead of the world's most celebrated young royal. "But I can't even leave here to sort things out. I'm followed wherever I go—and it's not just the paparazzi—but my bodyguards, my secretary, my ladies-in-waiting." Her slim shoulders shifted and her fingers curled until her hands were fists against the glass. "For just one day I want to be normal. Ordinary. Maybe then I could take care of something, make this nightmare I'm in go away."

The anguish in Emmeline's voice made Hannah's chest squeeze tight. "What's happened, Your Highness?"

Princess Emmeline gave her head the slightest shake. "I can't talk about it," she said, her voice breaking. "But it's bad… It'll ruin everything…"

"Ruin what, Your Highness? You can tell me. You can trust me. I'm very good at keeping secrets and would never break your confidence."

The regal princess lifted a hand to her face and swiftly wiped away tears before turning from the window to look at Hannah. "I know I can trust you. That's why I'm asking for your help."

The princess took a deep breath. "Tomorrow, switch places with me for the afternoon. Be me and stay here in the suite and I'll be you. I won't be gone long—a couple of hours, four or five at the most—and then I'll return and we'll switch back again."

Hannah sat down in the chair next to her. "I want to help you, but I have to work tomorrow. Sheikh Al-Koury doesn't give time off, and even if he did, I don't know the first thing about being a princess."

Emmeline crossed the rich crimson carpet to take a seat

opposite Hannah's. "Sheikh Al-Koury can't make you work if you're ill. Not even he would drag a sick woman from her bed. And you wouldn't have to leave the hotel. I could book some spa treatments for you tomorrow and you could be pampered all afternoon—"

"But I sound like an American, not a Brabant royal!"

"I heard you introduce your sheikh boss in French yesterday at the polo tournament. You speak French perfectly, without even an accent."

"That's because I lived with a family in France one year during high school."

"So speak French tomorrow. It always throws Americans." Emmeline suddenly grinned. "We can do this. Bring hair color with you in the morning, a blond color for you and your chestnut color for me, and we'll do our hair and change clothes and think what an adventure it'll be!"

There was something infectious in Princess Emmeline's laugh and Hannah reluctantly smiled back. If Hannah had met the princess in school she would have wanted to be her friend. There was something special about Emmeline, something engaging. "It'd only be for a couple of hours, just tomorrow afternoon. Right?"

Emmeline nodded. "I'll be back before dinner."

Hannah chewed the inside of her lip. "Will you be safe, going out on your own?"

"Why wouldn't I? People will think I'm you."

"But you're not doing anything dangerous, are you? Putting yourself in harm's way?"

"Absolutely not. I'm staying in Palm Beach, not traveling anywhere. Say you'll help me, Hannah, please."

How could Hannah say no? The princess was positively desperate and Hannah had never been able to say no to someone in need of help. "I'll do it, but just for the afternoon."

"Thank you! *Merci!*" Emmeline reached out and clasped Hannah's hand in her own. "You are an angel, and you won't regret this, Hannah. I promise you."

CHAPTER ONE

Three days later—Raguva

BUT Hannah did regret it. She regretted it more than she'd ever regretted anything.

Three days had passed since she'd switched places with Emmeline. Three endless days of pretending to be someone she wasn't. Three days of living a lie.

Hannah should have stopped this yesterday before heading to the airport.

She should have confessed the truth when she could have.

Instead she'd boarded the royal jet and flown to Raguva as if she really was Europe's most celebrated princess instead of an American secretary who just happened to look like the stunning Princess Emmeline...

Should have, could have, would have...

Hannah held her breath, trying to contain her panic. She was in serious trouble now, and the only way she—and Emmeline—would survive this disaster intact was by keeping a cool head.

Not that remaining cool and calm would be easy given that she was just about to meet Princess Emmeline's fiancé, the powerful King Zale Ilia Patek, a man rumored to be as brilliant as he was driven, in front of his entire court.

Hannah knew nothing about being royal, or European. Yet here she was, squeezed into a thirty-thousand-dollar couture gown with a delicate diamond tiara pinned to her artificially lightened hair after having spent a long, and very frantic night cramming everything she could learn about Zale Patek of Raguva into her head.

Only a fool would appear before a king and his court, pretending to be his fiancée.

Only a fool, she repeated, knowing no one was holding a gun to her head, no one was forcing her to pretend to be Emmeline. No one but herself. But she'd pledged her help to Emmeline, given the princess her word. How could she abandon the princess now?

Hannah stiffened and gulped air as the tall gold and cream doors swung open, revealing the palace's grand crimson throne room.

A long row of enormous chandeliers shone so brightly overhead that she blinked, overwhelmed by the glittering and hum of sound.

Hannah blinked again and focused on the throne dais at the far end of the room. A long red carpet stretched before her. Then a voice announced her, first in French, and then Raguvian, silencing the buzz of conversation— "Her Royal Highness, Princess Emmeline of Brabant, Duchess of Vincotte, Countess d'Arcy."

The formal introduction made Hannah's head swim. How could she have thought swapping places with Emmeline was a good idea?

Why hadn't she perceived the dangers? Why hadn't she realized that Emmeline's plan had been far from foolproof?

Because she'd been too busy enjoying the decadent spa treatments, thinking herself lucky to have this escape before she returned to her exhausting, but fascinating life as secretary for impossible to please Sheikh Makin Al-Koury of oil-rich Kadar.

Only Emmeline had never returned.

Instead she'd called and texted, begging Hannah to keep up the charade a few more hours, and then a day after that, saying there was a snag, and then another, but not to worry, everything was fine, and everything would be fine. All Hannah had to do was keep up the charade a little longer.

One of the ladies-in-waiting at Hannah's elbow whispered, "Your Royal Highness, everyone waits."

Hannah's gaze jerked back to the throne at the end of the long red carpet. It seemed so far away, but then suddenly, somehow, Hannah was moving down the plush crimson carpet, placing one trembling foot in front of the other. She wobbled in her foolishly high heels, and felt the weight of her heavy silk gown with the thousands of crystals, but nothing felt as uncomfortable as the intense gaze of King Zale Patek as he watched her from his throne, his unwavering gaze resting on her face.

No man had ever looked at her so intently and her skin prickled, heat washing through her, cheeks on fire.

Even seated, King Patek appeared imposing. He was tall, broad-shouldered and lean, and his features were handsome and strong. But it was his expression that made her breathless. In his eyes she saw possession. Ownership. They weren't to be married for ten days but in his eyes she was already his.

Hannah's mouth dried. Her heart raced. She should have never agreed to play princess here. Zale Patek of Raguva would not like being played the fool.

Reaching the dais, she gathered her heavy teal and blue skirts in one hand and sank into a deep, graceful curtsy. Thank God she'd practiced this morning with one of her attendants. "Your Majesty," she said in Raguvian, having practiced that, too.

"Welcome to Raguva, Your Royal Highness," he answered in flawless English. His voice was so deep it whispered through her, smooth, seductive.

She lifted her head to look up at him. His gaze met hers and held, demanding her full attention. She sucked in a quick breath of surprise. This was the thirty-five-year-old king of Raguva, a country adjacent to Greece and Turkey on the Adriatic Sea. He looked younger than thirty-five. Furthermore, he was ridiculously good-looking. The photographs on the Internet hadn't done him justice.

Impressions continued to hit her one after the other—short dark hair, light brown eyes and a slash of high cheekbone above a very firm chin.

The intelligence in his clear steady gaze made her think of all the great kings and Roman rulers who'd come before—Charlemagne, Constantine, Caesar—and her pulse quickened.

He was tall, imposing, powerfully built. His formal jacket couldn't hide the width of his shoulders, nor the depth of his muscular chest. He'd been born a prince but had trained as an athlete and become a star footballer through dedication to his sport. But he'd walked away from his incredible success when his father and mother had died in a tragic seaplane accident five years ago that had taken the lives of all onboard.

She'd read that Zale Patek had rarely dated during the decade he played for two top European football clubs because football had been his passion and once he'd inherited the throne, he'd applied the same discipline and passion to his reign.

And this man, this fiercely driven man, was to be sparkling, enchanting Princess Emmeline's husband.

At the moment Hannah didn't know whether to envy her or pity her.

"Thank you, Your Majesty," she answered, slowly lifting her head to look into his eyes. His gaze met hers squarely and she felt a sharp jolt to her heart, her chest squeezing tight in protest.

It was like a thunderbolt of sensation—hot, electric—and her knees buckled, and her whole body felt weak.

Trembling in her heels, she watched King Patek rise and descend the steps of the dais. He reached for her hand, carried it to his mouth, brushing his lips across the back of her knuckles. The touch of his mouth sent yet another shudder through her, her body tingling from head to toe.

For a moment silence hung over them, surrounded them, an

intimate, expectant silence that made her grow warm and her cheeks burn. Then King Patek turned her around to face his court. Applause filled the Throne Room and before she knew it, King Patek was introducing her to the first of his many advisors.

Moving down the crimson carpet, the king would pause to introduce her to this important person or that, but the sensation of his skin against hers made it impossible for her to concentrate on anything. The names and faces blurred together, making her head swim.

Zale Patek was in the middle of introducing Emmeline to yet another member of his court, when he felt her hand tremble in his. Glancing down at her, he saw fatigue in her eyes and a hint of strain at her mouth. Time for a break, he thought, deciding the rest of the introductions could wait until dinner.

Exiting the Throne Room, Zale led her through a sparsely furnished antechamber, and then a small reception room, ending in the Silver Room, a room that had been a favorite of his mother's.

"Please," he said, escorting her to a petite Louis IV chair covered in a shimmering silver Venetian embroidered fabric. An oversize silver and crystal chandelier hung from the middle of the room and Venetian mirrors lined the oyster-hued silk that upholstered the walls.

It was a pretty room and it sparkled from all the silk, silver and glass, but nothing in the room could compare to the princess herself.

She was stunning.

Beyond stunning.

As well as cunning, manipulative and deceitful, which he hadn't learned until after their engagement.

It'd been a year since he last saw Emmeline—at the announcement of their betrothal in the Palace of Brabant—and they'd only spoken twice before that, although of course he'd seen her at various different royal functions while growing up.

"You look lovely," he said as Emmeline sank gracefully into the fragile chair, her full teal and aqua skirts clouding around her, making him think of a mermaid perched on a rock. And like the sirens of lore, she used her beauty to lure men in—before dashing them on the rocks.

Which wasn't a quality Zale wanted in his wife, or Raguva's future queen.

Strong, calm, steady, principled—those were the qualities he wanted, qualities he'd come to realize she didn't possess.

"Thank you," she answered, a delicate pink appearing in her flawless, porcelain skin.

The bloom of pink in her cheeks stole his breath and made his body harden.

Had she truly just blushed? Did she think she could convince him she was a virginal maiden instead of a jaded, promiscuous princess?

And yet despite all her character flaws, in person she was nothing short of physical perfection with her exquisite bone structure, cream complexion and darkly fringed blue eyes. Even as a young girl Emmeline had been more than pretty with her wide blue eyes that seemed to see everything and know far too much, but she'd grown into an extraordinary beauty.

His father had been the one to suggest Princess Emmeline d'Arcy as a suitable bride. Zale had been fifteen at the time, Emmeline just five, and Zale had been horrified by his father's preliminary arrangements. A chubby little girl with blue eyes and dimples for a future wife? But his father had assured him that she'd be a stunning woman one day, and his father had been right. There wasn't a more beautiful or eligible princess in Europe.

"You're here at last," he said, hating that he derived so much pleasure from just looking at her. He should be distant, disgusted, turned off. Instead he was curious. As well as very physically attracted.

Her head dipped. "I am, indeed, Your Majesty."

She did that so prettily, he thought, the edge of his mouth

curving in a slightly cynical smile. The blushes, the shyness, the wide-eyed innocence. "Zale," he corrected. "We've been engaged this past year."

"And yet we've never once seen each other," she answered, lifting her chin, porcelain cheeks stained pink.

He raised an eyebrow. "By your choice, Emmeline, not mine."

Her lips parted as if to protest before she pressed them to- gether again. "Did that bother you?" she asked after a moment.

He shrugged, knowing what he couldn't—wouldn't—say. That he knew Emmeline had spent the past year continuing to see her Argentine playboy boyfriend, Alejandro, despite being betrothed to Zale.

He wouldn't say that he knew her seven-day trip to Palm Beach this past week had been to watch Alejandro play in a polo match. Or that for the past several days Zale hadn't even been sure Emmeline would actually get on the plane and come to Raguva for their wedding scheduled for June 4, ten days from now.

But she had.

She was here.

And he fully intended to use these next ten days before their wedding to discover if she was ready to honor her com- mitments to him, their countries and their families, or if she planned to continue playing games and playing him. "I'm glad you're here now," he responded. "It's time we began to get to know each other."

She smiled, a slow, radiant smile that lit her eyes from the inside out and he felt heat and pressure build in his chest.

How absurd that Emmeline's beauty literally took his breath away. Ridiculous that he could be so moved by a woman in a ball gown and jewels. Diamond and sapphire rings covered her fingers and the diamonds in the tiara perched on her golden head glinted, throwing off tiny prisms of light.

"So am I," she answered. "And it's a completely different world than Palm Beach."

"It is at that," he agreed, intrigued despite himself. Charmed by everything about her right now. "I'm sorry I couldn't welcome you last night when you arrived. There is so much tradition attached to the job. Five hundred years of protocol."

"I understand."

She should. She'd agreed to this arranged marriage, too, despite being passionately in love with her boyfriend of five years. "Do you need any refreshment? Dinner is at least an hour away."

"No, thank you, I can wait."

"I heard you hadn't eaten anything today, or even last night after you arrived."

She gave him a slightly mocking look, her finely arched eyebrows rising. "Which of my attendants tattled on me?"

"My cooks were worried when you refused your meals. They feared they'd failed to whet your appetite."

"Not at all. The breakfast and lunch trays looked delicious but I was very aware that at five I'd have to fit into this gown," she said with a gesture to her curvaceous body swathed in teal silk and intricate jeweled designs.

"You're not on a starvation diet, are you?"

She glanced down at her figure. "Do I look in danger of fading away?"

Zale's lips twitched. No, she did not look like she was starving. The gown's fitted bodice revealed full, firm breasts while her waist nipped in before curving out again over very feminine hips. The gown's rich hues highlighted her smooth, creamy skin, the startling blue of her eyes and the pink pout of her generous lips. She looked lush, ripe, edible.

He felt a hot shaft of desire, and Zale fought a sudden urge to touch her. Taste her. To take his tongue to her softly parted lips, to sink his teeth into their softness, then brush his lips along her satin skin—

He broke off as his body hardened, tightening, making the fit of his trousers almost unbearable. It'd been a year since he taken a woman into his bed, wanting to respect his engagement to Emmeline, but it'd been a long year and he looked forward to consummating their marriage in ten days.

Should they marry.

He glanced down at her and discovered she was staring steadily back at him, her blue gaze unflinchingly direct. As his gaze locked with hers, he felt raw, primal desire surge through him.

He'd have her, too, he vowed, even if he didn't make her his queen.

Breathlessly Hannah dropped her gaze, breaking that strange hold Zale had had on her. When looking into his eyes—all amber color and fire—she'd felt absolutely lost, snared by her senses, drowning in sex and sin.

It'd been forever since she'd felt this way.

Wanting something so much it almost hurt…

She drew a slow breath, trying to slow the racing of her heart, trying to pretend her cheeks and lips didn't burn. But oh, they did…

He was stirring something inside of her, something that hadn't been stirred in years…

It'd been a long, long time since she'd been serious about anyone, and even longer since she'd wanted to be loved by anyone. Hannah enjoyed sex when shared with someone special. The trouble was, there hadn't been anyone special, not since she graduated from Texas A&M University four years ago. Twenty-one and thrilled to have earned her degree, Hannah had expected her college boyfriend to propose. Instead he broke up with her, announcing that he was ready to move on and begin seeing other women.

But now, for the first time since Brad had dumped her, she felt something…

For the first time in four years she wanted something…

Restless, aching, Hannah crossed her legs beneath her gown's full silk skirt and petticoat, feeling the rasp of the lace garter belt against her thighs even as her inner thighs brushed delicate skin exquisitely bare. Emmeline's lingerie, she thought despairingly, remembering in a painful rush that gorgeous, virile Zale Patek belonged to Emmeline, too.

Hannah froze, her breath catching in her throat, shocked that she could forget for even a moment who she was, what she was doing here and why.

You are not Emmeline, she told herself furiously. *You will never be Emmeline, either.*

She rose, briefly glanced at Zale as she smoothed her skirt with quick, flustered hands. "If there's time, I'd like to freshen up in my room before dinner."

"They won't even call us to the dining room for another half hour."

"Will you excuse me then?"

"Of course. I'll send someone to escort you to the dining hall when it's time."

She left the Silver Room quickly, the heavy embroidered skirts swishing as she hurried to the stairs that would take her to her suite of rooms on the second floor. Madness, madness, madness, she chanted over and over, her stomach churning, heart racing as she climbed the stairs as fast as she could.

Please let Emmeline be on the way. Please, please let there be a message from Emmeline saying she was on the plane and everything was fine and Hannah would soon be free to leave.

Inside her suite, Hannah shut the door and dashed for the nightstand next to her bed where she retrieved her phone and checked for messages, first text, then voice, but there was nothing. Nothing. Not a word.

Nothing. *Nothing!*

Hannah put a hand to her queasy middle, dangerously close to throwing up all over the green, cream and pink antique Aubusson rug beneath her feet.

It'd been hours since Emmeline's last text. Where was she? Why wouldn't she respond?

Hannah struggled to calm herself. Maybe the princess was

already en route. Maybe she was on a plane flying to Raguva right now.

Hannah felt a ray of hope. It was possible. Emmeline might have been in such a hurry getting to the airport that she'd forgotten to send a message to Hannah saying she was on the way…

But even as Hannah comforted herself with the thought, the phone rang.

Emmeline.

Hannah answered immediately. "Are you here?" she asked hopefully. "Have you arrived?"

"No, I'm still in Florida," Emmeline's clipped precise voice suddenly wobbled, sounding very far away at the other end of the line. "I'm having a bit of trouble getting out as you have my plane. Could you send it back for me?"

"Were you able to work things out?"

"N-no." Again that wobble.

"Are you okay?"

"I'm not in physical danger, if that's what you're asking."

Hannah heard the threat of tears in the princess's voice. "Things aren't going well there?"

"No." Emmeline drew a slow breath. "How is Zale? As cold as ever?"

Hannah flushed. "I wouldn't call him cold…"

"Maybe not. But he is rather grim, isn't he? I don't think he likes me much."

"He's marrying you."

"For five million Euros!"

"What?"

"Hannah, it's an arranged marriage. What did you expect?"

Hannah pictured Zale's strong, handsome face, those fiercely intelligent eyes and his tall, powerful frame. He was gorgeous. How could Emmeline feel nothing for him? "Maybe you will fall in love, once you spend time together."

"Oh, I hope not. It'd just complicate everything—" Emmeline broke off, spoke to someone in the room with her, then returned to the phone. "Good news. I don't need to wait for my plane. A friend here has a jet I can take tonight. I'll be there in the morning. Once I land, I'll text you. With any luck, no one will be the wiser."

With any luck, Hannah silently echoed, closing her phone, heart strangely heavy.

CHAPTER TWO

HANNAH told herself she was relieved that this impossible charade was nearly over. She told herself she was glad to be going in the morning. But part of her was disappointed. Zale fascinated her.

In her dressing room, Hannah touched up her makeup and adjusted the tiara before following her lady-in-waiting through soaring galleries and elegant chambers on the way to the Grand Dining Hall.

They walked briskly, her skirts whispering with every step. Passing through the Empire Room, Hannah caught a glimpse of herself in a tall mirror over the high white marble fireplace.

The reflection startled her. Is that how she really looked? Elegant? Shimmering? *Pretty?*

She shook her head at her reflection and her reflection shook her head back—pink cheeks. Deep blue eyes. High cheekbones above a generous mouth.

Hannah couldn't believe she really looked like that. Didn't know she could look like that. She'd never felt beautiful in her life. Smart, yes. Hardworking, of course. But her father had never placed any value on physical beauty—had certainly never encouraged her to wear makeup or dress up—and for a moment she wanted to really be the beautiful girl in the mirror.

What if she was a princess in real life?

Would it change everything? Would it change her?

The lady-in-waiting paused outside tall paneled doors that opened onto the Grand Dining Hall. "We'll wait for His Majesty here," she said.

Hannah nodded, eager to see King Zale Patek again. She shouldn't care. Shouldn't feel anything.

Suddenly King Patek and his attendants were there and the atmosphere felt positively electric.

Hannah's breath caught in her throat as heat and energy crackled around them. Tall, lithe, strong, Zale Patek practically hummed with life.

She'd never met a man so vitally alive. Had never met a man with such confidence. Lifting her head she looked up into his eyes and the expression in the rich amber depths made her heart turn over.

"You look lovely," he said.

She inclined her head. "And you do, too, Your Majesty."

"I look *lovely?*"

"Handsome," she corrected, with a blush. "And royal."

He lifted an eyebrow but Hannah was saved from further conversation as the doors to the Grand Dining Hall opened simultaneously, revealing an immense, richly paneled hall easily two stories tall.

"Oh," Hannah whispered, awed by the medieval grandeur of the room. The huge room was lit almost exclusively by candlelight. Ivory tapers flickered in sconces and tall silver candelabras marched down the length of the table. Stone fireplaces marked both ends of the room and magnificent burgundy tapestries covered the richly paneled walls. The high ceiling was an intricate design of gold stencil against dark stained wood.

Zale looked down at her, a hint of a smile at his lips. "Shall we?" he asked, offering her his arm.

She looked up at him and her heart did a funny little hiccup. Beautiful face, beautiful eyes, broad shoulders, narrow waist, long muscular legs. A fantasy come to life.

Would it be such a bad thing if she were to enjoy playing Princess Emmeline for just one night?

Would it ruin everything if she liked Zale a little? Tomorrow morning she'd be heading home and would never see him again, so why couldn't she just be happy tonight?

Together they entered the crowded hall where the guests were already seated at the longest dining table she'd ever seen.

She could feel all their eyes on them, and conversation died as they walked to the two places still empty in the middle of the table. "Such a big table," she murmured.

"It is," he agreed. "Originally it was built to accommodate one hundred. But five hundred years ago people must have been considerably smaller—or perhaps they didn't mind a very tight squeeze," he answered with a hint of laughter in his voice, "because I don't think we ever seat more than eighty today."

A uniformed butler drew out a chair for Hannah while another held out Zale's and then they were sitting, and Zale leaned toward Hannah to whisper. "And even then," he added, "as you can see, eighty is still quite snug."

Snug was an understatement, she thought an hour later, feeling excessively warm and more than a little claustrophobic as the five-course meal slowly progressed. Her teal gown was too tight and pinched around her ribs, and Zale was a big man with very broad shoulders and he took up considerable space.

And then there were her emotions, which were all over the place.

Everything about him intrigued her, and it was impossible to ignore him, even if she wanted to. At least six foot three, he dominated the table with his broad shoulders and long legs.

All evening she was aware of him, feeling his warmth and energy even without touching him.

And then when they *did* touch—a bump of shoulder, a tap on the wrist and that one time his thigh brushed her own—her head spun from the rush of sensation.

Working for Sheikh Al-Koury, Hannah had arranged numerous events and dinners, and had sat next to countless wealthy men, and yet no one had ever made her feel like this before.

Nervous. Eager. Self-conscious. *Sensitive.*

Next to Zale she could hear her heart thud, feel the warmth of her breath as she exhaled, tingle with goose bumps as he turned his head to look into her eyes.

She loved that he did that. Loved that he was strong enough, confident enough, to look at a woman and hold her gaze. It was probably the sexiest thing she'd ever experienced.

But even when he wasn't looking at her, she liked the way he watched others, studying the world intently, listening with all of him—heart and mind, ears and eyes.

As one of the staff leaned over to take her plate, Hannah startled and bumped Zale.

He glanced at her with a half smile, and that barely there smile captivated her as much as his whiskey-colored gaze.

This man would be a force to reckon with—so alive, so vital—and she envied Emmeline, she did.

Imagine being loved by a man like King Patek. And that was the appeal, wasn't it? Zale wasn't a boy. He was a man. And unlike Brad, her college love, Zale was mature, successful, experienced. He was a thirty-five-year-old man in his prime.

To be loved by a man who knew what he wanted…

To be loved by a man who knew he wanted her…

Her chest squeezed hard, tight and she dragged a hand to her lap, fingertips trailing across the exquisite beading of her gown as she tried to think of something else. Something besides Zale and what was quickly becoming an impossible infatuation.

Zale's gaze met hers and held. The air bottled in her lungs. Her heart thudded in her ears.

"Not every dinner will be as long as this," he said to her in English, his voice pitched low. They'd been switching back and forth between French and English all night for the benefit of their guests but whenever he spoke to Hannah it was in English. "This is unusually drawn out."

"I don't mind," she said, careful to speak without a hint of her Texas twang. "It's a beautiful room and I have excellent company."

"You've become so very charming."

"Haven't I always been?"

"No." His lips curved in a self-mocking smile. "You didn't enjoy my company a year ago. It was our engagement party and yet you avoided me all night." His smile didn't touch his eyes. "Your father said you were shy. I knew better."

This was a strange conversation to have here, now, with eighty people around them. "And what did you know?"

He looked at her intently, his narrowed gaze traveling slowly over her face until it rested on her mouth. "I knew you were in love with another man and marrying me out of duty."

Definitely not a conversation to be having at a formal dinner party. Nervous, Hannah rubbed her fingers against the delicate beading on her skirt. "Perhaps we should discuss this later...?"

"Why?"

"Aren't you afraid someone will overhear us?"

His gaze pierced her. "I'm more afraid of not getting straight answers."

She shrugged. "Then ask your questions. This is your home. Your party. Your guests."

"And you're my fiancée."

Her chin lifted a fraction. "Yes, I am."

He studied her for an endless moment. "Who are you, Emmeline?"

"Excuse me?"

"You're so different now. Makes me wonder if you're even the same woman."

"What a strange thing to say."

"But you are different. You look me in the eye now. You have opinions. *Attitude*. I almost think I could get an honest answer out of you now."

"Try me."

His eyes narrowed, strong jaw growing thicker. "That's exactly what I mean. You would have never spoken to me like this a year ago."

"We're to be married in ten days. Shouldn't I be forthright?"

"Yes." He hesitated a moment, still studying her. "Romantic love is important to you, isn't it?"

"Of course. Isn't it important to you?"

"There are other things more important to me. Family. Loyalty. Integrity." He looked into her eyes then, as if daring her to disagree. "Fidelity."

Her brows pulled. "But doesn't romantic love incorporate all of the above? How can one truly love another and not give all of one's heart, mind, body and soul?"

"If you loved a man, you'd never betray him?"

"Never."

"So you don't condone affairs…no matter how discreet?"

"Absolutely not."

"You don't hope to take a lover later, after we're married and you've fulfilled your duty?"

Hannah was appalled by his questions. "Is that the sort of woman you think I am?"

"I think you're a woman who has been pressured into a marriage she doesn't want."

Her jaw dropped slightly, and she stared at him unable to think of a single response.

Zale leaned closer, his deep voice dropping even lower, his amber gaze intense. "I think you want to please others, even if it comes at a terrible price."

"Because I've agreed to an arranged marriage?"

"Because you've agreed to *this* marriage." His eyes held hers. "Can you do this, Emmeline, and be happy? Can you make this marriage work?"

"Can you?" she flashed, flustered.

"Yes."

"How can you be so sure?"

"I have discipline. And I'm older by ten years. I have more life experience and know what I need, and what I want."

"And what is that?"

"I want prosperity for my country, peace in my home and heirs to ensure succession."

"That's it? Peace, prosperity and children?"

"I'm a realist. I know I can't expect too much from life so I keep my desires simple. My goals attainable."

"Hard to believe that. You were the star footballer that carried Raguva to the finals of the World Cup. You don't achieve success like that without big dreams—"

"That was before my parents' death. Now my country and family come first. My responsibilities to Raguva outweigh everything else."

The fierce note in his voice made her tremble inwardly. He was intense. So very physical. Everything about him screamed male—the curve of his lip, the lean cheek, the strong masculine jaw.

"I need the same commitment from you," he added. "If we marry there will be no divorce. No room for second thoughts. No means to later opt out. If we marry it's forever, and if you can't promise me forever, then you shouldn't be here."

Zale abruptly pushed back his chair and extended a hand to her. "But that's enough serious talk for one evening. We're supposed to be celebrating your arrival and the good things to come. Let's mingle with our guests, and try to enjoy the evening."

The rest of the night passed quickly with everyone vying for an opportunity to speak with King Zale and the glamorous, popular Princess Emmeline.

But finally by ten-thirty, with the last guests departing, Zale escorted Emmeline back to her suite on the second floor.

It had been a strange evening. Perplexing, he thought, glancing down at her golden head with the delicate diamond tiara.

He'd been ambivalent about her arrival. He'd needed her here for duty's sake. Raguva needed a queen and he needed heirs. But at a purely personal level, he knew she wasn't the woman he would have ever picked as his wife.

Zale knew his faults—hardworking, no-nonsense, intensely dedicated—but he was loyal. It was a trait he respected in himself, and valued highly in others.

He realized belatedly that Emmeline might not.

He knew she'd never been spoiled by her parents. If anything, her parents had been hard on her, holding her to an exacting standard that she could never meet, which made Emmeline desperate to please. The world might see her as a glowing, confident princess but her father had warned Zale that she could be difficult and at times, terribly insecure.

King William d'Arcy's warning had worried Zale as he did not need a difficult and insecure wife, much less a fragile, demanding queen.

But Zale's late father had wanted this match very much. In his eyes, Princess Emmeline had been the perfect choice for Zale, and although his father had died five years ago, Zale wanted to honor his father's wishes, hoping that once the beautiful Emmeline reached Raguva she would settle in, settle down and become the ideal bride his father imagined her to be.

They'd reached her suite and for a moment neither said anything. "It's been a long day," he said at length, breaking the uncomfortable silence, even as he wondered how he could marry her with so many doubts.

But she was here, another part of his brain argued. She'd come when she'd said she would, and she'd behaved perfectly proper tonight. More than proper, she'd been beautiful, approachable, likable.

"It has," she agreed.

"Tomorrow night will be far less formal. There is no state dinner, just a quiet dinner together, so that should be relatively easy."

She nodded, looking up at him, her blue eyes dark with an emotion he couldn't decipher. "I'm sure it will be."

He stared down into her face, wondering how this warm, appealing woman could be the remote, cold Emmeline of the past year.

"Is there anything you need?" he asked now. "Anything that hasn't been provided?"

"Everything has been wonderful."

Her answer baffled him even more. "No special requests? You've my ear now. I'm happy to oblige."

She shook her head.

"You're happy to be here then?"

Her full mouth curved into a tremulous smile. "Of course."

He didn't know if it was the inexplicable shimmer of tears in her eyes, or that uncertain smile, but suddenly Europe's most beautiful princess looked so very alone and vulnerable that Zale reached for her, putting his hand low on her back and finding bare skin.

Her head tipped back, her blue gaze finding his. Zale's hand slipped lower, his palm sliding down warm satin skin.

He heard her soft intake of breath as he drew her closer, holding her against him, her full, soft breasts crushed to his chest. He dropped his head, covering her mouth with his.

It was to have been a brief kiss, a good-night kiss, but when her lips trembled beneath his he felt a rush of hunger. Desire.

Power.

He drew her closer still, molding her to him with pressure in the small of her back.

She shivered against him and his pulse quickened, blood pounding in his veins, making his body hot, and hard.

The need to possess her filled him, consuming him, and ruthlessly he deepened the kiss, taking her as if she already belonged to him.

The insistent pressure of his lips parted hers, and the tip of his tongue flicked the softness of her inner lip making her squirm. The urgent press of her hips against his made blood roar in his ears and he nipped at her mouth, small bites that made her shudder with pleasure.

God, she was sensitive. Responsive. Her body trembled against him, and he slid his hand from the small of her spine down, lower, over the pert curve of her backside, which made her gasp, her nipples hardening, pebbling against his chest through the thin silk of her gown.

Blood coursed through him.

Desire pounded through his veins.

She was deliciously smooth, deliciously curved and he wanted more of her, all of her. His body throbbed.

God, she was hot and tasted sweet. He wanted to rip her gown off her, strip her voluptuous body bare and explore her curves and hollows—like the dip of her spine, the space behind her knee, the softness between her thighs.

He wanted between her thighs. Wanted to part her knees as wide as he could—

Reality returned. What the hell was he doing? They were in the hall. In full view of the hidden cameras broadcasting images to his security detail.

His hand stilled on her hip. He removed the other from beneath her breast.

Slowly he lifted his head to look into her eyes. They were dark and cloudy, her lips swollen, her expression dazed.

"I'm afraid we've given my security a show," he said, voice pitched low and rough.

Color rushed into her cheeks. "I'm sorry."

He brushed a blond tendril from her flushed cheek, finding her nearly irresistible. "I'm not. Good night, Your Highness."

She looked at him for an endless moment. "Goodbye." Then she slipped into her room and closed the door.

CHAPTER THREE

ENTERING her suite Hannah gently closed and locked the door, heart racing, body shaking.

For a long moment she leaned against the locked door, a hand pressed to her mouth.

She'd kissed him. Kissed him madly, passionately, kissed him as if she were drowning, dying, and maybe she was.

How could she go tomorrow? How could she leave and never see him again?

But there was no way she could stay. He didn't want her, Hannah, he wanted Emmeline.

And even that hurt. How could he want Emmeline when the princess didn't care for him, would never care, while Hannah already cared too much…?

That was the part that confused her, infuriated her, most. How could she care already? She'd only met Zale today. She'd spent what—five hours with him? Six? Barely enough time to be infatuated. So why did she feel sick? Panicked?

Desperate?

Why did she think when she left here she'd never forget him?

Hannah choked back a frustrated cry and pressed her hand harder to her mouth to stifle the sound.

Her eyes burned and her throat ached and she hated herself for wanting something—someone—she couldn't have.

She wasn't the type of woman to set herself up for failure.

"Your Highness," Celine, Hannah's maid, said breathlessly, emerging from the dressing room, with Hannah's nightgown and robe. "I didn't hear you return. Have I kept you waiting?"

Hannah blinked back tears and pushed away from the door. "I just returned," she said, mustering a watery smile. "But I'd love your help getting out of this gown."

Leaving Emmeline, Zale forced himself to put her from his mind and focus now on other things—like Tinny.

He headed toward his own wing of the palace but first stopped at his younger brother's room. He never went to bed without a last check on Tinny.

Opening the door to Tinny's sitting room he saw that all the lights were out except for the small lamp on the top of the bookshelf on the far wall.

Tinny's night-light. He couldn't sleep without it.

Zale felt a rush of affection for his twenty-eight-year-old special-needs brother, a brother who'd needed him even more after their parents' death.

Constantine—or Tinny, as he'd always been called within the family—was to have been on the plane with his parents on that ill-fated flight, but at the last minute he'd begged his parents to let him fly to St. Philippe, their private Caribbean island, with Zale the next day instead.

Even five years later, Zale gave daily thanks that Tinny hadn't been onboard. Tinny was everything to him, and all the family he had left, but Tinny still missed his parents dreadfully, still asked for them, hoping that maybe today his beloved mama and papa would come home.

"Your Majesty," a voice whispered from the dark, and Mrs. Sivka, Tinny's evening nurse, emerged from the shadows in a dressing gown. "He's doing well. Sleeping like a lamb."

"I'm sorry I didn't come to say good-night earlier."

"He knew you wouldn't be coming. When you were here at tea this afternoon you told him tonight was a very important night." Mrs. Sivka smiled. "How did it go, Your Majesty? Is she as beautiful as they say?"

Zale felt a strange tightness in his chest. "Yes."

"Tinny can't wait to meet her. It's all he talked about today."

"He shall meet her as soon as possible."

"Tomorrow?"

Zale pictured Emmeline and then his brother, and knew that innocent, idealistic Tinny would immediately place her on a pedestal. He'd adore her, worship her and give her the power to break his heart. "Not tomorrow, but soon, I promise."

"He'll be disappointed it's not tomorrow."

"I know, but there are a few wrinkles to still iron out."

"I understand and Prince Constantine will meet your bride when the time is right." Mrs. Sivka smiled. "I'm proud of you. Your parents would be proud, too. You deserve every good thing coming, you do."

"But you have to say that, Mrs. Sivka," he said, teasing her gently, forever grateful she'd come out of retirement to help with Tinny after his parents' accident. "You were my nanny, too."

"That I was. And now look at you."

He smiled crookedly. "Good night, Mrs. Sivka."

"Good night, Your Majesty."

Zale left his brother's suite of rooms and headed to his own, feeling tightness and tension return to his chest.

He felt like he'd ridden a roller coaster of emotions tonight. He didn't like it.

He rarely let his emotions get the better of him. Little ruffled Zale. Virtually nothing got under his skin. But tonight everything about Emmeline had gotten to him. She wasn't the one he'd remembered. She was nothing like the cool ice princess of the past. And tonight she'd managed to turn him inside out.

Not good, he told himself, walking to his own suite of rooms in the next wing.

He wasn't supposed to be emotionally involved with Emmeline. As they both knew, their union wasn't a love match but a carefully orchestrated arrangement with significant financial incentives. Every step of their relationship had been outlined and detailed in the final draft of the seventy-page document they'd sign in the morning.

He could want her, desire her and enjoy her but he couldn't ever forget that their relationship was first, and foremost, business.

Business, he reminded himself sternly, which meant he couldn't allow himself to get distracted, not even by a beautiful face and lush body.

Fortunately Zale was famous for his discipline. That same discipline ensured success in school, in sport and then as Raguva's sovereign.

Growing up the second of three sons, no one placed pressure on him. No one had particularly high expectations for him. But Zale had high expectations for himself. From a young age he was determined to find his own place in the world, would carve a niche that was uniquely his. And so while his older brother, Stephen VII, Raguva's Crown Prince, had learned the fundamentals of ruling a monarchy, Zale had learned the fundamentals of football.

His older brother would be king one day and Zale would play professional sport.

Zale had been sixteen and attending boarding school in England when nineteen-year-old Stephen, in his second year at Trinity College, had been diagnosed with leukemia. His parents and Tinny had relocated to London to be with Stephen during the grueling chemo and radiation treatments.

For three years Stephen fought hard. For three years he endured horrific pain in hopes that the debilitating treatments would knock the leukemia into remission.

Zale had felt helpless. There was nothing he could do. Not for Stephen. Or his parents. And so he poured himself into his sport, needing a focus, a fight of his own. His self-imposed training regime had been grueling—three, four hours a day—running, weight training, sit-ups, push-ups, sprints, drills. He pushed himself to breaking point each day. He worked to muscle failure. It was the least he could do. Stephen was fighting for his life. Zale should struggle, too.

After passing his exams, Zale made the decision to follow his brother to Oxford, where in his first year he made the university's football club's first team, the Blues.

In his second year he carried the Blues to Oxford's newly created Premier League where they finished top.

Stephen was there for the last big game of their season. He'd insisted on attending and their father, Raguva's king, pushed frail Stephen into the stadium in a wheelchair and no one cheered louder than Stephen during the game.

A week after the game, Stephen had died. Zale blamed himself. The day at the stadium had been too much for Stephen. He shouldn't have gone.

Zale remembered nothing of his final year at Oxford. It was a blur shaped by grief. The only time he felt present in his skin was on the pitch. By the time he graduated, four different football clubs competed to sign him to their team.

He'd signed with a top Spanish club despite his parents disapproval. They had wanted him to return to Raguva—he was the Crown Prince now—but Zale didn't want to be king. He had a love, a passion, a dream. It was football.

Football, Zale silently repeated, entering his suite of four rooms, which had served every Raguvian king for the past five hundred years.

His valet was waiting for him in his dressing room, the King's Dressing Room, where the sumptuous curtains had been drawn across the wall of leaded windows, shutting out the night.

"Was it a good evening, Your Majesty?" his valet asked, assisting Zale out of his formal jacket.

"It was, Armand, thank you." Zale's jaw tightened as he began unbuttoning his vest and dress shirt.

No, he'd never wanted to be king, had no desire to rule, but when his parents' plane had crashed on landing, of course he came home. And he turned his tremendous discipline and drive to his reign.

He'd be a great king.

He owed it to his people, his parents and most of all, Stephen.

Hannah slept fitfully that night, tossing and turning in her ornate bed in her sumptuous bedroom, dreaming of Zale, dreaming of leaving, dreaming of finding Emmeline only to lose her again.

She woke repeatedly during the night to check the clock, anxious about the time, anxious about getting to the airport in the morning. At three she climbed out of bed to push the heavy drapes open, exposing the window with the night sky and quarter moon.

But finally it was dawn and pink and yellow light pierced the horizon. For a moment Hannah lay in bed watching the sun slowly rise, the yellow and pink sky deepening to gold and coral.

It would be a beautiful morning. Not a cloud in sight. There was nothing but soaring green mountains behind the walled city and the Adriatic Sea stretching before.

Hannah left the bed to stand at the window wanting to remember everything.

The rugged mountains. The pale stone houses and walls. The red tile roofs. Church spires and castle turrets. The sparkle of the sun on the water.

This morning Raguva's capital looked magical, as if it had been plucked from a fairy tale.

She felt a tug on her heart and that tug was enough to make her turn away.

She wasn't going to think today. Wasn't going to feel, either. There would be no remembering last night, not even guilt over that kiss in the corridor.

She was going home. Back to her work and world. Back to a life where she excelled and could make a difference.

But first she'd need to shower, and then she'd dress and pack the few personal things she'd brought with her into an elegant shopping bag she'd found a few days ago.

The shopping bag was part of her "escape" plan. It was really quite a simple plan, too.

She'd make arrangements to go out shopping this morning. A driver could take her to an upscale fashion boutique where she'd window-shop and wait for Emmeline's call. Once Emmeline phoned, Hannah would head to the airport where she and Emmeline would meet in the ladies' room, change into each other's clothes and swap places. Easy.

Once bathed, Hannah searched for a dress in Emmeline's wardrobe that would fit both she and Emmeline. Hannah settled on a plum dress with a jewel neckline and cutout cap sleeves that could be worn with an optional gold belt. Hannah would leave the belt off but take it in her purse so that Emmeline, who was at least ten pounds lighter, could cinch the belt around her waist to keep the dress from looking baggy on her more slender frame.

Hannah pinned her hair up in a casually chic French twist, and added classic gold earrings as her only other accessory. The less she had to put on and off the better.

Once dressed and packed, the only thing Hannah could do was wait. She called for coffee and a footman arrived with coffee and croissants.

Hannah nibbled on a croissant while waiting for Emmeline to call.

A half hour became an hour, and then two and soon it was nine o'clock and Lady Andrea arrived to cover the day's schedule with her.

"It's going to be a very busy day," Lady Andrea said, taking a seat in the suite's sitting room and pulling out her leather calendar to flip to the proper page. "At ten this morning you have an appointment with His Majesty, and the lawyers in His Majesty's chamber, and then at eleven you'll have your hair and makeup done for the first sitting for your official portrait.

Later, if there's time after tea, Mr. Krek, the Head Butler, will take you on a tour of the palace. Tonight you'll have a private dinner with His Majesty and a few guests."

Lady Andrea drew a breath and looked up at Hannah. "Any questions?"

A half dozen questions came to mind, but nothing as pressing as the meeting with Zale in just under an hour. "What is the purpose for the meeting with His Majesty and the lawyers?"

Lady Andrea closed the leather appointment book. "You're meeting to sign paperwork, I believe."

Hannah felt an icy rush of panic. "What paperwork?"

"The prenuptial agreement, Your Highness, spelling out division of assets, as well as custodial arrangements, in the event of the dissolution of the marriage."

Hannah's mouth opened and closed. Of course Zale and Emmeline would have a prenup, but Hannah couldn't, wouldn't sign a legal document in Emmeline's name.

Thank God Emmeline was on her way. Only problem was, Hannah didn't know when the princess would arrive.

Hannah stole a quick glance at her watch. Nine-fifteen. The meeting with Zale and the lawyers was only forty minutes from now and even if Emmeline landed right now, it would still be impossible for Emmeline and Hannah to switch places by then.

She'd have to stall. Have to get the meeting postponed until later.

"Could you please send word to His Majesty that I'd like to push back this morning's meeting to this afternoon, or even tomorrow morning?" Hannah said. "I'd like time to review the documents before I sign anything."

Lady Andrea hesitated, then nodded. "Of course, Your Highness, I'll send word to His Majesty's secretary and see if we can't get this morning's meeting rescheduled. I'll also request copies of the documents be sent to you immediately."

As soon as Lady Andrea left, Hannah checked her phone to see if she'd missed a call or text. Nothing.

But why nothing? Hannah pressed two fingers to her temple trying to ease the pressure building in her head.

Where was Emmeline?

Hannah sent her yet another text. *What's happening? Where are you? When will you arrive?*

Phone tightly clutched in her hand, Hannah paced her suite, desperate for a response. Call, call, call, she silently chanted, anxious beyond belief. But minutes crawled by without a word from Emmeline. Five, ten, twenty. And each minute made Hannah more nervous.

Lady Andrea returned, flustered. "Your Highness, His Majesty can't reschedule this morning's meeting. He asked that I remind you that you just approved the document and its contents two weeks ago—"

"I understand," Hannah interrupted, panic sharpening her tone, "but I'm not feeling well enough to meet him—much less sign anything—right now. Please send my apologies—" Hannah broke off as her phone suddenly buzzed. She glanced at her phone. Emmeline.

Thank God. She must have just landed. Everything would be okay. Hannah would just postpone the signing for an hour or two to allow Emmeline to arrive at the palace.

Hannah glanced at Lady Andrea, and smiled weakly. "Please see if we can't reschedule for after lunch. I'm sure my headache will be gone by then."

Hannah didn't even wait for the door to close behind Lady Andrea before reading the Emmeline's text message.

Couldn't get flight plan approved last night—
What? No. *No!*

Tiny spots danced before Hannah's eyes. She swayed on her feet, shocked, sickened. Emmeline hadn't even left Florida yet?

Hannah read the rest of the message with tears of frustration burning her eyes. *Trying to get permission now. Don't panic. Will be there soon! xxx Emme*

Don't panic? She nearly threw her phone across the room. How could she *not* panic?

"No!" Hannah choked, blinking tears, adrenaline making her heart race. "No, no, no!"

She was so furious and frustrated she missed the knock on the outer door, as well as the fact that it had opened.

Hannah might not have heard anyone enter but she felt it immediately, her nape tingling and goose bumps covered her arms. She wasn't alone anymore. Even the energy in the room felt different.

Hannah lifted her head, her fingers stilling about the phone's tiny keypad.

Zale.

And he was upset.

She saw his expression and it took her by surprise.

Why was he so angry? Was it because she had pushed back this morning's signing? But that didn't make sense. Why would rescheduling the meeting upset him so much?

"What's wrong?" she asked, taking a step back.

"What is this about?" he demanded imperiously, approaching her, his handsome features grim, his amber gaze holding hers, commanding her attention.

She sucked in a nervous breath, overwhelmed by his intensity. Zale Patek hadn't just entered her room, he owned it, dominated it and in turn, dominated her.

Was this the same man who'd kissed her senseless last night?

Was this the man she couldn't bear to leave?

"I don't understand," she said, taking another step back.

Zale kept walking toward her, tension radiating from him in waves. "Neither do I." His tone was clipped, hard. "Explain to me why you've canceled the meeting."

She bumped up against the delicate coffee table between the pink silk sofa and armchairs and had no more room to run. "I woke up with a headache and it's just gotten worse."

"I'm sure you could suffer through for a thirty-minute signing."

"But I can't. The pain's so bad I can't even read right now."

"I'll read it to you, then."

His sarcasm stung. Why was he being awful? Was it necessary to be rude? Necessary to be so inflexible? "I'm sure we can reschedule—"

"No."

"And why not?" she demanded, just as curtly.

He tipped his head, studying her, his short crisp hair dark, but definitely not black, just as his eyes were neither brown nor gold but a shade somewhere in between. This morning he wore a black suit with a white dress shirt open at the collar. His throat was the same bronze tone as his face. She could almost see him in the sun, his lean, chiseled features glazed by light.

Gladiator.

Warrior.

King.

"Because," he said slowly, clearly, "the lawyers are here, the paperwork is ready and the agreement is to be signed now."

"Even if I don't feel well?"

His features tightened, his mouth compressing. "I should have known the games weren't over."

Her hands knotted. "I'm not playing games—"

"What do you want now? How do you intend to up the stakes? Are you holding out for ten million for each child? What is it this time?"

"That's insane!"

"It is, isn't it? But that's how you play, Emmeline—"

"No. You couldn't be more wrong. I'm not changing anything or asking for anything other than a postponement so I can take some medicine and lie down and try to feel better."

"What's wrong?"

"I told you. I have a headache."

"Is that so?" His deep voice mocked her even as his gaze examined her, slowly scrutinizing her appearance from the top of her head down to her toes.

Hannah could see herself in his eyes—her perfectly coiffed French twist, the rich plum of her dress and the expensive designer shoes. She'd dressed smartly, elegantly, knowing that when she left the palace this morning she needed to look every inch the royal princess.

"Yes," she answered, lifting her chin, staring him in the eye, daring him to call her a liar. She'd been raised by a tough man. Her father didn't tolerate fools, either, but her father had also taught her that men were to be gentlemen. Men were to treat women properly—which meant with kindness and respect. And Zale Patek was definitely not treating her with respect right now. "But if you don't believe me, would you like to call a doctor? Have him examine me? Would that reassure you, Your Majesty?"

"That's not necessary," he said stiffly.

"But I think it is. Clearly you doubt my sincerity. You've questioned my integrity—"

"I haven't."

"You have. You've been rude. Why? For what? A prenup?"

Heat flared in his amber eyes, making them gold. "Your father was the one that wanted the contract. It was drawn up at his insistence and at great expense, so don't put that one on me."

Hannah blanched. The contract had been Emmeline's father's idea? What kind of father was this King William of Brabant? He certainly didn't sound supportive or loving.

"Everyone is here because of you," Zale added tersely. "Five lawyers, Emmeline. Two of whom flew in from your country, and one from overseas, and now I am to tell them to go to their rooms and twiddle their thumbs until the morning?"

He had a point. But what was she to do? Sign as Emmeline? Impossible. "Yes," she said firmly. "That's exactly what you do when your future queen is ill and unable to make the meeting."

Zale drew a slow breath. He exhaled. A small muscle pulled in his jaw.

"I apologize, Your Highness," he said from between clenched teeth, color darkening the high slash of cheekbone.

"I did not mean to appear insensitive. Your health is of course my first concern. Everything else can and will wait."

Then with a brief, icy bow, he walked out.

CHAPTER FOUR

HANNAH sank into the nearest chair after Zale left, heart racing so fast she felt like throwing up. For a long moment she couldn't think, too rattled by the intense confrontation with Zale to do anything but process what had just taken place.

He'd been so angry. And his anger had felt personal. As if he was disgusted with her.

Why?

Why would delaying the meeting upset him so much? She hadn't said she wouldn't sign it. She hadn't asked for changes. She'd just asked for time. But it seemed as if time wasn't something Zale was prepared to give her.

And then she remembered something he'd said, spitting the words at her as if they'd hurt his mouth—*I should have known the games weren't over.*

Then he'd added something about her raising the stakes, holding out for millions, because that's how she played.

How *she* played?

He was the one who had burst into her room, temper blazing, words coldly mocking.

I did not mean to appear insensitive. Your health is my first concern. Everything else can wait.

Liar! He didn't mean a word of it. He'd totally meant to be insensitive. He'd been deliberately rude.

From the moment he'd entered her suite he'd shown absolutely no concern for her health. Instead he'd bullied her. Tried to intimidate her. Accused her of playing games.

Who did he think he was, treating a woman like that?

Livid, Hannah chased after Zale, catching up with him as he descended the grand staircase. "Your Majesty, I'd like a word with you," she said sharply, stopping him midstep.

He slowly turned to look up at her, his straight eyebrow lifted in surprise. "Your head seems to be much better."

"It's not," she answered shortly, cheeks flushed, body shaking with tension, "and you owe me an apology. You were unforgivably rude."

"*I* was rude?"

"And cruel. You should be ashamed of yourself! I can't believe that's how your parents raised you."

Color darkened his cheekbones and his eyes glittered with anger. "I could say the same for you. Engaged to me and yet playing the field—"

"How dare you!"

"Save me the theatrics. I know, Emmeline. I know the truth."

"What truth?"

"I know why you were in Palm Beach. I know what you were doing there—"

"Attending fashion shows and dinners and a charity polo match."

"God, you're good," he said, moving back up the stairs with that stealthy animal grace that made her pulse leap and heart beat too fast. "Charity polo match! That's wonderful. Cling to your story. Keep to the facts, right?"

"I have no idea what you're talking about."

"Don't go there," Zale said, joining her at the top of the stairs, and his sheer size and intensity overwhelmed her. She didn't like how he towered over her. Didn't like that she had to tip her head back to see his expression. Being this close made her feel alarmingly vulnerable.

"What does that mean?" she demanded fiercely, her heart racing, her pulse unsteady.

"Emmeline, I *know*. I know why you were in Palm Beach. I know you went to meet him. I know you spent every free moment in Florida you could with him."

Hannah inhaled hard, stunned. Couldn't be... Emmeline couldn't have been with someone else when she was engaged to the King Patek...could she?

"No," she whispered, not wanting to believe it, not wanting to imagine that beautiful, charming Emmeline d'Arcy would be unfaithful. "That's not true."

"Don't add insult to injury! It's bad enough you were seeing him throughout our engagement, but don't lie to me, too. You were seen together—constantly—mutual friends were concerned enough to phone and let me know."

Hannah felt cold. His ugly, hurtful words made her sick. "What friends?" she murmured faintly, horrified that this was the kind of relationship Zale and Emmeline had. How could they marry when they mistrusted each other so? When they had so many secrets? Where was the warmth? And respect?

"Does it matter which friends?" he answered wearily, his expression shuttered. "Because it's the truth. You were with Alejandro every moment you could spare. I wasn't even sure you'd get on the plane to come here."

Hannah laced and unlaced her fingers, heartsick.

That's why Emmeline had wanted Hannah to switch places with her? She'd wanted more time with her lover. No. No, couldn't be...

Was Emmeline that cold? That calculating?

Hannah shook her head, confused, betrayed and wished with all her heart she'd never started this terrible charade. She'd thought it was an innocent prank, pretending to be Emmeline for a few hours, but instead there was so much more at stake.

Countries. Kingdoms.

A man's self-respect.

Hannah's eyes burned and she had to look away to cling to her control. "I'm sorry," she said, thinking the words didn't mean much because they'd change nothing. Emmeline still wasn't here. Hannah was pretending to be someone she wasn't. And the charade continued, making Zale Patek the fool.

Her father would be so ashamed if he saw her now. He'd raised her to be strong, independent and true.

True.

But oh, she wasn't being honest now. She was anything but. And Zale deserved better.

At the very least, he deserved the truth.

"But you did come," he said after a moment, breaking the strained silence. "Do you mean to stay? Or are you just waiting for an opportunity to escape?"

Hannah went hot then cold, lips parting—but what could she say?

Nothing.

So she closed her mouth and just looked at him, heart aching, wanting so badly to tell him everything but not knowing where to start.

And then he turned, jaw hard, tight, and continued on down the stairs, his broad shoulders squared.

Zale needed air. Badly.

He walked through the central hall down a corridor, leaving the beautifully restored palace for his favorite wing—the original castle keep, a stone tower built nearly a thousand years ago with thick walls and a proper parapet for soldiers to patrol.

As a boy this had been his favorite place to hide, a place neither of his brothers could find him and his parents wouldn't dream to go.

On top of the tower he felt free.

He needed that freedom now. Needed freedom to think, freedom to breathe.

Zale walked the parapet with the stunning views of the old medieval walled town nestled between the green slope of mountain and the blue Adriatic Sea.

He'd lost it earlier in Emmeline's room. Completely lost it. And he never did that. At least, he hadn't, not in years.

But oh, dear God, he felt like he was close to losing it again.

He knew there had been issues before she'd arrived. He knew he'd have to make a decision about her, and their future, once he'd spent time with her. But spending time with her didn't help. Spending time with her was making him mad.

Was she crazy, or was he?

How could one woman appear to be so many different things?

She was just so different than he'd expected. She'd always been beautiful, but she'd never been this fierce or strong. But the Emmeline now under his roof was downright fierce. Feisty. Warm. Complex.

He struggled now to remember the princess he'd met at the engagement party a year ago. She still looked like that Emmeline—well, a healthier, more athletic version—and she was still as intelligent and articulate, but everything else was different.

Her expressions.

Her mannerisms.

Her inflection.

Everything had changed since that evening, but he didn't understand it. Didn't understand her.

This was the part that bothered him most.

Which was the real Emmeline? The Emmeline that was so reserved and cool he'd once compared her to a beautiful marble statue—all sleek lines, stunning face and perfect proportions?

Or the warm, engaging, challenging Emmeline here? The Emmeline who blushed easily, spoke quickly and responded to his kiss last night with hot, sensual passion?

Maybe if he was just a man instead of a king, he could choose emotion and passion, but he was a king. And he was responsible for the future of his country.

He needed a proper princess.

He needed the right princess.

And as beautiful as Emmeline was, she didn't appear to be the right princess after all.

While he welcomed passion, he needed suitability.

He needed predictability.

Strength of character.

And the Emmeline that was here appeared strong, but was it real, or an act?

And the fact that he didn't know just nine days before their wedding was a huge red flag.

How could he afford to risk his country's future on an enigma? A question mark?

He couldn't. He wouldn't. But if he was going to end this, then he needed to do it soon. He'd accept the blame, pay the penalty and be free. The longer he put it off, the worse the repercussions would be.

In her suite, Hannah felt positively sick. Anxiously she paced the living room, stomach churning, nerves stretched to breaking.

Zale thought he knew the truth. He thought he knew everything. But he didn't, and Hannah should have told him.

She should have confessed who she really was and asked him to forgive her for her part in the deception and then headed to the airport to get a flight home.

But she hadn't done that. She'd allowed him to walk away thinking that maybe finally everything would be okay.

Hannah was still pacing when Lady Andrea gently knocked on the door and opened it. "Your Highness? Your stylists are here to prepare you for your sitting. Shall we get started?"

Hannah opened her mouth to protest but closed it, knowing she was in too deep now. And the only way she'd get out of this in one piece was for Emmeline to arrive so Hannah could escape.

"Yes."

Nearly three hours after the clash with Zale, Hannah still sat in a chair before the dressing-room mirror, watching Camille, Emmeline's personal hairstylist for the past seven years, spritz a tiny bit of hairspray on Hannah's hair to discourage fly-away strands.

It was all Hannah could do not to wiggle as Camille ran a light, practiced hand over Hannah's hair, ensuring all the ends hung straight. "No more do-it-yourself color, *oui,* Princess?" she said, tapping her on the shoulder. "If you want to go darker, or put in streaks, next time ask me. *Oui?*"

"Oui," Hannah agreed, thinking at that point she'd agree to anything just to get the marathon session over. She'd wanted a diversion, but two and a half hours in this chair while Camille colored, cut and then blew her hair dry using a large round brush to make it straight and glossy, was just too much. Hannah rarely did anything special with her hair, and was amazed that Emmeline could tolerate having her hair professionally styled every time she stepped out in public.

Teresa, Emmeline's personal makeup artist, had spent a half hour on her face and she moved forward now as Camille stepped back to apply one last coat of mascara and then another dab of soft gold gloss over Hannah's matte rose lipstick.

"Perfection!" Teresa murmured, nodding approvingly as both she and Camille critically examined their handiwork, looking for any flaws. "What do you think, Your Highness? Anything you'd like changed?"

Hannah forced herself to focus on her reflection. Her hair hung straight and very golden—she'd never been this blond in her life—even as her eyes had been subtly lined and lashes darkened to intensify the blue of her eyes. Her lips were full and a discreet golden pink. Her couture gown—the color somewhere between gold and sand—had a deep V neckline and long straight sleeves making Hannah feel unusually sophisticated.

"Nothing," Hannah answered, astonished by how much she looked like the real Princess Emmeline.

Now that her hair had been cut and colored, with her makeup applied by the same deft hand that did Emmeline's makeup, Hannah truly could pass for the princess.

If she didn't know better, even she would think they were

twins. "I look…I look…" She searched for the right words to express herself but couldn't find them.

"Stunning," a deep voice said quietly from the doorway, finishing her sentence for her.

Hannah's hands clenched the arms of her chair as her gaze met Zale's in the mirror. He was no longer angry, just somber, but she wasn't ready to see him. Too much had been said already for one day.

But he lifted a hand, dismissing the stylists. "We'd like some privacy, please."

She swallowed uneasily as they slipped away and the door to the dressing room closed, leaving her alone with him.

For a long moment after the others left he said nothing. "I was wrong," he said, breaking the silence. "I handled the situation this morning badly."

It was the last thing Hannah had expected him to say. "I don't suppose you'd ever cancel a meeting for a headache," she said.

"No."

"Just as I don't suppose you ever let a headache keep you out of a football game."

"Definitely not."

Her lips curved. "You played with pain?"

"My job was to play, not sit on the bench."

She'd expected as much. You didn't become a star midfielder without pain and sacrifice. "So, no excuses."

"No excuses," he echoed.

At least on this point, her father would agree with him. Her father was tough—physically and mentally—and he'd raised Hannah to be the same. She wasn't allowed to make excuses. *Always do your best,* he'd tell her, *no matter what.*

Not that being here, passing herself off as Emmeline, was her best.

"I can understand why you were so upset with me then," she added carefully. "But I didn't this morning. I thought you were being a bully."

"A bully?"

"An unreasonable one."

He looked startled and then he smiled, a quick smile that made him real and warm and sexy.

But she didn't want to find him sexy. Not if he was Emmeline's.

"Have we made a mistake, Emmeline?"

The quiet question in his deep, softly accented voice shocked her. *"What?"*

"I wonder if we're forcing something we shouldn't."

She looked at him, too stunned to speak.

"It's never been easy between us," he added, leaning against the wall, his big shoulders even broader in the black jacket. His brow furrowed. "I know why I've pushed ahead, but why have you? There are a half dozen eligible royals you could marry right now. You could have your pick of any of them—"

"But I chose to marry you," she interrupted softly, because Emmeline had chosen him, and while Emmeline might not love Zale, she must want to be Queen of Raguva.

"Why?"

"For all the same reasons you chose me—our families approved, our countries would forge a stronger alliance, the next generation would be secure."

He sighed and ran a hand along his jaw. "I wish I could believe you."

She sat up straighter. "Why can't you?"

"Your behavior this past year. The secret weekends with your Argentine boyfriend. The prolonged contract negotiations. Your refusal to spend time with me until now." His broad shoulders shifted. "One of those alone would give me pause, but all three? I'd be a fool to trust you."

She knew he was talking about Emmeline, but at the moment his anger and mistrust felt personal. "You'd be a bigger fool to let me go."

Something flickered in his eyes. "Why would I?"

"Your country has felt the same economic downturn that

the rest of Europe has experienced, but you have big plans to turn the economy around, and those plans hinge on me." Hannah was grasping at straws now, trying to piece together an argument based on the articles she'd read online about the impact the royal wedding would have on Raguva—increased tourism, greater financial resources, improved clout and visibility. "Since the announcement of our engagement, Raguva's popularity has skyrocketed. The scenic coast has become the new Riviera, and the public can't get enough about us and the wedding. The telecast of the ceremony will bring millions to your treasury—" She broke off, drew a quick breath. "Are you willing to throw all that away on a whim?"

"It's not a whim. I've been concerned about your suitability for a long time."

"Then why have you let it go this long? The wedding is in just nine days. The lawyers are here—all five of them. And the portrait artist is out there setting up his easel this very moment."

His gaze narrowed. His jaw tightened. He didn't speak for so long that the uncomfortable silence turned into exquisite tension. "I like confidence in women, Emmeline, but you're absolutely brazen. You've flaunted your boyfriend beneath my nose for months and yet you expect me to just ignore my better judgment and marry you anyway?"

Heat washed through her, scorching her cheeks, burning her skin. "There is no boyfriend."

"Emmeline, I know all about Alejandro. You've been together for years."

"But that was before we were engaged. We're not together anymore."

He gave her a cool look, features grim. "So how do you explain the photographs of you and Alejandro at the Palm Beach polo match?"

"You know I attended the match and posed for pictures afterward. It was a charity event and I took pictures with everyone. Why aren't you asking me about the photos I took with the English or Australian teams?"

"Because you're not involved with any of their players."

"But I'm not involved with anyone anymore. I'm here, engaged to you."

"Maybe here in body, but not in spirit."

"You don't know that. You can't say that!" She fought back. The last thing Hannah wanted was to be responsible for Emmeline and Zale's relationship. She hadn't come all this way, or struggled this much, to have Zale break off the engagement here and now. No, if Zale wanted to end the engagement, he had to end it with Emmeline, not with her. And if Emmeline wanted to break things off, then she needed to tell him—in person, which meant she had to get here and sort this out herself.

Princess Emmeline's presence was required. Immediately.

"You see only my faults and none of my strengths," she said.

"Maybe that's because your faults outnumber your strengths."

"So that's that? You've made up your mind, decided our fate, game over?"

"You make it sound like I'm an executioner about to take off your head."

"It feels like it."

"Emmeline!"

She shook her head. "You're not giving me a chance."

"I gave you chances—twelve months of them!"

"But I'm here. I came. Let's play the damn game, Zale!"

"What does that mean?"

"It means we're still early in the match and you're wanting to pick up the ball and walk off the field. But we have nine days until the ceremony, nine days to figure out what's real and what's not. So put the ball down. Give me a chance to play."

"And so what do you suggest?"

"We use this time right now to get to know each other. We

make every effort to see if this could work before you make a rushed, and rash, decision."

His expression looked skeptical.

"We commit the next nine days to discovering if we're compatible. If we are, we marry as planned. If we're not, we end this amicably."

"It sounds reasonable except for one thing. We can't cancel the wedding at the eleventh hour, not after everyone has traveled at great effort and expense to be here for the event. It would be a public relations nightmare."

"Five days, and we'll make a decision?"

"Four," he countered. "Four days should be more than sufficient if we use the time wisely. And then if I'm still not happy in four, it's over. Done. No more negotiating. Understand?"

His amber gaze burned into her but Hannah stared straight back, lifting her chin, her expression equally determined. "I understand perfectly, but you should know I'm tough. I play hard. And I'm playing to win."

CHAPTER FIVE

THE moment Zale left the dressing room, Hannah grabbed her phone and tried to call Emmeline.

The call went straight to Emmeline's voice mail.

"You need to get here, Emmeline. Zale is threatening to call the wedding off. Hurry." Hannah hung up just as Lady Andrea appeared.

"Your Highness, Monsieur Boucheron, the artist commissioned to do your portrait, is ready."

Hannah slipped the phone back into the drawer beside her bed before following Lady Andrea to the Queen's drawing room where Monsieur Boucheron had set up his easel.

For the next two hours Hannah sat in the small elegant armless chair holding herself perfectly still as the soft yellow afternoon light illuminated her shoulders and face.

Lady Andrea, Camille and Teresa hovered in the background as the artist sketched. Every now and then Camille or Teresa would move forward to smooth a strand of hair, or apply a dab of powder to Hannah's brow or nose.

But Hannah never moved, or complained, her gaze fixed on a distant point.

Her calm was an act. Beneath her cool, half smile, she felt wild.

What if Emmeline was deliberately delaying her flight to Raguva so she could spend more time with her boyfriend?

What if Emmeline's goal all along was to have a long romantic break with this Alejandro?

Hannah's hands clenched in her lap. Please don't let that be the case. Emmeline couldn't be so selfish—

"Maybe a break?" The artist suggested, setting down his paintbrush. "Her Highness looks unhappy. Perhaps it's time for a little stretch?"

Hannah nodded, and hurried to her room to try to call Emmeline again. This time she got through.

"I couldn't understand your message," Emmeline said, answering immediately. "The reception wasn't good and the message was broken up—"

"Are you with Alejandro?" Hannah demanded sharply.

"What?"

"You know, your Argentine boyfriend, a member of the polo team."

Emmeline exhaled hard. "How do you know?"

"Zale. He's not happy. You have to come now. Today. You have to sort this out before it's too late."

"You know I'm trying—"

"No, Emmeline, I don't know you're trying. I actually don't think you're trying very hard at all, because things are falling apart here—"

"Things are falling apart here, too!"

"Zale wants to end the engagement. He doesn't think you're compatible."

"How can he say that? He's never spent time with me!"

"Precisely. If you want to save the marriage, you have to get here quickly, because he's giving us—well, you—just four days to prove to him that you're the right one."

"Even at the soonest, I won't be able to get there before morning, so it's up to you to convince him for the next twenty-four hours that he does want to marry me."

"But, Emmeline, I'm not you!"

"So be yourself. Smooth things over. I know you can."

"Why should I? What have you ever done for me?"

"What do you want me to do?"

Good question. What did Hannah want? She already had the great job and good friends. She liked herself. Liked what she'd accomplished in life. All she really wanted now was to fall in love, but she wasn't going to find her Mr. Right if she was with another woman's man. "I just want you to come here and get me out of this. This is your relationship. Your engagement."

"I know!" Emmeline's voice suddenly broke. "Hannah, I know. But I'm in trouble. And I can't see my way clear yet."

"Do you even want to marry King Patek?"

"Yes," Emmeline said quickly then paused. "No. No, I don't. But I have to. It's what our families want. Zale's father and mine. They worked out an arrangement that essentially forces me into the marriage. If I don't marry Zale, it will cost my father five million euros. If I fail to fulfill my obligations in any way, my family pays."

"So you can't end the engagement."

"No. Not without disgracing my family."

"And what if King Patek breaks off the engagement?"

"If he breaks the engagement without cause, he pays my family two and a half million euros. But if he breaks it off with cause, my family still has to pay him five million."

"Why does he only have to pay half of what your family pays?"

"He's a king. I'm just a princess."

Just a princess, Hannah silently repeated, overwhelmed by this world of nobility, wealth and power.

"So you see why I need you," Emmeline said wearily. "I need you to convince Zale I am right for him and once I get there, I will make it work. I will walk down the aisle, and say my vows, and make him happy."

"Can't you talk to your family about this? Can't you go to your father—"

"No. My father would never understand. Or forgive me. My...parents...they aren't like me. They're very strict. Very old-fashioned. I know they mean well but they already disapprove of me, already view me as if I'm...tainted."

"Tainted? How?"

"Not truly noble."

"But why?"

Silence stretched across the line and it took Hannah a moment to realize that Emmeline was crying.

"Emmeline." Hannah felt for the princess. "It's going to be okay. Things always work out—"

"Not this time, Hannah. This time I lose no matter what happens."

Hannah's brows pulled together. She hated suffering in any form, and Emmeline was clearly suffering. "Don't give up. Stay calm. I'll do my best until you can get here."

"Thank you, Hannah, and I will be there. As soon as I can."

Hannah hung up the phone, exhausted. This was such a mess. An absolute disaster.

And none of this would have happened if Hannah didn't wear her heart on her sleeve.

Her father had always warned her that she was too tenderhearted, that people would—and did—take advantage of her. He'd predicted that one day her lack of backbone would come back to haunt her, and he was right. It'd happened.

A half hour later Lady Andrea entered Hannah's suite expecting to find her dressed and ready for dinner. Instead Hannah lay stretched on her bed using her high-tech phone to do some research on the Internet.

"Your Highness, His Majesty is expecting you in minutes."

Hannah looked up from the screen where she'd been doing a crash course on celebrity gossip so she'd know as much as she could about Emmeline's Argentine boyfriend, Alejandro.

It was just unfortunate that she'd waited until now to learn what she could about Emmeline, but celebrities and royals had never interested her, and growing up without a television or even Internet access, she'd never known such a world existed until she entered high school. But now she wished she'd spent a little more time paying attention to Hollywood celebrities and European royals, particularly the young royals today.

"I know. I'll be ready," she said. "I just need to finish this article and I'll go."

"But you aren't dressed for dinner. Do you even know what you're going to wear?"

"No. You can pick something for me, if you'd like."

Lady Andrea sent Hannah to dinner in a stunning marine blue gown that was loosely gathered at the throat and yet cut away to leave her shoulders and arms bare. Rich blue sapphire teardrops hung from her ears and a matching bracelet circled her wrist.

With her hair softly gathered at her nape and sleek high heels on her feet Hannah felt more glamorous than she ever had before.

They were to have a quiet dinner in the King's Chambers, which were four large rooms strung together. Zale's butler opened the living room door, inviting her in.

"I haven't had the pleasure of meeting you yet, Your Highness, but I look forward to serving you soon," Mr. Krek said with a formal little bow.

Hannah smiled warmly. "It's good to meet you. I've heard so much about you."

He flushed with pleasure. "I look forward to serving you, Your Highness."

"Thank you, Mr. Krek."

"Now if you'll excuse me, I'll see to your drinks and appetizers."

Hannah watched him walk out and she was alone, and then a moment later, she was not.

She knew the moment Zale entered the room. Felt a frisson of pleasure race down her spine. Turning slowly, Hannah looked over her shoulder.

There he was, Zale Patek, standing in the doorway, dressed in an elegant dinner jacket, crisp shirt and tie. His hair was combed, his jaw freshly shaven.

"Your Majesty," she said, suddenly breathless.

"Your Highness," he answered, allowing his gaze to slowly sweep over her, making her feel as if she was about to become his next favorite plaything. He moved from the doorway and walked toward her. "I like the dress."

Her heart beat double fast. "But not the lady?"

His piercing amber gaze met hers. "I'm still trying to decide."

She lifted a brow, her full lips pursing. "Well, when you've come to a decision, do let me know."

Heat shot through Zale, his body hardening instantaneously. My God, she was good. Interesting. *Clever.*

He was fascinated by the way she carried herself, her wit, her intelligence. She was beautiful and challenging and complex.

He'd fully intended to end it with Emmeline earlier today. He was going to make a clean break, wire the money he'd owe the d'Arcy family to the Bank of Brabant and move on so that he could find someone more suitable.

That's why he'd gone to her in her dressing room. That's why he'd been honest.

Blunt.

But now that she was fighting back, demanding a chance to prove herself worthy, he felt compelled to give her that opportunity.

Not out of any altruistic gesture, of course.

When it came to Emmeline he was appallingly carnal. He might not like her, but she was right—he wanted her. And the intensity of his desire surprised him.

He'd thought her beautiful at their engagement party but he hadn't felt this fierce physical attraction that evening. The truth was he hadn't felt much of anything for her throughout the year. Until now.

But ever since yesterday, whenever he looked at her, he

thought of one thing—getting her in his bed, naked beneath him.

He wanted to see her long blond hair tousled about her face, a golden ripple across the pillow.

He wanted to part her thighs as wide as he could and bury himself in her, thrusting deep and hard to make her come.

He wanted to shatter her control and make her fall apart and see if there was perhaps a real woman, a warm woman, underneath the shimmering hair and stunning face.

"We both have busy schedules," he said, "but I'll see if I can't have our appointments and appearances shuffled around to allow us to spend as much time together in the next few days—"

"Four," she interrupted. "You've promised me four starting tomorrow."

"I think that was four, starting today."

"Tomorrow," she insisted firmly. "Today was already half over when we made the agreement."

"Perhaps, but as I intend to spend all our time together, I think you might find four days excessively long, unless you don't think you'll weary of me after morning, noon and night?" His voice trailed off and he shrugged, as if to say it was entirely up to her.

Two bright spots of color burned high in her cheekbones deepening her blue eyes. "I would only weary of you if you were boring." Her full lips curved. "Do you intend to be boring?"

She was outrageous. She should be punished. With his hands, and mouth, and tongue.

His body hardened just thinking of how she'd feel beneath him.

Emmeline glanced around the room, her expression serene. "I'm starving. Do you know when dinner will be served?"

"I'm not so easily distracted," he said, "and a change of subject won't change my intentions."

"And I'm sure you've heard the expression, don't put the cart before the horse?"

He let his gaze travel slowly over her, resting provocatively on her breasts, hips and the juncture of her thighs. "Are you the cart? Or the horse?"

Her chin lifted. "Neither."

Hannah was thrilled when Mr. Krek invited them to dinner, which was served at an intimate round table before the living room's tall gold marble fireplace.

"I knew your English was excellent," Zale said, midway through dinner as the footmen removed one plate only to replace it with another. "But I hadn't realized you spoke it with an American accent. Did you study in the States or have an American tutor?"

She'd read that Zale Patek spoke more languages than any other royal—Spanish, Italian, French, English, Swedish, Turkish, Greek and of course his native language, Raguvian. He was that rare breed of scholar and athlete.

"American tutor," she said, trying to remember if Emmeline had ever studied in the United States but didn't think so. "And you?"

"I was educated in England—sent to boarding school at ten, and then on to university after."

"Why England?"

"Tradition. I attended the same schools as my brother, father, grandfather and great-grandfather."

"When you have children, will your son do the same?"

A slightly mocking note entered his voice. "You mean, *our* son?"

Hannah glanced up, straight into his eyes. They were such a unique color, not exactly brown, not exactly gold. "Yes, ours," she said, blushing as she imagined having Zale's child.

"Our one of two," he added. "The heir and spare. It's all you'd agree to give me, remember?"

Hannah just looked at him.

"Why, Emmeline, were you so adamant that it only be two? You never gave me a proper explanation." His lips curved in a lazy smile that failed to touch his eyes. "We finally have time to talk properly. To discuss all the things you wouldn't discuss this past year. I'd love to know why you insisted we limit our family to two. If we hope to save our relationship, then this is probably the best place to start."

"I don't know."

Zale took her hand, lifted it to his mouth. "Was it your figure you feared losing?"

She tugged her hand back, fingers tingling from the touch. "No!"

"Your freedom then?"

"That's silly."

"Well, it is hard to gallivant about when you're pregnant."

"I don't gallivant, and despite what you might think, I look forward to having a family."

"Just not a large family."

"Yes."

"Why?"

"Personal preference. Why do you want a large one?"

"Because I enjoyed having brothers. Their friendship and companionship meant a great deal to me." His lashes lowered concealing his expression as he toyed with the delicate stem of his wine goblet. "Do you ever think your fear of pregnancy might stem from your mother's death after childbirth?"

Hannah froze, suddenly chilled.

Emmeline's mother had died in childbirth?

But how was that possible? Emmeline's mother, Queen Claire, was alive and well and had just been in Spain on holiday last week.

"My mother is alive," she said numbly, finding the subject too close to home as Hannah's own mother had died in childbirth as well.

"I'm sorry. I should have said your birth mother. You were

adopted by your parents, King William and Queen Claire d'Arcy, when you were just six days old."

"How did you find out?" she whispered.

"Your father told me several months ago when we hit that impasse in our contract negotiations. He wanted me to understand that your reluctance to have children wasn't out of selfishness, but probably fear."

"So if my father gave you a reason, why put me through this?" Hannah fought to hang on to her temper.

"I wanted you to tell me."

"Why?"

He was angry now, too. "Because just once I'd like to hear the truth from you. I'd like to know the real you. I don't know who that person is, or what she wants, or what she really feels."

She flinched at the words, *real you,* but wouldn't linger on them.

"You want to know what I think?" she blazed. "I think it's a crime that women still die in childbirth. We can put men on the moon. Create weapons of mass destruction. Produce miracle drugs and design modern hospitals. So why can't we make childbirth safe? How can we allow women to die while creating life?"

"Because we're mortal. Life eventually ends for all of us."

Hannah's father, Jake, had said the same thing regularly while Hannah was growing up. "It's tragic." Her voice dropped, deepening. "Children need their mothers."

"Just as mothers need their children." His broad shoulders shifted uncomfortably. "It broke my mother's heart that she couldn't save my older brother. I heard her say more than once, that she wished she could switch places with Stephen."

"Didn't that hurt you?"

"Stephen was her firstborn. She'd always been close to him."

"Weren't you two close?"

"Not as close as I would have liked. But I was the middle child and my younger brother needed my mother more."

"Where is your younger brother?"

"Here, in the palace."

"Why haven't I met him?"

He hesitated, choosing his words with care. "Constantine has special needs and requires round-the-clock care. He forms attachments easily and doesn't comprehend loss."

Hannah frowned, puzzled. "Are you afraid I'll hurt him?"

"Not deliberately. But in order to protect him, I've decided to wait to introduce you until I know you're staying."

CHAPTER SIX

LATER that night, tucked in bed, Hannah took out her phone and researched the Patek Royal family.

There were dozens of articles online but very few references to the youngest Patek prince, Constantine. Once someone gave his date of birth—he was three years older than Hannah—and another time, he was referred to as the third son, but that was it. To the outside world, Prince Constantine didn't exist.

Hannah could see why Zale would want to protect his brother from the world, but to keep his future wife from meeting his only surviving family? It made Hannah think Zale had no intentions of marrying Emmeline.

Hannah turned off the phone, and then the lamp next to her bed, but couldn't sleep.

Zale wasn't an easy man. He was tough, proud and competitive. And the more she got to know him, the more certain she was that he'd crush Emmeline. Not intentionally, of course, but simply because he didn't understand his own strength.

He'd never win Emmeline's heart by browbeating her, either. He needed to court her. Needed to woo her. Needed to show that he had a softer side, and Hannah knew he did because she saw glimpses of it every now and then. Just not often enough.

It was time Zale exerted himself a little bit. Time he made an effort to win Emmeline over instead of judging her and criticizing her. He might be a king, but he needed to start treating his betrothed like the queen she would be.

Hannah woke early the next morning and rang for Celine to help her dress. "Can you send word to His Majesty that I'd like to meet him?" Hannah asked, stepping from her shower to dress.

Today she chose her own clothes, selecting a pale apricot linen dress from Emmeline's wardrobe paired with a slim-fitting cropped cashmere sweater the same hue. She slipped a gold bangle on her wrist and small gold hoops on her ears, before pulling her hair back in a ponytail. She did her own makeup, keeping it light, and was just finishing applying mascara when word arrived that His Majesty was waiting for her in the family dining room.

Hannah took a deep breath and squared her shoulders as a footman escorted her.

The family dining room was a cozy room on the second floor. Tall mullioned windows lined the walls and sunlight glazed the glass, casting bright rays across the rich walnut table and illuminating the centerpiece of pink and cream tulips in a crystal vase.

Zale sat at one end of the table reading a stack of newspapers, a cup of espresso at his elbow.

Briefly he lifted his head as she entered the room, his amber gaze sweeping over her. "This is a surprise," he said.

"A pleasant one, I hope," she answered, taking the chair the uniformed footman held for her and smoothing the hem of her crisp linen dress over her knees.

The footman poured her coffee and brought her fresh squeezed orange juice before handing her a small elegant printed menu. Her eyebrows arched. A printed menu for a family meal?

Zale must have been able to read her mind as he said from behind his newspaper, "Chef will make anything you like, but he also offers specialty items every morning based on what he's picked up from the local farmers market."

"How do you know what I was thinking?"

"You're easy to read." He folded the paper and set it down.

"So what am I thinking now?" she asked, stirring milk into her coffee.

Zale studied her for a moment, his expression inscrutable. "You're upset that I won't introduce you to my brother, and you're here to convince me otherwise."

"Not at all," she said, lifting her cup to sip the hot, strong coffee. "I think you're spot-on. Your brother should be protected. Until we are absolutely certain we want to proceed with the wedding, we should be careful. I'd hate to grow fond of your brother only to realize you're not entirely suitable for me."

His eyebrow lifted. "And now *I'm* not suitable?"

She offered the footman a sunny smile as he moved forward to offer her a selection of flaky pastries. She refused the pastries and turned her attention back to Zale. "I thought about what you said last night—about our lack of compatibility—and you might be right."

He shifted in his seat, shoulders becoming broader, expression harder, "Is that so?"

She nodded, took another sip of coffee. "We don't know each other, and the only way you'll know I'm right for you is if I'm myself. So from now on, I'm going to be myself, and hopefully, you'll like the real me. But if you don't, I'd rather go home than marry someone who doesn't enjoy my company."

Zale's brows lowered. "You would reject me?"

She smiled, the same patient smile she gave Sheikh Al-Koury when he gave her another impossible task. "Since we're being completely honest, I admit that I don't want to marry someone I don't like, either."

His lips thinned.

She nodded, as if he'd given a sign of agreement. "I'm really looking forward to the next four days and spending time together. I imagine you have some fun activities planned—" she lifted a finger, holding him off a moment "—activities other than signing documents, sitting for portraits and selecting china patterns."

"Those are all necessary if we're to marry."

"Yes, *if*. But as you made clear yesterday, we don't know that we will. In fact, you're fairly certain we won't. So perhaps selecting a china pattern is a bit presumptuous, never mind a colossal waste of time. Perhaps we should slow down and... date...first."

"Date?"

"Mmm. Lunches. Dinners. Activities that allow us to spend time together in a relaxed and enjoyable manner."

"Is this a joke?"

"No. I definitely wouldn't joke about our future."

Zale stared at her through narrowed lashes, his expression grim. "You're so different from a year ago. You were so quiet at our engagement party. You hardly looked at me. Where has all this *personality* come from?"

Hannah shrugged. "It was always there, just a bit squashed by my parents' disapproval. But my parents aren't marrying you. I am."

"And this entire epiphany came to you last night?"

"Yes. As I lay in bed." She gestured to the footman. "I think I'd like the eggs Florentine and some fresh fruit. Thank you." She lifted her white linen napkin from the table and placed it on her lap. "I thought you'd be pleased by my epiphany but you don't seem happy at all."

He didn't look happy, either. His brow was furrowed, his square chin jutted and he was practically glowering at her from across the table. "I find your attitude a trifle cavalier considering the circumstances. Your parents have invested a great deal of money into our alliance—"

"Five million euros."

A small muscle pulled in his jaw at her interruption. "And I, too, am invested."

"Two and a half million. Because you're a king and more important than I am."

"Emmeline," he growled.

It'd meant to be a warning.

Hannah ignored it. "But that's the reality, isn't it? You are a king and I'm just a princess—"

"Stop."

"It's true. You do have more power. You can afford to be critical. Judgmental. Unforgiving."

"That's not who I am."

"It's how you speak to me. You've told me repeatedly that I'm not suitable." Her shoulders lifted and fell. "So why would I want to marry you? Why would I want to spend my life with a person who treats me like my parents do?"

He leaned back in his chair and for a long moment said nothing and then he shook his head. "I respect your parents, but I'm nothing like them."

"Yet all I've heard from you since I arrived is that I'm a disappointment and you can't wait to get rid of me."

"I also think I've told you you're beautiful a half dozen times."

"But I'd rather you like who I am as a person than appreciate my looks. Beauty fades. Appearances change. It's the inside that matters and that's the part of me you don't like."

"I've never said that."

"Because there isn't anything about me—other than my bloodline and my looks—that you do like."

He fell silent. She knew she'd made a point. She could see it in his eyes and the twist of his lips.

Silence stretched. Zale drew a deep breath and slowly exhaled. "I like you right now," he said after a moment. "I like your candor. I appreciate honesty."

Hannah suppressed the twinge of guilt she felt at his mention of honesty. "Zale, I think there are a lot of things you'd like about me, given the chance to get to know me. I love adventure. I have a great sense of humor. I enjoy traveling and reading and learning about new cultures. But if you keep throwing the past in my face, you'll never get to know any of those things about me."

"It's hard to forget that until last week you were with Alejandro."

"Is that pride speaking?"

"No. It's the realist in me. The one that knows leopards don't change their spots."

"But the realist must also see that I'm here. I asked to join you at breakfast this morning. I want to spend as much time as I can with you—Zale, the man, not the king—over the next few days. But you have to want to be with me, too, because I don't want to marry my father. I want a man that likes me. Enjoys me. And could maybe even one day love me."

Zale stood up, walked across the room, then turned to face her. "Maybe we need to start over," he said quietly. "Wipe the slate clean."

"Can you?"

His broad shoulders shrugged. "I won't know until I try. But let's do what you've suggested. Try to act like a normal couple getting to know each other. We'll spend time together...date."

She smiled at the way he said date. He made it sound foreign and exotic, as if it was something he'd never normally do. "Good. It's the only way we'll know if we really have a chance."

"So let's have our first...*date*...today. I've morning meetings but once they wrap up we'll head out for the rest of the day." He paused, thought a moment and then added, "We'll plan to meet at eleven. Wear something comfortable, bring a sweater and a swimsuit, just in case."

A sweater and a swimsuit? She was immediately curious as to where they were going but didn't ask. "I'll be ready."

Hannah changed into white linen pants, a blue and white striped knit shirt topped by a navy jacket. It was rather nautical but the most casual thing Hannah could find in Emmeline's elegant wardrobe.

Reluctantly she packed one of Emmeline's two-piece swimsuits, thinking there was no way her curvy figure would be covered by the tiny scraps of material, but Zale had said to bring a suit and so she would.

She headed downstairs at five to eleven to find Zale already waiting for her. She'd expected a car would be waiting outside but discovered a helicopter in the enormous circular driveway instead.

The pilot gave both Hannah and Zale headsets to wear for the flight to reduce noise. The headsets came equipped with microphones but Zale was quiet as they lifted off the palace helipad and flew above the walled city over creamy colored bluffs, cypress pines and hillsides dotted with orange and red tiled houses.

Even with the microphones it would be impossible to really talk above the noise and Hannah didn't mind the silence as it gave her a chance to really see Raguva. It'd been nighttime when she'd arrived and she was fascinated by this jewel-like kingdom on the Dalmatian Coast.

"We're going to my island," Zale said, ten minutes into the flight. "I don't go often, haven't been there in years, but I thought we could both use some downtime away from the palace."

For twenty minutes they flew over sapphire water and the odd sailboat, barge and yacht until several rocky islands appeared below. The islands were almost barren with just a few gnarled trees above jagged cliffs. There were stone ruins on one island, and a simple stone house on another. That's the island they were landing on.

The pilot slowly touched down in a clearing before the house and Zale opened the door, climbed out and helped Hannah out. The pilot handed Zale a leather duffel and they spoke together for a moment before taking off.

Hannah watched the helicopter lift off, blades whirring, leaving them alone on a deserted island in the middle of the Adriatic Sea. "He's coming back for us, right?"

Zale's lips curved in a trace of a smile. "Don't worry. He'll be back before it's dark. But even if he isn't, my security detail has been in the water since midmorning. They've secured the island and they can be here in minutes."

"Do you come here often?" she asked, shouldering her beach tote bag and looking around. The simple farm-style house had thick stone walls, single-pane glass windows and a pale terracotta tiled roof.

He shook his head. "Haven't been here in years."

"Why?"

"Haven't had the desire, nor the time."

The sun was now directly overhead and it was hot in the sunlight. Hannah peeled her navy jacket off. "I should have brought shorts or worn a skirt."

"You'll be in your swimsuit soon. We're about to head down to the beach for lunch."

"Is that our picnic lunch?" she asked, gesturing to the small leather duffel.

"Nope. My suit, towels and sunscreen."

"Where's lunch?"

"Hungry?"

"Thirsty."

"Come. Let's go to the beach. Everything's already there."

They walked across the clearing toward the cypress trees and a steep staircase chiseled into the stone cliff.

Hannah followed Zale down the stairs slowly, careful not to trip in her heels. The sun beat down on the top of her head and she grew hotter by the moment. Her elegant sandals were totally impractical for the steep descent and her white trousers grew dusty at the hem. And yet the ocean sparkled far below, the sapphire and turquoise water lapping against ivory sand.

The deep blue water looked impossibly inviting. Hannah couldn't wait to get her feet wet. She loved to swim and looked forward to stretching out in the sun.

Zale waited for her at the bottom of the stairs. He'd taken off his shoes and rolled up his sleeves revealing strong tan forearms. "No more stairs till later."

She slipped off her high-heel sandals, flexing her toes. "Good. That was a little scary."

She'd thought they'd already reached the beach but Zale walked around the corner to another private beach. A large colorful blanket was spread out on the sand with a large basket anchoring one corner, and an ice chest on another.

Zale crouched next to the ice chest and opened the top. "Chef took care of us. Beer, wine, water, juice. What would you like to drink?"

"Beer, please," she said, kneeling down on the blanket, feet blistered and totally parched.

"Beer?"

"I love a cold beer on a hot summer day. Don't you?"

"Yes, but not many women do." He withdrew two chilled bottles and a chilled glass.

"I don't need a glass," she said, waving off the glass and taking one of the opened bottles from him. "How did this all get here?" she asked, gesturing to the basket and ice chest.

"My security detail brought it earlier when they secured the island."

"Is this a family island?"

He unbuttoned his shirt, giving her a tantalizing view of tan, taut skin over sinewy muscle. "No, I bought it back when I played football for a living. I wanted a place far from crowds, paparazzi and overly friendly fans."

Hannah almost licked her lips. He looked incredible. The dense curved muscles of his chest gave way to lean hard abs. "Did you bring your girlfriends here?"

"Just one, and only once. She found it too isolated for her liking."

"So what do you do when you're here?"

"Sleep. Read. Relax."

She sipped her beer. "What do you read?"

"Everything. Novels. Biographies. Histories. Whatever I can get my hands on."

Her lips curved and she settled onto the blanket. "Do you have a favorite author?"

"I do, but I don't think he's writing anymore. Most of his books were published nearly twenty years ago. James Clavell is his name. He wrote *Shogun, Tai-Pan, Noble House*—"

"King Rat," she supplied, smiling. "I loved his books. My father introduced me to him. For years I wanted to learn Japanese."

"Did you?"

"No. You couldn't find Japanese language classes in B—" Hannah broke off, realizing she came dangerously close to saying Bandera, her hometown in Texas. She flushed, took a quick sip of her beer. "I learned Spanish and Italian instead."

"You're fluent in both?"

"Yes. You are, too. I read somewhere that you know more languages than any other modern royal. Do languages just come easily to you?"

"I worked at it, the same way I worked at playing football. You don't improve if you don't apply yourself."

"Not everyone is willing to work that hard."

He shrugged, the thin fabric of his shirt clinging to his broad shoulders and outlining his muscles. "I don't mind hard work. Never have."

Hannah bit her lip, liking him more with every moment that passed. Zale was her kind of man—gorgeous, built and brilliant, too. Not fair, she thought breathlessly, far too attracted for her own good.

What she needed was to cool down. "Feel like swimming?" she asked.

"Good idea. It's hot." He pointed along the cliff to an opening in the rock. "There's a little alcove over there by the rock where you can change. Or if you don't like caves, you can just change here, and I promise not to look."

"Cave sounds great," Hannah answered, grabbing her suit and getting to her feet.

In the hollowed-out rock she stripped off her clothes and

stepped into the tangerine bikini bottoms before tying the strings of the bikini top around her neck and back. The tiny shiny orange triangles barely covered anything and she sucked in her stomach as if she could somehow make herself smaller.

It took all of her courage to walk back to the blanket in nothing but her suit.

It didn't help that Zale stood at the edge of the water, watching her walk. He'd changed while she was gone and was wearing black and red surfer-style board shorts instead of the traditional European men's suit.

She liked the long board shorts. They hung low on his lean hips, showing off his flat, chiseled stomach. He looked like a surfer—tan, lean, muscular—and she couldn't remember the last time she had found a man this sexy.

Dropping her clothes on the blanket, Hannah walked toward him. "I like your board shorts. Do you surf?"

"I do." He paused. "Well, I did. I grew up surfing—my brother Stephen was really good—but haven't gone on a true surf trip in years."

She waded into the water, gasping a little at the cool temperature. "Where would you go?"

"Wherever there were good waves. Rincon, Brazil, Indonesia, Costa Rica." He ran a hand through his hair, muscles in his thick bicep flexing. "I miss it. But then I miss football, too. I find it hard, being inside, sitting at a desk, as much as I do."

"So how do you handle it?" she asked, wading deeper and sinking down to her shoulders. The water felt warmer already.

"I run and work out. A lot."

There was a roughness in his voice, a sound of pain, and Hannah's chest squeezed. Everything about him was so real, so physical.

Here on this island he was a man, not merely a king, and she found the man incredibly appealing.

Her survival instinct told her to be careful, that allowing herself to feel anything for him would lead to danger. But Zale was so hard to resist. Who else had this combination of dense muscle, burnished skin, keen intellect and burning ambition?

"You need a proper vacation," she said huskily. "A chance to just unplug and unwind."

"It'd be nice."

"Why don't you take one?"

"Our honeymoon was supposed to be one."

Hannah inhaled sharply, feeling as if she'd gotten a kick to the ribs.

She'd forgotten yet again that she was supposed to be Emmeline. Forgot he would soon marry Emmeline. Would soon honeymoon with her.

The thought of Zale with Emmeline hurt. "Remind me, what are we doing for our honeymoon?" she asked, hating that she already felt jealous. Hating the idea of them together on a beach like this, talking like this...

"We're spending ten days on my yacht in Greece and then a few days in Paris so you can do some shopping."

Hannah chewed on her inner lip, thinking that Zale did not strike her as the type to enjoy cruising the Greek islands on a yacht. He struck her as too active for ten days of sunbathing on a yacht. Some rest was good but wouldn't he also want adventure, or some of an adrenaline rush? "That doesn't sound fun for you."

"It's what you wanted."

He meant, that was what Emmeline wanted.

Hannah shook her head, unaccountably angry. Emmeline and Zale were not a good fit. They didn't belong together. Emmeline didn't even want to marry him but was doing it out of obligation. How could this be a happy marriage?

But Hannah couldn't say anything. It wasn't her place to say anything. She was just here as a placeholder until Emmeline arrived.

And even that made Hannah furious.

She dived under a wave, exhaled until she needed air and then popped back to the surface. Still upset, she swam a few strokes before turning on her back to float. The sun shone brightly overhead. The water felt cool against her skin and she could taste the tang of salt on her lips.

Zale was not hers.

Zale would never be hers.

She had to remember that. Couldn't forget it. Couldn't let personal feelings cloud the commitment she'd made to Emmeline. Even if that commitment made her heart ache.

Hannah turned onto her stomach and swam slowly back to the beach where Zale sat on the sand waiting for her.

"You're a good swimmer," he said as she walked out of the water. His gaze was warm as it slowly swept over her, lingering on the small triangles that barely covered her full breasts as well as the scrap of fabric between her thighs.

She could tell from his expression that he liked what he saw and it made her nipples harden and thrust against the wet flimsy fabric of her bikini top.

Nervous, she slicked her long wet hair back from her face. "I love the ocean," she said, her legs feeling strangely weak. No man had ever looked at her like this. No man had ever made her feel special or beautiful. As if she were something to be touched...tasted... "Love being in the water."

"I like watching you."

His voice had dropped, deepened and she felt something coil deep in her belly. Nerves. Adrenaline.

She was wanting all kinds of things she never thought about. Wanting emotions and sensation she never felt.

"Well, I'd love to watch you surf one day," she answered, sitting down next to him. He was so close she could reach out and brush her fingers across his hard bronzed biceps, so close she could see every shadow and hollow of his flat ripped abs.

She wondered what his skin would feel like if she touched him. Wondered what he'd do.

Her fingers curled into a fist. She couldn't think like this. Couldn't be tempted.

"We'll have to plan a surf trip," he said, reaching out to lift her wet hair and twist the long strands, wringing water from the ends. "Where should we go? Bali? Perth? Durban?"

She shivered with pleasure as his warm fingers grazed her shoulder. She liked the way he twisted her hair, the tug on her scalp, the heat in his eyes.

He made her feel beautiful. Desirable.

Hungry.

She touched her tongue to her upper lip, dazed by the need to be touched. She craved his hands on her body, wanted his palms on her breasts.

"Anywhere," she whispered, her breasts aching, her nipples pressing in blatant invitation against her bikini top.

His gaze dropped to her breasts and she could feel the heat in his eyes as if he'd actually caressed her.

"What would you do while I surfed?" he asked, pushing her back against the sand to straddle her hips.

He was hard and she gasped, looking up into his eyes, her lips parting helplessly. It felt so good. She wanted more of him and was aching for him to touch her.

"I couldn't just leave you at the hotel bored," he added, reaching out to cup her breast, fascinated by her response.

"Wouldn't be bored," she choked, her voice failing her, her inner thighs squeezing tight as hot sensation rushed through her. She wanted him between her thighs, his mouth on her nipple, his hands stroking everywhere…

"What would you do?" he asked.

She could hardly think straight. "Read."

"I don't know if that would work," he murmured, slipping a hand into her thick wet hair, and drawing her head back so he could see her face.

"Why not?"

Desire burned in his eyes, formed lines at his mouth. A rich dusky color warmed his cheekbones. "I don't know if I could leave you alone long enough to go surf. I don't think I'd want to surf, not if I had you in my bed."

She just stared up into his eyes, lost in him.

He stretched out over her, bracing his weight on his elbows and lowered his head to touch his lips to the tender skin beneath her pale jaw. "I want you."

He'd only brushed his lips against her jaw in the most fleeting of touches and yet the place he'd kissed burned, her skin too hot and sensitive.

"But you know that, don't you?" he added, kissing yet another spot, making her nerves dance. "You know I can't stay away from you even when I should."

She shivered helplessly as his mouth melted her defenses, turning her inside out. She couldn't even focus on what he was saying, not when his lips were making her body ache for him.

"And yet I should," he added, voice pitched seductively low. "At least until we both know what we want."

Hannah quivered as his voice rumbled through her, making her squirm. She knew what she wanted. She wanted him. Zale. Wanted to wrap herself around him and never let go.

He pressed another kiss to the base of her throat before turning her over, pulling her on top of him. Gritty sand slipped between them. The sun shone hotly, but nothing was as hot as Hannah's hunger as he put his hands on her waist, sliding one hand down across her bottom while the other slid up to cup her breast.

His hands were so warm and they made her feel as if she were on fire. She ached and tingled and burned, shivering against him.

"I think I know what I want," she breathed, as his thumb found her taut, aching nipple and strummed it. "But maybe that's not what you're talking about."

"And what do you want?"

She could hardly think straight, wasn't even sure where she was or what was happening, only that she wanted more—more him, more skin, more sensation. "You."

"But for how long?" he asked, kissing the side of her neck and then brushing his lips over hers.

She kissed him back, lifting an arm and clasping the back

of his neck. He was so tall, so hard, so strong. She was safe with him. He'd never let anyone hurt her. "For ever," she whispered against his mouth, not caring if he heard her, not caring about anything anymore but him.

When would she ever meet someone like Zalc Patek again? When would she ever feel so alive and beautiful again?

He lifted his head to look into her eyes. His eyes were dark, his cheekbones jutted, his expression intense. He looked wild. Fierce. Primal.

"Be careful what you say," he murmured, molding her nearly naked body even closer to his. She could feel his warm skin against hers and his hard shaft press against her belly.

He cupped her backside in his hands, holding her hips firmly against him, making her gasp as he rubbed her over the head of his shaft once and again.

She could feel the thickness and length of his erection through his board shorts. Felt the corded muscles of his thighs and the thick muscles in his back. He was gorgeous, so very, very gorgeous. "I do want you," she said, her voice breaking. "Even if it's wrong."

His head dipped, his lips taking hers in a slow, deep, bone-melting kiss. "I can't make love to you now," he said, his voice hoarse in her ear. "But if you still feel this way tonight, Emmeline, you won't be able to keep me out of your bed."

CHAPTER SEVEN

"WHY won't you make love now?" Hannah asked dizzily, hands pressed to Zale's warm bare chest. The sun beat down on her back and Zale felt so good, his skin smooth and firm, the scent of him addictive, almost as addictive as his kiss.

His hands rested on her backside, his touch sending rivulets of pleasure through her.

"I don't want to take advantage of you."

Beneath her palms she felt the steady beating of his heart. "You think I'll regret it?"

"Possibly. And I'd hate it if that happened."

"Smart," she answered, voice husky. She sat up, disappointed. But she knew he was right. She probably would have regretted it. Obviously he had more control than she did.

He sat up, caught the back of her head and kissed her head. "Don't look so hurt." His voice was pitched so deep it rumbled through her. "I'm trying to protect you, Emmeline. But it's not easy doing the right thing."

She nodded and stood up, backed away a step, unsteady on her feet. "I understand," she said, horribly close to tears. She liked Zale so much. Wanted him even more.

Zale stood and brushed the sand off, his expression equally grim. "Shall we see what Chef packed us for lunch?"

"Yes," she answered, going to retrieve her towel to wrap around her waist.

They sat in the middle of the blanket and Zale opened the

hamper. Hannah watched, her head thick, senses drugged. If his kisses were this potent, Hannah couldn't even imagine how she'd feel if they had sex.

Zale unpacked the lunch hamper in silence and Hannah was good with that. She didn't think she could make small talk, not when her emotions felt so wild. How could she be falling for Zale this hard? How could she want him this much, even when she knew he belonged to Emmeline?

Her conscience felt stricken and yet there was something else primal fighting with her guilt.

Need.

Desire.

And the desire was so foreign to her. She never wanted a man like this. Hadn't needed a man in years.

"I'll let you help yourself," Zale said, handing her a plate.

Hannah looked at all the food Zale's chef had sent—roast chicken, baguettes, cheeses, potato salad, beet salad, fruit and more—but her appetite was nonexistent.

"Would *you* have regretted making love?" she asked abruptly, looking across at him.

Zale sighed. "You have an amazing body and I'd have no problem taking you, exploring you. But…considering there are still serious decisions to be made, I don't think we can just jump into bed."

"So you're still trying to make up your mind about me."

He hesitated, then nodded.

Hannah clenched her hands together. "Forgetting the past, what worries you most about me?"

He looked off into the distance, his narrowed gaze fixed on a distant point out at sea and then his shoulders shifted. "You're just so different, Emmeline. You're not the woman I thought I was marrying. And I don't understand what's changed."

Hannah's heart sank. "You don't like…me?"

"No, I do like you. I very much like the woman that is here on the beach right now. You're smart, playful, confident and sexy. But that wasn't the woman I proposed to a year ago. And that concerns me. People don't change this much. Not at our age."

"Would you feel better if I was more like the old me?"

"Maybe. Probably. I'd at least be on familiar ground."

Hannah mustered a smile even though she felt like crying. "Then I'll work on getting the old me back. Hopefully it won't take long."

They returned to the palace midafternoon after more swimming and sunbathing but there was tension between them and Hannah felt the strain. She was glad when the helicopter arrived to take them back to the palace and told herself she was glad when Zale let her walk away from him and return to her suite of rooms.

She wasn't glad, though.

She didn't want to be alone in her rooms. She wanted to be with him. Wanted what they'd had for a moment on the beach—tenderness, closeness, passion.

Hannah paced her living room absolutely desperate. She'd agreed to play pretend and it was killing her. She wanted to tell Zale who she was, wanted him to know the truth about her, but she knew once she told him, she'd lose him altogether.

It wasn't fair that the one man she wanted most in the world was the one man she couldn't have.

If only she really was Emmeline d'Arcy. If only she could be the princess he needed.

A soft, muffled sound reached her and Hannah paused in the middle of her suite to listen.

There it was again, a low cry—part whimper, part moan—and it sounded as though it were coming from her adjoining bedroom.

Hannah stiffened, her skin prickling. She was about to call for the palace guard when she heard the word *Mari,* Raguvian for Mama.

And then again.

Someone was crying for his mother.

Timidly she went to her bedroom door and pushed it slightly

open. Light spilled into the dark bedroom. She could hear the sound of crying more clearly.

Mama, Mama.

Hannah pushed the door all the way open and the light from the living room illuminated the bedroom. She could see all the way across the large room. And although the far corners remained shadowy, she saw a figure in one sitting on the floor, hunched over.

The figure rocked in the corner. "Mama?" he said, slowly lifting his head.

It was a child's voice coming from an adult body, and Hannah knew immediately who was it was. Dark brown hair, sloped shoulders, knees bent and held tightly against his body.

Prince Constantine.

"Tinny?" she whispered, not wanting to startle him.

He scrubbed his face with his forearm and looked at her hopefully. "Mama, home?"

For a moment Hannah couldn't breathe and her eyes burned with tears. She slowly crouched down in the doorway. "No, my love, your mama isn't home." And suddenly her heart felt as if it would break. Mothers needed their children. Children needed their mothers. But it didn't always work out that way. "Do you want to find Zale? I bet he'd like to see you."

"Zale," Tinny said. "My brother."

"That's right. Let's find Zale, shall we?"

Hannah called for a footman, and the footman summoned Mrs. Sivka since His Majesty couldn't be located.

Hannah was sitting with Tinny on the love seat in her living room looking at pictures in a magazine with him when a knock sounded on her door.

Hannah opened the door to a short, round woman in her late seventies. "Forgive me for intruding, Your Royal Highness, but I understand my missing boy is here."

"Yes, I found Prince Constantine in my bedroom." Hannah opened the door wider, inviting the woman in. "Although I don't know why he was there."

"These are the Queen's Chambers, Your Highness."

Hannah stared blankly at the elderly woman before it hit her. This was his mother's room. The prince came here looking for her. "He still misses her."

The woman smiled sadly. "He doesn't understand why she hasn't come back."

"He knows Zale, though—" Hannah broke off, corrected herself. "His Majesty. We talked about him."

"Prince Constantine adores his big brother." The elderly woman looked at Hannah closely. "And I'm sure you hear this often, Your Highness, but you're the spitting image of your mother."

Hannah's breath caught in her throat. "How do you know?"

"I knew her." She frowned. "My goodness, I don't think I even introduced myself. I am Mrs. Sivka. I'm His Majesty's nanny."

"His Majesty? Zale Patek?"

"The very same. I took care of all the Patek princes as babies, and am back again taking care of Prince Constantine now that his parents are gone."

Hannah gestured toward the couch. "Please, sit. I'd love to hear more about the royal family, about His Majesty as a boy. What was he like? Did he get into trouble?"

Mrs. Sivka's round face creased with a broad smile. "Yes, he did, but then all boys get into trouble, and Prince Stephen and Prince Zale were no exception. They were bright, energetic, mischievous children, eager for adventures and busy planning pranks. Prince Stephen was not as sly as Prince Zale and would get caught red-handed, but His Majesty was small and fast and far more sneaky."

"Small, fast and sneaky, Mrs. Sivka?" It was Zale, and he'd entered the room so quietly that neither Hannah nor the nanny had heard him come in. "That hardly sounds flattering."

Mrs. Sivka's round face was wreathed in smiles. "You were a scamp, Your Majesty, but a very, dear, sweet one."

Zale rolled his eyes and moved to crouch before his brother,

Zale's powerful thighs corded with muscles, his evening jacket stretched tight across his back. "Tinny," he said sternly, hands on his brother's knees. "You can't run away from Mrs. Daum. You gave her quite a scare. She's very upset."

Tinny pressed a hand to his mouth, eyes wide. "Playing, Zale. Tinny playing."

"I know you like to play, but you can't just leave her like that. She's crying."

"Tinny love Mmm Daum."

"I know you do. So you can't just go on your own. You must take Mrs. Daum or Mrs. Sivka with you when you want to go for a walk or come see me."

Tinny's dark brown eyes filled with tears. "Tinny see Mama. Tinny miss Mama."

Zale swallowed hard. His voice dropped, deepening. "I know you do, Tinny. I miss Mama, too."

Tinny wiped tears away with the back of his wrist. "Bed now. Story."

Zale nodded and patted his brother's knee. "Yes, let's get you to bed and we'll read you a story. Okay?"

Mrs. Sivka held Tinny's hand as they walked back to his suite. Zale and Hannah followed. Tinny was babbling to himself, and rocking back and forth as he walked.

"It takes him a while to calm down once he's upset," Zale said to Hannah.

"He still misses your mother."

Zale's expression was troubled. "It's hard, because there's nothing I can do. There's no way I can fix this. He was so attached to my mother, and she was very devoted to him. She spent nearly all of her time with him."

"How did he get to my room?"

"He slipped away from Mrs. Daum while they were out walking after dinner. There are hundreds of hidden doors and secret passage ways in the palace and when he disappeared, Mrs. Daum went one way, my brother went another and panic ensued."

"Does he go to the Queen's Chambers often?"

"He used to, but hasn't in almost a year. That's why no one went there first."

They'd reached Tinny's suite and Zale offered to help get his brother changed into his pajamas, but Mrs. Sivka refused, saying she thought His Majesty and Her Highness should spend the time together. "Once all the guests arrive for the wedding, you won't have time to be alone, so take advantage of the time now."

Hannah hugged Prince Constantine. "Good night, Tinny," she said in Raguvian, kissing his cheek. "Sleep tight," she added in English.

Tinny squeezed her hard. "Night, Em-mie."

Emmie. Such a sweet nickname for Princess Emmeline. Hannah fought the lump in her throat.

Zale was saying good-night to his brother now, and Hannah turned to Mrs. Sivka, her emotions raw. "You're absolutely wonderful, Mrs. Sivka," she said huskily, tears not far off. "I'm so glad I got to meet you tonight, and I think His Majesty was very lucky to have you as his nanny."

"I still think of him as mine," the nanny answered quietly. "They are my boys, even if they are now men." She hesitated, her gaze searching Hannah's. "Are you settling in all right, Your Highness? Is everything to your liking?"

"Everything is wonderful, thank you."

"I understand you visited His Majesty's island today. It was a good day to go to the beach."

"It was. A beautiful day. But then everything has been lovely here, and everyone has been so kind."

"Do you think you could be happy here?"

"I do."

"And His Majesty? Is he being good to you?"

Hannah shot Zale a swift glance. She couldn't help but notice he was listening. Of course he'd listen now. "He's trying," she said, lips twitching.

"I think it's time to separate the two of you," he interjected, taking Hannah's hand in his. "Come, Emmeline. And good night, Mrs. Sivka, I'll see you in the morning."

Still holding hands, Zale and Hannah walked back to the grand staircase and across to the other wing. Hannah loved the feel of Zale's large, strong hand against hers, his fingers intertwined. It was such a small thing to hold hands, not at all sexual, but rather loving and tender, which is maybe why it felt so special to Hannah. With Zale like this, she felt completely happy. Completely herself.

"Mrs. Sivka said that my rooms are the Queen's Chambers," Hannah said as they turned the corner and walked down the elegant corridor that led to her suite.

"They are," Zale answered, nodding acknowledgment to a palace guard stationed in the hall.

"But why would the Queen's Chambers be so far from the King's? Your rooms are in Tinny's wing, which is a good walk from here."

"Not all kings wanted their queens next door," Zale said, reaching her suite's outer door.

"Because the kings had lovers?"

"Possibly. But there's another explanation."

"What's that?"

"Not all kings liked their queens." Zale leaned past her, opened her door for her.

"Sounds like a common theme around here."

He released her hand but didn't move very far back. "Not to be completely contradictory, but I'm beginning to like you."

Her heart did a funny little jump. "How horrifying for you."

"I know," he answered dryly. "It complicates things."

"How so?"

His lashes lowered and his gaze moved slowly across her face. "I won't want you to go if I really like you."

Heat rushed to her cheeks. Her skin suddenly tingled. "But you don't *really* like me yet."

He looked down into her eyes, heat in his eyes, his expression intense. "I wouldn't be so sure, Your Highness. You've begun to grow on me."

Her pulse raced and her stomach did wild flips. "Heavens," she murmured, her heart suddenly so full it'd begun to hurt, "what a disaster."

"My sentiments exactly." And yet his voice was deep and rough, a sexy rumble of sound that made her feel absolutely breathless.

Hannah was falling for him, falling hard and fast. "Do you want to come in?"

"It's late—"

"Not that late. Just ten now. We could ring for coffee or a glass of port."

He gave her a long look. "If I came in, I wouldn't want coffee."

Blood rushed to her cheeks and her belly tightened, her body feeling impossibly hot. "We could just talk."

"You know we wouldn't." His gaze dropped, rested on her mouth, as if imagining the feel of it against his own. "If I had you behind closed doors I'd do what I've wanted to do since the night you arrived."

She struggled to breathe. "And what is that?"

"I'm trying hard to remain controlled here."

"I'm just curious."

"And you know what curiosity did to the cat."

She locked her knees, her inner thighs clenched tight. "Yes, but did it feel good?"

A light blazed in his eyes. His jaw thickened. Stark hunger hardened, was etched across his face. "So damn good," he said thickly, reaching for her, and pulling her to him.

She tipped her head back. "So it was pleasure that killed the cat?"

"You are impossible." His voice was a rasp of sound. "And completely irresistible. If you're not very careful, I'll strip you right here in the hall and kiss every inch of you."

She shuddered against him, desire making her womb ache.

She wanted him. Needed him. "That might be too much of a show for your palace security."

He drew a rough breath, color warming his cheekbones. "You are testing my resolve."

He was so hard and warm and his body felt amazing against hers. She pressed herself to him, rubbed like a cat against him. "You feel so good."

He was gritting his teeth, strain evident on his face. "Can't do this here. Won't. It'd feel wrong in my mother's room."

"Then let me come to yours."

He gazed down into her eyes. "You're serious?"

She nodded. "I want this… I want you."

"Wait one hour. Cool down. Think it through. Because once we do this, once we make love, there's no going back."

CHAPTER EIGHT

HANNAH entered the King's Bedchamber wearing a black coat over her nightgown and black velvet slippers on her feet. She tried to act nonchalant as she walked through the bedroom door even though butterflies were flitting wildly in her middle, making her heart beat too fast.

She saw Zale immediately, barefoot at the far end of the ornate chamber and her stomach flipped all over again. He'd shed his dark jacket, and had unbuttoned his white shirt at the collar and rolled the crisp sleeves back on his tan forearms.

"Brave girl," Zale said from the far end of the chamber where he stood before one of two gold marble fireplaces anchoring the room, and it was a magnificent room, the high ceiling covered in rich paneled wood and Flemish tapestries hung on the dark paneled walls.

But nothing was more awe-inspiring than the enormous canopied bed that dominated the room. The bed was huge, bigger than an American king-size—obviously designed for true nobility.

Gold and brilliant blue fabric draped the numerous windows, warming the chamber and shutting out the night while thick blue velvet lined in gold hung from the bed frame, creating an intimate cocoon inside.

"You're here," he said, hands on his hips, studying her from beneath lowered lashes.

Not so brave, she thought, feeling as if she'd entered the

lion's lair, with the lights dimmed and the bed prepared for seduction.

Hannah glanced once again at the immense bed, seeing how the brocade coverlet had been turned down, revealing pristine white sheets and pillows. For centuries powerful kings had slept, dreamed and prayed there. And soon she'd be in it, too.

She licked impossibly dry lips. "I am."

"And you've carefully thought this through?" His eyes met hers and held.

The room glowed in the soft candlelight, creating dancing shadows and Hannah plunged her hands into the deep pockets of her coat, self-conscious that Zale was still dressed and she had nothing on underneath her coat but the thin nightgown. "I have."

His lips curved and he began to unbutton the rest of the buttons on his crisp white dress shirt one at a time. "Then why stand so far away?"

But her feet wouldn't move. She was rooted to the spot, mesmerized by his long, lean fingers unfastening the small buttons on his shirt.

Was he really undressing before her?

Was she really going to do this? Then he shrugged out of the shirt, revealing bronzed skin over dense, sinewy muscle, and her mind went blank.

God, he was beautiful.

With perfect aim he tossed the shirt onto the back of a nearby chair. "Second thoughts?"

She shook her head, touched her tongue to her lips again. "No."

"Then come." He curled a finger, beckoning her, thick bicep curving.

He had an amazing body, an athlete's body with broad shoulders, deep chest and hard flat abs that tapered to narrow muscular hips, a body that had taken years to develop.

"Come," he repeated. "I'm hungry for you."

Hannah shivered at the rough urgency of his voice and the sexy command, *Come. I'm hungry for you.*

For a moment her conscience shrieked a protest, and then she silenced it. She needed him. Needed this.

It'd been forever since she'd been wanted, forever since anyone had touched her, loved her. And it was hard to pretend she never needed anything, much less love.

Not that this would be love.

But it'd be something. Zale liked her. Wanted her. And for tonight that was enough.

Hannah walked toward him. She felt his gaze travel over her face and down her body as she closed the gap between him, her breasts growing heavier and more sensitive with every step until she stood before him. He was tall, very tall, and muscular, and overwhelmingly male.

He reached out and unknotted the sash on her trench coat and discarded it. And then watching her from beneath heavy lids, he pushed the coat back from her slim shoulders and let it fall. His gaze dropped to the daring décolleté of her satin gown, the ivory fabric molded to her rounded breasts. Her nipples strained against the satin cups, the darker areola visible through the fabric.

"You are without doubt the most beautiful woman I have ever seen."

His voice was deep, rough with desire and she warmed all over, senses coming to life.

"Beauty isn't everything," she murmured.

A small muscle pulled at his jaw. "You're right." He ran the back of his fingers across her soft cheek. "So what does matter, Emmeline?"

She stared up into his face, seeing emotion darken his eyes and tighten his strong, handsome features. Tension rippled through him. "You. Me. Us."

His gaze dropped to rest on her mouth, his dense black lashes fanning his high cheekbones. "So you know I'm now playing for keeps."

Her cheeks burned, her body felt feverish. She cared about nothing right now but him, this. The future wasn't hers to have. All she had was tonight. All she had was now. "Good."

She took a step closer to Zale and placed her hands on his chest, slowly sliding her palms over the smooth, hard plane of muscle there.

"Make me forget everything," she whispered, voice breaking, as she lifted her mouth to his. "Make me forget everything but you."

Zale slid the straps of her nightgown down over her arms until it fell off her, pooling in a puddle of ivory silk at her feet.

He stood back and looked her over as the fire crackled and burned, light flickering over her, highlighting her curves before slowly drawing her into his arms.

He kissed her as if she tasted like wine and honey, his lips parting hers, his tongue probing her mouth and then teasing her tongue before sucking on it.

She kissed him back, wrapping her arms around his neck, but even then she felt as if she couldn't get close enough. She wanted more of him, wanted all of him, and she welcomed his hard chest crushing her breasts and the cool buckle of his belt grazing her naked belly.

"Want you," he said thickly.

She nodded and reached for his belt, unfastening the buckle, and then the button on his trousers and finally the zipper.

But before she could tug at his trousers he broke away, leaned over to remove his shoes, socks and then the pants fell, leaving just his snug briefs that barely contained him.

She found herself staring wide-eyed as he peeled the briefs away and he sprung free, very large, very hard and very erect. This king came well-equipped, she thought breathlessly, feeling a pinch of panic as it had been a long time since she'd done this and he looked maybe too big.

"You look nervous," he said.

Her head spun and she moistened her lips. "I am."

"Why?"

"You're…big. Not sure how this will work."

"Don't worry. I know how."

She heard the wicked note in his voice as well as the hint of something else, something that sounded like tenderness.

He took her hand, and tugged, drawing her to the carpet in front of the fire.

She glanced at the fire. "Not the bed?" Her voice wobbled with a fit of nerves. It'd been four years since she made love. Four years before she'd been intimate like this and suddenly she wasn't sure she could do it.

He pressed her gently back onto the carpet, and stretched out next to her, running his hand from her waist, over her ribs, across a full breast and down again. "Love your breasts," he murmured. "They're absolutely perfect."

He stroked her up and down again, his fingers each time brushing lower across her belly until he was caressing the top of her thigh to collarbone and back. She stirred restlessly beneath his hand, arching helplessly as he brushed her curls between her thighs.

"Beautiful," he said under his breath, moving over her, his mouth claiming hers, his weight braced on his arms.

He kissed her deeply, hands still caressing as his knees parted her own. He held her knees apart and then he shifted his weight, turning to press his mouth to her flat belly, his tongue flicking her navel and then lower, his lips brushing across her soft inner thighs and then the softer folds.

She groaned and clenched her hands at her sides, overwhelmed by the intense pleasure.

Zale's tongue traced her tender lips then stroked the tip of his tongue across her tight, engorged clitoris.

She bucked against him when he did it again.

Holding her hips securely, he licked and sucked her wet pink flesh, devoting excruciating attention to her.

Panting, Hannah fought against the hot, sharp sensation building inside her. She'd never done this before, had never been intimate this way with anyone.

But the more she resisted the pressure, the more intense it became. "No," she choked, shaking her head, her legs trembling violently.

"Come on," he said hoarsely. "Come for me."

She heard him, and she knew what he wanted but she didn't think she could it do, didn't think she could just let go, but when he slipped a finger inside her as he sucked, she shattered against his mouth, screaming his name. For an endless moment Hannah tumbled blindly, wildly through time and space, sensations too intense, her body beyond her control.

She was exhausted after, her body tingling and sensitive. She felt utterly spent, and didn't think she could ever want anything again, but when Zale moved over her, and drew a nipple into his mouth, lathing it with attention, fresh desire coiled inside her belly, making her want him again.

He shifted between her thighs but he didn't enter her right away. Instead he sucked and nipped on one pert nipple and then the other, making her grind her hips up against his.

It wasn't long before she was straining against him, desperate to be filled. "Zale." She groaned his name, feeling the thick tip of his shaft brush against her wetness. "Please."

He entered her with a deep, slow thrust and air caught in Hannah's throat. Even though her body was slick and ready for him, he was still big, still stretched her.

She struggled to catch her breath, wanting to relax, wanting it to be comfortable. He eased out and then moved forward again, sliding deeper this time. Again and again he withdrew only to return, deeper, harder and all of a sudden the tension turned to stunning pleasure. She wanted more, wanted him to keep thrusting, craving that intense sensation that told her she was on her way to another orgasm.

"More," she panted, hot, flushed, skin growing damp. "More."

His gaze found hers, held as he quickened his tempo, driving deep into her. She was breathing in little gasps now, shallow breaths as the pleasure built, tighter, sharper, the peak of the climax just out of reach.

"Come," he said, dropping his head to kiss her, and frantically she drew his tongue into her mouth even as he filled her all the way, his body possessing her completely. And just when she thought she couldn't come, that it was too elusive this time, she did, breaking, crashing, her world spinning out of control as she cried his name, again, in pleasure so intense it felt almost like pain.

He came then, in a last deep thrust, his body rigid, muscles tense. She felt his release, felt him shudder from the power of it, and then she sighed, and sagged against the carpet, spent.

After a moment he withdrew from her and rested next to her for a few minutes, his arm holding her close to his side. And then as the fire burned low, he scooped her into his arms, and carried her to the massive bed where he slid her between soft white sheets.

"Sleep," he said, smoothing her hair back from her face and kissing her forehead and then her nose and finally her lips. "You need your rest."

She murmured agreement, snuggling into the impossibly soft pillow and smooth, cool sheets that felt so good against her heated skin. "Will you sleep, too?" she whispered.

"Yes."

An hour later, Zale lay on his back in bed listening to Emmeline's soft even breathing. He'd told her he would sleep. He wished he could sleep. Instead his mind raced.

Making love to Emmeline tonight changed everything. They were committed now. As good as married.

He'd thought he'd be uncertain, or regretful. He wasn't. He was glad Emmeline was his.

But this hadn't just been sex. It'd been more like…love. He hadn't planned on love. He was only now starting to like her. Love was not part of the deal.

The fact that he felt so much made him just want her that much more.

In the past, sex was like exercise—a great workout and a welcome release, giving him a good night's sleep.

But tonight he couldn't sleep. Instead he was lying awake, seething with chaotic emotions, new emotions, intense emotions.

He did not want the emotions. He did not want anything to do with feelings, especially if they could trip him up, cloud his thinking.

He desired Emmeline, wanted Emmeline, would soon marry Emmeline, but he didn't know how she felt about him.

Yes, she desired him. After all, tonight she'd been hot, wet, astonishingly responsive. He'd made her come tonight—twice—but could there be more between them? Could there be love?

Tonight kissing her, buried deep in her, he'd felt lost in her, felt lost in something he'd forgotten even existed. Light. Warmth. Joy.

She felt like something you waited for…something special, magical…like the feeling you got as a child on Christmas morning.

Baffled by the dark tangle of his emotions, Zale rolled onto his side to look down at her, her elegant profile barely visible in the dark.

He'd known for years she was to be his. He'd known since he was fifteen she was the one chosen for him. But he'd never expected this…never expected this overwhelming desire to keep her, protect her, not just now, but forever.

CHAPTER NINE

HANNAH woke up early the next morning in a very dark room, in a strange bed, feeling utterly disoriented. And then turning over, she bumped against a very large, warm, solid person and it all came back to her.

She was in Zale's room, in his bed, naked.

Bits and pieces of the past night came to her. Guilt pummeled her. Why had she let this happen? How could she have let it happen?

Worse, how could she have enjoyed it so much?

But it had been amazing. *He'd* been amazing and last night he'd managed with his talented hands and mouth and body to sweep away her better judgment, as well as any inhibitions...

Blushing in the dark, she remembered how she'd practically screamed his name as she came...so really, truly mortifying. Hannah couldn't imagine Emmeline screaming during sex. Couldn't imagine that a proper princess would lose control like that...

Hannah rolled back over onto her stomach and pressed her face into her pillow, and let out a muffled shout.

"I can hear that," Zale said dryly, next to her in the dark. "Anything you'd care to share?"

She pushed up onto her elbows and looked his way although the heavy drapes and blackout shades made it impossible to see. "I threw myself at you."

"I liked it," he said, shifting onto his own back and plumping pillows behind his head. "You did, too."

"I know I did, but…" she gritted, throwing back the covers and about to leave the bed when Zale's hand shot out, caught her by the wrist and pulled her toward him.

"But what?" he demanded, rising over her, straddling her hips and pinning her arms down over her head.

The air against her bare breasts made her nipples tighten and goose bumps danced across her skin. She arched against the pressure of his hands, which just made her nipples pebble harder.

She felt Zale shift, his hips sinking against her as his head dipped, his lips claiming one of her taut nipples, taking it into his warm, damp mouth.

Hannah shivered as he sucked on the sensitive bud, his tongue lazily flicking and then stroking until her hips strained up, pushing against him. His body was hard, his shaft long and rigid, the thick, rounded head pushing at the juncture of her thighs. All she had to do was bend her knees, open her legs…

And then she did, sliding her legs open beneath the weight of his, allowing his body to settle lower, the head of his shaft teasing her inner lips, nudging her hot, slick opening.

She wiggled beneath him, needing more but he didn't push forward, didn't do anything other than lift his head and move to the other breast, giving the tender nipple the same attention he'd shown the first.

Hannah panted and wiggled again, lifting her hips up to grind against him. The smooth silken head of his shaft rubbed up and down her opening, sliding over her clitoris and then down over her wetness. She shivered and trembled and wiggled again.

He sucked harder on her nipple and she nearly screamed out loud. "Zale," she choked, skin hot, and unbearably sensitive. "Fill me."

He didn't need a second invitation. Using his knees he parted her thighs wider, and pushed against her entrance, stretching her open and sinking deeply into her body, which was definitely hot, wet, ready.

Last night the tempo had been slow, leisurely, but he took her hard now, driving into her as if he was trying to prove a point, teach her a lesson. But Hannah loved the sensation and friction, welcomed his hardness and heat and the way he filled her, making her forget everything but him.

There was just him. Him and her. Him with her. Him forever with her.

She was going to come again but the sensation of it was almost too much. She felt too much, felt pleasure and love.

Felt love.

Not possible, couldn't be, but that's what she felt. She loved him. Loved him completely.

She closed her eyes at the dizzying rush of white-hot sensation, the pleasure so sharp it was excruciating. She pressed her feet into the mattress and dug her fingers into his shoulders, skin pressed to skin as her control slipped and the orgasm took her.

"Emmeline." Zale ground out her name, loud, hoarse, his powerful body tensing, muscles clenching, as his body emptied into hers.

Emmeline.

Hannah slowly opened her eyes, aware of the warm weight of Zale on her, and the strength of his thighs between hers, and his thick erection still hot inside her body.

Emmeline.

Oh, God. This entire time, it hadn't been them, not him and her, but him and Emmeline.

Because that's who he wanted, Emmeline. Not Hannah, never Hannah. Hannah was nothing and nobody.

Her eyes burned. Hot. Scalding. She tried to blink but couldn't, frozen, shattered, stuck.

Stuck in a part she'd created, stuck in a lie she'd perpetuated.

If Zale found out the truth, he'd hate her. He'd never forgive her.

And did she blame him? She'd done everything he despised most—tricked, manipulated and played him.

Zale's hand touched her cheek, catching a tear as it fell. "Emmeline, why are you crying?"

"I'm not."

He gently touched the tip of his finger with the tear to her lips. "Trust me. You can tell me. You can tell me anything."

Trust me...you can tell me anything...

Her chest squeezed so tight her heart felt as if it would burst. "Everything's good," she said, fighting to keep her voice from breaking.

"Then why the tears?"

"Happy," she choked out, gulping air as fresh hot tears welled. "Just happy to be with you."

Hannah squeezed her eyes shut as Zale settled onto his side and drew her close, exhaling in a sigh of utter satisfaction.

He sounded relaxed, sated, happy, while she writhed inwardly, tormented by self-loathing.

She was bad, bad, bad...so bad. What had she done? How could she have done it?

Horrified and ashamed that she'd sleep with Emmeline's fiancé, Hannah pressed the soft sheets to her chest, regret filling her, making her conscience hurt and heart sting.

She should have told him the truth yesterday. Should have confessed her part in the charade, accepted the consequences and then gone home.

Or at the very least, she should have just gone home.

Instead she'd stayed, allowing herself to be seduced by her senses, and this impossible fantasy. As if she could be a princess. As if her life was a fairy tale.

Worse, she hadn't stayed for Emmeline. She'd stayed for herself. Stayed for the most selfish of reasons—she'd wanted Zale. And so she'd taken what wasn't hers.

And now the reality of her foolishness, and selfishness, was hitting her like a sledgehammer.

Zale stroked her hip, a slow, lazy caress. "We didn't get a lot of sleep last night and yet we both have busy days."

"Do we?"

"I've meetings this morning, and you need to finish sitting for your portrait. Once done with that, I'll have Krek give you a tour of our private wing and then hopefully we can meet for lunch."

"You don't have to worry about me. I don't need entertaining," she said, trying to ignore the warmth of his hand as it moved leisurely up and down her body making her feel cherished and beautiful. "I've got plenty to do."

"I'm sure you do, but you said that you wanted to learn everything you could about me so I've arranged for Krek to take you on a tour."

"I won't be adding to his workload, will I?"

"No. Krek lives for this sort of thing," he answered, kissing her cheek before pulling away. He left the bed and crossed to the window, to pull back the heavy drapes, allowing the morning light to flood the room.

Hannah blinked at the light, and rubbed her eyes before pushing a tumble of heavy hair back from her face.

Zale was still standing at the window, gazing out over the walled city to the sea. He was naked and completely comfortable with it. But of course he would be. He had that sinfully sexy body—big shoulders, rock hard stomach, a small, firm butt and those long, lean muscular legs.

He was so perfect. She was not. "Can I have my coat please?" she asked, sitting up and still holding the sheet to her breasts.

"I can't believe you're shy," he said, collecting her nightgown and coat and carrying it to her. "I've heard you sunbathe topless on friends' yachts."

Hannah wrinkled her nose, unable to imagine going topless in public.

But then, her father had been very strict when Hannah was growing up. He'd frequently reminded her that her mother had been a lady and Hannah would be a lady, too. Which meant no short shorts or revealing tops. She hadn't been allowed to date until she was sixteen and even then it had to be on a group date. Anyone she wanted to date had to come to the ranch and be grilled for an hour by her dad, so mostly, no boys in Bandera wanted to.

"It's chilly," she said, taking the coat from him and sliding one arm into a sleeve, and then the other before knotting the sash tightly about her waist.

Head held high, Hannah rose from the bed, prepared to dash out of the bedroom, but Zale caught her by the wrist as she passed, pulling her toward him.

"You keep surprising me," he said hoarsely, holding her against him. The coat provided little protection. She could feel the entire length of him, from his thick chest to his warm torso and firm, narrow hips.

She sucked in a breath, heat surging to her cheeks as his body hardened against her. "Is that good or bad?"

The expression in his eyes was possessive. "Both." He drew his thumb across her mouth, his gaze fixed to her soft lips as they parted in a silent gasp.

"How can it be both good and bad?" she whispered, licking her dry lips.

"You're more than I expected." He hesitated. "Which is good."

"So what is bad?"

He slowly dragged his thumb across her bottom lip, tugging it down, making her feel alarmingly exposed. "How much I want you. *Still.*"

His words and touch were unbearably erotic. She shuddered in response, her defenses caving. He made her feel so carnal. Made her want all the things that were forbidden.

Like him.

"I've just had you, three times in the past nine hours. I shouldn't need you again," he added, his voice deepening, rougher than usual, even as his shaft rose against her belly, an insistent nudge that made her feel weak. Every time he touched her, she melted. Just one touch and she became his.

His, she repeated silently, dazed by the waves of pleasure surging through her one after the other. He made her feel drunk but it was on passion and emotion.

She'd never felt anything close to this with anyone, and she didn't think she'd ever feel this way about anyone else, either.

"And that's bad?" she asked unsteadily.

He tugged the coat back from her shoulder, exposing one full pale breast.

"Yes." He cupped her breast and she exhaled at the warmth of his hand against her cool skin. He stroked the soft underside, a light teasing caress that made her nerve endings dance and her lower back tingle.

"But you don't really need me," she whispered, trying her best to stay coherent—rational, knowing she needed to focus. But thinking was virtually impossible when she was so overwhelmed by sensation. "You've had plenty—"

"But apparently not plenty enough," he contradicted, as his erection grew bigger, thicker.

She rubbed against him, feeling the broad rounded tip, remembering how amazing it had felt last night as he entered her, slowly, deeply.

The memory made her shudder and he groaned as she rubbed against him.

With a muttered oath he caught her hips in his hands, pressed her even more firmly to him, his breathing ragged. "I don't want to want you this much."

"I don't want to want you this much, either," she flung breathlessly at him, as his hand moved down to cup her backside. He was kneading her cheek, squeezing and lifting the cheek away from the other, as if to part her legs and make room for him between.

The sensation of his hands on her butt, the feeling of being opened for him, was so provocative her legs nearly gave away.

"Yes, you do," he answered, lowering his head to kiss her, his lips and teeth nipping at her lips. "You are so hot you're almost on fire."

It was true. Little stars exploded in her head and Hannah pressed her thighs tight, sending rivulets of pleasure everywhere. She wasn't just hot, she was wet, and desperate for him to fill her, answering the terrible ache throbbing inside of her. "You're deliberately turning me on, making it impossible to function—"

He cut her off with a kiss, the pressure of his mouth parting her lips, his tongue taking her mouth as if it belonged to him. She loved the way he kissed her—hard, fierce—and she wrapped her arms around his neck, holding him closer. With his cool tongue in her mouth and his hands against her heated skin she thought she'd let him do anything, have anything.

The handsome clock on the gold marble mantel suddenly chimed, and continued to chime repeatedly.

Zale lifted his head, listened to the chiming of the clock. "Can't be," he muttered, glancing at his watch then pushing her firmly away. "This is what I mean. I have a meeting in just a few minutes and yet I am still here."

"Not my fault!"

"No, I know. It's mine." His gaze swept over her. "But that's the part I don't like. Because self-control has never been a problem. Not until I met you." Then with a short, sharp shake of his head, he walked into his adjoining bath to shower, shave and start his day.

Dazed, body numb, Hannah climbed back into bed and drew the covers up to her chin.

She was lost. And she wanted her own life back. She needed it, and she needed to be herself. And Zale needed to know the truth.

She had to tell him.

Had to let him know she wasn't his Emmeline.

* * *

Hannah must have fallen asleep because the next thing she heard was the sound of Celine wheeling a breakfast trolley laden with tempting treats into her room.

Celine positioned the trolley next to the bed and began uncovering dishes—strawberries and cream, buttery croissants, warm savory meat pastries, poached eggs, Greek yogurt, granola, fresh squeezed orange juice and a tall silver pot of coffee.

"His Majesty thought you might enjoy breakfast in bed today," Celine said, transforming the trolley into a table next to the bed, acting as if it was perfectly normal for Hannah to be in the king's bed.

Hannah sat up. "All for me?"

"His Majesty said you've a long day of appointments, activities and meetings, starting with this morning's portrait sitting, so you'll need a good breakfast. And once you've eaten, we'll return to the Queen's Chambers and get you ready for your portrait sitting."

Emmeline's personal stylists were waiting for her as she emerged from her bathroom a half hour later, swaddled in a Turkish towel.

Camille had everything ready to do Hannah's hair and it wasn't long before Hannah was back in the dress she was wearing for her portrait, the pale shimmering gown clinging to her curves, the color highlighting her golden beauty, as Camille ran the flat iron over the ends of her hair making sure it was perfectly straight.

Teresa was passing time by sitting on a stool and flipping through a magazine, sometimes reading an article aloud. Suddenly she stopped flipping pages to stare at a photograph.

"There she is!" Teresa exclaimed. "That Hannah Smith, Your Highness, the American lookalike we told you about in Palm Beach."

"The one you said helped organize the polo tournament?" Hannah answered vaguely.

Camille smoothed a strand of hair with the flat iron. "Yes,

and it's a shame you didn't meet her. Teresa and I were dying to see the two of you together...would have been fascinating."

"Mmm." Hannah feigned boredom. "You said she's in the magazine?"

"Yes. This week's issue." Teresa drew the magazine closer to study the photo and caption. "They snapped her leaving a South Beach nightclub and she's with someone who isn't happy at all...oooh! Sheikh Makin Al-Koury. It looks like he's dragging her out of the club." Teresa glanced up at Hannah. "I wonder if that's her boyfriend?"

Hannah's brows flattened. "I thought she just worked for him?"

"I don't know, but he looks really ticked off. He's practically dragging her out of the club." Teresa grinned. "Just like a jealous boyfriend."

"What does the caption say?"

"Not much, just *Sheikh Al-Koury and unidentified friend leaving Lounge Mynt.*" Teresa looked up. "Although that is a really trendy club. Impossible to get into unless you're a VIP."

"I'm sure they're not dating," Hannah said firmly, staggered by the news that Emmeline and Makin Al-Koury were together. "Sheikhs do not date their secretaries." Hannah impatiently held her hand out for the magazine. "Can I see?"

Teresa slid off the stool and carried the magazine to Hannah. "There," she said, holding the magazine out to Hannah while Camille peeked over her shoulder for a look, too. "Doesn't he look angry with her?"

Hannah couldn't believe her eyes. It *was* Emmeline and Makin stepping out of a South Beach nightclub, which was all the more incredible because Sheikh Makin Al-Koury did not go to nightclubs, avoiding places celebs and paparazzi hung out. He was a very private man and never dated women who liked the limelight.

She glanced from Makin Al-Koury to Emmeline. Emmeline looked terrible. Gaunt. Frail. Eyes deeply shadowed. "She doesn't look well," Hannah said. "She's too thin."

Camille leaned closer to the photo. "She's probably partying too much. Everyone does everything in South Beach."

"Not Makin," Hannah said under her breath, thinking Teresa was right. Makin looked absolutely livid in the photo. What was going on between them? What were they doing together? And when had Princess Emmeline met up with Hannah's boss?

"What's everyone looking at?" Zale asked from the doorway.

Hannah jumped and shoved the magazine back into Teresa's hands. "Nothing."

"Nothing?" he drawled, entering the dressing room. "Then why do all three of you look guilty?"

"Because we were all drooling over clothes. Expensive clothes. Something you'd never do," Hannah answered with a laugh. "What brings you here, Your Majesty?"

"You."

His rich voice and Raguvian accent made everything he said sound sinful. Sexy.

Heat swept through her. Her cheeks burned as she turned in her chair to face him. He was wearing a dress shirt and dark slacks and yet he looked incredibly fit, as though he'd just returned from a long run. "I'm honored."

"How are the preparations coming for your sitting?"

"Good. Just need my makeup and I'm off."

Camille and Teresa discreetly disappeared and Zale approached her carrying a large black velvet box.

"I have a gift," he said. "Something I should have given you when you first arrived."

She tipped her head back, looked him straight in the eyes, loving the heat in his amber gaze. "But you haven't been sure about me."

"That's true." He handed the velvet box to her. "But I'm sure now."

Hannah opened the lid of the black box, revealing a tall, glittering tiara.

"It was my mother's," he said, "and my grandmother's before that."

It was stunning, beyond stunning, the delicate diamond arch sparkling, catching the light, reflecting it in every direction. It was classic and simple and breathtaking. "I can't possibly accept this," she whispered, "it's far too valuable. It's a family heirloom—"

"Of course you can. It's mine to give," he interrupted. "And I give it to you, just the first of many, Emmeline. Once you become my queen, you will be showered in jewels."

The possessive light in his eyes made her breath catch. "You really intend to marry me?"

"Yes."

"No doubts?"

"No. Once I made love to you, I committed myself. We're as good as married. There's no turning back."

CHAPTER TEN

HANNAH tried not to panic.

Zale said there was no turning back. They were as good as married. Which would be a huge problem if Emmeline failed to show up.

Emmeline had to show up.

What would Hannah do?

The wedding was a week away. The world expected a magnificent royal wedding, a wedding that was to be televised to the world. Emmeline couldn't just bail on Zale at the last minute. It wouldn't be right. Wasn't fair. To string him along throughout their engagement and then to fail to show for the wedding...

Hannah needed to tell him the truth. But how would she tell him? How to break the news?

Hey, King Patek, I'm not actually your betrothed, but Hannah Smith from Bandera, Texas, and I am here to keep you occupied while your real fiancée sorts some things out in Palm Beach.

Sick at heart, stomach churning like mad, Hannah pressed her hands together, and tried to push the anxious thoughts out of her mind. Emmeline would come. Emmeline had said she'd come. Emmeline wouldn't break her word.

A half hour later Celine helped Hannah change from the elegant evening gown into a pretty navy silk skirt and white blouse for Hannah's palace tour with Krek. She wore fat pearls at her throat, a pearl and diamond bracelet on her wrist and medium-heel shoes that would be comfortable to walk in.

"As you know, I am one of the most senior staff members," Krek said, meeting her in the sitting room of the Queen's Chambers. "I have served the Patek family for nearly thirty-five years now, starting as a footman to the late queen, before becoming butler for His Majesty. As head butler at the Patek Palace, I am responsible for all private and official entertaining both here and abroad. I organize and attend state banquets and receptions, ensuring that every detail is properly, professionally and elegantly handled."

"That's a great deal of responsibility," Hannah answered.

"It is, Your Highness, but this is what I've done my whole life. I can't imagine doing anything else."

They'd walked down the large corridor, descended the stairs and he opened the doors to a gorgeous light-filled room painted a vivid yellow contrasted by ornate white moldings.

"This was Queen Madeleine's favorite room," he said, leading her inside. The high ceiling of the room was painted sky-blue with white billowy clouds. "Yellow was Queen Madeleine's favorite color as it reminded her of the sun and this was where she preferred to entertain." He glanced at her. "Did you ever meet her? She was your grandmother's first cousin."

Hannah's mouth opened and shut. "I…I don't recall."

"You would if you had met her. She was a lovely woman. We had quite a good relationship and I was very happy working for her, but when Princess Helena—His Majesty's mother—arrived from Greece to marry His Majesty's father, King Stephen IV, I was assigned to the newlyweds' household."

"Did you mind the switch?"

"Not at all. King Stephen and Princess Helena were a delight to work for. They, too, were an arranged marriage but soon after the wedding fell in love."

"They had a happy marriage then?"

"The happiest." It was Zale who'd answered and Hannah

inhaled sharply, his deep voice sinfully sexy. Zale had entered through a side door and he walked toward them now.

"The two of them were inseparable through thick and thin, and they certainly had their fair share of challenges."

"Your Majesty," Krek said with a formal bow as Zale joined them. "We haven't made it very far yet."

"Perhaps I can take over?" Zale suggested.

Krek bowed again. "Of course, Your Majesty." He tipped his head in Hannah's direction. "Your Highness." And then he was gone, quietly, discreetly.

"Enjoying the tour?" Zale asked.

"Yes," she answered. "But we really only just started."

"Then let's continue," he answered, leading her to the adjoining room, the Crimson Room, which had been the favorite reception room for Zale's grandfather, King Stephen Mikal. "In this room my grandfather, King Mikal, entertained the Tsar, a Sultan, two British kings, a dozen dukes, as well as a Pope."

"Did you ever know him?"

"He died when I was fourteen months old, but apparently he spent a lot of time with Stephen and me. We have quite a few photos of us together."

"Were you and Prince Stephen close growing up?"

"Yes. But that didn't mean we always got along. We could be quite competitive." Zale's expression was rueful. "At least, I was."

"You fought?"

"Fistfights? No. But every now and then we'd challenge each other to a race or a wrestling match and then it was a battle to end all battles." Zale smiled. "Mind you, Stephen was two and a half years older than me, and I was scrawny until my midteens, but there was no way I'd let Stephen take me without a fight."

Hannah couldn't imagine Zale small. "Define scrawny."

"Skinny, lanky, short."

"I can't believe it."

"Neither could I. I hated it. But at least I had speed."

Her pulse quickened. Zale appealed to her at every level. "So when did you grow? Because no one could call you scrawny now."

"I shot up nearly six inches when I was seventeen. Grew another four inches at eighteen. And kept growing until I turned twenty. But it's hard being taken seriously in football when you're so small. Fortunately it forced me to work hard, harder than everyone around me, and my work ethic was born."

"I admire your work ethic."

"It helped make me who I am."

Zale opened the doors to a bright, vast, high-ceiling hall lined with portraits. "We're now entering the Royal Gallery. All the portraits of Raguva's kings and queens hang here. Your portrait will join mine after it's completed—"

"We're really going to marry?"

"Yes. Sex sealed the deal, Emmeline. I told you it would. It's in the prenup, part of our contract. By making love, you became mine."

They were standing before a large portrait of a dark-haired, brown-eyed king that looked remarkably like Zale.

She shivered. His.

He reached out to tuck a pale blond tendril of hair behind her ear. "We can be happy."

She felt lost in his eyes. "You really think so?"

"Yes."

Her eyes burned and her throat ached and she had to turn away so he wouldn't see her cry. "How can you be so sure?"

"Because I have strong feelings for you."

His tone had been light, teasing and yet suddenly her chest constricted, air bottled in her lungs. If she were good…

But she was not good. Nor was Emmeline. Because they were both duplicitous. Both betraying him.

"I think we've seen enough," he said. "Let's go to lunch. I have something special planned."

He led her downstairs, through a hall and then another, into an old wing of the palace that looked more like a castle than a palace.

"The original fortress," Zale said as soldiers before them opened a thick wooden door studded with metal that led to a narrow stairwell.

"This was the keep, built in the late fourteenth century and enlarged and strengthened in the 1500s," he said, taking her hand as they walked up the winding staircase, which was cool and dimly lit. "For hundreds of years kings have made new additions to the castle, and modernized existing wings, turning the fortress into something more palatial, but this part remains as it was five hundred years ago."

They climbed at least three floors until they reached the top of the tower and Zale pushed open another door, revealing blue sky and impossibly thick stone walls.

"The castle parapet," Zale said. "My favorite place growing up."

They were up high, in the tallest point of the castle and it was a gorgeous day with a blue sky and not a cloud in sight. The spring air was crisp and flags snapped below them in the wind, with the breeze carrying a hint of salt from the sea.

"I can see why you like it here," she said, joining him at the thick wall and leaning against the weathered stone warmed from the sun. "A place a boy can escape to, and where a king can think."

"That's exactly it." Zale leaned on the wall, too, his shoulders flexed, his weight resting on his forearms. "Here I have quiet and space. Perspective. I find perspective is essential. Far too easy sometimes to get caught up in emotions or the stress of a situation, whether real or imagined."

She would have never guessed he could get caught up in emotions. He seemed far too levelheaded for that. "Thank you for bringing me here."

"We're not done yet." He extended his hand to her. "Come. Let's eat."

But instead of leading her back down the stairs, they continued walking around the parapet to the other side where a round tower was in ruins, with just pieces of walls and without a roof. The stairwell had been cemented over and a new stone floor mortared into place.

In the center of the ruined tower was a small round table with two chairs. The table was covered in a pale rose linen cloth with a loose floral arrangement of roses, freesias and lilies in the middle. There were two place settings, with sterling cutlery, gold-rimmed china topped with silver covers and tall, delicate stemware adding sparkle to the table.

"Your Royal Highness," Zale said, drawing a chair out from the round table for her. "If you'd please."

"Thank you."

He helped scoot her chair in, the legs scraping against the stone. "I enjoyed our picnic on the beach so much I thought we should have another meal where it was just you and me. I rather like not having staff waiting on us. It's more relaxed."

"And more fun," she added, thinking that while she'd enjoyed the picnic on his island, this was the most gorgeous, romantic setting she could imagine. "Thank you."

"It's my pleasure," he answered, sitting opposite her and drawing a bottle of white wine from an impressive silver bucket where it'd been chilling. He opened the bottle and filled each of their goblets. "To you, to me, and our future together," he said, his gaze holding hers and lifting his glass in a toast.

Her eyes burned hotter and she had to smile to keep the tears back. "To our future," she echoed, clinking the rim of her glass to his.

He searched her eyes, looking for something, but what, she didn't know.

"Cheers," he said.

They clinked glasses again and then drank and Hannah had never been so grateful for the warmth of the wine as it slipped down her throat and heated her stomach. She was cold on the inside, cold and scared.

This was going to end badly. So badly.

And then to cover the almost unbearable pain, she leaned forward to smell one of the sweetly scented roses. "They smell like real roses. Thank goodness."

He looked at her, mildly amused. "When did roses stop smelling like roses?"

"A number of years back when someone got the idea to make them more hardy and disease resistant. The flowers grew bigger but the fragrance disappeared."

"I didn't know that."

"I don't suppose there's a section on rose horticulture in your how-to-be-a-king manual."

"Regrettably there isn't such a manual. I could have used one."

"Why?"

"The first few years were hard. Every day I wished I'd spent time with my father learning about my responsibilities before he died. There's so much he could have taught me, so much I needed to know."

"But that would have meant giving up your career sooner."

"I know. I wasn't ready to give up football. I probably would never have been ready. But then they died and their accident forced me to grow up."

She was silent a moment. "Is that how you really view it?"

"I was the Crown Prince. I should have been here, learning from my father."

"But football was your passion. You loved it since you were a boy."

His broad shoulders shifted. "Boys become men."

She reached out, covered his hand with hers. "It's none of my business, but I'm glad you were able to do what you loved to do. So many people are miserable. They hate their jobs, hate their lives. It's not the way I want to live."

"You're happy then?"

"I love my work. I'm lucky I get to do what I do."

He smiled at her then and his smile transformed his face from handsome to absolutely gorgeous.

If only she could tell him the truth. She needed him to know.

Her eyes burned and she took a quick sip of her wine to hide her pain.

Zale reached out and brushed a long pale strand of hair back from her cheek. "You keep tearing up today. What's wrong? What have I done?"

"Nothing. I'm just thinking about the past and the future and our families."

"There's been a lot of pressure from our families, hasn't there?"

She nodded.

"You know my father was the one that wanted us to marry. He picked you for me when I was fifteen." His lips twisted. "You were five. And chubby. I was horrified."

Hannah smiled crookedly. "I would have been horrified, too."

"My father assured me that you'd grow up, and once you did, you'd be a rare beauty. He was right. You…fit me."

"I'm glad."

"Are you?"

"Very much so."

"So no regrets about last night?"

"None at all. I love—" She broke off, aware that she'd come so close to telling him how she felt. Because she did. "I loved every moment of it."

"We should probably get the prenup signed. Your father calls me every day, sometimes twice a day, to ask why we haven't done it yet."

"And what do you tell him?"

"That we'll sign it when we're ready."

"I can't imagine he likes that."

"No. But this is between you and me now, and I intend to keep it that way."

"Do we need the prenup then? Can't we just get married without it?"

Zale studied her from across the table. "You'd marry me without any financial agreement in place?"

"I trust you."

"You should. I'd never betray you."

Guilt flooded her. Guilt and grief.

But even as she battled her conscience, she told herself to remember it all.

Every word.

Every smile.

Every detail.

She wanted to remember it all so that even when she was gone she'd have at least the memories to hold, memories of lunch with Zale in the crumbling tower overlooking the walled city nestled between mountains and sea.

Because this wasn't just the day she fell in love, but the day she fell in love with him forever.

Less than a week ago she knew practically nothing about Raguva, Zale's small independent country overlooking the sapphire Adriatic Sea, and even less about him, Zale Ilia Patek, Raguva's king, but now Hannah knew far too much.

Like how driven Zale Patek was, and how determined he could be.

How his country meant so much to him and his brother even more so.

It'd break her heart to leave. And she would leave. If not tonight, then tomorrow. It wasn't a maybe, it was definite. Simply a matter of time.

A question of when.

"Would you have been attracted to me if we'd met a different way?" she asked.

He seemed intrigued by her question. "You mean, if we'd just met randomly…two people on the street?"

She nodded.

His brow lowered and he studied her so intently that she felt as though he could see all the way through. "Yes. Definitely."

If anyone else had looked at her so closely it would have

made her uncomfortable, but when Zale looked at her like this she felt beautiful…safe.

Yes, safe. He was a warrior. A protector. A man with courage and integrity.

"Would you like me?" he asked, leaning back in his chair.

Her eyes stung.

Absolutely. Most definitely. "Yes."

His lips curved, and his amber gaze warmed. "So the prince and princess rode off into the sunset and lived happily ever after?"

The lump in her throat was making it hard to breathe. "I hope so."

"Me, too." Still smiling, he looked down at the silver dome covering his plate. "And maybe while we're in agreement, should we eat?"

She nodded and lifted the silver cover off her plate revealing a cold seafood salad with a small plate of fresh rolls and sweet butter. "Looks delicious," she said, knowing she wouldn't be able to swallow more than a mouthful.

"Yes," he agreed, looking at her instead of his plate. "Absolutely delicious."

She blushed, her body coming alive, lower back tingling, breasts aching. "How can I possibly eat now?"

"Maybe we just skip lunch and head back to my room—"

"No!" she cut him off with a breathless laugh. "Absolutely not."

"Absolutely not? Was last night that bad?"

She choked on a muffled laugh, even as bittersweet emotion filled her, flooding her, reminding her to again remember everything…his expression, his strong features, the sensual curve of his lip, the searing heat in his eyes.

Remember, she told herself, remember his warmth and the smell of his cologne and the way he smiles when he looks at you and likes what he sees…

Like now.

"You know it was great."

"Thank God. I was beginning to worry there."

She smothered another laugh, loving him like this…light-hearted, teasing, entertaining. "I just wanted to stay because it's so beautiful here and you went to so much trouble arranging this lunch. But if you want to go, we can."

"You're letting me make the decision?"

She made a face. "You are the king."

His warm gaze moved slowly across her face, lingering on her full lips. "We'll stay," he said at length. "We'll eat. But as soon as we're done, I'm taking you to my bed."

CHAPTER ELEVEN

HANNAH struggled to chew her food but it was nearly impossible with all the butterflies flitting inside her belly. Zale didn't help matters by giving her that I'm-so-hungry-I-could-eat-you look throughout the meal.

After a half dozen bites she gave up and sipped her wine, drinking one glass, and then another. By the time she'd finished the second glass, she knew she'd drunk too much.

Not because she was drunk. But because she was a little too hot, a little too turned on. Already.

"You're not eating," Zale said, noticing her plate was virtually untouched and his was nearly empty. "Didn't care for the lobster? It's one of my favorites."

"I do. It was good."

"How would you know? You ate nothing."

She took a quick breath, cheeks warm, limbs unusually heavy. Even her pulse felt slow. "I'm happy, though."

"Are you?"

"I'll never forget it. The view. The flowers. The conversation with you."

He smiled, amused. "That's a lot to remember."

"I know, but it's worth it. How many women get to do something like this? Lunch with King Zale Patek in one of his parapet towers overlooking the sea? Not many."

"No. Just you."

Something in his eyes made her heart jump. He was look-ing at her as if she mattered.

"We'll have to do it again one day," he promised, that faint smile playing at his lips while his amber eyes held hers. "Maybe on our first anniversary."

"I'd like that," she whispered, knowing that she wouldn't be the one here, that she'd never have any of this again but she wouldn't think about leaving, not now, not when she had the rest of the day, the night and possibly tomorrow.

"There's something else I'd like, Your Majesty," she said, voice barely audible.

"And what is that, Your Highness?"

For a moment Hannah couldn't speak, not when her throat squeezed closed and her heart felt as if it were being torn to pieces. And then she pressed the intense emotions back, re-fusing to let pain steal a single minute of what was left of the day. "I'd like you to kiss me."

Heat burned in his eyes. His nostrils flared. Hannah could practically feel his desire.

He left his chair, pulled her from her seat and pressed her back against one of the remaining walls. He leaned close, crowding her, his chest against her breasts, his lean hips teas-ing hers. He was lean, hard, hot and dropping his head he brushed his lips across hers in a kiss so soft and light that she groaned deep in her throat.

"How's that?" he murmured, his lips pressing a kiss to the hollow beneath her ear. "Was that good?"

"No."

"No? Why not?"

His breath was warm on the cool curve of her ear and made her tingle with pleasure. "Not enough," she murmured, slid-ing her hands up the broad planes of his chest. His chest was hard, thickly muscled, and she ran her hands over the firm, dense muscle.

"Want more," she said. "Want you to kiss me properly."

"Like this?" he asked, nibbling at her earlobe.

She felt the coiling of desire in her belly and the dampness between her thighs. Her womb actually ached, her innermost places empty, wanting him. "No. A real kiss. A proper kiss to make the day perfect."

"You've already made it perfect," he said, catching her face in his hand, and lifting her chin up to look down into her eyes before capturing her mouth with his.

He kissed her slowly, gently, coaxing a response from her, at first warm and sweet, and then warm and sweet became desperate and hot. His lips parted hers and his tongue took her mouth and Hannah wound her arms up around his neck, unable to get close enough.

She needed him, wanted him, wanted everything with him—marriage, and babies, and growing old together—but she wouldn't have that, she'd only have this.

And she'd take this, all of this, and somehow she'd make it be enough.

She could feel the stubble on his jaw, smell that subtle cologne he wore, taste the wine on his tongue.

"Need you," she murmured against his mouth, as she slipped her fingers into the short crisp hair at his nape. "Need you so much…"

He broke off the kiss, lifting his head to look down at her. His chest rose and fell with deep breaths and his eyes were cloudy with desire and she reached up to touch his mouth with her fingertips, awed by everything she felt for him.

It was magnificent.

And terrifying.

"You are so damn beautiful," he said, pressing a kiss to her fingertips. "I honestly can't get enough of you."

"Then don't."

Jaw thick, eyes narrowed, he lifted her into his arms, carried her to a broken stone in the shadows of the turret and set her on the edge. Pushing back her skirt he exposed her bare legs and parted her pale thighs to reveal the scrap of thong she wore. "Unbelievably hot," he growled, lightly running a fingertip over the damp silk thong between her thighs, making the fabric even wetter.

She gasped as his finger traced her swollen lips again and again, making her thighs quiver and her insides clench with need.

"So wet," he muttered, fascinated by the bit of silk outlining her most intimate places, and stroking it even more slowly to feel her shudder against his hand.

"And so eager for more," he added, voice rough, raspy, before pulling the scrap of silk away from her body. He swore beneath his breath as he caught sight of her inner lips and her pink, glistening core.

Hannah clutched the sides of the broken stone she sat on, unable to breathe. No man had looked at her so closely, so intently and she tried to close her thighs but Zale was crouching between, his thighs holding hers open.

"What is it about you?" he groaned, lightly sliding his fingers up and down the wet tender flesh. "Why do you do this to me?"

She jumped and cried out as his fingertips brushed against her, the nub already so sensitive she thought she might explode. "It's not...me..." she panted, fire licking her skin, making her burn, ache. "It's...you."

"No. I've never needed or wanted a woman the way I want you."

She gripped the stone even harder as he focused his attention on her, teasing the small nub, using the pad of his thumb to draw small light circles against the slick ridge.

Hannah could feel the pressure building within her, the coil of desire growing hotter, tighter, fiercer. She was close to climaxing but was too aware that Zale watched her face as he touched her, reading her emotions and reactions. It was sexy and yet scary—to be so open in front of a man—physically and emotionally.

There was so much at risk, she thought, struggling to breathe, already too dizzy. If she wasn't comfortable he'd see just how much she wanted him to take her, own her, make her forever his.

"Come," he said, "I want to watch you come."

She shook her head even as her body jerked and jumped, nerve endings stretched to breaking. "Can't," she choked, skin hot, body burning, desperate to find release but unable to let go when he'd watch her fall apart. She'd never been wild, never sexually adventurous, her college boyfriend going so far as to complain that she was boring in bed, but with Zale she felt positively daring.

Desperate.

Wanton.

"Yes, you can," he insisted.

"N-n-noooo. I c-c-c-can't," she stuttered, unable to meet his gaze even as her thighs trembled with the building pressure.

"Why not?" he murmured, gaze intent on her flushed face.

"You're…watching."

"I like watching. It gives me pleasure."

She shook her head, her lower lip caught between her teeth. The tension within her was overwhelming. She couldn't hang on much longer.

"Then close your eyes."

She shook her head again and with a growl he parted her knees wider, and leaned in to cover her clitoris with his mouth. He sucked hard and when she bucked against him, he slid a finger into her, a slow upward thrust that hit a certain spot at the exact moment he suckled the nub.

She screamed, the sound wrenched from her as he shattered her control with an orgasm so intense her hips lifted off the stone.

But he didn't stop.

He kept sucking and thrusting a finger into her, deeper, steadily, rubbing against that magic invisible spot making her feel hot and tingly all over again. She wanted to tell him it'd never work, wanted to tell him she'd never come again but then he blew on her, a warm breath of air before slowly licking the taut ridge and sucking on the tiny tip.

She exploded a second time, screaming his name.

This time Hannah pushed him back with a shaking hand. "No more."

Still shuddering, she adjusted the wet thong over her swollen sensitive parts and pulled her skirt down over her legs.

"What did you do to me?" she choked out, her entire body rippling with aftershocks.

"What you do to me every time I look at you."

Hot salty tears stung her eyes and she wiped them away. "I think you broke me," she whispered, still shuddering and shaking.

He smiled crookedly and kissed her knee through her skirt and then higher on her thigh before standing.

She tipped her head back to look up at him. "What about you?" Her gaze dropped to his trousers and the fabric straining over his thick erection. "Don't you want anything?"

He looked at her for what felt like forever before extending his hand to her. "Yes. But in my room. Putting you on your hands and knees here won't be comfortable on the stone."

She gulped a breath. Hands and knees next? She'd never tried that yet. "Maybe we should."

Zale laughed softly and they made their way back across the parapet and down the circular staircase in the tower until they reached the ground floor.

They were on the way to the King's Chambers when one of the footmen stopped Zale and said that Mrs. Sivka needed him to help her with Prince Constantine.

Zale's jaw tightened, concern etched in his features. "I'll go directly," he told the footman, before turning to Hannah. "I'll find you in your room."

"Is there anything I can do?"

"Just wait for me."

She watched Zale walk with the footman toward Prince Constantine's suite, his stride long, quick. He was worried.

He's a good brother, she thought, an amazing man.

In her suite, she washed her hands and was still running a brush through her hair when she heard her phone vibrate in the nightstand drawer.

Emmeline!

Hannah raced to retrieve her phone. "Hello?"

"Hannah, it's me."

Hannah glanced behind her, making sure none of the staff members were nearby able to hear. "Are you okay?"

"I…I don't know."

"Are you coming?"

"I…don't…know."

Stunned, Hannah pressed a hand to her forehead, feeling as if she was close to losing her mind. "What do you mean, you don't know?"

"I'm in Kadar."

"Kadar? Sheikh Makin's country? Why?"

"He thinks I'm you."

"Tell him you're not!"

"I can't."

"Why not?"

"It'd ruin everything!"

Hannah darted another quick look over her shoulder and added more urgently. "But everything's already ruined! You have no idea what's happened—"

"I'm sorry, I am." Emmeline cut Hannah short, tears thickening her voice. "But everything's out of my control."

"*Your* control. *Your* life. It's always about *you,* isn't it?"

"I didn't mean it that way."

"But you did mean to send me here in your place and you didn't intend to come right away." Hannah was so angry she was practically shouting. "You used me. Manipulated me. But how do you think I feel being trapped here, pretending to—" She broke off as the floorboards creaked behind her.

She wasn't alone. Hannah spun around.

Zale.

She felt the blood drain from her face and for a moment there was just the roar in her ears and then nothing.

Silence and nothing.

She snapped the phone closed and it nearly slipped from her fingers.

"How is our good friend Alejandro?" Zale asked, taking a step into the room and closing her bedroom door behind him.

Hannah's heart thudded hard and she darted a panicked glance at the now closed door. "W-w-who?"

"Emmeline."

"It wasn't what you think."

"Of course you'd make it a game. Nothing is ever straightforward with you." He walked to the bed and sat down on the edge and then patted the mattress beside him. "So come, sit, we'll try to make this fun."

He smiled at her but his expression was cold. Angry. "Shall we play twenty questions? I'll ask, you answer—"

"Zale, it wasn't a man. It wasn't Alejandro. It was one of my girlfriends."

"And you expect me to believe that?"

"Yes."

"I know what I heard. You were begging him to come get you and take you home."

"No! That wasn't it. I promise. Cross my heart—"

"Don't." His voice dropped, his tone pitched low and dangerous. "Don't do that."

Hannah crossed the carpet, shaking from head to toe. She thrust her phone out to him. "Call. Call the last number back. See who answers. It's not a man."

But he refused to take the phone and it fell between them, hitting the mattress and then sliding onto the floor next to the bed.

She'd never seen him this angry. He seethed with fury, amber eyes glittering like cut stone. After a moment he rose from the bed, circled her where she stood.

"Every time I get comfortable with you, you do this. Every time I commit to you, you play me for a fool."

"No." She laced her fingers together, skin prickling with unease. He was dangerous like this. Unpredictable. "I would never do that to you. Never." And then she heard herself and her vehemence and realized she *was* playing him for a fool. She had ever since she arrived.

Pretending to be Emmeline.

Pretending to be working out the differences in their relationship...

Pretending to get to know him before they married, when in reality, she wasn't even the one he'd ever marry...

"You're not a damsel in distress, Princess." He spit the words out as if they hurt his mouth. "There's no lock on any door. No guard keeping you here. If you want to go. Go. As for me, I have things to do and I'm not going to stand here and waste another minute with you."

"Zale—"

He lifted a hand to silence her. "Enough. Have some respect. Please." Hand still lifted, he walked out the door.

CHAPTER TWELVE

ZALE left his room and returned to the old castle keep, crossing through the once grand medieval hall still lined with heraldic banners and suits of armor, to the new wing on the far side, a wing which he'd had built five years ago to house his personal gymnasium and sport facility.

The sport facility was really a world-class sport complex, containing a regulation football field on the first floor with real grass, nets and stadium lighting. The second floor was divided into various sport courts—one for tennis, basketball and handball—plus a weight room where he still trained every other day.

A locker room adjoined the weight room, outfitted with a sauna, a whirlpool and a massage table for rehabilitating injuries.

Not that Zale got injured anymore. But it made him feel connected to the person he'd been, the one who'd lived and breathed sport above everything. The sport facility hadn't been cheap, either. It'd cost him millions to build, but he'd used his own money and he maintained it with his own money, too. In this part of the palace he wasn't a king but a man. A man who needed nothing but a ball, a net, an expanse of grass.

In his locker room he stripped out of his dress shirt and trousers, changing into sweatpants, a T-shirt and his running shoes.

Today he wouldn't run on the treadmill. Today he ran on the

track that circled his field, running fast, hard, one kilometer and then another and another but no matter how fast he ran he couldn't escape himself.

Couldn't escape his thoughts.

It was madness to have trusted her. Madness to have cared.

They hadn't signed the prenup and they had had sex. But she was cheating on him, still seeing Alejandro. It was within his rights to send her away. But ending it with Emmeline wouldn't be a small thing. It would be a huge crisis, personally and politically. But once she was gone, and once the shock of the news had worn off, people would move on. He'd move on.

But when Zale imagined her leaving, when he imagined her gone, he didn't feel relief.

He felt...pain.

Loss.

Her fault, he thought. The hollow emptiness within him, this sense of loss, was her fault. She was a witch, not a princess, and she'd cast a spell on him.

But it was a spell he had to break. Sooner than later.

And so he ran harder, ran faster, leaving the track to do tortuous wind sprints down the center of the field, again and again, pushing himself for an hour, running until his legs shook, and his heart pounded and he couldn't catch his breath.

Finally, finally his mind was calm. His thoughts were quiet. Yes, his chest still ached, but now it was due to exhaustion not emotion. And he could handle that.

In the Queen's Chambers, Hannah paced the sitting room for a half hour after he left her, in case he should change his mind and return. He didn't.

After thirty minutes she went to his rooms but he wasn't there, either. She returned to her room, sank onto the small pink silk couch and picked up one of the French fashion magazines Lady Andrea had bought but she couldn't read, or even look at the pictures.

She wanted to fix things with Zale, make amends somehow,

but he didn't return to their rooms or summon her, and the afternoon slipped away and then evening came and the maids and footmen slipped in and out of rooms turning on lamps and building fires.

Numb, Hannah watched Celine build the fire in her sitting room's hearth with the pink marble surround. She listened to the pop and crackle as the dry kindling caught, and fed the bigger logs until flames danced and licked making the fire bright. But even with the fire's warmth next to her, Hannah remained chilled.

What if this was her last day here?

What if Zale sent her away?

What if he was making plans this very moment to put her on a plane?

Her stomach heaved and acid rose up in her throat. She couldn't leave, not like this. She had to see him. Had to make him understand. Hannah left the sofa even as the thought hit her—

What was she to do to make him understand?

That she'd tricked him, yes, but she'd had good intentions…?

Or that she'd deliberately deceived him because she'd fallen in love with him at first sight?

Hannah sank back down on the sofa cushion knowing she could never confess any of that.

Knowing she could never make any of this okay.

Some things were too bad, too horrible to forgive.

When seven o'clock rolled around and Zale still hadn't put in an appearance or sent word about dinner, Hannah ate the meal Celine brought for her on one of the silver trolley tables they sent up from the kitchen.

At nine o'clock Celine asked Hannah if she'd like help changing into her gown and robe for bed.

Hannah shook her head. "Not yet," she answered huskily. "But there's no need for you to stay. I can change later when I'm ready. I know where everything is."

"You're certain, Your Highness?"

Hannah winced at the Highness part, feeling anything but royal. "Very certain. Good night, Celine. Sleep well."

At ten Hannah had had enough of sitting, waiting, worrying. She had to do something. Take action of some sort. Move. Walk. Find Zale.

Find Zale. Yes, that's what she needed to do. Immediately.

Ignoring the uniformed guards posted outside her room and throughout the palace, she went downstairs to the wing that contained his suite of offices—his library and office space, as well as adjoining rooms for secretaries and various assistants. But he wasn't there. The rooms were dark, the doors locked.

Where else would Zale be at ten o'clock at night?

With his brother maybe?

Hannah returned to the family wing but on reaching Tinny's suite, she discovered it dark and Mrs. Daum in her nightgown and robe as it was Mrs. Sivka's night off.

Hannah stood on the grand staircase, confused. A footman approached her. "Is there something you're looking for, Your Highness?" he asked.

She struggled to hold her smile. "Yes, His Majesty. I seem to have misplaced him."

The footman appeared truly apologetic. "I'm sorry, Your Highness. I have not seen him, but I can certainly ask and see if someone knows His Majesty's whereabouts."

"That would be wonderful. Thank you."

"And will you be in your rooms, Your Highness?"

"Yes."

Fifteen minutes later Krek knocked on her door, arriving with the message that His Majesty hadn't gone out, nor was he with his brother, or in his private gym, but most definitely somewhere in the palace. Just where, no one knew.

It wasn't until Krek left that Hannah thought she knew where Zale would be. The parapet. Where they'd had lunch today. Hadn't he said he liked to walk there when he had things on his mind or wanted to be alone?

Hannah took a soft velvet blue cloak from the dressing room

and left her room to head downstairs, walking quickly through the now deserted grand rooms and corridors of the palace for the old castle keep.

The lights were dim in this part of the palace and her footsteps echoed eerily loud in the medieval hall as she searched for the right hallway that would lead to the tower stairs. But finally she found the stone arch and the circular staircase that wound to the top of the tower.

A guard was at the top of the stairs in front of the door, but he bowed and immediately opened it for her.

Hannah sucked in a quick breath at the chill in the air as she stepped into the night. It was a clear night and the lights of the city below played off the bright stars overhead.

She drew her dark blue velvet cloak closer and set off, walking along the high thick wall in search of Zale, imagining all the people who must have walked the same path in the eight hundred years since the castle was built.

She imagined the worries people must have had, the hopes and dreams, as well as the pain. In eight hundred years, politics, fashion and technology had changed, but the human heart hadn't.

"What are you doing?"

It was Zale's voice, coming from the dark and she jumped and turned, peering uneasily into the night. "Where are you?"

He moved away from the shadowed wall and into the open. Moonlight silhouetted his tall frame and lit his profile. "Here."

She couldn't read his expression but his voice was hard, his tone impatient. For a moment her courage wavered and then she gathered her strength and pushed on. "I am so sorry you had to hear any of that earlier, but it isn't what you think. It wasn't Alejandro. I haven't spoken to him since Palm Beach and even then, there was nothing." The words tumbled from her, one after the other, hoping somehow to get through to him.

He wasn't listening, though. "I don't care," he said brusquely.

"But I do, which is why I had to find you." She took a deep breath, nervously crushing the soft velvet fabric between her fingers. "I know I haven't been easy. I know I'm not the woman you wanted. And I wish I had been. I wish I could be the right woman, the one that could make everything perfect for you—"

"I don't need perfect," he interrupted roughly. "But I also won't tolerate dishonesty or deceit."

"I'm sorry. I am. But you must know that since I arrived I've only wanted one thing, and that is you."

He made a sound of disgust.

She moved toward him. "I mean it, Zale. There is no one else for me. I need you to believe me."

"Emmeline," he said warningly.

She ignored the threat in his voice. "I hate it that you're angry. Please forgive me—"

"Em—"

She cut off his protest by rising on tiptoe to kiss him. His lips were cold, rigid beneath hers but she couldn't give up, couldn't not try. And so she kissed him slowly, sweetly, reaching up to clasp his face between her hands. She could feel the rasp of his beard against her palms and the gradual warming of his mouth beneath hers.

And then he was kissing her back, hard, almost aggressively. She welcomed the punishing pressure of his mouth on hers, and in an instant the kiss exploded into something hot and hungry and fierce. Zale dragged a hand into her hair and knotted the silken strands around his fingers, drawing her head back to give him better access to her mouth. He parted her lips, his tongue plundering the soft recesses of her mouth.

He kissed her until her head spun and little stars danced before her eyes, kissing her senseless, kissing her until he was all and everything.

He pushed her back, pressing her against the cold stone wall, as his hands took hers, trapping them above her head, holding her immobile. "This isn't working," he said, leaning into her, his voice a rasp in her ear. "We don't work."

She could feel the warmth of his fingers wrapped around her slender wrists and the pressure of his hips grinding against hers. His hard, broad chest crushed her breasts and his knee pressed between her thighs, rubbing against her most sensitive place, and she felt absolutely no fear. Just pleasure. And desire.

She needed him. Wanted him. Wanted him even when he was savage and furious and intent on punishing her because he'd never hurt her. He'd always protect her. Even if it was from himself.

"But we do work," she answered. "At least this part does… when we're together like this."

"But sex, even great sex, doesn't make a marriage work. There has to be more. I want more." His voice was hard, sharp, and yet his head dipped and he kissed the corner of her mouth and then her soft lower lip.

"But we could have more," she protested, tipping her head back, eyes closing, as his lips traveled down the side of her neck setting her skin and body on fire.

"Yes, more drama," he answered, lips at the base of her throat, breath warm on the small hollow there. "More lies. But I can't do it. I won't."

"You promised me four days, Zale. We still have two days. Give me those days—"

"No."

"Please."

"Absolutely not."

"But isn't the Amethyst & Ice Ball tomorrow night? I know it's a huge fundraiser of the year for your personal charity. Won't it seem strange to not have me there?"

"It'd be worse trying to get through the evening acting like I like you."

Hannah flinched.

He released her and moved back a step, setting her free. "That was harsh, and I hate being cruel, but, Emmeline, we both know that you are not right for me, or good for me."

She realized then she was fighting a losing battle. Zale was finished with her. He did intend to send her away. And maybe this was the right thing to happen. Maybe this was the way it was to end.

She could leave in the morning and Zale would never know the truth…he'd never know that it wasn't Emmeline who was here, but Hannah. He'd never have to know he'd been deceived.

He turned his back on her, moving to the stone balustrade to look out over the city that glimmered with light. "I'm tired," he said after a moment. "Tired of talking. Tired of arguing. Tired of trying to make this work."

She could feel his exhaustion, too. It was in his voice, the slump of his shoulders, the bite of his words. "I understand."

"I will phone your father in the morning and tell him we've realized it won't work. I'll tell him it was a mutual decision and that our differences were just too great to overcome."

"Okay."

He looked at her from over his shoulder. "It's better this way, doing it now, instead of waiting until the last minute to cancel the wedding."

"I agree."

He dropped his head, closed his eyes, fingers digging into the stone wall. "So why does it feel like hell?"

A lump filled her throat and her eyes burned. "Because despite our differences, we did have feelings for each other."

He drew a slow, heavy breath. "I'm sorry."

She went to him, and wrapped her arms around his waist, pressing her cheek to his back. "It's my fault. It's you that needs to forgive me."

He covered her hands with one of his. "It's late," he said roughly. "We should go to bed. The morning will be here soon enough."

"Can I sleep with you tonight?"

"That's just asking for trouble."

She kissed his back. Zale was warm and felt so good. But then everything about him was strong. Solid. Like the tough Texas men she'd known growing up, men with integrity, men who understood honor. "I won't cause trouble," she whispered.

"I just want to be near you. Just want to sleep with you one last time."

"I won't change my mind, Emmeline. You'll still leave in the morning."

"I will."

He was silent so long she was sure he was going to refuse her, but then he lifted her hand to his mouth, pressed a kiss to her palm. "Then we'll spend our last night together and say our goodbyes in the morning."

They made love in his big bed with the brocade fabric panels down creating a cocoon for just the two of them. It was as if the rest of the world had fallen away and they were the only two who existed.

In the darkness Zale loved her slowly, holding back his own orgasm until he'd brought her to a climax, once and then again. Tonight there was a sweetness in their lovemaking, a poignancy in every kiss and caress. Closing her eyes, Hannah savored his hard body stretched over hers, his skin so warm and delicious to touch.

When she came a second time, her heart seemed to shatter along with her body and it was all she could do to hold back the tears, and keep him from feeling her pain. The pain was considerable.

She loved him, loved him, loved him and he'd never know it.

Tears burned beneath her lids and she shuddered in his arms, her body rippling with aftershocks even as her heart exploded with fresh pain.

Forgive me, Zale, she whispered silently, kissing his chest, just above where his heart would be.

Forgive me for not being who you needed me to be.

Zale couldn't sleep even though his body was spent. His mind wouldn't turn off. His thoughts raced. His chest ached.

Zale had always needed order. He did not do well with uncertainty. For him, ambivalence was akin to chaos. And chaos was a synonym for loss.

Loss of peace.

Loss of focus.

Loss of control.

And Zale needed control. He needed to be in control. Always. And the few times he wasn't in control terrible things happened, things with a tragic outcome.

Stephen's leukemia.

His parents' crash.

Tinny's seizures.

No, control was everything. Which is why he'd trained so hard in his sport. He knew that if he worked hard, relentlessly hard, he would be successful. He knew he had talent, but it was his commitment that drove him to the top. And it hadn't been by chance. His success was the direct result of drive, discipline and sacrifice.

He had put in the work and was rewarded.

He'd made the necessary sacrifices and earned peace of mind.

It was basic. Straightforward. Black and white.

But with Emmeline it was different. With Emmeline his emotions were chaotic. Primitive.

He felt wild around her. Fierce. As if he was barely clinging to control. Lately he wanted to grab her by the hair and haul her caveman-style to his lair and keep her there just for him. Even now he longed to lock her up, secure her, take away all the uncertainty.

Maybe then he'd be comfortable.

Maybe.

Hannah suddenly sighed, and murmuring something unintelligible in her sleep, pressed herself closer to his side, snuggling against the warmth of his chest as if that was the only place to be.

And just like that, he felt a hot, wrenching pain.

How could he love her? How could he—even now—want to hold her?

CHAPTER THIRTEEN

IT TOOK Hannah just a moment after waking to realize she was alone. Stretching out a hand to the space near her the sheets were cool.

Zale had been gone for a while.

The realization sent her heart tumbling and she rolled onto her stomach and buried her face in her pillow. It was morning. Zale was gone. And she'd be leaving here now.

Sometime in the next half hour or hour, she'd pack her things and say her goodbyes.

The idea of saying goodbye to Zale, though, made her heartsick.

She loved him but would leave him.

How was this right? How was it fair?

And how would Zale say goodbye to her? Would he come to her room and say goodbye there? Or would he meet her at the door? Or would he refuse to see her, and say nothing at all?

Hannah's heart contracted, her chest aching with the pressure and pain. *But you can't cry,* she told herself. *You must keep it together for Zale's sake. You must stay calm until you're gone.*

And she would stay calm. She'd focus on the future, on returning to her life, her own life, the life of an ordinary twenty-five-year-old woman working to pay her bills, make her car payment and cover her rent.

She once liked being ordinary, and she'd always loved her

independence and autonomy. She'd enjoyed working and then coming home at night to her apartment, and curling up on the sofa and watching her favorite shows and reading her favorite books.

She could do this, she repeated, throwing back the covers to face her day.

Hannah had barely finished her shower in her bathroom in the Queen's Chambers when Lady Andrea came knocking on the door to discuss Hannah's day with her.

"It's going to be a busy day with the ball tonight," Lady Andrea said, consulting her calendar with the scrawl of events and notes. "You'll join His Majesty for morning coffee in his office, and then directly after you'll have a fitting with Monsieur Pierre who has flown in this morning with your gown for tonight's Amethyst & Ice Ball."

So that's how this would play out, Hannah thought, unable to speak. He was summoning her to his office where he'd say a few brief words and then have her shown to the door. How perfectly professional. How wonderfully regal. "Thank you," she said. "I'll dress quickly."

"I'm not supposed to say anything," Lady Andrea said, dropping her voice, "but I've seen the ballroom. The decorations are breathtaking. The entire room has been transformed into a winter wonderland with floor-to-ceiling ice sculptures."

Hannah didn't care about the ball. She wouldn't be there. But she did care about Zale. She cared very much about saying goodbye, and handling herself right. She had to keep it together. Had to be as calm and controlled in Zale's study as possible.

Twenty minutes later, Hannah found herself seated in Zale's personal study, a room lined with floor-to-ceiling books that made her think of a library, sipping a cup of coffee in a chair across from Zale's desk, wishing he'd speak.

He'd barely looked at her since she arrived a few minutes ago. Nor had he touched his coffee. Instead he stared at a spot on his desk, fingers drumming on the rich polished wood.

"Did you sleep well?" he finally spoke, breaking the unbearable silence.

She nodded. "Yes, thank you."

"Yesterday I was very upset. I overheard you on the phone and felt betrayed—"

"It's okay, Zale. I understand. I'm not going to make a scene—"

"I owe you an apology," he interrupted tersely. "I had it all wrong. You were telling me the truth. You weren't speaking to Alejandro."

She felt a shiver of alarm. "How do you know?"

"He was badly injured in a polo accident yesterday in Buenos Aires. He was in surgery for hours, and he remains unconscious in intensive care." He finally looked at her, his expression blank, his jaw hard. "I imagine you already knew that—"

"I didn't."

He looked away, swallowed hard. "I'm sorry, Emmeline. I know you have...strong...feelings for him."

She stared at her hands, fingers interlocked. "I'm sorry he was hurt, but I'm not in love with him."

"No?"

She shook her head and lifted it to meet his gaze. "How could I, when I care so much about you?"

For a long moment he searched her eyes before taking a deep breath. "You still do? Even though last night I was determined to throw you out?"

Her lips curved into a tremulous smile. "Yes."

He looked pale and tense and unhappy. "I'm sorry. I should have trusted you."

Guilt clawed at her. She struggled to hang on to her smile. "Mistakes happen."

"Can you forgive me?"

"Yes."

"And will you please stay? I don't want to host the ball tonight without you at my side."

"Yes. Absolutely. I'd love to be there with you."

"Thank you." He sounded relieved but his expression remained grim. "And in that case, I'm to send you straight back to your room for a final fitting for tonight's ball gown."

She nodded, forced another smile and quietly slipped away.

He watched her leave, listened as the door closed soundlessly behind her.

For a moment he felt strangely bereft. Hollow and empty and alone. He didn't like it.

He'd liked having her in his study. He enjoyed her company. Loved having her around.

She'd said last night that she knew she wasn't the woman he'd wanted, but she was wrong. She was exactly what he wanted. Now he just needed to prove it to her.

It was time he stopped trying to control everything so much. Time to stop defining everything as black or white. Could he open a little? Grow a little? Change for her?

Yes.

He pictured her sleeping so trustfully in his arms last night and he wanted that every night. He wanted a life with her, a future together. Marriage and babies and everything that went with it.

Across the palace in the Queen's Chambers, Hannah stood in her dressing room on the small, low stool in a thin white Grecian gown that wouldn't zip closed, her image caught reflected in the numerous mirrors.

And no one said anything.

Not Lady Andrea who sat in the corner with her notebook. Or Camille and Teresa who stood against the far wall. Or Celine, who hovered behind Anton Pierre, the designer from Paris who'd just flown in that morning hand carrying the two commissioned gowns—the ball gown for tonight's gala and the wedding dress for Saturday's ceremony.

No one spoke because what could anyone say?

The thin, slim chiffon gown should have cascaded effortlessly in an elegant column of white. Instead the fabric rode up in Hannah's armpits and the back wouldn't zip. Turning her head, Hannah could see her thin bra strap across her back and even that looked tight.

"Suck in your stomach," Anton Pierre said, tugging hard on the zipper of the gown, lips pursed, expression critical.

"I am," Hannah answered, wincing a little as the zipper pinched her back, catching at her skin.

"More," he insisted.

She yelped as he zipped another bit of skin. "Ouch, stop! Stop. That hurts."

Anton threw his hands up in displeasure. "If this gown is too tight, your wedding gown isn't going to fit, either. Your breasts and hips are huge, Your Highness. What have you been eating?"

"Not a lot," Hannah answered, knowing she'd actually lost weight in the past week, at least five pounds.

"Nonsense. I think you're bingeing on butter and bon bons, Your Highness. I've dressed you for years and you've always asked me to tell you the truth. So I'm telling you the truth. You're fat. You have chub." He grabbed an inch on her back near her bra strap and pinched. "This is bad. You must lose ten pounds quickly—immediately—or you won't be wearing my wedding gown. It's made for a princess, not a midfielder."

"Get out!" Zale's voice thundered through the dressing room, rattling a mirror on one wall. He looked huge and violently angry as he gestured toward the door. "Get out, Pierre, before I personally throw you out."

Then he turned on Lady Andrea. "How dare you allow a designer to speak to Her Highness that way? Where is your loyalty? Where is your allegiance? Perhaps you need to pack up your things, too, and join Monsieur Pierre on his plane home."

Lady Andrea covered her mouth, holding back a sob. "Your Majesty, forgive me. I was just about to intervene—"

"When?" He interrupted. "I stood outside the door listen-

ing. I heard it all. When were you going to intervene? How far did you intend to let it go?"

Lady Andrea shook her head and wiped away tears that were falling fast and furious.

"That's all the answer I need," Zale retorted. "Pack your things."

He turned to Celine, Camille and Teresa next. "And you three? What is your excuse? Why did none of you protect Her Highness?"

Celine's eyes were huge in her face. "I should have, Your Majesty. I wanted to. But I was scared."

"Why?"

Celine glanced at Hannah and then back to Zale. "I didn't think it was my place because Monsieur Pierre is so famous and Princess Emmeline's favorite designer…" Her voice drifted off and she pressed her hands together. "Should I pack my things, too?"

Zale looked at Hannah who still stood on the stool with the gaping chiffon gown clutched to her chest. His jaw jutted, eyes blazed and for a moment he just looked at her, expression impossible to read, then turned back to Celine. "I will let Her Highness make that decision. But I want all of you to leave us now. I'd like to speak to Princess Emmeline alone."

The staff escaped from the dressing room and closed the outer door to the suite.

Zale crossed to the stool where Hannah was standing. "Give me your hand."

She did and he helped her step off the stool and onto the ground.

"Turn around," he instructed.

She did and he drew the zipper down so she could step from the dress.

"How could you let him speak to you that way?" He gritted, his features hard, his expression savage.

"I'm supposed to be thin," she whispered.

"Utter nonsense. You are perfect. I wouldn't change one thing about you."

Her eyes burned and she blinked. "Yes, but fashion designers prefer very slim models. Clothes look better that way."

"I couldn't care less about clothes. I care about you."

Her heart staggered a bit inside her chest. "You do?"

"Can't you tell? I haven't kept my hands off you since you arrived."

"I figured you had a healthy sex drive."

"I do, but I've had no problem managing it until I met you."

She smiled crookedly. "You still make that sound like a problem."

"It is. I pride myself on my self-control but you have challenged it, and challenged me, at every turn. But I'm glad. It's made me realize just how strong my feelings are for you." He drew a rough breath, his expression darkening all over again. "My God, how dare Pierre talk to you that way? I nearly thrashed him! I still want to go after him, teach him a thing or two."

He did sound angry, crazy angry, which was so not Zale Patek, King of Cool. "But what about tonight's ball? I need something to wear."

"We'll get that one altered," he said. "I know a Raguvian designer who puts Anton Pierre to shame."

"You think she can fix it?"

"Not just fix. Eva will improve the design." He looked at her, shook his head. "She'll take what I think is a rather boring dress and will make it extraordinary. You are an extraordinary woman and deserve no less."

Her heart skipped.

He'd just called her extraordinary. The words her father had used for her late mother. The words she'd always wanted to hear. "Thank you," she said, her voice breaking.

He reached for her, pulling her into his arms. His head dipped and his mouth covered hers, lips traveling slowly, leisurely over hers, drawing a hot, hungry response.

Hannah gloried in his warmth, and slipped her hands up his broad chest to wrap her arms around his neck.

His hands moved to her hips and he molded her against him. He was hard and hungry for her but after another long, melting kiss he pushed her gently away. "If I don't make some calls now, and track Eva down, you won't have a dress to wear tonight."

She gave him a naughty smile. "That's okay. I'll go naked."

"The hell you will," he said on a growl.

Hannah laughed as he swatted her backside and was still smiling after he left and she threw herself onto her bed.

She stretched happily, recalling how Zale had swept into the dressing room and ordered Pierre out. It was like a scene from a movie. Zale Patek, rushing in on his white stallion to save the lady in distress.

Hannah's smile faded as she thought of Lady Andrea. Poor Andrea. Hannah wasn't sure that Andrea deserved to be fired. Monsieur Pierre was intimidating. No one knew how to handle him...well, no one but Zale. Hannah decided she'd talk to Zale and ask him to hire Andrea back.

Hannah was still lounging on the bed when her phone in the nightstand drawer buzzed with an incoming message.

Hannah knew it was from Emmeline. She could feel it in her bones. And this time she didn't want to know what Emmeline had to say.

A minute passed. And then another. Finally, reluctantly, Hannah retrieved the phone and opened it.

It was from Emmeline. The text was brief.

I'm not coming to Raguva. The wedding is off. Once you leave I'll break the news to Zale. Text me when you're gone. Sorry.

Hannah blinked, read it again and when the words were the same, she felt everything tilt and slide, crashing into disaster.

It had all been for naught.

Emmeline wasn't going to marry Zale. Zale would be embarrassed and angry beyond measure.

She read the message again. And then again. But each time it was the same.

Emmeline wasn't coming. She wouldn't be marrying Zale after all. And Hannah had to go.

Little spots danced before Hannah's eyes. She had to go. Had to leave.

A knock sounded on the bedroom door. "Your Highness?" It was Celine. "Can I come in?"

Hannah couldn't speak. Breathe, breathe, she told herself, air bottled in her lungs.

"Your Highness?"

Tears filled Hannah's eyes. It had happened. She had to leave. But she couldn't go tonight, not hours before the ball. She couldn't humiliate Zale like that. No, she'd go in the morning, first thing tomorrow.

"Yes," she called out at last, her voice faint, strangled. "Please, come in, Celine."

Celine opened the door and saw Hannah sitting on the bed wiping away tears. "Is everything all right, Your Highness?"

"Everything's great."

CHAPTER FOURTEEN

THE ball was less than three hours away, and Hannah was getting a Swedish massage on a special table in her dressing room. The lights were dimmed, candles burned and soft instrumental music played. It was supposed to be a treat, something Zale had arranged for her, but Hannah was too keyed-up to enjoy it.

"Take a nice slow, deep breath," the masseuse said soothingly, rubbing fragrant lavender oil into Hannah's tense shoulders. "Now exhale. Slowly, slowly, Your Royal Highness. Good. Now again."

Hannah tried to do as she was told, she did, but it was hard to relax when everything inside her was tied up in knots.

She hated Emmeline right now. Hated Emmeline for what she'd done. Hannah should have never come here. She shouldn't have ever agreed to play acting for an afternoon much less a week.

If only she hadn't gotten on the plane. If only she'd refused to continue the charade at that point.

But she hadn't. She'd been too worried, afraid that the princess was facing a crisis all alone.

"Your Highness," the masseuse said gently, but firmly, kneading Hannah's shoulders. "Let go of everything. Just focus on your breathing. Focus on feeling good for the next half hour."

And somehow, beneath the magic hands of the masseuse, Hannah did relax, shutting everything from her mind for the

next thirty minutes, but once she was in her bathroom, showering off the oil and shampooing her hair, the anxiety returned.

So how did she fix this with Zale? There had to be something she could do…some magical fix, but standing in the
shower, hot water pounding down, Hannah could think of nothing.

Hannah had always prided herself on being able to handle
whatever her difficult, demanding boss, Sheikh Koury, sent her
way. The Sheikh had been through a dozen secretaries before
he found Hannah who could speak four languages fluently and
handle the endless and challenging work he tossed her way.

No matter what he dropped in her lap, she handled it with
aplomb. Arrange an environmental awareness meeting with
the world's leading oil executives? No problem.

Plan activities for the oil executives' wives, many of whom
had to be segregated from men? Hannah didn't even blink.

Organize an international polo tournament in Dubai? Then
move it to Buenos Aires? And provide transportation for all
players and horses? Consider it done.

Hannah loved puzzles and thrived on good challenges, but
the one thing she couldn't do, and the one thing she was desperate to do, was protect Zale from what was to come.

The truth.

Eva, the Raguvian designer, had reworked the ball gown for
Hannah, changing the design from a simple off-white column
dress, to a shimmering chiffon gown with jeweled embroidered flowers unfurling across the bodice and to bloom down
one hip in a profusion of purple and amethyst jewel petals that
reached her feet.

She wore pale gold sling-back heels with more jewels at
the toe, and her blond hair was piled high on her head and
held in place with glittering citrine and amethyst hairpins.
Rectangular rose-gold, diamond and amethyst earrings hung
from her ears, a cuff circled her wrist, and on Zale's arm she
felt like a princess.

"You're a goddess tonight," Zale said as they paused inside the ballroom doors and took in the glittering winter wonderland anchored by a dozen massive ice columns. "More beautiful than any woman has a right to be."

She flushed with pleasure, heat radiating out from the tight coil of desire in her belly to the tingle in her fingers and toes. "I don't know what to say."

Zale was dressed in black coat and tails, white shirt, white vest and tie and looked devastatingly attractive, especially when he smiled, and he was smiling now. "Just say thank you."

And then they were being announced and swept into the immense white and gold palace ballroom that glittered with floor-to-ceiling ice sculptures and potted trees brought in just for the occasion. The trees' white, frosted limbs were covered by strands of miniature white lights and the only spot of color in the glittering white room was the ladies' elegant gowns in shades of purple, violet and lavender.

Zale and Hannah circled the room on their way to the head table, Zale's hand resting lightly on her back. She could feel the heat from Zale's hand and she shivered as exquisite sensation raced through her. There was something about his touch… something in the way her body responded to him that made her feel so alive.

"What do you think?" he asked as they took their places on the platform, several feet higher than the rest of the room.

"It's absolutely magical. I feel like a princess from a fairy tale."

He grinned. "Which one?"

"Cinderella." She reached down to lightly touch one of the jeweled blossoms on her waist. "Eva waved her magic wand and voilà! I'm a princess at your ball."

Uniformed footmen filled their tall, slender flutes with champagne. Zale lifted his flute. "To my princess," he said, a half smile playing at his lips.

"To my king," she replied, clinking the rim of her glass to his.

They drank and the champagne's tiny bubbles fizzed in her mouth and the cold liquid warmed as it went down.

"Have all Raguvian kings married royalty?" Hannah asked, setting her flute back on the table. "Has no one married a... commoner?"

"Only once in the past two hundred years and he gave up his throne to marry her."

"Why is a blue-blood bride essential?"

"Our monarchy grew out of a tribal kingship that spanned nearly a thousand years, and the Raguvian people have fought hard to preserve the monarchy, although today we are—like Brabant—a constitutional monarchy."

Hannah knew the differences between monarchies from working for Sheikh Koury.

There were absolute monarchies like those in the Middle East—Brunei, Saudi Arabia, Qatar—and then there were constitutional monarchies like those in Belgium, Sweden, Monaco and the United Kingdom. A constitutional monarchy gave a king power as defined by each country's constitution.

Her brow furrowed. "Does it actually say in your constitution that you must marry a royal?"

"Yes."

"You couldn't marry a commoner?"

"Not without relinquishing the throne."

"And you wouldn't do that?"

"I could not."

She noticed his word choice. It wasn't that he wouldn't. He couldn't. "Why couldn't you?"

"I could never be selfish enough to put my needs before that of my country."

She ran a fingertip around the base of the flute stem, watching the tiny gold bubbles of champagne rise to the surface and pop.

Even if Zale wanted Hannah Smith, he wouldn't choose her. Even if Zale should love her, he wouldn't keep her. "Have you ever dated a commoner?" she asked, voice breaking.

"All my girlfriends were commoners." His lips curled, slightly mocking. "You are my first princess."

And she wasn't even a real princess, either.

Her heart grew even heavier during dinner. It didn't help that when Zale looked at her, she lost track of time. In his eyes there was just now, only now, and right now she was happy. Lucky. Good.

Suddenly Zale was standing and extending his hand to her. "Your Highness," he said, his smile warming his eyes, warming her, making her feel so very alive. But then, he was so very alive. "May I have this dance?"

She looked up into his lean face with the strong brow, firm mouth and uncompromising chin and a frisson of feeling raced through her. "Yes."

She rose, putting her hand into his, inhaled as sensation exploded inside her, making her body go hot and cold. Again. He'd done it again. Made her want, made her feel, making her aware of just how much she loved him.

Zale led her toward the dance floor as the orchestra started playing the first notes of an achingly familiar love song she'd played endlessly on her guitar growing up.

"Your favorite song," Zale murmured as he pulled her into his arms and close to his tall lean frame.

Hot emotion rushed through her. How did he know?

And then as his hand settled low on her back, his warmth scorching her through her thin gown, she remembered he meant Emmeline.

Of course he meant Emmeline. But Emmeline wasn't coming. It all ended tonight.

For a moment she couldn't breathe, suffocated by crushing pain.

Early tomorrow morning she'd slip away, leaving him a note. He'd hate her when he found the note. She'd never forgive herself for deceiving him, either.

"You're a good dancer," she whispered.

"That's because you're my perfect partner."

Eyes burning, heart on fire, she tipped her head back and was immediately lost in Zale's eyes. She loved his face. Loved everything about him far too much. "You are full of compliments tonight, Your Majesty."

He smiled at her. "I'm happy."

He did look happy. His light brown eyes glowed. "I'm glad."

"Marry me, Emmeline."

"I thought we were?"

"I'm proposing again so we can start over. Start fresh. This isn't about our families or our countries. This is about us. Will you marry me?"

Her eyes filled with tears. She blinked to clear her vision. "You're sweeping me off my feet."

"It's what I should have done from the beginning."

"I had no idea you were such a romantic."

His steady gaze held hers. "So is that a yes, Your Highness? Or do you need time to think about it?"

Her chest ached. How could she say no? How could she ever refuse him anything? "Yes."

He smiled, a great boyish smile that lit his face and made him look utterly irresistible. "Thank God. For a moment I thought you intended to leave me standing at the altar."

He was teasing. Trying to be funny. But Hannah shivered, chilled by reality.

Zale felt the goose bumps on her arms and drew her closer. "Cold?"

"A little."

He held her even more snugly against him and she pressed her cheek closer to his jacket, her ear resting on his chest just above his heart. And remembered Cinderella.

In *Cinderella,* at the stroke of midnight the magic ended. The glass coach turned back into a pumpkin. Cinderella's gown became rags. And Cinderella became no one.

The song was ending and Zale lifted her hand to his mouth, kissing her fingers. "Thank you."

She looked up into his face, that handsome face, which owned every bit of her heart. "Have you ever been in love?"

"Yes."

"She was a commoner?"

He nodded.

"What happened?"

His jaw tightened. "My parents died and I became king."

She stared up at him. "You gave her up?"

He nodded again and she exhaled in a rush. Tenderly Zale brushed a wisp of hair from her flushed cheek. "It hurt," he admitted, "but it was meant to be. Because if I hadn't ended it with her, I wouldn't be here with you."

Zale saw her cheeks turn pink and her blue eyes deepen, a sheen of tears making the color look like sapphires, a perfect complement to the jewels in her hair and at her ears.

She'd never looked more beautiful, and yet she hadn't been this emotional, or fragile, since their engagement party. But he understood her exhaustion. It had been a hard night without either of them getting a lot of sleep.

"I see some friends across the room," he said, taking her hand. "Let's go say hello."

All evening he'd introduced her to different people he thought she should know—members of his cabinet, members of parliament, influential men and women from all over the world. But now he was taking her to old friends, close friends, people Emmeline loved.

Crossing the ballroom they joined the Greek prince, Stavros Kallas, and his bride of one year, the stunning Greek-English heiress, Demi Nowles. Prince Stavros was a first cousin of Zale's, their mothers were half sisters and Stavros had been a friend of Emmeline's since childhood.

When Stavros had proposed to Demi Nowles after a whirlwind engagement, no one had been happier than Emmeline who'd socialized with Demi for years. One year they'd been the inseparable dancing duo, hitting every exclusive nightclub on the Continent.

"I do believe you know these two," Zale said. "Perhaps *you* should introduce *me,* Your Highness?"

Emmeline didn't reply and glancing down at her he saw panic in her eyes.

"Your Highness," he prompted, gently, teasingly. "If you'd do me the honor…?"

Emmeline smiled, but her features were tight, and her expression looked frozen.

She extended a hand to Prince Stavros. "It's a pleasure," she said politely. "Good to see you again."

Stavros looked at Emmeline's hand, glanced at Zale and then back at Emmeline before slowly taking her hand. "Yes," he agreed uncomfortably. "You look well, Emmeline."

Zale frowned, and Demi watched the exchange, equally baffled.

For a moment Demi didn't seem to know what to do and then her expression suddenly cleared. "Oh, Emi, I get it now! You're making fun of those Americans and their strange manners. You were just there in Palm Beach for that polo tournament. Heard it was quite the crush."

"Yes, it was," Emmeline agreed pleasantly. "How long are you here for?"

Silence followed Emmeline's question, a most awkward silence, and even Demi's smooth brow furrowed. "Until the wedding, of course," Demi answered, perplexed. "Unless you've decided to replace me as one of your bridesmaids."

Again there was silence and Zale caught Stavros and Demi exchanging puzzled glances.

Zale reached for Emmeline's hand. She was trembling. He didn't understand what was happening.

"No," Emmeline answered, breaking the excruciating silence. She smiled but she looked alarmingly brittle. "Don't be ridiculous. How could I get married without you at my side?"

Stavros smiled. Demi hugged Emmeline. But Zale wasn't fooled. Something was wrong with Emmeline.

They moved on, just a short distance from Prince and Princess Kallas. "Are you all right?" Zale asked, his head bent to hers, his voice pitched low.

She swayed on her feet. "I don't feel well."

He slipped an arm around her waist to support her weight. "I can see that," he said, leading her through a narrow door hidden in the ballroom's ornate white and gold paneling, exiting the ballroom for a small cream room where he swept her into his arms and carried her to a chaise in the corner.

He settled her on the chaise and she lay still with her eyes closed, her lashes black crescents against her pallor. "Do you feel faint?" he asked.

She nodded.

"A little."

"What can I get for you?"

Tears seeped from beneath her lashes. "Nothing."

Zale summoned a footman. "Brandy and water," he said crisply.

The footman returned quickly and Zale carried the snifter of brandy to Emmeline. "Drink. It'll help."

She sat up, brushing away tears and took a sip, gasping a bit as the alcohol burned her throat.

He waited for her to take another sip before standing up. "How do you feel now?" he asked.

"Better."

But her teeth were chattering and she was still too pale.

Zale slipped his coat off and draped it around her shoulders before moving to stand in front of the fireplace. He stared into the cold hearth. "You didn't recognize them," he said bluntly. "You still don't know who they are."

She lifted her head, looked at him then, her blue eyes shadowed. "No. I don't."

"And you shook Stavros's hand. He's a childhood friend."

"I...embarrassed you."

"No. That's not the issue. I just don't understand. How can you not know them?"

She didn't answer, her head hung in shame.

But he didn't want shame. Nor did he want an apology. He wanted answers. "Are you on something? Taking something? Pills...uppers, downers, pain medicine?"

"No."

"Diet pills, or an appetite suppressant?"

"No."

"Snorting anything? Smoking anything?"

Her head jerked up and she gave him a horrified look. "No!"

"Then what?" His voice throbbed with emotion. "What the hell happened in there?"

"I'm tired, Zale. Confused. I haven't been sleeping much lately—"

"That doesn't hold up. You always travel. You are a globe-trotting royal, never long in the same place."

"But there's been so much stress. We've had problems and the wedding is just days from now—"

"I don't buy it. Not from you. You are Emmeline d'Arcy. You thrive on stress. So tell me what happened in there. Tell me why you're acting like this."

"I'm telling you but you're not listening."

"No. What you're telling me are lies. I can see it in your face. You haven't told me the truth yet. And I want the truth."

Hand trembling, she reached for the brandy, took another sip and then set the glass back down. "Maybe you should sit."

His temper flared. "I prefer standing."

She nodded once, a small nod that said nothing and yet everything. "This isn't going to be easy."

"Please," he groaned impatiently. "Spare me the theatrics."

Her chin lifted and she looked up at him, expression blank. For a long moment she said nothing and then she shrugged. "I'm not Emmeline."

CHAPTER FIFTEEN

ZALE gritted his teeth. Not Emmeline? It was ridiculous. She was being ridiculous.

"This isn't a good time for drama," he said, striving to stay pleasant, and trying not to think of the three hundred and fifty guests in the ballroom awaiting their return. "We're throwing a party. A huge fundraiser. Until now it's been quite a success. Let's sort this out so we can return—"

"I'm not Emmeline," she repeated flatly, no emotion anywhere in her voice, her expression equally vacant. "I'm Hannah. Hannah Smith."

Again he felt that need to laugh but then he saw her face and finally understood she wasn't joking. She was serious.

Zale abruptly sat down. "What do you mean you're not Emmeline?"

"I've just been pretending," she whispered, hands clenched into a fist in her lap. "I was doing Emmeline a favor. I was only supposed to be her for a few hours while she went to see friends, but she never came back, and I got onto the plane and then I was here."

He stared at her in shock.

She'd lost her mind. She needed help. "I'll get you a doctor," he said gently. "We'll get you care—"

"I'm not sick," she interrupted, her voice low but steady. "Just very foolish. Inexcusably foolish. And I don't expect you to forgive me, but it's time you knew the truth."

She looked up at him, eyes bright, cheeks finally taking on some color. "I'm an American. I work in Dallas as a secretary for an Arab sheikh named Makin Al-Koury—"

"I know Sheikh Al-Koury. He just hosted the Palm Beach Polo Tournament."

"I organized the event." She drew a quick breath. "And that's where I met Her Highness, Princess Emmeline d'Arcy. We were mistaken for each other so often that she requested a meeting with me. The princess needed to take care of something and asked for my help—"

"To impersonate her?"

She nodded. "Her Highness said she would never be able to leave without a disguise, and so she left the hotel as me."

"Where was she going?"

"I don't know. She never told me. She just said she needed to take care of something and she'd be back in a few hours." Hannah laced and unlaced her fingers. "But she never returned that day. Or the next. So here I am."

They never returned to the ballroom. The Amethyst & Ice Ball finished without them.

Instead Zale had Emmeline escorted back to the Queen's Chambers, his tuxedo jacket still draped across her shoulders. He headed to the parapet where he walked the tower for half an hour.

He didn't believe her. Couldn't.

Emmeline wasn't Emmeline but an American secretary named Hannah Smith?

Impossible.

There weren't two Emmelines in the world, and Emmeline d'Arcy was such a rare beauty, so distinctive that there couldn't be another woman who looked like her.

Or moved like her.

Or smiled like her.

Which meant that Emmeline wasn't well, and he needed to get her away from Raguva, away from the pressures of the palace, far from the wedding preparations and all the attention that came with both.

She needed rest and medical care and he'd make sure she got the help shc needed.

Back downstairs he gave instructions for his jet to be prepared for an early morning departure. He sent for Krek and told his butler that he needed a suitcase packed. "I'm not sure how long I'll be gone...one week, two. See to it that Her Highness's maid packs for her, too."

Krek stood there a moment looking confused. "Pack another suitcase, Your Majesty?"

"No, Krek. She just needs one."

"But Her Highness went downstairs with a small suitcase a little while ago. Her maid found this on the floor in the living room. She must have dropped it on the way out." The butler reached into the pocket of his black pin-striped trousers and withdrew Emmeline's phone. "Perhaps you could give it to her when you see her?"

Zale took the phone, turning it over in his hand. The infamous phone. The source of so much tension.

Silent, gut hard, chest tight, Zale flipped the phone open to scroll through her in-box. Text from Emmeline.

Text from Emmeline.

Text from Emmeline.

His chest squeezed tighter. He drew a rough, unsteady breath as Krek quietly left. For a moment Zale wanted to hurl the phone across the room but instead he sat down in the nearest chair to read the messages. He went back to the very beginning and read them all, incoming as well as outgoing since he had time, because Emmeline, or Hannah, or whoever she said she was, wouldn't be going anywhere. The palace gates were always locked, and no one came or went without Zale's knowledge and permission.

Just as Krek said, Hannah had packed a suitcase, and changed into traveling clothes, but she couldn't get out of the palace.

The gates were locked. The palace guard stood at attention. They refused to even make eye contact with her. She tried to persuade one guard and then another to open the gates but each one stared straight ahead as if she wasn't even there.

Hannah gave up pleading and sat down on the palace's front steps. It was a clear night, a cool night, and she was growing cold but she'd rather freeze to death on the steps than go back inside.

She was beginning to think she'd freeze to death, too, when Zale's very deep voice spoke on the top step behind her. "Hannah Smith, you have some explaining to do."

Her stomach plummeted. Goose bumps covered her arms. Slowly she rose knowing that this next conversation with Zale would be horrendous.

She was right. He grilled her for hours, repeating the same questions over and over. It was three-thirty in the morning now and Zale was growing angrier by the minute.

"It's illegal what you've done," he said harshly after she finally fell silent, worn-out from talking, exhausted from trying to make him understand. "You've broken too many laws to count. You didn't just impersonate Princess Emmeline, you committed fraud as we well as perjury."

She stared at him dry-eyed, her body trembling from fatigue. "I *am* sorry."

"Not good enough."

"How can I make amends? I want to make amends."

"You can't," he answered brusquely. "And the more I think about it, the more certain I am that I should have you arrested. Locked up. Let you sit in jail for a couple of years—"

"*Zale.*"

But he couldn't be placated. "What sort of person are you? Who does what you did?"

"I was never supposed to come here. I'd never agreed to come—"

"But you did."

Hannah's shoulders twisted helplessly. "I kept thinking that any moment Emmeline would show up. Any moment she'd return and we'd switch places again and that would be that."

"What you did was a crime! It's a serious offense to enter the country under false pretenses, use a fake identity, interfere with state business. Any one of those would earn you a stiff prison sentence, but all three together?" He shook his head. "How could you do it?"

"I don't know." Hannah felt horrible, beyond horrible. "And there isn't a good excuse. I was stupid. Beyond stupid. And I knew I was in trouble once I got here but I didn't know how to put a stop to it. I liked you immediately. Fell for you hard—"

"Please don't go there."

"It's true. I fell for you at first sight. And I knew you weren't mine. I knew you belonged to Emmeline but she wouldn't come, and yet she wouldn't let me leave."

"So you decided to just stay and play princess, thinking no one would ever find out the truth?"

She bit her lip, unable to defend herself. Because yes, that's what she'd naively hoped.

Stupid, stupid, Hannah.

The silence hung between them, tense, agonizing, and then Zale turned away, making a rough sound in his throat. "To think I nearly fell in love with you. A fake. An impostor! My God, I even took you to my bed—"

"You can't blame me for that. You wanted to sleep with me, too!"

"Yes, because I thought you were mine. I thought you were to be my wife. I had no idea you were an American girl getting her thrills pretending to be my fiancée."

"It wasn't like that. I didn't want to betray you or Emmeline—"

"But you did, and you did come to my bed, and you enjoyed it." He went to her, tangled his hand in her hair and forced her face up to his. "Didn't you?"

Her jaw tightened and she stared up at him in mute fury. Zale saw the blaze of anger in her eyes and he welcomed it.

Good, let her be angry. Let her hurt. Let her feel a tenth of his pain and shame.

To be tricked like that…

Played for a fool…

He'd never forgive her. Never.

Zale released her, disgusted with her, him, all of it. "So where is Emmeline now?" he demanded, taking a step away. "Why isn't she here?"

Hannah shook her head. "I don't know. She never said."

He turned his back on her, walked across the room toward the windows. The drapes had not been drawn against the night and the lights of the walled city twinkled below. "I have to call her father. Tell him what's happened. We'll need to let our guests know the wedding is off."

She knotted and unknotted her hands. "Can I do something?"

"Yes. You can go." He spoke without turning around, keeping his back to her. "I want you gone first thing in the morning, and I never want to see you again."

Hannah left before daybreak. This time the palace guard allowed her to leave and she walked through the palace gates and out onto the cobbled streets, her footsteps unsteady.

The worst had finally happened. Zale had found out the truth. He knew who she was now, knew Emmeline wasn't coming, and now she was free to return to her own life, resume her work, see her friends.

This is what she'd wanted. This is what her goal had been. And yes, she was sad now—shattered, actually—but eventually she'd be okay. Hannah knew she was tough. Resilient. And maybe one day if she was lucky, she'd fall in love again.

Reaching the old city center, Hannah went to the train station to purchase a ticket and discovered she didn't have enough money to get across Raguva much less out of the country as she'd left her credit cards in her hotel room in Palm Beach. She'd need her father to wire her money and get one of the secretaries at the office in Dallas to overnight her passport to her.

Hannah reached into her coat pocket to call her dad but her phone was missing. She searched the rest of her pockets before opening her small suitcase to check there. But no, nothing, which meant she must have left the phone at the palace or dropped it while walking into the city center.

Her heart fell as she imagined returning to the palace, only to be confronted by Zale.

She couldn't handle seeing him again. Couldn't handle his disappointment and anger.

Last night she'd felt like Cinderella at the ball—a beautiful princess dancing with the handsome king—and just like the fairy tale, today she was no one. She'd been tossed into the streets.

Exhausted, Hannah closed her suitcase and got to her feet and stood in the middle of the train station, wishing she had a fairy godmother who could come wave a magic wand and make everything good again.

But fairy godmothers didn't exist, and real life women like Hannah Smith had to sort out their problems and mistakes on their own.

Only her plight hadn't gone unnoticed. An old gentleman working at the station ticket counter left his booth and approached her, speaking a mixture of broken English and Raguvian. "Do you need help?"

She nodded, hating the lump in her throat. "I need to find a hotel, something cheap, for a night or two until my father can send money."

He pointed to a building across the street. "Nice and clean," he said, with a sympathetic smile. "And not too much money. Tell them Alfred sent you."

She shot him a grateful smile. "I will, thank you."

He nodded and watched her hurry across the plaza to the small hotel tucked into the stone building on the other side of the cobbled street.

The woman at the front desk seemed to be waiting for Hannah at the front door. She ushered her in and got her registered at the small reception desk in minutes before personally showing Hannah to her room, explaining through gestures and smiles how the small ancient television and room thermostat worked.

When Hannah told her she needed a phone to make a collect call to the United States, the woman handed Hannah her own from her dress pocket.

But the phone operator couldn't reach Hannah's father for him to accept the collect call. They tried twice before Hannah gave up.

"You can try again later, as many times as you need," the front desk clerk assured her. "I will be here all day."

Hannah did try three more times, but each time she had the operator try to place the collect call, her father's answering machine picked up.

By the end of the day, Hannah had resigned herself to the fact that she'd be stuck in Raguva at least another day. If not longer.

For the first twenty-four hours after Hannah left, Zale wanted revenge. He fantasized about hunting Hannah down and making her suffer as he was suffering.

He was still angry the second day after she'd left, and plotted her downfall, but now when he imagined doing something to her, he was doing something to her body. Something...pleasurable.

He hated himself for even thinking of her, much less desiring her.

The fact that he could imagine taking pleasure in her body baffled him after everything that had happened.

Why was he even thinking about her? How could he want her? She'd manipulated him and played him and he should hate her.

He didn't. He couldn't. Not when he loved her.

Zale ran a hand through his short hair, knowing he'd only been in love once before. It'd been six years ago when he'd lived in Madrid. She had been young, brilliant and vivacious, a breathtaking Spanish beauty, but when his parents had died he'd retired from football and ended their love affair, moved back to Raguva and never once looked back.

Zale knew how to move on without looking back. He knew how to be ruthless, relentless, hard.

And he'd force himself to be ruthless and hard now.

She was gone. And there would be no forgiveness. No second chances.

But when he pictured Hannah, he didn't want to be ruthless and hard.

On the third day Zale woke, even more angry and frustrated than when he went to bed.

He would find her. He would. He'd take her in his hands and make her pay.

But first he had to find her.

Zale spent the morning making inquiries before turning to Krek at noon. Turns out he should have started with Krek as his butler already knew where Hannah could be found. "The Divok Hotel, Your Majesty, under the name of Hannah Smith."

Zale tried to hide his irritation. "How did you know where she was?"

"Her Highness is distinctive. Word quickly spread."

"No one told me."

"Everyone knew you were unhappy with her—"

"Does *everyone* know why?"

Krek shrugged vaguely. "Lovers' quarrel, something of that nature."

"They are aware the wedding has been called off?"

"Yes, Your Majesty, but they're all hoping that you'll come to your senses and forgive her so the wedding can be on again."

"It's not going to happen."

"Whatever you think is best, sir."

"Krek, I know you heard us fighting. I know you and half the palace must know the truth. She isn't Emmeline d'Arcy. She's an American impostor."

"Yes, Your Majesty."

"Krek."

The butler bowed. "Will you be going out, sir?"

Zale glowered at him. *"Yes."*

"Very good, sir."

Zale was annoyed that he'd be showing up at the unassuming Divok Hotel with full escort, but he couldn't very well go alone. He was a king. There was protocol. And safety was always an issue, even in his own country.

Zale waited in his armored car as his security guard checked out the hotel, securing the front and back entrances before allowing him inside.

The front desk clerk's welcome was effusive. Beaming and bowing, she showed him and four of his bodyguards up to the top floor, which was where she'd given Hannah Smith a room. "It's one of our best rooms," she said, "and every day I make sure she has fresh flowers."

Zale thanked the clerk for the kindness she'd shown Hannah Smith, and knocked on Hannah's door.

He waited a moment, gut tensing, and then knocked again. Finally she opened the door a crack and peered out, her long hair messy, her face pale with deep shadows beneath her eyes. The interior of her room was dark with the blinds still drawn although it was almost noon.

She blinked at him, obviously stunned but sleepy. "What are you doing here?"

"I don't know," he answered grimly before gesturing to her room. "May I? The hallway isn't the most private place for us to talk."

She nodded, tucked her hair back behind her ears and opened the door wider. "Come in."

* * *

While his security detail waited in the hall, Hannah turned on the lights and opened her blinds and smoothed the covers of her rumpled bed.

He glanced around the small, Spartan room with the bouquet of violets in a little glass vase next to the bed. "Why are you still here?"

She winced at his sharp tone. "Because I can't afford to leave."

"You should have told me."

"And what would you have done? Laughed in my face? Or thrown me in prison?"

He shrugged. "I was angry. I still am."

She sat cross-legged on the foot of the bed and tilted her chin up at him. "My father has sent me a credit card and my passport by express mail. It should arrive this afternoon. I'll be leaving soon."

"Not if I arrest you."

"Is that why you brought so many of your palace guard? Expecting me to put up quite a fight, aren't you?"

"You don't sound remorseful at all."

"What can I say that I haven't already said? I've apologized again and again, and I meant every word—"

"So say it again."

A tiny frisson of sensation raced down her back. Something in his voice hinted at danger. Or perhaps it was the expression in his eyes. But suddenly the room felt sexually charged. "I'm sorry."

"That's it? That's your most sincere, heartfelt apology?"

"I gave you my sincere, heartfelt apology two nights ago and you threw it back in my face."

"So? I want to hear it again. I want to feel your sincerity. I want you to prove your sincerity."

"How?"

His hot amber gaze raked her from head to toe. "I'm sure you can think of something."

A shiver raced through her—nerves, anger, as well as anticipation. "You can't kick me out of your palace and then expect me to invite you into my bed."

"Why not?"

"Because I don't want to sleep with you," she retorted fiercely.

"Good, because I can assure you we won't be sleeping."

"It's not going to happen. You were horrible. Mean. Cruel."

"Yes, yes, I was all of the above. So how will you pleasure me?"

"I won't."

"You will." He closed the distance between them, stopping in front of the bed, his thighs inches from her knees. He was standing so close that Hannah's skin prickled and the fine hair at her nape lifted. Unfortunately there was nowhere to run. Not on the third floor with four security guards outside the door.

"And why would I?" she whispered, licking her dry lips.

"Because I remember what you said, the night of the ball. You said you fell hard for me. You fell in love at first sight. Or did you just make that up along with everything else?"

She stared up into his eyes, feeling his tension. He was hanging on to control by a thread, barely mastering his emotions. "No," she whispered. "I did fall for you, right from the beginning. I knew it was wrong to continue to pretend to be Emmeline but I loved being with you...near you...loved everything about you."

"You loved being with me."

She nodded. "More than I've ever enjoyed being with anyone."

He reached down, slipped a hand into her thick hair, his fingers tangling the long golden strands. "Just as I've never enjoyed anyone as much as I enjoyed being with you."

The husky note in his voice and the heat in his eyes made her pulse leap and her body warm. Her skin tingled and her nerves fizzed and she had to remind herself to breathe.

"So what do we do now?" he asked, allowing the long strands of her hair to slip through his fingers.

"You're not angry with me?"

His hand moved to her neck, and down, caressing the base of her throat to the pulse that beat so erratically there. "I am, but that doesn't seem to change what I feel for you."

She shivered at his touch. Her mouth had gone dry. "And what do you feel for me?"

Emotion burned in his eyes, making the rich amber irises glow. "Love."

Her heart stuttered and stopped. Air bottled in her lungs, she looked up at him in wonder. "You...love...me?"

He dropped his head, his lips brushing hers. "Fool that I am...yes."

She closed her eyes, heart racing. "Not a fool, Zale, because I love you so very, very much."

"Say it again."

She opened her eyes, looked up at him, seeing the hunger and hope in his eyes. "I love you, Zale. I love you more than I've ever loved anyone."

CHAPTER SIXTEEN

ZALE lay in bed with Hannah in his arms, blinds still open so they could watch the sun set. Moments ago the sky had been a spectacular red and orange but the fiery colors were fading, leaving long lavender shadows to stretch across the plaza. The elegant street lamps at the train station were coming on, shining soft yellow pools of light onto the cobbled street.

They'd been in bed for hours. Had made loved for hours. Their lovemaking warm and tender and bittersweet.

Zale had known since birth he'd have to marry a blue blood, a true princess. He'd known since he was fifteen that princess would be Emmeline.

But in the blink of an eye it had all changed.

He wouldn't be marrying Emmeline.

The woman he loved was definitely not royal.

Duty required that he walk away from Hannah. Common sense suggested the same, and yet somehow she felt as essential to his life as Tinny. And he'd never walk away from Tinny.

But who would assume the throne if he chose Hannah? Who knew this country well enough to lead?

There were cousins, of course, but none of them even lived in Raguva anymore, choosing instead to make their home in far flung places like Sydney and Paris, London, San Francisco and Buenos Aires. Places that were urban, sophisticated, exciting.

On the other hand, he hadn't been living in Raguva when

his parents died. He'd been in Madrid, but he had returned, and learned what he needed to know to get the job done and he'd served Raguva well.

Others could do what he had done. His oldest cousin, Emmanuel, was first in line, and a compassionate, educated man. He'd be a quick study but his health was poor. So poor in fact that he and his wife hadn't started a family yet due to Emmanuel's weak heart, which meant succession would once again be an issue.

Emmanuel's younger brother, Nicolas, was next in line and Nicolas was charismatic but a notorious spendthrift. Despite a sizable allowance, he was always in debt and looking for a quick bailout from one family member or another.

No, Nicolas was not an option. He'd ruin Raguva within a year or two.

So who then would be Raguva's king should Zale step down? Who would protect Raguva? Who could put Raguva first?

Hannah reached out, placing her hand on his chest. "Stop," she murmured. "There's nothing to do, nothing to decide. We both know how this plays out. I'm leaving in the morning."

"No."

Her hand caressed the smooth plane of muscle. "I don't want to go, but I can't give you heirs, and you need heirs. Not just an heir and a spare, but a whole brood."

"I won't lose you."

"It will be better once I go. Better to make a quick, clean break. We both know the longer I stay the worse it'll be."

"I've lost so much in my life, Hannah. How can I be expected to give you up, too?"

She was silent a long moment. "I don't know," she said at last. "But it's the only real option. You can't forsake your country, and you need to be here for Tinny."

"Tinny can go wherever we go."

"But the palace is the only home Tinny has ever known. You can't take him from his home. Nor can you walk away from your responsibilities here. You are the king. This is your country. This is your destiny."

He cupped her face in his hands, his expression fierce, his amber eyes burning. "*You* are my destiny. I am sure of it. More sure of it than I've ever been of anything."

She kissed him, once and again. "I love you, Zale, but you're wrong. I can't be your destiny, not when Raguva needs you."

"It's so easy for you to go?"

"No! It's not easy, but if you relinquished your throne for me, you'd come to resent me, and I'd always feel guilty."

"There has to be another way."

Hannah curled closer to him, her cheek pressed to his chest so she could listen to the strong, steady beat. The even steady beat soothed her, reassured her. He was a good man and a true king. "But there isn't, darling. Is there?"

So it was decided. She'd be leaving in the morning. Zale would take her to the airport, and put her on his plane for Dallas.

Decision made, Zale called the palace requesting Chef to send dinner over, and they ate in her room, and drank a bottle of red wine and talked for hours about everything but Hannah's departure in the morning.

At midnight they made love again and talked some more, and then somehow it was dawn, and the sun was rising from behind the mountains, turning the sky pale yellow.

Hannah lay in Zale's arms watching the sky gradually lighten.

She felt Zale's hand in her hair, his fingers threading through the long strands. He hadn't spoken in hours but she could feel the emotion inside of him.

"I know I'm not in a position to be asking for favors," she said softly, breaking the silence, "but I'd like to ask for one anyway. Can I see Tinny one more time before I go?"

Zale didn't answer.

"Just a brief visit," she added. "I'll keep it light. Won't get emotional. Won't make a big deal about saying goodbye."

"I don't know, Hannah. Tinny already thinks you're going to be his sister and he won't understand why you're not there anymore."

"But won't he already be confused as to why I'm not there?" She turned in his arms to better see his face. "I can tell Tinny I have to go to Texas to see some of my family, and I'll tell him about Texas and ranches and cowboys." Her eyes searched Zale's. "Please, Zale. It would help me to leave, help me know I haven't just walked away from Tinny as if he didn't matter."

Zale's jaw flexed, his expression taut. "Fine. I'll call Mrs. Sivka and let her know we're taking morning tea with Tinny."

"Thank you."

Three hours later they were sitting down in Tinny's suite at a small table in the living room for morning tea. The table was covered with a cheerful yellow check cloth and a bowl of daisies sat in the middle. Teacups and plates were at each of the three places and Tinny rocked excitedly back and forth in his chair, delighted that he was entertaining.

Mrs. Sivka poured the tea for them, and presented Tinny with his hot chocolate as Hannah entertained Prince Tinny with stories as she'd promised, telling him about Texas and all the animals on their ranch. He liked that they had horses and cows and chickens. He was really excited she'd had a goat.

Hannah loved Tinny's laughter and the way he clapped his hands with excitement. But all too soon teatime was over and they were having to say their goodbyes.

Tinny gave her a big hug and kiss. Hannah hugged him back. And then she was holding Mrs. Sivka's plump, cool hands in her own.

Mrs. Sivka's blue eyes watered, she squeezed Hannah's hands tightly. "I'm sorry, Your Highness."

Hannah gulped a breath, fighting tears of her own. "Oh, Mrs. Sivka, you can't call me that anymore. I'm just plain Hannah Smith."

"Never plain." Mrs. Sivka's hands squeezed hers. "Take care of yourself."

"I will," Hannah assured her.

"And be happy."

Hannah's smile faltered. "I'll try."

Then Zale's hand was at her elbow and he was ushering her out the door and down the grand staircase to the waiting limousine. The drive to the royal airport was a quiet one and it was even more strained as he escorted her onto his private plane.

Zale could hardly look at Hannah as she sat down in the jet's leather armchair, his handsome features hard, expression savage. "And I'm just supposed to leave you like this?" he demanded, voice harsh.

She'd made up her mind in the limousine she wouldn't cry as they parted, had told herself she'd keep it together for both their sake, and she was determined to keep her vow. "Yes."

His jaw clamped tight. His cheekbones jutted. "And what am I supposed to say now?"

A lump filled her throat, and a terrible tenderness ached in her chest. Her eyes drank him in, trying to remember every feature, every expression. How she loved this man. How she'd miss him.

Her nails dug into her palms. Her eyes were scalding hot. "You say goodbye."

"No."

She would not cry. Not cry. Not, would not. Rising, she caught his handsome face in her hands, looked into his eyes then kissed him gently, tenderly. "Goodbye, Zale. It's time to let me go."

Zale was in hell. A hell unlike any other hell he'd ever known, and he'd known hell before. He'd suffered terribly when Stephen was fighting leukemia. He'd raged when his brother later died. He'd mourned his parents after their plane crashed and cried in private for Tinny who missed his mother every night, not understanding why she wouldn't come home.

But none of that sorrow, none of that loss, was like the pain he felt now because Hannah had given him something no one else had—peace. With Hannah he felt complete. Strong. Whole.

He hadn't realized until she'd arrived in Raguva how empty he'd been, how hollow he'd felt.

Yes, he'd known duty and he'd fulfilled his responsibilities but he'd been like a man sleepwalking. He'd been numb, just going through the motions. And then she arrived and brought him to life.

And now she was gone. His woman. And she'd taken his heart.

For two endless weeks Zale barely spoke, moving silently from bedchamber to office, to parapet and back again.

He ate little. Slept less. He wouldn't even allow Krek to attend to him. When he wasn't working he ran. He ran early in the morning, in the middle of the day and late into the night. And when he couldn't run anymore, he stretched out on his bed and prayed.

He prayed as he hadn't prayed in years. Not since Stephen was ill and Zale wanted him cured.

Zale's prayers hadn't been heard then but he prayed anyway now.

He loved her. He needed her. Fiery, passionate, fierce, funny Hannah.

She was flawed and stubborn, impetuous and emotional and he'd never loved anyone more.

His eyes stung and he rubbed at them. He hadn't cried since he'd had to comfort Tinny after their parents funeral, and he wouldn't cry now, but his heart was breaking and there was nothing he could do about it. Life was life and it'd dealt him a bitter hand.

It had been nearly a month since Hannah had gone and Zale had run himself to the point of exhaustion. But the exhaustion failed to dull the pain. His heart hurt—burned—constantly and he couldn't understand how that part of him could hurt so much when the rest of him felt dead.

He was standing at his window in his study, staring out at nothing when a knock sounded on his door.

The door opened and Mrs. Sivka entered looking so much frailer than she had a month ago. It was as if she'd aged ten years in thirty days. "Forgive me for intruding, Your Majesty, but I insisted that your staff let me in to see you."

Zale had been pacing his office, unable to sit, unable to rest and he walked away from her, to the window overlooking the garden. He kept his back to her so she couldn't see his face. "Is Tinny not well?"

"The prince is fine. He's with Mrs. Daum right now. But I need a word with you."

"What is it?"

She was silent so long that he glanced over his shoulder. "Mrs. Sivka?" he prompted impatiently.

Anxiety was etched into her features and worry in her eyes. "There is something I've never told anyone. Something I swore I would never tell. It was a blood oath. One of those promises you cannot break, for any reason, ever. And I haven't."

Zale sighed, irritated. He was tired, not in the mood for this. The past month had been absolute hell and the last thing he wanted was to play word games. "And yet you feel the need to break it now?" he drawled sarcastically.

"Yes."

He turned around, folded his arms across his chest. "Why?"

"It might change everything."

No, he really couldn't deal with her now, not if she insisted on talking about secrets and blood vows and other silly games. "What would?"

"The truth."

"Mrs. Sivka, *please*."

Her round face creased. "There were two babies, Your Majesty. Two baby girls, not one. Princess Emmeline and the infant princess, Jacqueline."

Zale blinked. He'd heard what she said but it hadn't fully registered. "What?"

"Princess Emmeline was one of two. She had a twin sister."

"That's nonsense. Absolute fiction. King William would have told me if Emmeline had a twin—"

"He didn't know. No one knew—"

"Listen to yourself, Mrs. Sivka! I'm not Tinny. Not interested in make-believe."

"This is true. I was there. I was there for Princess Jacqueline's delivery at Marmont, the royal family's hunting lodge in northern Brabant. Her Royal Highness's nanny had been my best friend since childhood, and she'd asked me to be there, too, at the delivery. I was to take care of the newborn for the first few days while she tended to Princess Jacqueline."

Mrs. Sivka took a quick breath, expression pleading, wanting him to understand, needing him to understand. "Of course I went, and we thought we were prepared for the delivery. It was a difficult delivery. No one expected twins, and although there was a midwife on hand, it became apparent that something was very wrong. Her Highness needed surgery. She was bleeding internally. But as you know, Marmont is remote, at least an hour's drive from the nearest city, much less a modern hospital. We called for help but there was no helicopter available, no emergency medical team near us." Her eyes turned pink and her mouth pressed thin. "Her Highness knew she was dying—"

She broke off as tears fell and she struggled to keep control. "Her Royal Highness was very brave, and quite calm. She was also very specific about what she wanted us to do. One baby was to go to her brother at the palace in Brabant. And the other baby was to go to the babies' father in America. I took infant Princess Jacqueline to him with the news that Her Royal Highness had died in childbirth but she wanted him to have their child—"

"He knew Jacqueline had been pregnant?"

Mrs. Sivka nodded. "Her Royal Highness had written to him, told him, but her family wouldn't give him access to her."

"I can't believe this."

Mrs. Sivka's shoulders twisted. "But I never told him he had another daughter. I couldn't, not after the vow I made."

Zale was absolutely numb. "Why tell me this now?"

"Because it changes everything."

"It changes nothing."

"You're not listening then."

"I am listening. Fairy tales and secrets and blood vows—"

"You don't have to be afraid, Your Majesty."

"Afraid?" he roared, hands clenched, fury blinding him. "You think I'm afraid?"

"Yes." She folded her arms across her middle. "You did this very same thing when you were just a boy. You hated to be disappointed, hated pain, so you'd hurt yourself first so no one could make you hurt worse."

"You can go, Mrs. Sivka."

Mrs. Sivka didn't budge. "Your Majesty, prayers do get answered, and there is goodness and justice in the world, not just pain. Because in your heart you already know the ending of my story."

Zale ground his teeth together, muscles so tense he ached all over. "That what? This infant princess…this Jacqueline…?"

"Is your Princess Hannah."

Zale sat down abruptly on the windowsill, his legs no longer able to hold him.

Can't be.

Can't.

Impossible.

"You shouldn't tell tales," he said roughly, hating Mrs. Sivka in that moment for torturing him like this when he had nothing left to go on. He needed to eat, needed to sleep, but most of all, he needed her, Hannah, his woman.

"I've never lied to you, Your Majesty. I wouldn't start now." Mrs. Sivka went to the door, opened it, revealing a wan-looking Hannah dressed in jeans and a white blouse, her hair loose and her stunning face scrubbed free of all makeup.

Hannah looked at him from across the library, blue eyes huge in her pale face. "Hello, Your Majesty."

Zale couldn't breathe. Hannah. Here.

Here.

And his. Princess or not. It didn't matter. It would never matter. He'd gladly give up everything for a chance at a life with her.

Mrs. Sivka smiled broadly. "Your Majesty, may I present to you, Her Royal Highness, Hannah Jacqueline Smith."

Zale didn't know who moved first—he or Hannah—but suddenly she was in his arms in the middle of the study, her arms wrapped tightly around his neck.

"I never thought I'd see you again," she choked out, voice wobbling as she looked up into his face. "And never is such a long, long time."

"I know. I've been so angry this past month. I was going mad without you here."

"I heard."

"How?"

"I called the palace every day and talked to Mrs. Sivka or Krek, asking about you. It killed me to hear that you were so unhappy."

He clasped her face in his hands. "My staff talked about me behind my back?"

"Yes. Sorry. But I badgered them until they told me the truth. I had to know." Her eyes filled with tears. "And I'd lose it, absolutely lose it when I heard you were running fifteen, twenty miles a day and not eating. I wanted to jump on a plane and come see you but I was afraid that if I came, I'd never leave."

"But you're here now."

She blinked, and tears fell in streaks. "Because I don't ever intend to leave. Not unless you forcibly throw me onto the streets."

Her blue eyes had turned aquamarine from crying and her long black lashes were wet and matted and her nose was pink and she was the most beautiful woman he'd ever seen. "I need you here, Hannah. I can't do this without you. I don't even want to live without you."

"That's what Mrs. Sivka said when I called her on Tuesday. She said she feared for you, feared you'd become too self-destructive, and that's when she told me who I was." She bit into her lip to stop it quivering. "The name on my birth certificate is Hannah Jacqueline Smith. I always wondered where my father got the name Jacqueline. He never told me, not until this week after Mrs. Sivka told me everything."

Zale turned to look at Mrs. Sivka. "I can't believe you waited this long to tell her the truth! You could have cleared this all up weeks ago—"

"I'd made a promise, Your Majesty."

"Ridiculous," he muttered, adding something under his breath about old women and blood vows before clasping Hannah's face in his hands and kissing her brow, her damp cheek, her salty lips.

Hannah laughed against his mouth. "Don't be mean," she whispered. "At least she told us."

"I should fire her. Throw her out—"

"Zale!" Hannah drew back and gave him a stern look. "She's your nanny!"

Zale gazed down into her eyes, his expression hard and then turning to awe. "And she knew you before I did. She was there at your birth. Incredible." And it was incredible, he thought, drinking her in. Hannah wasn't ordinary Hannah Smith, but Emmeline's twin sister, and a true princess of Brabant. "It's a miracle."

"It is," she agreed. "And my father supports Mrs. Sivka's story. She did bring me to him when I was just a week old."

"He must be stunned to discover he has another daughter."

Hannah hesitated. "I haven't told him that part yet. I thought I would, when he flies in for our wedding."

The corner of Zale's mouth slowly curved. "And when is our wedding, Your Highness?"

Hannah grinned back. "Mrs. Sivka and I were thinking maybe a week from today?"

Zale glanced at his beaming nanny. "You're planning my wedding now, are you, Mrs. Sivka?"

"Why not? I used to change your nappies."

"You may go, Mrs. Sivka," Zale said with mock sternness.

"Yes, Your Majesty," she answered, heading for the door. But Zale called to her before she could close the door. "Mrs. Sivka?"

His nanny looked at him with terrible tenderness. "Yes, Your Majesty?"

"Thank you." His eyes were warm, his expression grateful. "Thank you for everything."

"My pleasure."

Once she was gone, Zale lifted Hannah onto the corner of her desk and moved between her legs to get as close to her as he could. "What kind of wedding do you want, Hannah?"

"I don't care, as long as you and I are both there." She reached for his hips, pulled him even closer, so that his zipper rubbed up against her inner thighs. "People are going to talk, though," she added, sliding a hand over his crotch and his growing erection. "How will you explain that I'm not Princess Emmeline, but Hannah?"

"Princess Hannah," he corrected, trying not to be distracted by the heat of her hand on his aching shaft. "Emmeline's twin sister, and a Princess of Brabant." He lowered his head, brushed his lips across hers and then kissed her again, wetting her lips with a flick of his tongue. "My Princess of Brabant."

She gasped and shivered against him, her hands pressed to his chest. "Um, King Patek, can we lock the door?"

"I think that's an excellent idea." He cupped her face, kissed her deeply, parting her lips to take her mouth completely. "Can't wait to do that to your body," he growled. "I've missed you. Missed everything about you."

She kissed him back, legs wrapping around his hips, so turned on she was trembling. "Zale, I love you."

"Not as much as I love you."

The corner of her mouth tilted in a wicked little smile as she lightly scratched her nails down his chest. "Prove it."

"Don't you worry, Princess. I will."

EPILOGUE

IT WAS late. It had been a long day, and Zale was only now heading for Tinny's rooms to say good-night to his brother.

But reaching Tinny's living room, Zale's tension and exhaustion eased, his shoulders relaxing as he spotted Hannah already there, sitting on the couch with Tinny reading him his favorite bedtime story.

Zale stood in the doorway a moment, content to just look at them and listen.

Hannah, his beloved princess, pregnant with his first child. And sweet, innocent Tinny who absolutely adored Hannah with all his heart.

What could be better? What more could a man want?

What more could a king need?

And for a moment his chest squeezed so tight Zale couldn't breathe.

To think that the randomness of life could take Stephen and his parents, but save Tinny, and then give him Hannah?

To think that an impostor princess could turn out to be the real thing?

Impossible that Hannah was Princess Jacqueline's other daughter, Emmeline's missing twin and the keeper of his heart.

Zale felt hot emotion sweep through him, constricting his chest.

If Hannah and Emmeline hadn't met in Palm Beach…

If Emmeline hadn't asked Hannah to switch places…

If Hannah hadn't come to Raguva…

If Mrs. Sivka hadn't broken her vow…

He gave his head a faint shake, overwhelmed all over again by fate. So many things could have gone wrong. So many things could have kept him from Hannah…

But they hadn't.

Suddenly Hannah looked up, brow furrowed and then seeing him, she smiled. "You're just in time for the last chapter."

Her smile made him ache and it was almost too much, almost too strong, this fierce love he felt for her.

"Good," he said, moving into the room and sitting down on the couch next to Hannah and Tinny. "This is my favorite part."

"Because you love happy endings," she said, smiling at him, her love for him so transparent, warming her beautiful blue eyes and curving her generous mouth.

"I do," he answered, taking her hand and carrying it to his mouth. "Are you tired? Is the baby kicking too much?"

She touched her round belly. "He was, but now I think he's listening. He knows his daddy is here."

"Shall I read the last chapter then? Would you like that, Tinny?" Zale offered.

"Yes, Zale," Tinny said, taking the book from Hannah's hands and pressing it into his brother's. "Yes, read it. Read it right now."

Hannah laughed softly as the baby inside her kicked hard just then, a vigorous one-two. "I think your future footballer agrees," she said, running her fingers across her ribs where the kick had been.

Zale's eyes gleamed. "He does have a good kick, doesn't he?"

"Most definitely." She leaned back, resting her head on his shoulder. "Now read, please. I'm anxious to get to the part where the prince marries the princess and they all live happily ever after."

"And they did, didn't they?" he said, opening to the first page of the last chapter.

Her voice grew husky. "Yes. Yes, Your Majesty, they did. Very happily."

* * * * *

HELIOS CROWNS
HIS MISTRESS

MICHELLE SMART

This book is for Aimee – thank you for all the support and cheerleading over the years. You're one in a million.

This book is also dedicated to Hannah and Sarah – the mojitos in this are for you!

xxx

CHAPTER ONE

'Do you really have to shave it off?' Amy Green, busy admiring Helios's rear view, slipped a cajoling tone into her plea.

Helios met her eye in the reflection of the bathroom mirror and winked. 'It will grow back.'

She pouted. Carefully. The clay mask she'd applied to her face had dried, making it hard for her to move her features without cracking it. Another ten minutes and she would be able to rinse it off. 'But you're so sexy with a beard.'

'Are you saying I'm not sexy without it?'

She made a harrumphing sound. 'You're always sexy.'

Too sexy for his own good. Even without a beard. Even his voice was sexy: a rich, low-pitched tone that sang to her ears, with the Agon accent which made it dance.

Impossibly tall and rangy, and incredibly strong, with dark olive colouring and ebony hair, currently tousled after a snatched hour in bed with her, Helios had a piratical appearance. The dangerous look was exaggerated by the slight curve of his strong nose and the faint scar running over its bridge: the mark of a fight with his brother Theseus when they were teenagers. Utterly without vanity, Helios wore the scar with pride. He was the sexiest man she'd ever met.

Soon the hair would be tamed and as smooth as his face would be, yet his innate masculinity would still vibrate through him. His rugged body would be hidden by a formal black evening suit, but his strength and vitality would permeate the expensive fabric. The playful expression emanating from his liquid dark brown eyes would still offer sin.

He would turn into Prince Helios Kalliakis, heir to the throne of Agon. But he would still be a flesh and blood man.

He lifted the cut-throat blade. 'Are you sure you don't want to do it?'

Amy shook her head. 'Can you imagine if I were to cut you? I would be arrested for treason.'

He grinned, then gave the mirror a quick wipe to clear away the condensation produced from the steam of her bath.

Smothering a snigger, she stretched out her right leg until her foot reached the taps, and used her toes to pour a little more hot water in.

'I'm sure deliberately steaming up the bathroom so I can't see properly is also treasonous,' he said with a playful shake of his head, striding lithely to the extractor fan and switching it on.

As with everything in his fabulous palace apartment it worked instantly, clearing the enormous bathroom of steam.

He crouched beside the bath and placed his gorgeous face close to hers. 'Any more treasonous behaviour, *matakia mou*, and I will be forced to punish you.'

His breath, hot and laced with a faint trace of their earlier shared pot of coffee, danced against her skin.

'And what form of punishment will you be forced to give me?' she asked, the desire she'd thought spent bubbling back up inside her, her breaths shortening.

Those liquid eyes flashed and a smirk played on the bowed lips that had kissed her everywhere. It was a mouth a woman could happily kiss for ever.

'A punishment you will never forget.' He snapped his teeth together for effect and growled, before throwing her a look full of promise and striding back to the mirror. Half watching her in the reflection, Helios dipped his shaving brush into the pot and began covering his black beard with a rich, foamy lather.

Amy had to admit watching him shave as if he were the leading man in a medieval film fascinated her. It also scared her. The blade he used was sharp enough to slice through flesh. One twitch of the hand…

All the same, she couldn't drag her eyes away as he scraped the cut-throat razor down his cheek. In its own way it had an eroticism to it, transporting her to a bygone time when men had been *men*. And Helios was all man.

If he wanted he could snap his fingers and an army of courtiers would be there to do the job for him. But that wasn't his style. The Kalliakis family were direct descendants of Ares Patakis, the warrior whose uprising had freed Agon from its Venetian invaders over eight hundred years ago. Agon princes were taught how to wield weapons with the same dedication with which they were taught the art of royal protocol. To her lover, a cut-throat razor was but one of many weapons he'd mastered.

She waited until he'd wiped the blade on a towel to clean it before speaking again. 'Do I take it that despite all my little hints you haven't put a space aside for me tonight?'

Her 'little hints' had taken the form of mentioning at every available opportunity how much she would love to attend the Royal Ball that was the talk of the entire island, but she hadn't seriously expected to get an invitation. She was but a mere employee of the palace museum, and a temporary employee at that.

And it wasn't as if they would be together for ever, she thought with a strange stab of wistfulness. Their relationship had never been a secret, but it hadn't been flaunted either. She was his lover, not his girlfriend, something she had known from the very start. She had no official place in his life and never would.

He placed the blade back to his cheek and swiped, revealing another line of smooth olive skin. 'However much I adore your company, it wouldn't be appropriate for you to attend.'

She pulled a face, inadvertently cracking the mask around her mouth. 'Yes, I know. I am a commoner, and those attending your ball are the *crème de la crème* of high society.'

'Nothing would please me more than to see you there, dressed in the finest haute couture money can buy. But it would be inappropriate for my lover to attend the ball where I'm to select my future wife.'

The deliciously warm bath turned cold in the beat of a moment.

She sat up.

'Your future wife? What are you talking about?'

His reflected eyes met hers again. 'The underlying reason for this ball is so that I can choose a wife.'

She paused before asking, 'Like in *Cinderella*?'

'Exactly.' He worked on his chin, then wiped the blade on the towel again. 'You know all of this.'

'No,' she said slowly, her blood freezing to match the chills rippling over her skin. 'I was under the impression this ball was a pre-Gala do.'

In three weeks the eyes of the world would be on Agon as the island celebrated fifty years of King Astraeus's reign. Heads of state and dignitaries from all around the world would be flying in for the occasion.

'And so it is. I think the phrase is "killing two birds with one stone"?'

'Why can't you find a wife in the normal way?' And, speaking of normal, how were her vocal cords performing when the rest of her body had been subsumed in a weird kind of paralysis?

'Because, *matakia mou*, I am heir to the throne. I have to marry someone of royal blood. You know that.'

Yes, that she *did* know. Except she hadn't thought it would be now. It hadn't occurred to her. Not once. Not while they were sharing a bed every night.

'I need to choose wisely,' he continued, speaking in the same tone he might use if he were discussing what to order from the palace kitchen for dinner. 'Obviously I have a shortlist of preferred women—princesses and duchesses I have met through the years who have caught my attention.'

'Obviously...' she echoed. 'Is there any particular woman at the top of your shortlist, or are there a few of them jostling for position?'

'Princess Catalina of Monte Cleure is looking the most likely. I've known her and her family for years—they've attended our Christmas Balls since Catalina was a baby. Her sister and brother-in-law got together at the last one.' He grinned at the scandalous memory. 'Catalina and I dined together a couple of times when I was in Denmark the other week. She has all the makings of an excellent queen.'

An image of the raven-haired Princess, a famed beauty who dealt with incessant press scrutiny on account of her ethereal royal loveliness, came to Amy's mind. Waves of nausea rolled in her belly.

'You never mentioned it.'

'There was nothing to say.' He didn't look the slightest bit shamefaced.

'Did you sleep with her?'

He met her stare, censure clear in his reflection. 'What kind of a question is *that*?'

'A natural question for a woman to ask her lover.'

Until that moment it hadn't been something that had occurred to her: the idea that he might have strayed. Helios had never promised fidelity, but he hadn't needed to. Since their first night together their lust for each other had been all-consuming.

'The Princess is a virgin and will remain one until her wedding day whether she marries me or some other man. Does that answer your question?'

Not even a little bit. All it did was open up a whole heap of further questions, all of which she didn't have the right to ask and not one of which she wanted to hear the answer to.

The only question she *could* bring herself to ask was 'When are you hoping to marry the lucky lady?'

If he heard the irony in her voice he hid it well. 'It will be a state wedding, but I would hope to be married in a couple of months.'

A couple of months? He expected to choose a bride and have a state wedding in a few months? Surely it wasn't possible…?

But this was Helios. If there was one thing she knew about her lover it was that he was not a man to let the grass grow beneath his feet. If he wanted something done he wanted it done now, not tomorrow.

But a couple of months…?

Amy was contracted to stay in Agon until September, which was five whole months away. She'd imagined… Hoped…

She thought of King Astraeus, Helios's grandfather. She had never met the King, but through her work in the palace museum she felt she had come to know him. The King was dying. Helios needed to marry and produce an heir of his own to assure the family line.

She *knew* all this. Yet still she'd shared his bed night after night and allowed herself to believe that Helios would hold off his wedding until her time on Agon was up.

Gripping the sides of the free-standing bath, she got carefully to her feet and stepped out. Hands trembling, she pulled a warm, fluffy towel off the rack and held it to her chest, not wanting to waste a second, not even to wrap it around herself.

Helios pulled his top lip down and brought the blade down in careful but expert fashion. 'I'll call you when the ball is finished.'

She strode to the door, uncaring that bathwater was dripping off her and onto the expensive floor tiles. 'No, you won't.'

'Where are you going? You're soaking wet.'

From out of the corner of her eye she saw him pat his towel over his face and follow her through into his bedroom, not bothering to cover himself.

She gathered her clothes into a bundle and held them tightly. A strange burning buzzed in her brain, making coherent thought difficult.

Three months. That was how long she'd shared his bed. In that time they'd slept apart on only a dozen or so occasions, when Helios had been away on official business. Like when he'd gone to Denmark and, unbeknownst to her, dined with Princess Catalina. And now he was throwing a ball to find the woman he would share a bed with for the rest of his life.

She'd known from the start that they had no future, and

had been careful to keep her heart and emotions detached. But to hear him being so blasé about it…

She stood by the door that opened into the secret passageway connecting their apartments. There were dozens and dozens of such secret passageways throughout the palace; a fortress built on intrigue and secrets.

'I'm going to my apartment. Enjoy your evening.'

'Have I missed something?'

The fact that he looked genuinely perplexed only made matters worse.

'You say it isn't appropriate for me to come tonight, but I'll tell you what isn't appropriate—talking about the wife you're hours away from selecting with the woman who has shared your bed for three months.'

'I don't know what your problem is,' he said with a shrug, raising his hands in an open-palmed gesture. 'My marriage won't change anything between us.'

'If you believe that then you're as stupid as you are insensitive and misogynistic. You speak as if the women you are selecting from are sweets lined up in a shop rather than flesh and blood people.' She shook her head to emphasise her distaste, watching as her words seeped in and the perplexity on Helios's face darkened into something ugly.

Helios was not a man who received criticism well. On this island and in this palace he was celebrated and feted, a man whose words people hung on to. Affable and charming, his good humour was infectious. Cross him, however, and he would turn with the snap of two fingers.

If she wasn't so furious with him Amy would probably be afraid.

He strode towards her, magnificently naked. He stopped a foot away and folded his arms across his defined chest. A pulse throbbed at his temple and his jaw clenched tightly.

'Be careful in how you speak to me. I might be your lover, but you do not have a licence to insult me.'

'Why? Because you're a prince?' She hugged the towel and the bundle of clothes even tighter, as if their closeness could stop her erratically thumping heart from jumping out of her chest. 'You're about to make a commitment to another woman and I want no part of it.'

Benedict, Helios's black Labrador, sensed the atmosphere and padded over to her, his tongue lolling out as he sat on his haunches by her side and gave what looked like a disapproving stare at his master.

Helios noticed it too. He rubbed Benedict's head, the darkness disappearing as quickly as it had appeared, an indulgent smile spreading over his face as he looked at Amy. 'Don't be so dramatic. I know you're premenstrual, and that makes you more emotional than you would otherwise be, but you're being irrational.'

'Premenstrual? Did you really just say that? You really are on a different planet. God forbid that I should become "emotional" because my lover has had secret dates with other women and is about to take one of them for his wife and still expects me to warm his bed. But don't worry. Pat me on the head and tell me I'm premenstrual. Pat yourself on the back and tell yourself you've done nothing wrong.'

Too furious to look at him any more, she turned the handle of the door and pushed it open with her hip.

'Are you walking away from me?'

Was that *laughter* in his voice? Did he find this *amusing*?

Ignoring him, Amy raised her head high and walked up the narrow passageway that would take her to her own palace apartment.

A huge hand gripped her biceps, forcing her to twist around. He absolutely dwarfed her.

Regardless of the huge tug in her heart and the rising

nausea, her voice was steady as she said, 'Get your hands off me. We're over.'

'No, we're not.' He slid his hand over her shoulder to snake it around her neck. His breath was hot in her ear as he leaned down to whisper, 'While you're sulking tonight I will be thinking of you and imagining all the ways I can take you when the ball's over. Then you will come to me and we will act them all out.'

Despite her praying to all the gods she could think of, her body reacted to his words and to his closeness the way it always did. With Helios she was like a starved child, finally allowed to feast. She craved him. She had desired him from the moment she'd met him all those months ago, with a powerful need that hadn't abated with time.

But now the time had come to conquer the craving.

Pressing a hand to his solid chest, resisting the urge to run her fingers through the fine black hair that covered it, she pushed herself back and forced her eyes to meet his still playful gaze.

'Enjoy your evening. Try not to spill wine down any princess's dress.'

His mocking laughter followed her all the way to the sanctuary of her own apartment.

It wasn't until she arrived in her apartment, which was spacious compared to normal accommodation but tiny when compared to Helios's, and caught a glimpse of her reflection that she saw the clay mask was still on her face.

It had cracked all over.

Helios led his dance partner—a princess from the old Greek royal family—around the ballroom. She was a very pretty young woman, but as he danced with her and listened to her chatter he mentally struck her off his list. Whoever he married, he wanted to be able to hold a conversation with them about something other than the latest catwalk fashions.

When the waltz had finished he bowed gracefully and excused himself to join his brother Theseus at his table, ignoring all the pleading female eyes silently begging him to take their hand next.

Amy's words about him treating the women here as sweets in a shop came back to him. He was man enough to admit they held the ring of truth. But if he had to choose someone to spend the rest of his life with and to bear his children, he wanted a woman as close to being perfect on his palate as he could taste.

If Amy could see the ladies in question and their eager eyes, the way they thrust their cleavages in his direction as they passed him, hoping to garner his attention, she would understand that they *wanted* to be tasted. They wanted him to find them exactly to his taste.

Theseus's gaze was directed at their younger brother, Talos, who was dancing with the ravishing violinist who would play at their grandfather's Jubilee Gala in three weeks.

'There's something going on there,' Theseus said, swigging back his champagne. 'Look at him. The fool's smitten.'

Helios followed his brother's gaze to the dance floor and knew immediately what he meant. The other couple of hundred guests in the room might as well not have been there for all the attention Talos and his dance partner were paying them. They had eyes only for each other and the heat they were producing…it was almost a visible entity. And strangely mesmerising.

Not for the first time Helios wished Amy could be there. She would adore waltzing around the great ballroom. For a conscientious academic she had a fun side that made her a pleasure to be with.

Theseus fixed his gaze back on Helios. 'So what about you? Shouldn't you be on the dance floor?'

'I'm taking a breather.'

'You should be taking it with Princess Catalina.'

Helios and his brothers had discussed his potential brides numerous times. The consensus was that Catalina would be a perfect fit for their family.

Only a generation ago, the marriages of the heirs to the Agon throne had been arranged. His own parents' marriage had been arranged. It had been witnessing the implosion of their marriage that had led his grandfather King Astraeus to abandon protocol and allow the next generation to select their own spouses, providing they were of royal blood.

For this, Helios was grateful. He was determined that whoever he selected would have no illusions that their marriage would be anything but one of duty.

'You think...?' he asked idly, while his skin crawled at the thought of dancing another waltz with any more of the ladies in attendance, no matter how beautiful they were. Beautiful women were freely available wherever he went. Women of substance less so.

He glanced at his watch. Another couple of hours and this would be over. He would call Amy and she would come to him.

Now, *she* was a woman of substance.

A frisson of tension raced through him as he recalled their earlier exchange. He'd never seen her angry before. There'd been a possessiveness to that anger too. She'd been jealous.

Usually when a lover showed the first sign of possessiveness it meant it was time for him to move on. In Amy's case he'd found it highly alluring. Her jealousy had strangely delighted him.

Helios had long suspected that she kept parts of herself

hidden from him. She gave her body to him willingly, and revelled in their lovemaking as much as he did, but the inner workings of her clever mind remained a mystery.

She'd been different from his usual lovers from the very start. Beautiful and fiercely intelligent, she held his attention in a way no other woman ever had. Her earlier anger hadn't repelled him, as it would have done coming from anyone else; it had intrigued him, peeling away another layer of the brilliant, passionate woman he couldn't get enough of. When he was with her he could forget everything and live for the moment, for their hunger.

The seriousness of his grandfather's illness clung to him like a barnacle, but when he was with Amy it became tamed, was less of a thudding beat of pain and doom. When he was with her he could cast aside the great responsibilities being heir to the throne brought and simply be a man. A lover. *Her* lover. She was a constant thrum in his blood. He had no intention of giving her up—marriage or no marriage.

'Has anyone else caught your attention?' Theseus asked him.

'No.'

Helios had always known he would have to marry. There had never been any question about it. He had no personal feelings about it one way or another. Marriage was an institution within which to produce the next set of Kalliakis heirs, and he was fortunate to be in a position where he could choose his own bride, albeit within certain constraints. His parents hadn't been so lucky. Their marriage had been arranged before his mother had been out of nappies. It had been a disaster. His only real hope for his own marriage was that it be *nothing* like theirs.

Princess Catalina, currently dancing with a British prince, caught his eye. She really was incredibly beautiful. Refined.

Her breeding and lineage shone through. Her brother was an old school friend of his, and their meals together in Denmark had shown her to be a woman of great intelligence as well as beauty, if a little serious for his taste.

She had none of Amy's irreverence.

Still, Catalina would make an excellent queen and he'd wasted enough time as it was. He should have selected a wife months ago, when the gravity of his grandfather's condition had been spelt out to him and his brothers.

Catalina had been raised in a world of protocol, just as he had. She had no illusions or expectations of love. If he chose her he knew theirs would be a marriage of duty. Nothing more, nothing less. No emotional entanglements. Exactly as he wanted.

Making a family with her would be no hardship either. He was certain that with some will on both their parts a bond would form. Chemistry should ensue too. Not the same kind of chemistry he shared with Amy, of course. That would be impossible to replicate.

A memory of Amy heading barefoot down the dimly lit passageway, her clothes and towel huddled to her, her dark blonde hair damp and swinging across her golden back, her bare bottom swaying, flashed into his mind. She'd been as haughty as any princess in that moment, and he couldn't wait to punish her for her insolence. He would bring her to the brink of orgasm so many times she would be *begging* him for release.

But this was neither the time nor the place to imagine Amy's slender form naked in his arms.

With titanium will, he dampened down the fire spreading through his loins and fixed his attention on the women before him. For the next few hours Amy had to be locked away in his mind to free up his concentration for the job in hand.

Before he could bring himself to dance again he beckoned a footman closer, so he could take another glass of champagne and drink a large swallow.

Theseus eyed him shrewdly. 'What's the matter with you?'

'Nothing.'

'You have the face of a man at a wine-tasting event discovering all the bottles are corked.'

Helios fixed a smile on his face. 'Better?'

'Now you look like a mass murderer.'

'Your support is, as always, invaluable.' Draining his glass, he got to his feet. 'Considering the fact I'm not the only Prince expected to marry and produce heirs, I suggest you get off your backside and mingle with the beautiful ladies in attendance too.'

He smirked at Theseus's grimace. While Helios accepted his fate with the steely backbone his upbringing and English boarding school education had instilled in him, he knew his rebellious brother looked forward to matrimony with all the enthusiasm of a zebra entering a lion enclosure.

Later, as he danced with Princess Catalina, holding her at a respectable distance so their bodies didn't touch—and having no compulsion to bridge the gap—his thoughts turned to his grandfather.

The King was not in attendance tonight, as he was saving his limited energy for the Jubilee Gala itself. It was for that great man, who had raised Helios and his brothers since Helios was ten, that he was prepared to take the final leap and settle down.

For his grandfather he would do *anything*.

Soon the crown would pass to him—sooner than he had wanted or expected—and he needed a queen by his side. He wanted his grandfather to move on to the next life at peace, in the knowledge that the succession of the Kalliakis line was secure. If time was kind to them his grandfather might just live long enough to see Helios take his vows.

CHAPTER TWO

WHERE THE HELL was she?

Helios had been back in his apartment for fifteen minutes and Amy wasn't answering his calls. According to the head of security, she had left the palace. Her individual passcode showed that she'd left at seven forty-five; around the time he and his brothers had been welcoming their guests.

Trying her phone one more time, he strolled through to his bar and poured himself a large gin. The call went straight to voicemail. He tipped the neat liquid down his throat and, on a whim, carried the bottle through to his study.

Security monitors there showed pictures from the cameras that ran along the connecting passageways. Only Helios himself had access to the cameras' feeds.

He peered closely at the screen for camera three, which faced the reinforced connecting door. There was something on the floor he couldn't make out clearly...

Striding to it and unbolting the door, he stared down at a box. Crammed inside were bottles of perfume, jewellery, books and mementos. All the gifts he had given Amy during their time together as lovers. Crammed, unwanted, into a box and left on his doorstep.

A burst of fury tore through him, so sudden and so powerful it consumed him in one.

Before he had time to think what he was doing he raised his foot and brought it slamming down onto the box. Glass shattered and crunched beneath him, the sound echoing in the silence.

For an age he did nothing else but inhale deeply, trembling with fury, fighting the urge to smash what was left of the box's contents into smithereens. Violence had been his father's solution to life's problems. It was something Helios had always known resided inside him too but, unlike in his father's case, it was an aspect of himself he controlled.

The sudden fury that had just overtaken him was incomprehensible.

Acutely aware of how late she was, Amy slammed her apartment door shut and hurried down the stairs that led to the palace museum. Punching in her passcode, she waited for the green light to come on, shoved the door open and stepped into the private quarters of the museum, an area out of bounds to visitors.

Gazing longingly at the small staff kitchen as she passed it, she crossed her fingers in the hope that the daily pastries hadn't already been eaten and the coffee already drunk. The *bougatsas*, freshly made by the palace chefs and brought to them every morning, had become her favourite food in the whole world.

Her mouth filled with moisture as she imagined the delicate yet satisfying filo-based pastries. She hoped there were still some custard-filled ones left. She'd hardly eaten a thing in the past couple of days, and now, after finally managing to get a decent night's sleep, she'd woken up ravenous. She'd also slept right through her alarm clock, and the thought made her legs work even quicker as she climbed another set of stairs that led up to the boardroom.

'I'm so sorry I'm late,' she said, rushing through the door, a hand flat on her breathless chest. 'I over...' Her words tailed off as she saw Helios, sitting at the head of the large round table.

His elbows rested on the table, the tips of his fingers rubbing together. He was freshly shaven and, even casually dressed as he was, in a dark green long-sleeved crew-neck top, he exuded an undeniable power. And all the force of that power was at that very moment aimed at her.

'Nice of you to join us, Despinis Green,' he said. His tone was even, but his dark brown eyes resembled bullets waiting to be fired at her. 'Take a seat.'

Utterly shaken to see him there, she blinked rapidly and forced herself to inhale. Helios was the palace museum's director, but his involvement in the day-to-day running of it was minimal. In the four months she'd worked there, he hadn't once attended the weekly Tuesday staff meeting.

She'd known when she'd stolen back into the palace late last night that she would have to face him soon, but she'd hoped for a few more days' grace. Why did he have to appear today, of all days? The one time she'd overslept and looked awful.

Unfortunately the only chair available was directly opposite him. It made a particularly loud scraping sound over the wooden floor as she pulled it back and sat down, clasping her hands tightly on her lap so as not to betray their tremors. Greta, one of the other curators and Amy's best friend on the island, had the seat next to her. She placed a comforting hand over hers and squeezed gently. Greta knew everything.

In the centre of the table was the tray of *bougatsas* Amy had hoped for. Three remained, but she found her appetite gone and her heart thundering so hard that the ripples spread to her belly and made her nauseous.

Greta poured her a cup of coffee. Amy clutched it gratefully.

'We were discussing the artefacts we're still waiting on for my grandfather's exhibition,' Helios said, looking directly at her.

The Agon Palace Museum was world-famous, and as such attracted curators from across the world, resulting in a medley of first languages amongst the staff. To simplify matters, English was the official language spoken when on duty.

Amy cleared her throat and searched her scrambled brain for coherence. 'The marble statues are on their way from Italy as we speak and should arrive in port early tomorrow morning.'

'Do we have staff ready to welcome them?'

'Bruno will message me when they reach Agon waters,' she said, referring to one of the Italian curators accompanying the statues back to their homeland. 'As soon as I hear from him we'll be ready to go. The drivers are on call. Everything is in hand.'

'And what about the artefacts from the Greek museum?'

'They will arrive here on Friday.'

Helios *knew* all this. The exhibition was his pet project and they'd worked closely together on it.

She'd first come to Agon in November, as part of a team from the British Museum delivering artefacts on loan to the Agon Palace Museum. During those few days on the island she'd struck up a friendship with Pedro, the Head of Museum. Unbeknownst to her at the time, he'd been impressed with her knowledge of Agon, and doubly impressed with her PhD thesis on Minoan Heritage and its Influences on

Agon Culture. Pedro had been the one to suggest her for the role of curator for the Jubilee Exhibition.

The offer had been a dream come true, and a huge honour for someone with so little experience. Only twenty-seven, what Amy lacked in experience she made up for with enthusiasm.

Amy had learned at the age of ten that the happy, perfect family she'd taken for granted was not as she'd been led to believe. *She* wasn't what she'd been led to believe. Her dad was indeed her biological father, but her brothers were only half-brothers. Her mum wasn't her biological mother. The woman who'd actually given birth to her had been from the Mediterranean island of Agon.

Half of Amy's DNA was Agonite.

Since that bombshell discovery, everything about Agon had fascinated her. She'd devoured books on its Minoan history and its evolution into democracy. She'd thrilled at stories of the wars, the passion and ferocity of its people. She'd studied maps and photographs, staring so intently at the island's high green mountains, sandy beaches and clear blue seas that its geography had become as familiar as her own home town.

Agon had been an obsession.

Somewhere in its history was *her* history, and the key to understanding who she truly was. To have the opportunity to live there on a nine-month secondment had been beyond anything she could have hoped. It had been as if fate was giving her the push she needed to find her birth mother. Somewhere in this land of half a million people was the woman who had borne her.

For seventeen years Amy had thought about her, wondering what she looked like—did she look like *her*?—what her voice sounded like, what regrets she might have. Was she ashamed of what she'd done? Surely she was? How could anyone live through what Neysa Soukis had done and *not* feel shame?

She'd been easy to locate, but how to approach her...? That had always been the biggest question. Amy couldn't just turn up at her door; it would likely be slammed in her face and then she would never have her answers. She'd considered writing a letter but had failed to think of what she could say other than: *Hi, do you remember me? You carried me for nine months and then dumped me. Any chance you could tell me why?*

Greek social media, which Greta had been helping her with, had proved fruitful. Neysa didn't use it, but through it Amy had discovered a half-brother. Tentative communications had started between them. She had to hope he would act as a conduit between them.

'Have you arranged transport for Friday?' Helios asked, the dark eyes hard, the bowed, sensual mouth tight.

'Yes. Everything is in hand,' she said for a second time, as a sharp pang reached through her as she realised she would never feel those lips on hers again. 'We're ahead of schedule.'

'You're confident that come the Gala the exhibition will be ready?'

His voice was casual but there was a hardness there, a scepticism she'd never had directed at her before.

'Yes,' she answered, gritting her teeth to stop her hurt and anger leeching out.

He was punishing her. She should have answered one of his calls. She'd taken the coward's way out and escaped from the palace in the hope that a few days away from him would give her the strength she needed to resist him. The best way—the only way—of beating her craving for him would be by going cold turkey.

Because resist him she must. She couldn't be the other woman. She couldn't.

But she hadn't imagined that seeing him again would physically *hurt*.

It did. Dreadfully.

Before her job had been rubber-stamped, Helios had interviewed her himself. The Jubilee Exhibition was of enormous personal importance to him and he'd been determined that the curator with the strongest affinity to his island would get the job.

Luckily for her, he'd agreed with Pedro that she was the perfect candidate. He'd told her some months later, when they'd been lying replete in each other's arms, that it had been her passion and enthusiasm that had convinced him. He'd known she would give the job the dedication it deserved.

Meeting Helios… He'd been *nothing* as she'd imagined: as far from the stuffy, pompous, 'entitled' Prince she'd expected him to be as was possible.

Her attraction to him had been immediate, a chemical reaction over which she'd had no control. It had taken her completely off guard. Yet she hadn't thought anything of it. He was a prince, after all, both powerful and dangerously handsome. Never in her wildest dreams had she thought the attraction would be reciprocated. But it had been.

He'd been much more involved with the exhibition than she'd anticipated, and she'd often found herself working alone with him, her longing for him an ever-growing fire inside her that she didn't have a clue how to handle.

Affairs in the workplace were a fact of life, even in the studious world of antiquities, but they were not something she'd ever been tempted by. She loved her work so much it took her entire focus. Her work gave her purpose. It grounded her. And working with the ancient objects of her own people, seeing first-hand how techniques and social mores had evolved over the years, was a form of proof that the past didn't have to be the future. Her birth mother's actions didn't have to define her, even if she did feel the taint of her behaviour like an invisible stain.

Relationships of any real meaning had always been out of the question for her. How could she commit to someone if she didn't know who she truly was? So to find herself feeling such an attraction, and to the man who was effectively her boss, who just happened to be a prince... It was no wonder her emotions had been all over the place.

Helios had had no such inhibitions.

Long before he'd laid so much as a finger on her he'd undressed her with his dark liquid eyes, time and again. Until one late afternoon, when she'd been talking to him in the smaller of the exhibition rooms, she on one side, he on the other, and he'd gone from complete stillness to fluid motion in the beat of a heart. He'd walked to her with long strides and pulled her into his arms.

And that had been it. She'd been his for the taking. And he'd been hers.

Their three months together had been a dream. Theirs had been a physically intense but surprisingly easy relationship. There had been no expectations. No inhibitions. Just passion.

Walking away should have been easy.

The eyes that had undressed her a thousand times now flickered to Pedro, giving silent permission for him to move the discussion on to general museum topics. There might be a special exhibition being organised, but the museum itself still needed to be run to its usual high standards.

Clearly unnerved—Helios's mood, usually so congenial, was unsettling all the staff—Pedro raced through the rest of the agenda in double-quick time, finally mentioning the need for someone to cover for one of their tour guides that Thursday. Amy was happy to volunteer. Thursday was her only reasonably quiet day that week, and she enjoyed taking on the tours whenever the opportunity arose.

One of the things she loved so much about the museum was the collaborative way it was run, with everyone helping each other when needed. It was a philosophy that came from the very top, from Helios himself, even if today there was no sign of his usual amiability.

Only at the very end of the meeting did Pedro say, 'Before we leave, can I remind everyone that menus for next Wednesday need to be handed in by Friday?'

As a thank-you for all the museum staff's hard work in organising the exhibition, Helios had arranged a night out for everyone before the summer rush hit, all expenses paid. It was a typically generous gesture from him, and a social event Amy had been very much looking forward to. Now, though, the thought of a night out with Helios in attendance made her stomach twist.

There was a palpable air of relief when the meeting finished. Today there was none of the usual lingering. Everyone scrambled to their feet and rushed for the door.

'Amy, a word please.' Helios's rich voice rose over the clatter of hurrying feet.

She paused, inches from the door, inches from escape. Arranging her face into a neutral expression, she turned around.

'Shut the door behind you.'

She did as she was told, her heart sinking to her feet, then sat back in her original place opposite him but also the greatest distance possible away.

It wasn't far enough.

The man oozed testosterone.

He also oozed menace.

Her heart kicked against her ribs. She clamped her lips together and folded her arms across her chest.

Yet she couldn't stop her eyes moving to his, couldn't stop herself gazing at him.

His silver chain glinted against the base of his throat. That chain had often brushed against her lips when he'd made love to her.

And as she stared at him, wondering when he was going to speak, his eyes studied her with the same intensity, making her mouth run dry and her hammering pulse race into a gallop.

His fingers drummed on the table. 'Did you have a nice time at Greta's?'

'Yes, thank you,' she replied stiffly, before she realised what he'd said. 'How did you know I was there?'

'Through the GPS on your phone.'

'What? You've been *spying* on me?'

'You are the lover of the heir to the throne of Agon. Our relationship is an open secret. I do not endanger what is mine.'

'I'm not yours. Not any more,' she spat at him, running from fear to fury in seconds. 'Whatever tracking device you've put in my phone, you can take it out. Now.'

She yanked her bag onto the table, pulled out her phone and threw it at him.

His hand opened to catch it like a Venus flytrap catching its prey. He laughed. But unlike on Saturday, when he'd thought he'd been indulging her, the sound contained no humour.

He slid the phone back to her. 'There's no tracking device in it. It's all done through your number.'

'Well, you can damn well *un*track it. Take it off your system, or whatever it's on.'

He studied her contemplatively. His stillness unnerved

her. Helios was *never* still. He had enough energy to power the whole palace.

'Why did you leave?'

'To get away from you.'

'You didn't think I would be worried?'

'I thought you'd be too busy cherry-picking your bride to notice I'd gone.'

Finally a smile played on his lips. 'Ah, so you were punishing me.'

'No, I was not,' she refuted hotly. 'I was giving myself space away from you because I knew you'd still expect to sleep with me after an evening of wooing prospective brides.'

'And you didn't think you'd be able to resist me?'

Her cheeks coloured and Helios felt a flare of satisfaction that his thoughts had been correct.

His beautiful, passionate lover had been jealous.

Slender, feminine to her core, with a tumbling mane of thick dark blonde hair, Amy was possibly the most beautiful woman he'd ever met. A sculptor wouldn't hesitate to cast her as Aphrodite. She made his blood thicken just to look at her, even dressed as she was now in an A-line navy skirt and a pretty yet demure lilac top.

But today there was something unkempt about her appearance that wasn't usually there: dark hollows beneath her taupe eyes, her rosebud lips dry, her usual glowing complexion paler than was normal.

And he was the cause of it. The thought sent a thrill through him. Whatever punishment she had hoped to inflict on him by disappearing for a few days, it had backfired on her.

He would never let her know of the overwhelming fury that had rent him when he'd seen the box she'd left by his door.

Which reminded him...

He slid the thick padded envelope he'd placed on the table towards her. Smashing the box when his anger had got the better of him had caused the perfume bottles to spill and ruin the books, but the jewellery had been left undamaged.

Her eyes narrowed with caution, she extended an elegant hand to it and opened it gingerly. Her mouth tightened when she saw what was inside.

She dropped the envelope back on the table and got quickly to her feet. 'I don't want them.'

'They're yours. You insult me by returning them.'

She didn't blink. 'And you insult me by giving them back when you're about to put an engagement ring on another woman's finger.'

He got out of his chair and stalked over to her. With the chair behind her she had nowhere to retreat. He pulled her to him, enfolding her in his arms so that her head was pressed to his chest. He was too strong and she was too slender for her to wriggle out of his hold, and in any case he knew her attempts didn't mean anything.

He could feel her heat. She *wanted* to be in his arms.

Her head was tilted back, her breaths quickening. He watched as the pupils of her eyes darkened and pulsed, as the grey turned to brown, with a passionate fury there that set his veins alight.

'There is no need to be jealous,' he murmured, pressing himself closer. 'My marriage doesn't change my feelings for you.'

Her left eye twitched, an affliction he'd never seen before. Her top teeth razed across her full bottom lip.

'But it changes my feelings for you.'

'Liar. You can't deny you still want me.' He brushed his cheek against hers and whispered into her ear, 'Only a few days ago you screamed out my name. I still have your scratches on my back.'

She reared back. 'That was before I knew you were looking for an immediate wife. I will not be your mistress.'

'There is no shame in it. Generations of Agon monarchs have taken lovers after marriage.' His grandfather had been the exception to the rule, but only because he'd been fortunate enough to fall in love with his wife.

Of the thirty-one monarchs who'd ruled Agon since 1203, only a handful had found love and fidelity with their spouses. His own father, although he'd died before he could take the throne, had had dozens of lovers and mistresses. He'd revelled in waving his indiscretions right under his loving wife's nose.

'And generations ago your ancestors chopped your enemies' limbs off but you've managed to wean yourself off that.'

He laughed at her retort, running a finger over her chin. Even with her oval face free of make-up Amy was beautiful. 'We don't marry for love or companionship, as other people do. We marry for the good of our island. Think of it as a business arrangement. *You* are my lover. You are the woman I *want* to be with.'

His mother had been unfortunate in that she'd already loved his father when they had married, and it was that love which had ultimately destroyed her, long before the car crash that had taken both his parents' lives.

He would never inflict the kind of pain his father had caused, not on anyone. He had to marry, but he was upfront about what he wanted: a royal wife to produce the next generation of Kalliakis heirs. No emotions. No expectations of fidelity. A union founded on duty and nothing more.

Amy stared at him without speaking for the longest

time, searching for something. He didn't know what she hoped to find.

He brought his face down to meet her lips, which had parted, but she pulled back so only the faintest of touches passed between them.

'I mean it, Helios. We're finished. I will never be your mistress.' Her words were but a whisper.

'You think?'

'Yes.'

'Then why are you still standing here? Why is your breath still warm on my face?'

Brushing his lips across the softness of her cheek, he gripped her bottom and ground her against him, letting her feel his desire for her. The tiniest of moans escaped her throat.

'See?' He trailed kisses over her delicate ear. 'You do want me. But you're punishing me.'

'No, I...'

'Shh...' He placed a finger on her mouth. 'We both know I could take you right now and you would welcome it.'

Heat flared from her eyes but her chin jutted up mutinously.

'I am going to give you exactly five seconds of freedom. Five seconds to leave this room. If after those five seconds you are still here...' he spoke very quietly into her ear '...I will lift up your skirt and make love to you right here and now on this table.'

She quivered, a small tell but one so familiar he knew the expression that would be in her eyes when he looked into them.

He was right. The taupe had further darkened; the pupils were even more dilated. The tip of her pink tongue glistened between her parted lips. He knew that if he placed his hands over her small but beautifully formed breasts he would feel her nipples strain towards him.

He released his hold on her and folded his arms across his chest.

'One.'

She put a hand to her mouth and dragged it down over her chin.

'Two.'

She swallowed. Her eyes never left his face. He could practically smell her longing.

'Three… Four…'

She turned on her heel and fled to the door.

'One week,' he called to her retreating back. She was halfway out of the room and made no show of listening to him, but he knew she heard every word. 'One week and you, *matakia mou*, will be back in my bed. I guarantee it.'

CHAPTER THREE

AMY GAZED AT the marble statues that had arrived on Agon by ship that morning and now sat in the grand entrance hall of the museum on their plinths. Three marble statues. Three kings at the height of their glory. All named Astraeus. The fourth, specially commissioned for the exhibition, would be transported from the sculptor's studio in a week's time. It would depict the current monarch, the fourth King Astraeus, as a young man in his prime.

Helios had personally commissioned it. She didn't want to think of Helios. But she couldn't stop.

He was everywhere. In every painting, every sculpture, every fragment of framed scripture, every piece of pottery. Everything was a reminder that this was all his. His people. His ancestors. Him.

Her attention kept flickering back to the statue of the second King Astraeus, a marble titan dating from 1403. Trident in hand and unashamedly naked, he had the same arrogant look with an underlying hint of ferociousness that Helios carried so well. If she had known nothing of the Agon royal dynasty, she would have known instinctively that her lover was a descendent of this man. Agon had been at peace for decades but their warrior roots dated back millennia, were ingrained in their DNA.

Helios had warrior roots in spades.

She had to stop thinking about him.

God, this was supposed to be easy. An affair with no promises and no need for compromise.

She'd been so tempted to stay in the boardroom with him. She'd *ached* to stay. Her body had been weighted down with need for him. But in the back of her mind had been an image of him exchanging his vows with a faceless woman who would become his wife.

Amy couldn't be the other woman. Whatever kind of marriage Helios had in mind for himself, it would still be real. He needed an heir. He would make love to his wife.

She could never allow herself to be the cause of pain and humiliation in another. She'd seen first-hand the damage an affair could cause. After all, she was the result of an affair herself. She'd spent seventeen years knowing she was the result of something sordid.

She was nothing but a dirty secret.

Helios's driver brought the car to a stop at the back of the palace, beside his private entrance. Dozens and dozens of schoolchildren of all shapes and sizes were picnicking on the lawn closest to the museum entrance: some playing football, some doing cartwheels and handstands. In the far distance a group were filing out of the Agon palace's maze, which was famed as one of the biggest and tallest mazes in the world.

Helios checked the time. He was always too busy to spend as much time with the palace visitors as he would like.

He had a small window before he was due at a business meeting he'd arranged with his brothers. His brothers ran the day-to-day side of their investment business, but he was still heavily involved. Then there were his royal duties, which had increased exponentially since the onset of his grandfather's illness. He was in all but name Prince Regent, the highest ranking ambassador for his beloved island. It was his duty to do everything he could to bring investment and tourists to his island, to spread his country's influence on the world's stage and keep his islanders safe and prosperous.

As he neared the children, with his courtiers keeping a discreet distance, their small faces turned to him with curiosity. As often happened, it took only one to recognise him before his identity spread like wildfire and they all came running up. It was one of the things he so liked about children: their lack of inhibition. In a world of politeness and protocol he found it refreshing.

One thing he and Catalina were in agreement about was the wish for a minimum of two children. They agreed on many things. Most things. Which was a good omen for their forthcoming marriage. On paper, everything about their union appeared perfect. But...

Every time he tried to picture the children they would create together his mind came up blank. The picture just would not form.

Despite her ravishing beauty, his blood had yet to thicken for her. But this was only a minor issue, and one he was certain would resolve itself the more time he spent with her. Tomorrow he would fly to Monte Cleure so he could formally ask her father for Catalina's hand in marriage. It was only a formality, but one that couldn't be overlooked.

At least times had moved on from such issues as a dowry having to be found and trade alliances and so on being written into the contract of any royal betrothal. Now all he had to worry about was his bride having blue blood.

He'd always found blue so cold.

He turned his attention on the English children and

answered a host of questions from them, including, 'Is it true your toilet is made of gold?'

His personal favourite was 'Is it true you carry a sub-machine gun wherever you go?'

In answer to this he pulled from his pocket the pen-knife his grandfather had given him on his graduation from Sandhurst; an upgraded version of the one he'd been given on his tenth birthday. 'No, but I always carry *this*.'

As expected, the children were agog to see it. It was termed a penknife only in the loosest sense; on sight any-one would recognise it for the deadly fighting instrument it truly was. Children loved it when he showed it to them. Their basic human nature had not yet been knocked out of them by the insane political correctness infecting the rest of the Western world.

'Most Agonites carry knives with them,' he said to the enthralled children. 'If anyone wants to invade our island they know we will fight back with force.'

Their teacher, who had looked at the knife as if it had come personally from Eurynomos himself, looked most relieved as she glanced at her watch. Immediately she clapped her hands together. 'Everyone into their pairs—it's time for our tour.'

Today was Thursday... Amy was taking on some of the tours...

The hairs on the back of his neck lifted. He looked over at the museum entrance. A slender figure stood at the top of the steps. Even though she was too far away for him to see clearly, the increasing beat of his heart told him it was her.

He straightened, a smile playing on his lips. Only two days had passed since she'd called his bluff and walked out of the boardroom, leaving him with an ache in his groin he'd only just recovered from. He would bet anything she had suffered in the same manner. He would bet she'd spent the past two days jumping every time her phone rang, waiting for his call.

Her pride had been wounded when she'd learned he was taking a wife, but she would get over it. She couldn't punish him for ever, not when she suffered as greatly as he did. Soon she would come crawling back.

After a moment's thought, he beckoned for one of his courtiers and instructed him to pass his apologies to his brothers. They could handle the meeting without him.

The time was ripe to assist Amy in crawling back to him.

The Agon palace dungeons never failed to thrill, whatever the visitor's age. Set deep underground, and reached by steep winding staircases at each end of the gloom, only those over the age of eight were permitted to enter. Inside, dim light was provided by tiny electrical candles that flickered as if they were the real thing, casting shadows wherever one stood. Unsurprisingly, the children today were huddled closely together.

'These dungeons were originally a pit in which to throw the Venetian invaders,' Amy said, speaking clearly so all twenty-three children on the tour could hear. 'The Venetians were the only people to successfully invade Agon, and when Ares the Conqueror, cousin of the King at the time, led the uprising in AD 1205, the first thing he ordered his men to do was build these pits. King Timios, who was the reigning King and whom the Agonites blamed for letting the Venetians in, was thrown into the cell to my left.'

The children took it in turns to gawp through the iron railings at the tiny square stone pit.

'The manacle on the right-hand wall is the original manacle used to chain him,' she added.

'Did he die in here?' a young boy asked.

'No,' said a deep male voice that reverberated off the narrow walls before she could answer, making them all jump.

A long shadow cast over them and Helios appeared. In the flickering light of the damp passageway in which they stood his large frame appeared magnified, as if Orion, the famously handsome giant, had come to life.

What was he *doing* here?

She'd seen him only an hour ago, standing in the gardens talking to the school parties, as at ease with the children as he was in every other situation. That had been the moment she had forgotten how to breathe.

It will get better, she kept assuring herself. *It's still early days and still raw. Soon you'll feel better.*

'King Timios was held in these cells for six months before Ares Patakis expelled him and, with the consent of the people, took the crown for himself,' Helios said to the captivated children. 'The palace was built over these dungeons so King Ares could have personal control over the prisoners.'

'Did he kill anyone?' asked the same bloodthirsty boy.

'He killed many people,' Helios answered solemnly. 'But only in battle. Prisoners of war were released and sent back to Venice.' He paused and offered a smile. 'But only after having their hands chopped off. King Ares wanted to send a warning to other armies wishing to invade—*Step on our shores and you will never wield a weapon again.* That's if they were lucky enough to live.'

The deeper they went into the dungeons, which were large enough to hold up to three hundred prisoners, the more questions were thrown at him as the children did their best to spook each other in the candlelit dimness.

It was with relief that Helios handled everything asked

of him—his presence had made her tongue tie itself into a knot.

'Have *you* ever killed anyone?' an undersized girl asked with a nervous laugh.

He shook his head slowly. 'But since I could walk and talk I've been trained to use knives, shoot arrows and throw a spear. My brothers and I are all military trained. Trust me, should any other nation try to invade us, Agonites are ready. We fight. We are not afraid to spill blood—whether it's an enemy's or our own—to protect what's ours. We will defend our island to the death.'

Utter silence followed this impassioned speech. Twenty-three sets of wide eyes gazed up at Helios with a mixture of awe and terror. The teacher looked shell-shocked.

It had had the opposite effect on Amy.

His words had pushed through her skin to heat her veins. It had never so much been his looks, as gorgeous as he was, that had attracted her. It had been his passion. The Kalliakis family was a dynasty whose blood ran red, not blue. And no one's blood ran redder than Helios's. On the outside he was a true prince. Beneath his skin lay a warrior.

'And that, children, proves that it's not only Ares the Conqueror's blood Prince Helios has inherited from his ancestor but his devotion to his homeland.' Amy spoke quickly, to break the hush and to distract herself from the ache spreading inside her. 'Now, who here would like to be adopted by the Prince? Any takers? No? Hmm... You surprise me. Come on, then, who wants to visit the museum gift shop?'

That brought them back to life; the thought of spending their money on gifts for themselves.

'It's a good thing you'll never have to be a tour guide as your day job,' Amy couldn't resist saying to Helios as she climbed the stairs a little way behind the school party. 'They'll all have nightmares.'

He followed closely behind her. 'They're learning my family's history. I was putting it into the context of the present day for them.'

'Yes. They were learning about your *history*. There's a big difference between hearing about wars and blood-spilling from centuries ago and having it put into the here and now, especially in the dungeons, of all places. They're only ten years old.'

'The world is full of bloodshed. That's never changed in the history of mankind. The only way to stop it creeping to our shores is through fear and stability.'

Her hand tightened on the railing as she carried on climbing. 'But Agon *is* stable. You have an elected senate. You are a democracy.'

'The people still look to us, their royal family, for leadership. Our opinions matter. Our actions matter even more so.'

'Hence the reason you're marrying Princess Catalina,' she stated flatly.

'We are a prosperous, stable island nation, *matakia mou*, and it's the hard work of generations of my family that has made it so. Until the entire world is stable we are vulnerable to attack in many different forms. We lead by example, and as a people we are united as one. Stability within the royal family promotes stability for the whole island. My grandfather is dying. My marriage will bring peace to him and act as security to my people, who will be assured that the future of my family is taken care of and by extension their own families too. They know that with a descendant of Ares Patakis on the throne their country is not only ready to defend itself but able to weather any financial storm that may hit our isles.'

Somewhere during his speech they'd both stopped climbing. Amy found herself facing him from two steps above, coming to eye level with him. His eyes were liquid, the shadows dancing over his features highlighting the strength of the angles and planes that made him so darkly handsome. Her fingers tingled with the urge to reach out and touch him...

'I need to catch up with the children,' she breathed, but her rubbery legs made no attempt to move.

'They know where they're going,' he murmured, placing a hand on the damp wall to steady himself as he leaned in close.

His other hand caught her hip, jerking her to him. Delicious heat swirled through her; moisture pushed out the dryness in her mouth. Her skin danced and her lips parted as she moved her mouth to meet his...

She only just pulled away in time.

Swiping at his hand to remove it from her hip, she said, 'I haven't said goodbye to them.'

'Then say your goodbyes.' His eyes were alight with amusement. 'Keep running, *matakia mou*, but know you can't run for ever. Soon I will catch you.'

She didn't answer, turning tail and racing to the top of the steep staircase, gripping tightly onto the rail, and then out into the corridor.

At least in the corridor she could breathe.

What had just happened? She'd been a breath away from kissing him. Did she have no pride? No sense of preservation?

She wanted to cry with frustration.

Whether Helios believed it or not, they were over. He was marrying someone else. It was abhorrent that she still reacted so strongly towards him.

There was only one thing she could do.

She had to leave.

As soon as the exhibition was officially opened, to co-incide with the Gala in just over a fortnight, she would leave the palace and never come back.

After a long day spent overseeing the arrival of artefacts from the Greek museum Amy should have been dead on her feet, but the email she'd just received had acted like a shot of espresso to her brain.

After months of searching and weeks of tentative communication, Leander had agreed to see her. Tomorrow night she would meet her half-brother for the first time.

She looked at her watch. If she moved quickly she could run to Resina and buy herself a new dress to wear for their meal, before late-night shopping was over. She wouldn't have time tomorrow, with Saturday being the museum's busiest day.

After hurriedly turning her computer off and shuffling papers so her desk looked tidy, and not as if she'd abandoned it whilst in the middle of important work, she rushed out of her office and headed downstairs to see if Pedro was still about and could lock up.

She came to an abrupt halt.

There, in the museum entrance, talking to Pedro, stood Helios.

She wasn't quick enough to escape. Both of them turned their faces to her.

'Speak of the woman and she shall appear,' said Pedro, beaming at her.

'What have I done?' she asked, squashing the butter-flies in her stomach and feigning nonchalance.

Pedro grinned. 'Don't look so worried. Helios and I have been discussing your future.'

Within the confines of the museum the staff addressed Helios by his first name, at his insistence.

'Oh?' Her gaze fell on Helios. 'I thought you were going to Monte Cleure,' she said before she could stop herself.

'My plane leaves in an hour.'

Her chest compressed in on itself. Stupidly, she'd looked up the distance between Agon and Monte Cleure, which came in at just over one thousand two hundred miles. Just over two and a half hours' flying time. With the time difference factored in he would be there in time to share an intimate dinner with the Princess.

She pressed her lips together to prevent the yelp of pain that wanted to escape and forced her features into an expression of neutrality. Helios had so much power over her she couldn't bear for him to know how deeply it ran.

Oblivious to any subtext going on around him, Pedro said, 'I was going to leave this until tomorrow, but seeing as you're here there's no time like the present—'

'We were saying how impressed we are with your handling of the exhibition,' Helios cut in smoothly. 'You have exceeded our expectations. We would like to offer you a permanent job at the museum when your secondment finishes.'

'What kind of job?' she asked warily. A week ago this news would have filled her with joy. But everything was different now.

'Corinna will be leaving us at the end of the summer. We would like you to have her job.'

Corinna was second only to Pedro in the museum hierarchy.

'There are far more qualified curators than me working here,' she said non-committally, wishing Pegasus might fly into the palace at that very moment and whisk her away to safety.

'Pedro is happy to train you in the areas where you lack experience,' said Helios, a smile of triumph dancing in his eyes. 'The important thing is you can do the job. Everyone here likes and respects you...curators at other museums enjoy collaborating with you. You're an asset to the Agon Palace Museum and we would be fools to let you go.'

If Pedro hadn't been there she would have cursed Helios for such a blatant act of manipulation.

'What do you think?' he asked when she remained silent. His dark eyes bored into her, a knowing, almost playful look emanating from them. 'How do you like the idea of living and working here permanently?'

She knew exactly what he was doing and exactly what he was thinking. He knew how much she loved her job, his island and its people. Helios was working tactically. He thought that if he threw enough incentives at her she would be so overcome with gratitude she would allow him back into her bed.

She'd entered their relationship without any illusions of permanency. It had suited her as much as it had suited him. Desire was what had glued them together, and it scared her to know that despite all the protective barriers she'd placed around herself he'd still slipped inside. Not fully, but enough for pain to lance her whenever she thought of him and the Princess together. When she thought of her own future without him in her life.

How could she continue to be his lover feeling as she did now, even putting aside the fact of his imminent engagement?

His engagement had hammered home as nothing else could that she was good enough to share his bed but not good enough for anything more.

She knew she was being unfair—Agon's constitution and Helios's position in life were not his fault or within his control—but for the first time she felt the reality on an emotional level and that terrified her.

In her heart of hearts she'd always longed to meet someone she could trust with the truth about her conception and not fear they would turn away in disgust or believe that the fruit never fell far from the tree. To meet someone who could love her for herself.

During their time together she had come to trust Helios. He was a man she'd thought she could confide the truth to, and she was almost certain he wouldn't turn away in disgust. But still she'd kept her secrets close. He couldn't give her the other things she'd always secretly craved but had never quite believed she deserved. Love. Fidelity. Commitment. It had been wiser to keep her heart as close as her secrets.

She considered her words carefully, although her head swam. 'I'm going to need time to think about it.'

'What is there to think about?' he asked, his dark eyes narrowing slightly.

'My lifc is in England,' she said evenly, although she knew there was really nothing to think about. He could offer to quadruple her salary and the answer would be the same.

She was saved from elaborating by Helios's phone ringing.

'My cue to leave,' he said, flashing her a grin. 'We can continue this discussion another time soon.'

She knew what 'soon' meant. He meant to visit her on Sunday evening, when he returned.

With Pedro there she was in no position to refuse or challenge anything. And even if she'd wanted to Helios didn't give her the chance, wishing them both a good weekend before striding off and out of the museum. On his way to Monte Cleure to spend his weekend with the Princess and her family.

And she...

As soon as she returned from her last-minute shopping trip she would write her resignation letter. She would give it to Pedro tomorrow, safe in the knowledge that Helios would be over a thousand miles away.

CHAPTER FOUR

AMY PUT THE lip gloss tube to her mouth, but before she could squeeze the gel-like substance on, a loud rap made her jerk her hand back. The banging had come from the door outside her bedroom that connected the passageway between her apartment and Helios's.

She pressed her hand to her pounding heart.

What was he doing here?

He was supposed to be spending the whole weekend in Monte Cleure, using his time there to officially ask Princess Catalina's father's blessing for their marriage. He should still be there, celebrating their forthcoming union, not here on Agon, banging on his ex-lover's door.

Breathing heavily, she closed her eyes and willed him away.

Another loud rap on the door proved the futility of her wish.

Suddenly galvanised into action, she dropped the lip gloss into her handbag and slipped out of her room, hurrying past the connecting door as another knock rang out. Snatching her jacket off the coat stand, she left her apartment through the main exit and hurried down the narrow stairs. With her heart battering against her chest she punched in the code that opened the door and stole outside into the warm spring evening air.

She felt like an escaped convict.

Security lights blazed everywhere, and she kept as close to the palace wall as she could for as long as she could until she had to dart out to cross into the courtyard used by the palace staff. The car she'd ordered earlier was already waiting for her. She jumped straight into the passenger side, making Eustachys the driver, who was busy on his phone, jump.

'You're early,' he said with a grin, before adding, 'Where do you want to go?'

She forced a smile. Whenever she needed one of the pool of cars and drivers that were on permanent standby for the palace staff she was invariably given Eustachys, who spoke excellent English. 'Resina, please.'

She gave him the name of the restaurant she was dining at and tried not to betray her impatience as he inputted it into his satnav, especially as she was perfectly aware that he knew every inch of the island and had no need for it.

A minute later they were off, starting the twenty-minute drive to Agon's capital, a cosmopolitan town rich in history and full of excellent shops and restaurants.

She didn't want to think of Helios, still standing at her door demanding entry. She didn't want to think of him at all.

All she wanted at that moment was to keep her composure as she met the man who shared her blood for the first time.

When Eustachys collected her from the restaurant later that evening Resina's streets were full of Saturday night revellers and stars were twinkling down from the black sky above them.

Amy's head throbbed too hard for her to want to be out amongst them.

Although not a complete disaster, her meeting with Leander had been much more difficult than she'd anticipated. It hadn't helped that she'd still been shaken from Helios's unexpected return to Agon and that she'd been half expecting him to turn up at the restaurant. Discovering where she'd gone would have been as easy for him as buttoning a shirt.

Leander hadn't helped either. She'd already gathered from his social media profile and his posts that he wasn't the most mature of men, but now, reflecting on their meal together—which she had paid for with no argument from him—she came to the sad conclusion that her newly found half-brother was a spoilt brat.

He'd been honest as far as he'd wanted to be. He'd told his mother—Amy's birth mother—about their meeting. He'd made it clear to Amy that it would be his judgement alone that would determine whether Neysa would meet the child she'd abandoned, and that power was a wonderful thing for him to crow about.

Scrap being a spoilt brat. Her half-brother was a monster.

Through all the crowing and the sniffing—she was almost certain he was on drugs—Amy had gleaned that his wealthy father had no idea of her existence. The Soukises had a nice, cosy life, and Amy turning up was in none of their interests. As far as Leander was concerned, Amy was a can of worms that was one twist of the can opener away from potentially destroying his comfortable life.

So, their meeting hadn't been a *complete* Greek tragedy. But not far off.

After being dropped back in the courtyard she made her way on weary legs to her apartment, removing her heels to walk up the staircase to her apartment.

She couldn't elicit the tiniest bit of surprise at finding Helios on her sofa, feet bare, in snug-fitting faded jeans and a black T-shirt, his muscular arms folded in a manner she knew meant only one thing—trouble.

'How did you get in here?' she asked pointlessly. This was his palace. He could go where he pleased.

'With a key,' he answered sardonically, straightening up and rolling his shoulders. 'Where have you been?'

'Out.'

Helios threw her a stare with narrowed eyes, taking in the pretty mint-green dress that fell to her knees, the elegantly knotted hair and the hooped earrings. It was an outfit he'd never seen her wear before. 'Have you been on a date?'

She gazed at him with tired eyes. 'It doesn't matter where I've been. Shouldn't you be with your fiancée? I assume she *is* your fiancée now?'

'Her father gave his blessing. We will make the official announcement during the Gala.'

'So why aren't you in Monte Cleure, celebrating?'

'Some unwelcome news was brought to my attention, so I came back a day early.'

A flicker of alarm flashed across her pretty features. 'Has something happened to your grandfather?'

'My grandfather's fine.' As fine as an eighty-seven-year-old man riddled with cancer could be.

He visited his grandfather every day that he was in the country, always praying that a miracle had occurred and he would see signs of improvement. All he ever saw was further deterioration. The strong, vibrant man who'd been not just the head of his family but the very heart of it was diminishing before his eyes.

Helios and his brothers' business interests had been so successful that their islanders no longer had to pay a cent of tax towards the royal family's upkeep and security. They had enough money to keep their people afloat if the worst economic storm should hit. But not even their great wealth was enough to cure the man who had given up so much to raise them, and it hadn't been enough to cure their beloved grandmother of the pneumonia that had killed her five years ago either. Her death was something their grandfather had never recovered from.

But for once, this evening, he had hardly thought of his grandfather. He'd been sitting rigidly on Amy's hard sofa, trying to keep a lid on his temper as the hours had passed and he'd waited for her to return.

And now here she was, dressed for a romantic night out *with someone else*. It was the final punch in the guts after what had been a hellish day.

The straightforward task of asking the King of Monte Cleure for his daughter's hand in marriage had turned into something infinitely more stomach-turning. The King had received him as if he were a long-lost son, his pride and happiness in his daughter's choice and her future prospects evident.

Throughout the entire private audience a bad taste had been lodged in Helios's throat. Words had formed but he'd spoken them as if they were being dragged over spikes. And throughout all the formalities his brain had been ticking over Amy's less than enthusiastic response to his offer of a permanent role at the palace museum.

To Helios it had been the perfect solution—a way to prove to Amy that she still had a role to play in his life for as long as she wanted, and that he wasn't throwing away what they had for the sake of a piece of paper tying him to another woman. And, besides, she'd earned the job offer. All his reasoning, everything he'd said to her, had been the truth.

Her response had grated on him.

And then he'd received that message from Pedro and taken his jet straight back to Agon.

'Where have you been?' he asked for a second time, noting the way she avoided his gaze at the question.

She sank onto the armchair in the corner, put a palm to her eye and rubbed it, smearing a trail of smoky-grey make-up across her cheek. 'You have no right to ask. Who I see and what I do with my time is my own business.'

'If you have taken another lover then I have every right to question you about it,' he retorted, smothering the nausea roiling in his guts. If she'd taken another lover...

'No, you *don't*,' she said hotly. 'You're the one marrying someone else, not me. That makes me a free agent. I don't owe you anything.'

Staring at her angry face, it struck him for the first time that Amy was serious about their relationship being over. Until that precise moment he'd assumed her pride and jealousy had been speaking for her. That she'd been punishing him.

'Who have you been with?' he demanded. 'Was it a man?'

She met his eyes and gave a sharp nod.

'Is it someone I know?'

'No.'

'Where did you meet him?'

'That doesn't matter.' She sucked in a breath. 'Look, Helios—please—leave me alone. What we had...it's over...'

'So you've jumped straight into bed with another man? Is this your way of punishing me for doing my duty to my family and my country?'

The distaste that flashed over her face answered for her. 'That's disgusting.'

He hid the immediate rush of relief that she hadn't been intimate with this elusive man. The relief died as quickly as it had been born.

'If you're not punishing me then why were you out with someone else? Are you so keen to prove your point that we're finished that you'd humiliate me?'

'How is me dining with someone else humiliating? And how can you dare say that when you're the one *marrying* someone else?'

'And how can *you* dare think I'll let you walk away?'

She stilled, her eyes widening, the flicker under her left eye returning.

'The reason I came back early from Monte Cleure is because Pedro called to inform me that the curator in charge of my grandfather's Jubilee Exhibition—a woman who, may I remind you, was taken on despite her lack of experience, because Pedro and I were both convinced she had the knowledge and enthusiasm to pull it off—has decided to quit five months early.'

His anger burned, enflaming him. He would never have believed Amy could be so underhand.

'Helios…' She reached out a hand, then dropped it back to her side with a sigh. 'What other choice do I have? I can't stay here now.'

'You're not the heroine of some old-fashioned melodrama,' he said scathingly. 'What did you think would happen? That I would hear you had resigned and shrug my shoulders and say that it's okay? Or that I would be so upset at the thought of you leaving my life permanently I would abandon my plans to marry Catalina, renounce my claim to the throne and marry you?'

She clutched at the knot of hair at the nape of her neck. 'I hoped you would accept it and at least try to understand where I'm coming from.'

'Well I don't understand or accept it. Your resignation has been refused. You will stay until your contracted period is up or I will sue you for breach of contract.'

Her shock was visible. 'You wouldn't...'

'Wouldn't I? Leave before September and see for yourself.'

'The exhibition is almost complete,' she said, breathing heavily, angry colour heightening her cheeks. 'Come the Gala and we'll be ready for visitors—my job will be done. Anyone else can carry on.'

'"Anyone else" will not have the breadth of knowledge you've developed about my grandfather and our ancestors. You signed that contract and you will damn well fulfil it.'

She jumped to her feet, her hands balled into fists. 'Why are you doing this? Why can't you just let me go?'

'Because we belong together,' he snarled. 'You're mine—do you understand that?'

'No, the *Princess* belongs to you. Not me. I belong only to myself. You can insist I work the rest of my contract—that's absolutely within your rights—but that doesn't change anything else. I will work out the contract if I must, but I will not share your bed. I will not be your mistress.'

Helios could feel the blood pumping in his head. His veins were aflame; needles were pushing into his skin. Deep in his gut was something he couldn't identify—but, *Theos*, whatever it was, it hurt.

He'd known from the outset that Amy was a woman of honour. Her excitement at his job offer had been so evident it had been contagious, but she'd refused to agree or to sign the contract until she'd spoken to her bosses at the British Museum face-to-face. If there had been any hesitation from them in letting her take the role she would have refused it, even though it was, by her own admission, a dream come true.

If it was such a dream then why was she prepared to walk away from it now?

And if she was so honourable how could she already be actively seeking a new lover?

He needed to get out of this apartment before he did something he would regret. So many emotions were riding through him it was impossible to distinguish them. He only knew his fists wanted nothing more than to smash things, to take every ornament and piece of furniture in this apartment and pulverise it.

For the second time in as many weeks the violence that lived in his blood threatened to boil over, and he despised himself for it almost as much as he despised Amy right now for seeking to leave him. But, unlike his violent father, Helios knew his own temper would never be directed at a woman. It was the only certainty he could take comfort from.

Striding over to her, he took her chin in his hand and forced her to look at him. *Theos*, she had such delicate features and such gorgeous skin. He didn't think there was an inch of her he hadn't stroked and kissed. He refused to believe he would never make love to her again. He *refused*.

'If you understand nothing else, understand this—you will *always* belong to me,' he said roughly, before dropping his hold and walking out of her apartment.

Amy's phone vibrated, breaking her concentration on the beautiful green sapphire ring she was supposed to be categorising but instead could only stare at with a lump in her throat.

This ring had belonged to Helios's mother. This ring would one day soon slide onto Princess Catalina's finger.

The message from Leander was simple and clear.

She doesn't want to meet you. Do not contact me again.

She read it a number of times before closing her eyes

and rubbing at the nape of her neck. A burn stung the back of her retinas.

She had never expected her birth mother to welcome her long-abandoned daughter with cheers and whistles, but she had expected *something*. Some curiosity, if nothing else. Did she not even wonder what Amy looked like? Or who she had become?

But there was too much shame. To Neysa Soukis, Amy was nothing but a scar on her memories; a scar that had to remain hidden.

If Amy were a different person she would force the issue. She would stalk Neysa at her house until she was browbeaten into seeing her. But even if she was capable of doing that what would it accomplish? Nothing more than Neysa's further contempt and probably a restraining order to boot.

All she wanted was to talk to her. Just once. But clearly she wasn't worth even that.

'Are you ready to go yet?'

Blinking rapidly, she looked up and found Greta standing in the doorway.

Amy turned her phone off. 'She doesn't want to meet me.'

At least with Greta she didn't have to pretend.

Greta came over to her and put an arm around her back. 'I'm sorry.'

Amy sniffed. 'I just thought…'

'I know,' said Greta softly. 'But learning you were here probably came as a big shock to her. She'll change her mind.'

'What if she doesn't?'

'She will,' Greta insisted. 'Now, turn your computer off. We've a night out to get ready for.'

'I'm not going.'

'You are. A night out is exactly what you need.'

'But Helios will be there.'

'So what? This will be your chance to let him see you having a great time and that you're completely unaffected by your break-up.'

Amy gave a laugh that came out as more of a snort than anything else. Thank God for Greta. Without her cheering friendship and positive attitude life on Agon would be unbearable right now.

Was it only four months ago that she'd arrived on this island full of excitement for what the future held? With a handsome prince as her boss and the opportunity to find the woman who'd given birth to her?

Now she was stuck here for another five months, and she would have to watch the handsome prince marry his princess and her birth mother wanted nothing to do with her.

She wished she'd never come to Agon.

Greta rubbed her arm in solidarity. 'Let's get your dress and go back to my flat. There's a bottle of ouzo waiting for us.'

'But...'

'Are you going to give that man so much power over you that you'd give up a free night out with all your friends and colleagues?'

Amy sighed and shook her head. Greta was right. She'd spent the past four days hiding away, mostly holing herself up in the museum's enormous basement, on the pretext of categorising artefacts, desperate to avoid bumping into Helios. And she'd been successful—other than one brief glimpse of him in the palace gardens she'd not had any dealings with him. Of course he was incredibly busy, with the Gala being only ten days away.

'Maybe he won't come,' she said with sudden hopefulness.

'Maybe...' Greta didn't look convinced.

But the thought of him not coming made her feel just as rotten as the thought of him being there.

If he did come, she had to pray he didn't bring the Princess as his guest.

To meet his future wife in the flesh would be one wound too many.

CHAPTER FIVE

THE MAIN REASON Helios had chosen Hotel Giroud for the staff night out was because his staff deserved to enjoy themselves in the most exclusive hotel on Agon. The fact its gardens led to a private beach was a plus.

Owned by Nathaniel Giroud, an old friend from his schooldays, it was the sister establishment of Club Giroud, the most exclusive and secret club on the island. The hotel was only marginally more inclusive, provided one had the funds and the connections. The quality of Helios's connections went without saying, and of course he had the funds, more than he could ever spend. He didn't begrudge spending a cent of his money on the staff who worked so hard for him.

He took his museum staff out twice a year: once at the beginning of the summer season, and once right at the end. Although the events weren't compulsory everyone attended, even those curators and conservators who would live in the museum basement if he'd let them. Most of his museum staff were a breed unto themselves, deeply dedicated to their work. He'd never imagined he would *desire* one of them.

And yet he had. He did.

During what was possibly the busiest time of his life, he couldn't flush Amy from his mind. Even after the news his brother Theseus had given him a couple of days ago he couldn't rid himself of her. Here he was, wrestling with the bombshell that Theseus had a secret child, a Kalliakis heir, and still she remained at the forefront of his mind.

It was taking everything he had to keep away from the museum. There was far too much going on for him to spend any time there, but knowing Amy was within its spacious walls meant the place acted like a magnet to him.

There were only ten days now until the Gala, and he had a mountain of work to do for it. He was determined to make it a success for his grandfather and for all his people.

On Agon, heirs traditionally took the throne at the age of forty. His father had died a few years short of that age and so his grandfather—without a word of complaint—had abandoned his retirement plans to hold the throne for Helios. His grandparents had sacrificed their dreams of travelling the world and his grandmother had put aside her thoughts of returning to her first love of performing as violin virtuoso. Those dreams had been abandoned so they could raise their orphaned grandchildren and mould them into princes the whole of Agon could be proud of. They had sacrificed everything.

There was no person on this earth Helios respected more or felt a deeper affection for than his grandfather. He would do anything for him. And, out of everything, it was marriage he knew his grandfather wanted the most for him. King Astraeus the Fourth wanted to leave this world secure in the knowledge that his lineage would live on and that the monarchy was in safe hands.

Although his engagement was now an open secret, the official announcement would bring his grandfather peace. That more than anything was Helios's overriding concern. He didn't like to think what it would bring for his own state of mind.

Catalina wouldn't return to Agon until the Gala. He'd dissuaded her from coming any earlier, using his busyness as an excuse to keep her away. A shudder ran through him as he recalled her obvious disappointment when he'd left Monte Cleure a day early. When he'd said goodbye she'd raised her chin in anticipation of his kiss. The most he'd been able to do was brush his lips against her cheek. She'd smelled fantastic, and she'd looked beautiful, but he might as well have been dead from the waist down for all she did for him.

Catalina knew what she was marrying into, he reminded himself. She had no illusions that their union would ever be about love. She'd assured him of that herself. But now he wondered if mutual respect would be enough when he couldn't even bring himself to kiss her.

He stood in the hotel lobby, personally greeting his staff and their partners. In all, over one hundred people were expected. He always enjoyed seeing their transformation, enjoyed seeing the back-room staff, who tended to live in jeans and baggy tops, and the front-line staff, who wore smart uniforms, all dressed to the nines in smart suits and cocktail dresses.

As each person entered he welcomed them with an embrace while Talia, his private secretary, handed them all an envelope.

Soon the lobby was full and waiting staff with trays of champagne were circulating. Conversation was stilted, as it always was at the beginning of such evenings, but he knew that wouldn't last long. Once everyone had had a drink or two their inhibitions would fall away and they would enjoy themselves properly. They all worked so hard they deserved to let their hair down.

Through the lobby's wide glass doors he saw two figures approach, their heads bent close together, laughing. His heart jolted, making him lose the thread of the conversation he'd struck up with one of the tour guides. Closer they came, until they reached the doors and showed their identification to the guards on duty, who inspected them closely before standing to one side to admit them.

The doors opened automatically and in they walked.

He greeted Greta first, with the same kind of embrace he'd shared with everyone else. She returned it warmly, gushing about how excited she was. And then it was time to greet Amy.

The same smile she'd entered the lobby with stayed fixed on her face, but her eyes told a different story.

His throat ran dry.

He'd seen her dressed up on a few occasions before: when he'd taken her out on dates away from the palace, and last weekend for her 'date' with someone else, but tonight...

Theos. She looked stunning.

She wore a sleeveless navy blue chiffon dress that floated just above her knees, with silver diamond-shaped beads layered along the hem and across the high round neckline. On her feet were simple high-heeled black shoes that showcased her slender legs. She'd left her dark blonde hair loose, so that it fell across her shoulders and down her back. Her large taupe eyes were ringed with dark grey eyeshadow and her delectable lips were painted nude.

He couldn't drag his eyes away.

For what had to be the first time ever he found himself at a loss for words.

Judging by the expression in her wide eyes, pain emanating from them as she gazed back at him, she was struggling to form words on her own tongue too.

It was Greta who broke the silence, with a shout of, 'Champagne!' She grinned at Helios, slipped her arm through Amy's and whisked her off to find them a glass each.

'Thanks,' Amy muttered the second they were out of

his earshot. Her heart was hammering so hard she could swear she was suffering from palpitations.

'You're welcome. Here,' said Greta, thrusting a glass into Amy's hand. 'Drink this.'

'I've had enough already.' They'd had a couple of shots of ouzo each in Greta's flat, before the car had arrived for them, and while not drunk she definitely felt a little light-headed.

Greta shook her head. 'You're going to need a lot more than this to get through the night without throwing yourself at him.'

'I'm not going to throw myself at him.'

'You could have fooled me from the way you were just staring at each other.'

'We're over,' Amy stated flatly.

'So you keep telling yourself.'

'I mean it.'

'I know you do. The problem is I don't think your heart believes it.' Greta squeezed her hand. 'Don't worry. I'll stop you from entering the big bad wolf's clutches again.'

Fighting to stop her gaze flickering back to him, Amy nodded and swallowed half of her champagne.

'Let's see what's in these envelopes,' Greta said, ripping hers open.

Amy followed suit and found inside a personalised card, thanking her for all her hard work since joining the museum, and two hundred euros to spend in the casino.

'Last year we spent a day on Helios's yacht,' Greta confided, fingering her own pile of notes lovingly. 'It was amazing—when we got back to shore Talia was so drunk Pedro had to carry her off.'

Her words did the trick, making Amy laugh at the image of Helios's prim private secretary, brought along to keep events ticking along smoothly, losing control of herself in such a manner.

Some of her angst loosened and she made a pledge to enjoy herself. At some point just about *everyone* who'd had a work-based affair had to deal with an ex being present. She didn't have to make a big deal of it. If she stuck to Greta's side and avoided even looking at Helios she would be fine.

But stopping herself from staring became harder when they were taken through to the restaurant, which had been put aside for their private use. The seating plan meant she had an excellent view of the top table, where Helios was seated. So good was her view that the moment she took her seat his eyes found her.

She cast her eyes down to her menu, ostensibly familiarising herself with her selections. When she dared to look back up he was engaged in conversation with Jessica, an American curator who had worked at the museum for two decades.

'You're staring,' Greta hissed.

Smiling tightly, Amy forced small talk from her lips, taking a small breath of relief when the starters were brought out.

Her plate was placed before her, and the waiter removed the silver lid with a flourish to release the beautiful aromas of roast sea scallops and smoked celeriac purée sitting in a shellfish broth. It tasted as wonderful as it smelled, and she wished she could appreciate it more, but as hard as she tried her awareness of Helios two tables away was all-consuming.

She was powerless to stop her eyes flickering to him, taking in the strong brown throat exposed by his unbuttoned white silk shirt—all the other men wore ties—and the way his dark blue dinner jacket emphasised the breadth of his chest. If she could only ever stare at one thing for the rest of her life it would be him.

He was laughing at something Jessica had said, his generous smile wide, his liquid eyes lively. A burst of jealousy ripped through her to see him enjoying Jessica's company so much, a totally irrational feeling, considering that Jessica was old enough to be his mother, but real nonetheless.

It was some consolation that he hadn't brought the Princess with him. If she'd had to watch him talking and laughing with her, Amy was certain she would have been sick.

And then his gaze found hers again and her stomach somersaulted. He raised his glass of wine slowly and took a long swallow.

An elbow in her ribs brought her back to earth.

'Stop it!' Greta whispered fiercely.

But she couldn't.

Even when her main course of fillet of beef and truffle mash was brought out to her she couldn't stop her eyes from constantly darting to him.

There was nothing wrong in looking, she told herself helplessly. So long as she kept away from him she could look. She just couldn't touch.

After what felt like hours the meal was over. Before she could flee into the casino, away from the magnetism of Helios's stare, he was on his feet and making a speech, which ended with him raising his glass and offering a toast to them all.

'If you'd all make your way to the private beach at midnight you'll find a last surprise for you,' he finished with a grin. 'Until then, enjoy the casino and the music and most of all have fun—you've earned it.'

Keeping herself glued to Greta's side, Amy headed into the casino, which was every bit as opulent as she'd expected and very busy. However, Helios had arranged for them to have their own private poker, blackjack and roulette tables. She had no interest in playing but it was fun to observe, especially to watch Jessica, who seemed to be cleaning up on the blackjack table, to everyone's amazement. There was soon a crowd forming around her.

The only blot on the landscape was a prickle on her neck: the weight of Helios's stare upon her. It took everything she had not to return it. Without the dining tables separating them she felt vulnerable. It was only a matter of time before he sought her out.

Except it never happened. From out of the corner of her eye she watched him make his way around the casino and the adjoining dance room, speaking to all his staff in turn, his easy smile evident.

So many free drinks were being pressed into their hands that Amy felt herself becoming more light-headed by the minute. Soon it was enough to make herself switch to coffee.

She couldn't stop her heart from jolting every time Helios moved away from one person and on to another. Irrationally, she longed for him to bestow his attentions on her. But other than with his eyes he made no such attempt. She must be the only member of staff he hadn't made an effort to speak to. Apart from Greta, who hadn't let Amy out of her sight all evening.

Maybe he'd finally accepted that they were over, despite his proclamation that she would always be his. Maybe their short time apart had convinced him she had been right to end things between them.

A dagger speared her stomach at the thought of never feeling his strong arms around her again, or the heat of his kiss.

She needed to get out of there, to go back to her apartment and lick her wounds in peace before she gave in to the howl building in her throat. She'd done her best tonight, but not even the alcohol had numbed the ache pounding beneath her ribs. If anything, it had got worse.

But what peace could she find in her apartment when Helios was only the other side of a secret passageway? How could she survive another five months of living so close to him? With her resignation rejected and his threat of legal action if she left hanging over her head, her choices were limited. Her career would be ruined. Who would trust her if she were to breach her contract and be sued by the heir to the throne of Agon?

Because she believed that if she were to leave now he *would* carry out his threat.

He wasn't a cruel man, but when provoked Helios was hot-tempered, passionate and filled to the brim with pride. Her attempted resignation had punctured his ego.

But then, if he had finally accepted they were finished maybe he'd be more understanding and amenable to her leaving if she broached the subject again, once the Gala was over.

She wished so hard that she could hate him, but she couldn't. How could anyone hate him?

'It's nearly midnight,' Greta said animatedly. 'Let's go to the beach.'

Amy nodded. The low buzzing noise of all the surrounding chatter was making her head ache. Some fresh sea air would do her good. She'd go out and watch the last of the entertainment and then she would slip away and lick her wounds in earnest.

The hotel's curved private beach brought gasps of delight from everyone. Helios was pleased by their reaction. Indeed, the whole evening had been a marked success. He was sure there would be plenty of foggy heads in the morning, but he doubted anyone would regret them.

Rows of wooden tables with benches had been set along the sand, and gas lamps had been placed on them for illumination under the moonless sky. The hotel's beach bar was open and cocktails were being made.

To get to the beach you had to cut through the hotel's garden and follow a gentle, meandering trail, then take half a dozen steep steps down to it. It wasn't until the tables were half-full that he spotted Amy, making her way down with Greta, whom she'd clung to like a shield for the entire evening.

He knew why.

Amy didn't want to be alone because she was scared he would pounce the second he had the chance. And if she was scared of him pouncing there could only be one reason— she knew she would struggle to resist.

Her eyes had followed him everywhere that evening. She might try, but she could no more deny the chemistry between them than he could. Soon she would realise resistance was futile. Did the tide resist the pull of the moon? Of course not. Nature worked in perfect harmony, just like the desire that pulled him and Amy together.

And yet... Shadows darkened her eyes. There was pain there, the same pain he'd seen when she'd arrived at the hotel. Seeing it had made him...uneasy. It disturbed him in ways he couldn't explain, not even to himself.

It had made him think twice about approaching her. Could *he* be the cause of that pain?

When she got to the bottom of the pathway she held Greta's arm while she took her shoes off, then the pair of them took themselves to a table where some of their fellow curators were seated. Within moments of her sitting down her eyes roamed until they found him.

Even with only the soft glow of the lamps to illuminate her face he could see her yearning. He could sense her resistance waning. The uneasiness that had pulled at him all evening abated. He'd been imagining it.

With all the stress in his life—from his grandfather's deteriorating health, Theseus's shocking news, the forthcoming Gala, his own engagement and everything in between—it was no wonder his mind was playing tricks on him and making him see things that weren't there.

Music from the DJ's deck began to play; a soft dance beat for everyone to tap their bare feet to, its pulse riding through his veins.

Soon Amy would be his again. And when he got her back in his bed he was never going to let her go.

CHAPTER SIX

DESPITE HER LONGING to be away from the hotel, far from the pull of Helios, Amy was enchanted by what surrounded her. The beach, under the light of the twinkling stars, was the most perfect scene imaginable. The noise of the lapping waves mingled with the dance beat playing behind them and gave her a sense of serenity that had been missing from her life since Helios had announced his intention to marry.

'I need to use the bathroom,' Greta murmured, rising from the table. 'Are you coming?'

'I don't think you need me to hold your hand, do you?' Amy said drily.

Greta laughed and set off into the hotel on decidedly unsteady feet.

Amy shook her head with a smile. Greta had been enjoying the steady stream of free cocktails even more than Amy had enjoyed the steady stream of free coffee.

No sooner had Greta gone than two men with matching goatee beards and dreadlocks pulled back into ponytails appeared. Both were dressed in black outfits that brought to mind samurai warriors crossed with pirates. These men were Agonites; Amy would bet her savings on it.

With interpreters translating from their Greek, the two men insisted that the table Amy was seated at be moved back ten feet. As soon as that was done they drew a line in the sand, marking a semicircle which they made clear no one should cross.

Curiosity drove everyone to their feet. Without her heels on Amy had trouble seeing anything, so she ducked out of the crowd to stand at the top of the steps leading down to the beach. The extra height and distance allowed her to see unhindered.

As the men set themselves up, removing objects she couldn't see from two huge crates, Greta came out of the bathroom and made her way to the semicircle of people crowding around them.

The sun had long gone down and standing alone, without the shared body heat of the people below, Amy felt the slight chill in the air. Rubbing her arms for warmth, she kept her gaze on the men, pretending to herself that she hadn't seen Helios step out from the bar with two large cocktail glasses in his hands...

'I thought you looked thirsty,' he said, climbing the steps to stand with her.

Her heart and throat catching, she shook her head. Deep down she'd known that separating herself from the group would be perceived as an open invitation.

His smile was knowing as he handed her one of the drinks. 'Try this. I think you'll like it.'

The glass was full of crushed ice, and the liquid within it was pink. Fresh strawberries had been placed around the rim, and sprigs of mint laced the cocktail. Wordlessly, she took it from him and placed the straw between her lips.

He knew her tastes too well. 'It's delicious. What is it?'

'A strawberry mojito.'

'Did you make it?'

He laughed lightly and shook his head. 'I wouldn't know where to begin.'

She took another sip. The combination of fresh mint and crushed strawberries played on her tongue, as did the taste of rum.

'What are you drinking?'

'A Long Island iced tea. Try some?'

She shouldn't. Really, she shouldn't.

With the moonless sky filled with twinkling stars, the scent of the sea, the background throb of music, the laughter coming from the crowd of people before them…it was a scene for romance, one she should turn and run away from.

Yet her hand disobeyed her brain, reaching out to take the glass from him, bringing the straw his own lips had wrapped around to her mouth so she could take a small sip.

Her eyes widened. 'That packs a punch!'

He grinned and took the glass back from her, brushing his fingers against hers for a second too long.

Little darts raced through her hand and up her arm. She took another sip of her mojito, fighting desperately to stop herself from leaning forward and into him. He was so close…

'I found out the other day that I'm an uncle,' Helios said, making conversation before she could remember to flee again. Besides, this was something he really needed to talk about, before his head exploded with the magnitude of it all.

'Really?'

Her shock mirrored his own initial reaction to the news. 'Theseus. He had a one-night stand with a woman he met on his sabbatical.'

'Wow. That was a few years ago, wasn't it?'

'The boy is four. His name's Toby. Theseus only found out by accident and a quirk of fate—he lied about his identity to the mother, so she was never able to tell him. And then she turned up at the palace to work on the official biography.'

'That really *is* a quirk of fate. Is he going to recognise him?'

'Yes. And he's going to marry the mother to legitimise him.'

She took another long sip of her mojito, her eyes wide as she finally met his gaze. 'Does your grandfather know?'

'Theseus is going to tell him after the Gala. We've agreed it's best to let that day be for our grandfather.'

She looked down at the ground. He wondered if she was thinking the same thing, that he was using the Gala to make the announcement of his marriage. But his announcement was different—for his grandfather it would be the pinnacle of the day, confirmation of the security that would come with knowing his heir was going to embark on matrimony.

'Theseus's relationship with my grandfather is complicated. Being a Prince of Agon is not something he's ever liked or adjusted to. It's the reason why he's been working so hard on the biography, to prove that he is ready to embrace who he is.'

'Whereas you've always embraced your destiny?' she said softly.

'I am who I am,' he answered with a shrug, not admitting that for a fleeting moment his brother's news had given him pause for thought. Theseus had a ready-made heir and a fiancée he certainly was not indifferent to…

But, no, the thought had been pushed aside before he'd allowed it to float too far into his mind. The throne would be his. It was his destiny. It was his pride. Being King was a role Theseus would hate with every fibre of his being.

Seeing Amy using her straw to fight through the ice to

the liquid left in the bottom of her glass, he signalled to a passing bartender for two more drinks.

'The news about Toby is confidential, of course,' he said, once the man had returned to the bar. 'Only you and I and Theseus's private staff know.'

'Which means half the palace knows.'

He laughed. 'The palace grapevine has a life of its own, I admit, but I hadn't heard anything before Theseus told me, so I don't think word has got out yet.'

'No one will hear anything from me.'

'That goes without saying.' In their time together he had learned to trust Amy completely. He'd never had to watch what he said to her... Apart from the time he'd failed to tell her about the real purpose behind the pre-Gala ball.

Something glistened in her eyes, a spark that flew out to touch him and cut the last of the smile from his face. Had it not been for the bartender, carrying their fresh drinks up the steps, he would have leaned in to kiss her.

Amy blinked herself out of the minor stupor she'd been in danger of falling into and took a grateful sip of her fresh mojito.

It was crazy, but Helios's news about his nephew had brought a spark of hope within her. If there was a ready-made heir in the family...

But, no. Such hopes were futile. Helios had been born to rule this great nation with a royal bride at his side. It was his destiny. And she, Amy, was a nobody.

'The entertainment's about to begin.'

'Sorry?'

That knowing smile spread once again over his handsome face. He nodded at the crowd on the beach.

Following his gaze, she saw the two piratical men standing side by side in the semicircle they'd created, their legs parted in a warrior stance. What ensued was an acrobatic display of perfect synchronicity that on its own would have been marvellous but which then switched to a whole new level.

The men ducked out of Amy's eyesight before reappearing with thick, long sticks, the ends of which were ablaze. Her mouth opened in awe as she watched them dancing and twirling and leaping and whirling whilst the fire made patterns in the darkness, bringing the very air to life.

'You look cold,' Helios murmured, stepping behind her and wrapping an arm around her waist to secure her to him.

Transfixed by what was happening on the beach, her skin dancing with something like the same flames that were playing out before her, Amy didn't resist, not even when he brought his mouth down to nuzzle into her hair. Her insides melted and despite herself she leant back into his hardness, dizzying relief rushing through her at the sensation of being back where she belonged. In Helios's arms.

She gasped as she felt his hand slide over her stomach and drift up to rest under her breasts. She knew she should throw off his hand and walk away, that allowing herself to be held like this was the height of stupidity and danger, but no matter how loudly her brain shouted at her feet to start walking her body refused to obey.

A thumb was raised up to brush against the underside of her breast and he pressed his groin into the small of her back, letting her feel his arousal. The fire-wielding acrobats became a blur in her vision as her senses all turned inwards to relish the feel of Helios against her.

She should be like a marble Minoan statue. Unresponsive. Cold. But his touch turned her molten.

Send her to hell, but she rubbed against his arousal. He hissed in her ear, dropping his hand to her hip and gripping it tightly. She could feel his racing heart beating against her back.

Only the loud sound of applause cut through the sensuous fog she'd fallen into.

The show had finished.

The crowd was dispersing.

Blinking hard, aware of Greta searching for her, Amy finally managed to make her body obey, grabbed Helios's hand and pushed it away.

She took a step to distance herself from the security of his hold and drank the last of her mojito.

'Come back with me,' he said. For once, there was no arrogance in his voice.

She kept her eyes from his, not wanting him to see the longing she knew would be written all over her face. 'I can't.'

'You can.'

Greta had spotted them and was heading for them, or rather weaving unsteadily towards them.

'Come back with me,' he repeated.

'No.' She propelled herself down the steps, desperate to be away from him before her vocal cords said the *yes* they so yearned to speak.

He followed her, grabbing her hand when she reached the bottom step and spinning her around.

She waited breathlessly for him to say something, but all he did was stare at her as if he was drinking her in, his thumb brushing little swirls over the inside of her wrist. The message he was sending didn't need words.

Tugging out of his hold, she hurried away before she could respond to his silent request.

Helios pressed a hand to his forehead and growled to his empty bedroom. He'd been back for over an hour and not even his two Long Island iced teas, which had virtually every spirit imaginable in them, had numbed his brain enough to allow him to sleep.

His body still carried remnants of the arousal that had been unleashed by holding Amy in his arms. One touch was all it had taken. One touch and he'd been fit to burst.

If he'd been one of his ancestors from four hundred years ago he would have marched down the passageway, broken down her door and demanded she give herself to him. As he was a prince of these lands she wouldn't have been allowed to refuse him. She would have had to submit to his will.

But good Queen Athena, Agon's reigning monarch from 1671, had been at the forefront of the abolition of the law which had allowed women to be little more than chattels for the royal family's pleasure.

And even if he could he wouldn't force Amy into his bed. If she came back to him he wanted it to be under her own free will.

He knew she'd returned to the palace. After the fire show she'd disappeared into the throng, and then the last he'd seen of her had been when she'd climbed into one of the waiting palace cars with some of the other live-in staff.

Why was she doing this to him? To *them*? She was as crazy for him as he was for her, and he struggled to understand why she was resisting so hard.

He knew that she wanted to punish him because he had to marry someone else—if he were in her shoes he would probably feel the same way. The mere idea of her with another man was enough to make his blood pressure rise to the point where his veins might explode.

As ashamed as he was to have done so, he'd got his security team to find out who she'd dined with on Saturday night. Leander Soukis, a twenty-two-year-old layabout from a small village on the outskirts of Resina. How Amy had met this man was a mystery. And there was something about their meeting that ground at him.

Never mind that Leander was five years younger than Amy, when Helios distinctly remembered her saying she couldn't relate to younger men, he was also a slight, skinny thing, with a bad reputation. He came from a wealthy family, but that counted for nothing—Leander had been kicked out of three schools and had never held a job for longer than a week. Indeed, he was an ideal candidate for his brother Talos's boxing gym, which he'd opened in order to help disaffected youths, teaching them to channel their anger and giving them a leg up in life.

Why had she gone on a date with him of all people? Had it been her way of proving to Helios that she was serious about their relationship being over? Maybe he should have accepted her resignation rather than let his pride and ego force her into staying. If she was gone from Agon he wouldn't be lying in his bed with a body aching from unfulfilled desire.

But he knew such thoughts were pointless. Amy didn't need to be in his sight to be on his mind. She was there constantly.

And he would bet the palace that right at that moment she was lying in her bed thinking of him.

A soft ping from the security pad on his wall broke through his thoughts.

Jumping out of bed, he pressed a button on it, which brought up the screen issuing the alert. It was from the camera and the sensors in the secret passageway.

Peering closely, he saw a figure moving stealthily along the passageway, getting closer and closer to his room. With his heart in his mouth he watched as she hesitated, and willed her to take the final step and knock on the door.

* * *

Amy stared at Helios's door, not quite certain what she was doing or how she had got to this point.

Knowing she was vulnerable to temptation, she'd accepted an invitation to go to one of the other curator's apartments for a drink: a mini-soirée she would usually have loved attending. She'd tried so hard to pull herself out of the trance she'd fallen into, but her contribution to the conversation had been minimal. She couldn't remember a word of it. It was as if she'd been floating above it all, there in body but not in spirit.

She wanted to blame the alcohol, especially the mojitos Helios had given her, but that would have been a lie. It was all down to him.

She'd gone back to her own apartment after just one drink, but before she'd even stepped into her bedroom she'd stopped and stared at the door that led to the secret passageway. Her breaths had shortened as a deep yearning had pulled at her.

Impulse had overridden common sense. She'd unlocked the connecting door and stepped into the passageway in the same dreamlike state she'd ridden back to the palace in, not consciously thinking about where she was going. But now, standing at his door, sanity had pushed its way back through into her mind.

She couldn't do this. It was all wrong.

Closing her eyes, she pressed the palm of her hand to his door, holding it there.

This was as far as she dared go. If she were to knock and he were to answer...

She heard the telltale click of the lock turning.

She snatched her hand away, her breath catching in her throat.

The door opened.

Helios stood in the doorway, naked, nonchalant, as if Amy sneaking up to his room and doing nothing but touch his door was an everyday occurrence. Except the nonchalance was only on the surface. His chest rose and fell in tight judders. His jaw was taut; his nostrils flared. His eyes bore through her as he did nothing but stare.

And then he moved, sending out a hand to wrap around the nape of her neck and pull her to him and over the threshold. As soon as they were in his room he held her firmly and pushed the door shut. He pressed her against it, trapping her.

'Why are you here?' he asked roughly, leaning close enough for his warm, faintly minty breath to touch her skin.

'I don't know,' she whispered.

She *didn't* know. The closest she could come to describing it was her subconscious overriding her resolve. Now, though, the opposite was true. The sensations darting through her had overridden her subconscious and every inch of her had sprung into life. There was not a single atom of her body that wasn't tilting into him, yearning for his kiss, his touch.

'*I* know.'

Then, with a look that suggested he wanted to eat her alive, he brought his mouth to hers and caught her in his kiss.

CHAPTER SEVEN

IF HIS KISS had been the demanding assault she'd anticipated Amy would have been able to resist and push him away. But it wasn't. His lips rested against hers but he made no movement, stilling as if he was breathing in her essence. Amy inhaled deeply in turn, letting the warmth of his breath and the scent of him creep through her pores and inhabit her.

It was as if everything that had happened in the past ten days had been blown away, and with it all the reasons why being alone with him in his apartment and in his arms was all wrong. This was everything she wanted, everything she needed. How could something so wrong feel so *right*?

And now she didn't even want to think about right and wrong. All she wanted was to be in his arms. For ever.

She was the one to part her lips, to dart her tongue into the darkness of his mouth, to wind her arms around his neck and press into him. She was the one to break the kiss and drag her lips over his stubble-roughened cheeks and jaw and down the strong length of his neck, to run her tongue over the smooth skin, tasting his musky, masculine scent. And she was the one to draw her tongue back up his throat, dig her nails into his scalp and capture his lips with her own.

A tiny sob escaped her mouth when Helios growled and drew his arms around her. He crushed her to him. His lips parted and he kissed her so deeply and so thoroughly that in the breath of an instant she was lost in him.

A large hand dived into her hair whilst his other hand roamed down her back to clutch her bottom, which he squeezed before spreading his palm over her thigh and lifting it. He ground into her and she gasped to feel him huge against her, her underwear the only barrier to stop him entering her there and then.

In a mesh of lips and tongues he pushed her back against the wall, kissing her as if she were a banquet to be feasted on, before pulling away, tugging at her bottom lip painlessly with his teeth as he did so. His chest rising and falling in rapid motion, the palm of one hand held against her chest to still her, Helios lowered himself, pinched the hem of her dress and slowly raised it up. He kissed her stomach as he lifted the dress to her abdomen, his tongue making a trail upwards, through the valley of her breasts, into her neck, until he'd pulled it over her head and thrown it onto the floor.

Amy dug her toes into the hard flooring, her head spinning. Everything inside her blazed as fiercely as the whirling fires she'd seen on the beach. Her skin was alive to his touch. *She* was alive to his touch. Her senses had sprung to life from the very first moment she'd looked at him all those months ago and since then she'd been helpless to switch them off.

He straightened to his full height and stared down at her, his throat moving as his liquid eyes took in her semi-nakedness. He clasped her cheeks in his hands and brought his nose to hers. 'Not being able to touch you or make love to you has driven me crazy,' he said hoarsely. '*You've* driven me crazy.'

She pulled at his hair, wanting to hurt him, wanting him to experience the pain she'd gone through at the separation she'd had no choice but to force upon them. 'It's hurt me every bit as much as you,' she whispered, bringing her mouth back to his.

Holding her tightly, Helios lifted Amy into his arms, staring at her as he carried her through to his bedroom, delighting in the heightened colour of her cheeks and the dilation of her pupils.

All his dreams and fantasies had come true.

She'd come to him.

He hadn't realised how badly he'd prayed for it until he'd opened the door to her.

But he could still see the last vestiges of doubt and fear ringing in her eyes and he was determined to drive them away.

How could she not know that *this*, here, being together, was exactly how it was supposed to be?

Laying her down on his bed, he kissed her rosebud mouth and inhaled the sweet scent he had come close to believing he would never delight in again. All that separated them was her pretty black underwear. He remembered how once he'd peeled it off with his teeth, in those early hedonistic days when the desire between them had been so great he'd been certain it would *have* to abate. But it had only developed into something deeper, something needier.

Whatever it took, he would keep her in his bed.

As he gazed down, seeing the pulse beating in the arch of her neck, the way she stretched out her legs before raising her pelvis, the urgency grew. *Theos*, but he needed to be inside her.

She raised a lazy hand and pressed it to his chest, then spread her fingers over him, touching him in the way that always filled him with such gratification, as if he were one of the Seven Wonders of the World.

The knowledge that she would explore him in the same manner with which he delighted in exploring her had always been indescribable. There was not a fraction of her he had not tasted and not a fraction of him she had not touched. He would *never* tire of tasting her and making her his.

He slipped a hand behind her back and unclasped her bra, then carefully pulled the straps down her arms, kissing the trail they made and throwing it onto the floor with a flick. With her delectable breasts now bare, the dusky nipples puckered in open invitation, he dipped his head to take one tip in his mouth, groaning as she immediately arched her back to allow him to take more of her in.

Her fingers tugged through his hair as she twisted and writhed beneath him, the urgency in her movements matching the urgency flowing through his veins. She skimmed a hand down over his back before slipping it across his stomach, reaching for him. His attentions now on her other breast, he raised himself a little to make it easier for her to take his erection into her hand, groaning again as she held it in the way she knew he adored, rubbing her thumb over the head and guiding him to the apex of her thighs.

Gritting his teeth and breathing heavily, he kissed her neck and moved her hand away, squeezing her fingers between his own. Immediately she raised her thighs and rubbed against his length, moaning, begging him with soft murmurs.

But there was still the final barrier of her underwear between them.

He kissed her hard on the mouth, then pulled back, drifting his lips down the creaminess of her neck and breasts until he reached her abdomen. There, he pinched the elastic of her underwear between the fingers of both hands and tugged it down, past her thighs and calves and delicate ankles, until she was fully naked before him.

'Please…' she beseeched him, raising her thighs higher and reaching out a hand to touch him. *'Please.'*

Swallowing hard at the sight of her, so full of desire and need for him it made him heady, he guided his erection into her welcoming heat.

He pushed himself in with one long drive and buried his face in her neck, biting gently into the soft skin. And as she gripped him tightly within her he knew without a shadow of a doubt that *this* was where he belonged.

Skin against skin, heartbeat to heartbeat, arms and legs entwined, he made love to her.

And she made love to him.

He could sense the tension within her building, could hear it in the shortening of her breaths, the shallowness of her moans, feel it in the way she gripped his buttocks, deepening his thrusts. And then he felt her pulses pulling at him, pulling him even deeper inside her, her slender frame stilling, her teeth biting into his shoulder.

He didn't want it to end. He wanted it to last for ever, to be locked in her tight sweetness with her legs wrapped around him and her nails digging into his back for eternity…

And then there was no more consciousness. His own climax surged through him, tipping him over a precipice he hadn't known he was on the edge of and exploding in a wash of bright colours that took him to a place he'd never been before.

Amy awoke in the comfort of Helios's embrace, her face pressed against his chest, his arm hooked across her waist, his thigh draped heavily over hers.

Remorse flooded her in an instant.

What had she done?

Everything she'd sworn she wouldn't do had been ripped away in one moment of madness.

She should go. She had to go. She couldn't stay here.

How many times had she awoken in the night in his arms and felt the stirring to make love to him all over again? How many times had she lifted her head a touch and met his kiss? Had him fully hard and inside her in an instant? Too many to count. Sometimes she would wake in the morning and wonder if she'd dreamt their lovemaking in the early hours.

But at this moment Helios's breathing was deep and even. If she was careful she might be able to sneak out without him waking. Then she could flee to her apartment, pack a suitcase and check into a hotel. That was it. That was what she had to do.

Because she couldn't stay here—not now when she knew how hopeless she was at resisting him.

She'd tried so hard to stay away.

Oh, God, what had she *done*?

She could dress it up any way she liked but she'd given in to temptation, and now the ecstasy of being back in his arms had gone, replaced with an acrid taste in her mouth and a gutful of guilt.

She had to leave. Right now.

Carefully, after stealthily slipping out of his arms, she edged her way out of the bed, holding her breath until her feet touched the floor.

Scrambling, half-blind in the dark, she found her dress thrown across an armchair. She had no idea where her underwear had got to and was in too much of a panic to escape to hunt for it for long. She shrugged her dress on and, fearful of choking on the swell rising in her chest, tiptoed to the door.

'You wouldn't be running away, would you?'

Helios watched as Amy's silhouette froze at the bedroom door. Switching on the bedside light, he propped himself up on an elbow as she slowly turned around to face him with wide, pain-filled taupe eyes. To see her mussed-up hair and her beautiful face contorted in such misery... Something sharp pierced him.

'I'm sorry,' she whimpered. 'I know it's cowardly to sneak away.'

'Then why are you?'

'I shouldn't be here. We shouldn't have...' Her voice tailed away and she looked down at the floor.

'Made love?' he supplied.

She gave a tiny nod. 'It was wrong. All wrong.'

'It felt damn right to me.'

'I know.' She gave a sudden bark of harsh laughter and her eyes flashed. 'It's what I keep thinking. How can something so wrong feel so right?'

'If it feels so right then how can it be wrong?' he countered.

'It just is. You're getting *married*.'

That little fact was something that constantly played on his mind. Only being in Amy's arms had driven it and the accompanying nausea away.

Tightness coiled in his stomach. Throwing off the covers, he climbed out of bed and strode over to her, slamming his hand on the door to prevent her from escaping.

He spoke slowly, trying to think the words through before he vocalised them, knowing that one wrong word would make her flee whether or not he barricaded the door. 'Amy, I might be getting married, but it's *you* I want.'

'We've been through this before. It doesn't matter what you want or what I want. It doesn't change the reality of the situation. Tonight was a mistake that can't be repeated.'

'Running away won't change anything either. Admit it, *matakia mou*. You and I belong together.'

Her jaw clenched in response.

'So what are you going to do?' he asked scathingly, leaning closer to her ashen face. 'Run away and start a relationship with Leander? Is that how you intend to prove we're over?'

'How do you know about Leander?' She shook her head and took a deep inhalation. 'Don't answer that. I can guess.'

He felt no guilt for seeking information about her date. Helios looked out for those he cared for. 'He's too young for you. I know you, Amy. You don't need a boy. You need—'

'He's my brother,' she snapped suddenly, angry colour flushing her cheeks.

Her declaration momentarily stunned him into silence. Stepping back to look at her properly, he dragged a hand through his hair. 'But Leander is from Agon. Your brothers are English, like you...'

'I'm only half-English.'

'Your parents are English.' *Weren't* they? Wasn't this something they had talked about...?

'My father's English. Elaine—my mum—didn't give birth to me. My birth mother's from Agon.'

How had he not known this?

Amy must have sensed the direction his mind was travelling in. 'Do you remember once asking me how I'd developed such an obsession and a love for your country?'

'You said it was... You never gave a proper answer...'
Realisation dawned on him as he thought back to that

conversation, months ago, when they had first started sleeping together. She'd brushed his question aside.

'And you never pursued it.' She shook her head in a mixture of sadness and anger.

'I didn't know there was anything to pursue. I'm not a mind reader.'

'I'm sorry.' She gave a helpless shrug. 'A huge part of me wanted to tell you, and ask for your help in finding her, but I knew that confiding in you would change the nature of our relationship.'

'What would have changed?' he asked, completely perplexed.

From the first the chemistry between them had been off the charts. Making love to Amy had always felt different from the way it had felt with his other lovers. He'd never felt the urge to ask her to leave at night—he liked sharing his space with her, this incredibly sexy woman with a brain the size of a watermelon. He loved it that she could teach him things he didn't know about his own country.

To learn now that she had *roots* in his country...

'I didn't keep any secrets from you,' he added, his head reeling.

'Apart from throwing a party to find a wife?'

He inhaled deeply. Yes, the real purpose of the ball *was* something he'd kept from her for as long as he could. But this information was on a different scale. He'd known Amy had kept a part of herself sheltered from him, but he'd had no idea it was something so fundamental.

Her eyes held his. 'I was scared.'

Another stabbing pain lanced him. 'Of me?'

'Of what you would think of me. At least I was in the beginning.' Her voice lowered to a whisper. 'And I was scared because you and I came with time constraints. We had a fixed marker for when we would end, we both knew that. We both held things back.'

'I never held anything back.'

'Didn't you?' There was no challenge in her eyes, just a simple question. 'Helios, I couldn't take the risk of what we had developing into something more—of us becoming closer. We can't be together for ever. I was trying to protect myself.'

For an age he stared at her, wishing he could see into her mind, wishing he could shake her...wishing that everything could be different.

'Do not go anywhere,' he said, turning his back to her and striding to his dressing room. 'You and I are going to talk, and this is not a conversation to have naked. We're long past the point of keeping secrets from each other.'

While Helios slipped on a pair of boxers Amy used the few moments alone to catch her thoughts before he reappeared.

It wasn't long enough.

She pressed her back tightly against the door, her vocal cords too constricted for speech.

'I mean it, Amy,' he said with a hard look in his eye. 'You're not going anywhere until we've talked this through.'

'What's the point?' she asked, her voice hoarse.

'If your history is what's stopping us from being together then I damn well deserve to know the truth.' He strolled back to the bed and sat in the middle of it, his back resting against the headboard. 'Now, come here.'

What an unholy mess. It had never been supposed to end like this. Her memories of her time with him were supposed to be filled with wonder, not sorrow and despair. Losing him wasn't supposed to *hurt*.

She perched on the end of the bed and twisted to face him. Blowing out a puff of air, she gazed at the ceiling.

'My father had an affair with the au pair. She dumped me on him when I was two weeks old and has wanted nothing to do with me since. Her husband and her parents don't know I exist.'

CHAPTER EIGHT

OTHER THAN A slight shake of his head and a tightening of his lips, Helios gave no response.

'My birth mother had me when she was nineteen. I know very little about her—she didn't work for them for long.'

'When you say *for them*...?'

'My parents. My mum—as in the woman who raised me—was pregnant and had a three-year-old son when they employed Neysa, my birth mother, as an au pair. She quit after a couple of months but then turned up at my dad's workplace seven months later and left me with the receptionist.'

Amy studied Helios's reaction carefully. She no longer really feared, as she had at the beginning of their relationship, that he would think any less of her, but nagging doubts remained. Cruel words spoken in the playground still haunted her, clouding her judgement.

'You must have been one ugly baby for your own mum to dump you.'

'Do you have 666 marked on the back of your head?'

'Your real mum's a slut.'

She'd had to force herself to rise above it and pretend the taunts didn't affect her when in reality they had burned. For years she had tortured herself, wondering if the taunts held the ring of truth. For years she'd tried to live a life as pure as the driven snow to *prove* she wasn't intrinsically bad.

For years she'd wondered how Elaine—to her mind, her mum—could even bring herself to look at her.

Helios stared at her as if she'd just told him that all the scientists and even physics itself were wrong and the world was actually flat.

'Did she leave a note?' he asked quietly. 'Give a reason?'

'Her note to my father said only that I was his and that she couldn't keep me.'

'So your father had an affair with the au pair when your mum was pregnant? And they're still together?'

She nodded. 'God knows how Mum found it in her to forgive him but she did, and she raised me as her own.'

Helios shook his head, amazement in his eyes. 'She raised you with her own children?'

'Yes. Danny was born five months before me. We were in the same school year.'

He closed his eyes with a wince. 'That must have been difficult.'

'At times it was horrendous—especially at secondary school. But we coped.'

Amy's existence could have caused major friction between her and her siblings, but both Danny and their older brother, Neil, had always been fiercely protective of her, particularly during their teenage years.

'Did you always know?'

'Not when I was a young child. My family was my family. Danny being five months older than me...it was just a fact of our lives. Neil always knew I was only his half-sister but, again, it was just a fact of our lives and something he assumed was normal. My parents never mentioned it so he didn't either. Then we got older and other kids started asking questions… Mum told me the truth when I was ten.'

She shuddered at the memory of that sudden realisation that her whole life had been a lie.

'She'd been waiting until I was old enough to understand.'

It had been the most significant moment of Amy's life. It would have been easy to feel as if her whole world had caved in, but Danny and Neil had simply shrugged it off and continued to treat her as they always had—as their sister. That, more than anything, had made it easier to cope with.

'Did you not have *any* idea you weren't hers?'

'Not in the slightest. She loved me. Any resentment was hidden.'

'What about your father? Where does he fit in with all this?'

'He left it to my mum to tell me. When it came out he carried on as normal, trying to pretend nothing had changed.'

But of course everything had changed. *She'd* changed. How could she not? Everything she'd thought she knew about herself had been a lie.

She looked back at Helios, wanting him to understand. 'When I was told the truth it became important, I guess, to pretend that nothing had changed. They still treated me the same. They still scolded me when I was naughty. My mum still tucked me up in bed and kissed me goodnight. Outwardly, nothing did change.'

'And how does she feel about you being here now, trying to find your birth mother?'

'She understands. She's adopted herself—I think that's why she was able to raise me without blaming me for the sins of my birth mother. She knows what the urge to find out who you really are is like.'

Her mum had encouraged Amy's quest to learn all there was to know about Agon. She'd been the one to take her to the library to seek out books on Agon and Minoan culture and to record any television documentary that featured the island. So encouraging had she been that a part of Amy had been scared her mum *wanted* her to go to Agon and stay there. She'd been afraid that she wanted to get rid of the living proof of her husband's infidelity, that all the love she had bestowed on Amy had only been an act.

But Amy couldn't deny that she'd seen the apprehension in her mum's eyes when she'd left for Agon. Since she'd been on the island she'd received more daily calls and messages than she had when she'd first left home for university. Was she secretly worried that Amy would abandon her for Neysa…?

Secretly worried or not, wanting to get rid of her or not, being adopted herself meant her mum had first-hand experience of knowing what it was like to feel a part of you was missing. Helios had always known exactly who he was. There hadn't been a single day of his life when he hadn't known his place in the world or his destiny.

'She sounds like a good woman.'

'She is. She's lovely.' And she was. Loving and self-less. Amy knew her fears were irrational, but she had no control over them. They were still there, taunting her, in the deepest recesses of her mind.

'So why do you want to meet your birth mother?' Helios asked, puzzled that Amy could want *anything* to do with someone who'd caused such pain and destruction. 'She abandoned you and destroyed your mum's trust.'

She looked away. 'I don't want a relationship with her.

I just... I want to know what she looks like. Do I look like her? Because the only thing I've inherited from my dad is his nose. And I want to know why she did what she did.'

'Even if the truth hurts you?' If her birth mother was anything like her layabout son, he would guess she'd abandoned Amy for purely selfish reasons.

'I've been hurt every day of my life since I learned the truth of my conception,' she said softly. 'I know there are risks to meeting her, but I can't spend the rest of my life wondering.'

'Has your father not been able to fill in any of the gaps for you?'

'Not really. He doesn't like to talk about her—he's still ashamed of his behaviour. He's a scientist, happily stuck in a laboratory all day, and what he did was completely out of character.' She gave a sad smile. 'Even if he did want to talk about it there's not much for him to say. He hardly knew her. She was hired on a recommendation from one of Dad's colleagues who left his research company before I was dumped on him. All he and my mum knew was that Neysa—my birth mother—was from Agon and had come to England for a year to improve her English.'

And so the Greens had allowed a stranger into their home, with no foreknowledge of the havoc that would be wreaked on them.

'Everything else I've learned since I came here,' she added wistfully. 'Greta has helped me.'

But she hadn't confided in *him* or approached him for help.

Helios tried to imagine the pain and angst she'd been living with during all the nights they'd shared together. She hadn't breathed a word of it, although she must have known he was in the best position to help her.

'How's your parents' marriage now?'

Amy shrugged. 'When it all happened I was still a new-born baby. They patched their marriage up as best they could for the sake of us kids. They seem happy. I don't think my dad ever cheated again, but who knows?'

'My mother was a good woman too,' he said.

He was realising that Amy was right in her assertion that they had both kept things hidden. Both of them had kept parts of their lives locked away. And now it was time to unlock them.

'And my father was also a philanderer. But, unlike your father, mine never showed any penitence. The opposite, in fact.'

Her taupe eyes widened a touch but she didn't answer, just waited for him to continue in his own time.

'My father was hugely unfaithful—to be honest, he was a complete bastard. And my mother was incredibly jealous. To shut her up when she questioned him about his infidelities he would hit her. She deserved better than him.'

This was not a subject he'd ever discussed with anyone outside of his family. His father's infidelities were well documented, but his violence...that was something they'd all closed ranks on. Being the sons of such a vicious, narcissistic man was not something any of the brothers had found it easy to reconcile themselves with.

'I'm sorry,' Amy said, shaking her head slowly as if trying to take in his words. 'Did you know it was going on? The violence, I mean?'

'Only on an instinctual level. It was only ever a feeling.'

'How was *your* relationship with your father?' she asked quietly.

He grimaced as decades-old memories flooded him. 'I was the apple of his eye. He adored me, to the point that he excluded my brothers. It felt good, being the "special" one, but I also felt much guilt about it too. He was cruel—especially to Theseus. My mother struggled to make him treat us all fairly.'

Amy didn't say anything, just stared at him with haunted eyes.

'I was a child when they died. My memories are tainted by everything I learned after he'd gone, but I remember the looks he would give my mother when she stood up for Theseus or made a pointed remark about his other women. I would feel sick with worry for her, but he was always careful to make sure I was out of sight and earshot before hitting her. It got worse once I left for boarding school,' he continued. 'With me gone, he didn't have to hide it any more.'

'You surely don't blame yourself for that?'

'Not any more. But I did when I first learned the truth.' He met her gaze. 'It took me a long time to truly believe I couldn't have stopped him even if I had known. But, like you when your life fell apart, I was a child. Talos tried to stop it—that last day, before my parents were driven to the Greek Embassy and their car crashed, Talos was there, right in the middle of it. He got hurt himself in the crossfire.'

'Oh, the poor boy. That must have been horrendous for him.'

'It screwed up his ideas of marriage. He has no intention of ever marrying.'

'Not an option for you,' she said softly.

'No.' He shook his head for emphasis. 'Nor for Theseus. The security of our family and our island rests in our hands. But I swear this now—my parents' marriage will not be mine.'

'What if it was an option?' she asked suddenly, straightening. 'What if you'd been born an ordinary person? Who would you be now?'

'I don't know.' And he didn't. 'It's not something I've ever thought about.'

'Really?'

'Theseus spent most of his life fighting his birthright and all it brought him was misery. Why rail against something you have no control over? I had no control over my conception, just as I had no control over my parents' marriage or their deaths. My destiny is what it is, and I've always known and accepted that. I am who I am and I'm comfortable with that.'

It was only in recent weeks that the destiny he'd always taken for granted had gained a more acrid tang.

During their conversation Amy had moved fully back onto the bed and was now facing him, hugging her knees. Reaching forward, he took her left foot into his hands and gently tugged at it so it rested on his lap.

A strange cathartic sensation blew through him, and with it a sense of release. His father's violence and complete disrespect to his mother were things that he'd locked away inside, not wanting to give voice to the despicable actions he and his brothers felt tainted by. But Amy was the last person who would judge a child for the sins of its parents. In that respect they shared something no other could understand.

'The main reason I selected Catalina is because she has no illusions about what our marriage will be,' he said, massaging Amy's foot. 'She has been groomed from birth to marry someone of equal stature. I will be King, but I will never be like my father. Marrying Catalina guarantees that she will never expect more than I can give.'

'But your mother was a princess before she married your father.'

His mouth twisted. 'Their marriage was arranged before she could walk. She grew up knowing she would marry my father and she built an ideal in her head of what their marriage would be like. She loved him all her life and, God help her, she was doomed to disappointment. The only person my father loved was himself. Catalina doesn't love me any more than I love her. There will be no jealousy. She has no expectations of fidelity.'

'Has she said that?' Amy asked doubtfully.

'Her only expectation is that I be respectful to her and discreet, and that is something I will always be. Whatever happens in the future, I will *never* inflict on her or on anyone the pain my father inflicted on my mother.'

'I know you wouldn't hurt her intentionally. But, Helios, what she says now...it doesn't mean she'll feel the same way once you've exchanged your vows.' Amy closed her eyes and sighed. 'And it doesn't change how I feel about it. I won't be the other woman. Marriage vows should be sacred.'

Helios placed her foot gently onto the bed before pouncing, grabbing her hands and pinning her beneath him.

Breathing heavily, she turned her face away from him.

'Look at me,' he commanded.

'No.'

'Amy, look at me.' He loosened his hold only when she reluctantly turned her face back to him. 'You are not Neysa—you are Elaine's daughter, with all *her* goodness. Catalina is not your mother. Nor is she mine. And I am *not* my father. The mistakes they all made and the pain they caused are not ours to repeat. That's something neither of us would ever allow to happen.'

He came closer so his lips were a breath away from hers.

'And I'm not married yet.'

Her eyes blazed back at him, desire and misery fighting in them. He leaned down and placed a kiss to her neck, smoothing his hand over her breasts and down to her thighs. He inched the hem of her dress up and slid between her legs.

'Neither of us are ready for this to end. Why deny ourselves when my vows are still to be made and we're not hurting anyone?'

Amy fought the familiar tingles and sensations spreading through her again as the need to touch him and hold him grew stronger than ever. How was it possible to go from wanting to wrap him in her arms, to chase away what she knew were dreadful memories for him, to sensual need in the blink of an eye?

She writhed beneath him. Her words came in short breaths. 'I can't think when you're doing this to me.'

'Then don't think. Just feel. And accept that we're not over.'

In desperation she grabbed at his hair, forcing *him* to look at *her*. 'But you've made a commitment.'

'A commitment that won't be fulfilled for two months.' He slid inside her, penetrating as deep as he could go.

She gasped as pleasure filled her.

'Until then,' he continued, his voice becoming heavy as he began to move, 'you are mine and I am yours.'

Amy tightened her hold around Helios, wishing she didn't feel so complete with his weight upon her and his steadying breaths softly tickling the skin of her neck. She was a fool for him. More so than she could have imagined.

They'd laid their pasts bare to each other and the effect had been the very thing she'd been scared of. She felt closer to him, as if an invisible emotional bond had wrapped itself around them.

He finally shifted his weight off her and she rolled over and burrowed into his arms.

'Don't even think about trying to sneak out,' he said sleepily.

'I won't.' She gave a soft, bittersweet laugh. Her resolve had deserted her. Those bonds had cocooned her so tightly to him she could no longer envisage cutting them. Not yet. Not until she really had to. 'You and I...'

'What?' he asked, after her words had tailed off.

'No one can know. Please. Everyone who knew we were together knows we split up. I couldn't bear for them to think we're having an affair behind the Princess's back.'

When they'd been together originally Helios had made no secret of her place in his life. She might not have accompanied him to official functions, or been recognised as his official girlfriend, but she had been his almost constant companion within the palace.

She'd spent far more time in his apartment than she had in her own, and whenever he had come into the museum he would seek her out. He would touch her—not sexually... he at least had a sense of propriety when it came to *that* in public...but he would rest his hand in the small of her back, lean close to her, all the little tells of a possessive man staking his claim on the woman in his life. And if work or duty took him away from the palace she would be the one to look after Benedict.

It had only been on the inside, emotionally, that they had been separated. But not any more. At this moment she didn't think she had ever felt as close to anyone in her life.

'Discretion will be my new name,' he acquiesced.

'And when you marry you will let me go.'

He stilled.

Watching for his reaction, she saw his eyes open. 'That gives you two months to find my replacement,' she whispered. 'I want to know that you'll release me from the palace and from your life. I appreciate it means bringing my contract to an early end, but I don't think I'll be able to cope with living and working here knowing it's the Princess you're sleeping with.'

When he married their bonds would be destroyed.

He breathed deeply, then nodded. 'I can agree to that. But until then…'

'Until then I am yours.'

CHAPTER NINE

HELIOS CLICKED ON Leander Soukis's profile and stared hard at it. There was something about the young man's chin and the colouring of his hair that reminded him of Amy, but that was the only resemblance he could see. How could Amy share half her DNA with this layabout? Amy was one of the hardest workers he'd ever met, which, in a palace and museum full of overachievers was saying something.

And how she could be from the loins of Neysa Soukis was beyond his comprehension. Helios had done his homework on Amy's birth mother and what he had learned had not given him hope of a happy ending.

Neysa was a social climber. Approaching fifty, she still had a refined beauty. She had a rich older husband, who doted on her, and a comfortable lifestyle. Helios vaguely recalled meeting her husband at a palace function a few years back. Neysa had married him when she was twenty-one, less than two years after having Amy. Why she hadn't confessed to having had a child he could only speculate upon, but his guess was that it had nothing to do with shame and everything to do with fear. No doubt she'd been scared of losing the wealth that came with her marriage.

Neysa had put money before her own flesh and blood. If Helios had his way Amy wouldn't be allowed within a mile's radius of the woman. But he understood how deep blood could go. That morning he'd met his nephew for the first time. He'd felt an instant thump in his heart.

This little boy, this walking, talking dark-haired creation was a part of *him*. His family. His bloodline. He was a Kalliakis, and Helios had felt the connection on an emotional level.

It might break her heart in the process, but Amy deserved to know her bloodline too.

Whether the Soukis family deserved *her* was another matter...

If they did break her heart he would be there to pick up the pieces and help her through it, just as Amy had been there with a comforting embrace whenever the pain of his grandfather's illness had caught him in its grip.

Thinking quickly, Helios drafted a private message. If having a decree from the heir to the throne didn't motivate Leander to bring his mother and half-sister together, nothing would.

'Amy, you're late for your meeting.'

'What meeting?' she asked Pedro in surprise, looking down at him from her position on a stepladder, from where she was adjusting the portraits lining the first exhibition room. She wanted them to be hung perfectly, not so much as a millimetre out of alignment.

The museum and the palace tours had been closed to visitors all week in order to prepare for the Gala. As a result the palace and its grounds were in a state of absolute frenzy, with helicopters landing on the palace helipad on a seemingly constant basis. And the Gala was still a day away!

She'd never known the palace to be such a hive of activity. There was a buzz about the place, and information and gossip were being dripped in from so many sources, including the more serious museum curators, whose heads were usually stuck in historical tomes, that it seemed like a spreading infection.

The Orchestre National de Paris had arrived to great fanfare, a world-famous circus troupe had been spotted lurking in the grounds, the gardens had been closed off to allow even more blooms to be planted... Everywhere Amy went something magical was occurring.

The exhibition was to all intents and purposes ready for the *very* exclusive private tour that would be conducted after the pre-Gala lunch. Another, less exclusive tour would take place on Sunday, and the museum and exhibition would open to the public on Monday. From then on it really would be all systems go. Ticket demand had exceeded expectations.

She wanted it to be perfect—not just because of her professional pride, but also for Helios, his grandfather and his brothers.

'Your meeting with Helios,' Pedro said. 'He's waiting for you in his private offices.'

'Oh.' She rubbed at her lips, avoiding Greta's curious stare, willing them both not to notice the flames licking at her face.

Helios had been as good as his word. No one knew they were sharing a bed again, not even Greta. It wasn't just guilt preventing Amy from confiding in her friend, but the feeling that what she and Helios had now was just too intimate to share.

'Yes. Yes, I remember.'

Excusing herself politely, still not meeting their eyes, Amy hurried away. When she'd kissed Helios goodbye that morning, before coming to work, she'd assumed that he would be flat-out busy all day. His itinerary had given her a headache just looking at it. A frisson ran up her spine as she imagined what he might be wanting from her. She doubted very much that it had anything to do with the museum.

Helios's private offices were attached to his private apartment. Getting there was a trek in itself. She could cut through her own apartment and use their secret passage-way, but during daylight hours it wasn't feasible, not when this was an 'official' meeting, even if it would shave ten minutes off her walk.

The usual courtiers guarded his quarters. They were expecting her and opened the door without any questions. She stepped inside, into a large reception area. The door to the left led to his apartment. She turned the handle of the door to the right.

Talia, Helios's private secretary, rose to greet her, a pastry in her hand. 'Hello, Amy,' she said with a welcoming smile. Usually immaculately presented, today Talia had a wild-eyed, frazzled look about her. 'He's expecting you.'

Did Talia suspect Amy and Helios had resumed their relationship? Did *anyone* suspect?

Amy smiled back politely. 'How are things?'

Talia crossed her eyes and pulled a face. 'Busy. This is the first time we've stopped all day.' She pressed a key on one of her desk phones. 'Despinis Green is here,' she said.

'Send her in,' came the response.

Amy found Helios sitting behind his sprawling desk with Benedict, his black Labrador, snoozing beside him. Benedict cocked an ear and opened his eyes when she walked into the office, then promptly went back to sleep.

'Take a seat,' Helios said politely, his eyes following her every movement with a certain knowingness.

As soon as the door was closed and they had some privacy he rose from his chair and stepped round the desk to take her in his arms.

'Was there a reason you made up a non-existent meeting

other than to make out with me in your office?' she asked with bemusement when they came up for air.

His hands forked through her hair and he kissed her again. 'The French Ambassador's flight was slightly delayed, giving me an unexpected half-hour window.'

'It took me that long to get here,' she said teasingly.

'I know.' He gave a mock sigh. 'I suppose a few kisses are better than nothing.'

She laughed and rested her head against his chest. 'Should I go now?'

He looked at his watch. 'Five minutes.'

'That's hardly any time.'

Not that she could do anything more than share a few kisses with him in his office, with Talia on the other side of the door and the palace full of Very Important People who all demanded his time. How he kept his good humour was a mystery...

'There's always time for kissing,' he said, tilting her chin up so he could nuzzle into her cheek. 'Especially as I won't get the chance to touch you again for at least another ten hours...' Before she could get too comfortable, however, he stepped away. 'To answer your original question—yes, I did have an ulterior motive for seeing you other than the insatiable need to kiss you.'

She rolled her eyes.

'Before I tell you... I don't want you to think I've been interfering.'

'What have you interfered with?'

'I told you, I'm not interfering. I'm helping,' he added, with a deliberate display of faux innocence.

'What have you done?'

His features became serious. 'I've been in contact with your birth mother.'

Her heart almost stopped. 'And?' she asked breathlessly.

'She has agreed to meet you in a neutral place on Monday.'

She shook her head, trying to clear the sudden buzzing that had started in her brain at this unexpected development.

'Are you angry with me?'

'No. Of course not.' She wrapped her arms around him and breathed him in. His scent was so very reassuring. 'It's in your nature to take charge and boss people around.'

He laughed and rubbed his hands down her back. 'I wrote to her in my capacity as your boss. And in my capacity as her Prince.'

'It's amazing how people are able to do an about-turn on the basis of a simple word from you.'

'It certainly is,' he agreed cheerfully.

'If I were a princess I would throw my weight around everywhere.'

He pulled back and tapped her on the nose. 'No, you wouldn't... And I don't throw my weight around,' he continued, feigning injury.

She grinned. 'You don't need to.' Stepping onto her toes, she pressed a kiss to his lips. 'Thank you.'

'Don't thank me yet—there are no guarantees the meeting will go well.'

She shrugged. 'Having met Leander, I have no expectations. I don't want to be part of her family or cause trouble for her. I just want to meet her.'

'Just...be careful. Don't build your hopes up.'

'I won't,' she promised, knowing his warning came from a place of caring, just as his interference had. If their roles had been reversed she would be warning him too.

'Good. I'll email you the details.'

'Thank you.'

One of the landlines on his desk buzzed. Sighing, Helios disentangled his arms from around her and pressed a button. 'Yes?'

'The French contingent have landed and are expected in twenty minutes.'

'Thank you. I'll leave in a moment to greet them.' Disconnecting the call, he shook his head and grimaced. 'One more kiss before duty calls?'

Obliging him, Amy leaned closer, raised herself onto the tips of her toes and brought her mouth to his, giving him one last, lingering kiss before he broke away with a rueful smile.

'I'll see you later and we'll do a *lot* more than kissing,' he said, then strode to the office door and opened it.

'The Koreans will be arriving within the hour,' Talia called as he walked past her.

He shook his head. 'Whose idea was it to have so many guests arrive a day early?'

'Yours,' Talia said, her expression deadpan.

'The next time I come up with such an idea you're welcome to chop my hands off.'

Hoping her demeanour was as nonchalant as his, Amy said goodbye to Talia. When she stepped out into the corridor Helios had already gone.

Gala day had arrived.

If Helios had been busy the day before, it was nothing compared to today. His whole morning had been spent meeting and greeting guests and making sure everything was running perfectly.

This was a day he'd looked forward to. No one could organise an occasion better than the Agon palace staff and he always enjoyed celebrating the events they hosted. He was immensely proud of his family and his island, and never turned down an opportunity to discuss its virtues with interesting people.

With his grandfather's situation as it was, he'd expected

the day to feel bittersweet, with the joy of celebrating the great man's life certain to be shadowed by the knowledge that it would soon be ending.

What Helios hadn't expected was to feel flat.

There was a strange lethargy within him which he was fighting against. Merely shaking hands and making eye contact felt like an effort. His mouth didn't want to smile. He hadn't even found the energy to be disappointed by the news that the solo violinist Talos had been working so closely with would not be able to perform due to severe stage fright.

One bright spot had been the unveiling of his grandfather's biography, which he and his brothers had looked through with their grandfather privately before the pre-Gala lunch. To see the man who'd raised them make his peace with Theseus had warmed him. And King Astraeus had surprised them all by revealing that he knew about Theseus's son and his plans to marry the boy's mother, and had given his blessing.

These were all things that should have had Helios slapping his brothers' backs and calling for a glass of champagne.

They'd gone through to the lunch together. Again, he should have revelled in the occasion, but the food had tasted like cardboard, the champagne flat on his tongue.

His fiancée, who'd arrived with her father and her brother, Helios's old school friend, had sat next to him throughout the lunch. He'd had to force the pleasantries expected of him. When Catalina's father, the King of Monte Cleure, had commented about the announcement of their engagement it had taken all his willpower not to slam his knife into the table and shout, *To hell with the announcement!*

And now, with the lunch over, the clock was ticking

furiously fast towards the time when he would make his engagement official to the world.

First, though, it was time for his grandfather to have a very exclusive viewing of his exhibition. It would include just the King and his three grandsons. Above everything else occurring that day, taking his grandfather to the exhibition created in his honour was the part Helios had most been looking forward to. The biography was the culmination of Theseus's hard work—a tangible acknowledgement of his love and pride—and this exhibition was the pinnacle of his own.

With his brothers by his side, Helios and a couple of courtiers now led his grandfather out into the palace grounds and along the footpath that led to the museum.

The joy and pride he'd anticipated feeling in this moment had been squashed by a very real sense of dread. And when they arrived at the museum doors he understood where the dread had come from.

Amy, Pedro and four other staff members closely involved in the exhibition were there to greet them at the museum's entrance. All were wearing their official uniforms and not a single hair was out of place. This was their big moment as much as his.

Talos wheeled their grandfather up to the line of waiting staff so they could be spoken to in turn. When they reached Amy the thuds in Helios's heart became a painful racket.

This was the first time she would meet his family. It would also be the last.

Bracing himself, he said, 'This is the exhibition curator, Amy Green. She's on secondment from England to organise it all.'

Not looking at Helios, Amy curtsied. 'It is an honour to meet you, Your Majesty.'

'The honour is mine,' his grandfather replied with that

wheeze in his voice Helios didn't think he would ever get used to. 'I've been looking forward to seeing this exhibition. Are you my tour guide?'

Her eyes darted to Pedro, who, as Head of Museum, was supposed to take the role of the King's guide.

Sensing her dilemma, Helios stepped in. 'Despinis Green would be delighted to be your guide. Let's get you inside and we can make a start.'

Inside the main exhibition room the four King Astraeus statues were lined up on their plinths. The sculptor of the fourth, which was covered and ready for unveiling, awaited his introduction to the King. When that was done, and the official photographers were in position, in a hushed silence the cover was removed and the King was able to see his own youthful image portrayed in marble for the first time.

For the longest, stillest moment the King simply stared at it, drinking in the vibrant, enigmatic quality of his statue. There was a collective exhalation of breath when he finally spoke of his delight and reached out a wizened hand to touch his own marble foot.

It was a moment Amy knew would be shown in all the world's press.

From there, the group progressed through to the rest of the exhibition.

The thought of being the King's personal tour guide should have had Amy in fits of terror, but it was a welcome relief. She had to concentrate so hard to keep up with etiquette and protocol that she could almost act as if Helios meant nothing to her other than as her boss.

But only almost.

After the King had examined and admired all of the military exhibits, they moved through to the room dedicated to his marriage to Queen Rhea, who had died five years previously. It was heartbreaking and yet uplifting to see the King's reaction first-hand.

Their wedding outfits had been carefully placed on mannequins and secured inside a glass cabinet. Queen Rhea's wedding dress was one of the most beautiful creations Amy had ever been privileged to handle, covered as it was with over ten thousand tiny diamonds and crystals.

King Astraeus gazed at it with moist eyes before saying to her, 'My Queen looked beautiful that day.'

Amy murmured her agreement. On the opposite wall hung the official wedding portrait. Queen Rhea had been a beauty by anyone's standards, but on that particular day there had been a glow about her that shone through the portrait and every photo that had been taken.

What would it be like to have a marriage such as theirs? Her own parents' marriage had seemed mostly happy, but once Amy had learned of her true parentage her memories had become slanted.

Her father's infidelity, although mostly never spoken of, remained a scar. Danny knew their father had cheated on his mother whilst she'd carried him. Neil knew their father had cheated on his mother back when he'd still been talking in broken sentences. They might love Amy as a true sister, and have nothing to do with anyone who saw things differently, but their relationship with their father bordered on uncomfortable. They didn't trust him and neither did Amy. She loved him very much, but the nagging doubts remained. When they'd still been living at home, and he'd been kept late at work, although they'd never said anything they'd all wondered if his excuses were true. And as for her mum…

To anyone looking in, their marriage would seem complete. They laughed together and enjoyed each other's company. But then Amy thought of the times she'd caught her mum going through her father's phone when she'd thought no one was looking and knew the pain she'd gone through had never fully mended. Once trust had been broken it was incredibly hard to repair.

King Astraeus and Queen Rhea's marriage had bloomed into that rarest of things: enduring, faithful love. The kind of love Amy longed to have. The kind of love she could never have when the man she loved was going to marry someone else...

The truth hit her like a bolt of lightning.

She *did* love him.

And as the revelation hit her so did another truth of equal magnitude.

She was going to lose him.

But he'd never been hers to lose, so she already had.

There was nothing for her to hold on to for support. All she could do was keep a grip on herself and wait for the wave of anguish to pass.

The only man she could ever be happy with, the only man she could ever find enduring love with, the only man she had trusted with the truth of her conception... He was marrying someone else. The happy ending she'd always hoped she would one day have would never be hers.

When she dared to look at Helios she found his gaze on her, a question resonating from his liquid eyes. He was as sensitive to her changes of mood as she was to his.

She forced a smile and straightened her posture, doing her best to resume her professional demeanour. Whatever personal torment she might have churning inside her, she still had a job to do.

This was King Astraeus's big day, one he'd spent eighty-seven years of duty and sacrifice working towards. This was his moment. It was also Helios's and his brothers' moment too. The three Princes loved their grandfather, and this day was as much for them to show their appreciation of him as to allow their great nation to celebrate. She wouldn't do anything to detract from the culmination of all their hard work.

Amy kept her head up throughout the rest of the tour, but as soon as it was over she fled, using the pretext of needing to change her outfit for the Gala. Thankfully all the other staff wanted to change too, so saw nothing strange in her behaviour.

Finally alone in her apartment, she sank onto the edge of her bed and cradled her head in her hands. The tears that had threatened to pour throughout the exhibition tour had now become blocked. The emotions raging inside her had compacted so tightly and painfully that the release she needed wouldn't come.

The truth of her feelings and the hopelessness of her love had hit her so hard she had shut down inside.

CHAPTER TEN

FIVE THOUSAND PEOPLE were settled in the amphitheatre, watching the Gala, enjoying the multitude of performances taking turns on the stage, the glorious sunshine, the food and the drink.

Amy, sitting with the rest of the museum staff, tried to enjoy what was a truly spectacular occasion. A world-famous operatic duo from the US had just completed a medley of songs from *The Phantom of the Opera*, and now a Russian ballet troupe had taken to the stage, holding everyone spellbound.

When they were done, the compère came bounding back on. 'Ladies and gentlemen, boys and girls, in a small addition to our official programme, I am proud to welcome to the stage His Royal Highness, Prince Helios.'

Huge cheers broke out around the amphitheatre as the crowd rose to their feet to applaud the popular Prince.

Amy's stone-filled feet moved of their own accord and she stood too. The coldness rippling through her was such that it felt as if someone had injected ice into her veins. All the hairs on her arms had sprung upright. Nausea didn't churn—no, it turned and twisted, as if her stomach had been locked in a superfast waltzer. And yet the tightness in her chest remained, coiling even tighter if that were possible.

Helios started his address by thanking everyone for attending, then launched into a witty monologue about his grandfather, which led him neatly into entreating the audience and the hundreds of millions of worldwide viewers to visit the exhibition of the King's life now being held in the palace museum.

And then he cleared his throat.

Amy's own throat closed.

'I would also like to take this opportunity to confirm the speculation about my private life that has been documented in the world's press for these past few weeks. I am honoured to announce that Princess Catalina Fernandez of Monte Cleure has consented to be my wife.'

Such raucous cheers broke out at the news that they drowned out the rest of his speech. The crowd was still whooping when Helios bowed to them all and left the stage, with a grin on his handsome face that looked to Amy's eyes more like a grimace.

Looking around the crowd, blinking to clear the cold fog enveloping her mind, Amy saw that the happiest faces were those of the Agonites who'd been lucky enough to get tickets for this event.

So now it was official.

Helios and the Princess were betrothed. There could be no backing out of the marriage now; not when the pride of two nations was at stake.

And the tiny spark of hope she hadn't even realised she carried in her extinguished into nothing.

Helios shook the hand of yet another post-Gala party guest and silently cursed Talos for disappearing with the violinist, who'd overcome her stage fright and wowed everyone that evening. His grandfather had retired to bed, exhausted after such a full day, leaving Helios and

Theseus to welcome all the people on the three-hundred-strong guest list.

Thank goodness protocol dictated that his fiancée acted in no official capacity until their nuptials had been exchanged. He still couldn't imagine her by his side. Or in his bed.

For the first time he accepted that Amy leaving Agon when he married would be a good thing. The best thing. For all of them.

All he knew was that he wouldn't be able to commit himself to Catalina as a husband if Amy resided under the palace roof and worked in the palace museum.

He'd thought when she had come back to him that everything would be all right and they could return to the way they'd been. But everything was not all right. Everything was worse.

His feelings for her...

There was a trapdoor looming in front of him and every step he made took him closer to falling through it. But he couldn't see in which direction the trapdoor lay. He just knew it was there, readying itself to swallow him whole.

As was normal at a Kalliakis party, none of the guests was in a hurry to leave. But, as was not normal, Helios was in no mood to party with them.

He did his duty and danced with the Princess. Again he felt nothing. His body didn't produce the slightest twinge. Nothing.

When Catalina finally left to catch her flight back to Monte Cleure with her father and brother Helios sought out Theseus, who was still going through the motions with the last of the straggling guests, and bore him away to his apartment.

From the look on his brother's face he needed a drink as much as Helios did.

For someone with a newly discovered son he adored, and a wedding to the boy's mother on the horizon, Theseus was acting like someone who'd been told he was to spend the rest of his life locked in the palace dungeons.

Much as Helios himself felt.

He'd never thought of alcohol as a tool for making problems better—on the contrary, he knew it tended to make matters worse. But he wasn't trying to make himself feel better. That wouldn't be possible. All he wanted was a healthy dose of numbness, even if only for a short time.

Was Amy waiting up for him?

They hadn't made their usual arrangement. It had been on the tip of his tongue to say his customary 'I'll come to you when I'm done' that morning, but this time something had stopped him. A sense of impropriety. Indecency. To parade the news of his fiancée to the world, then expect to slip between the covers with his mistress...

An image flashed into his mind of Amy standing in the cathedral in a wedding dress, of his mother's sapphire ring sliding onto her finger... It was an image he'd been fighting not to see for weeks.

He closed his eyes and breathed deeply.

This was madness.

He took another swig of neat gin and said without thinking, 'Those people watching the Gala. They have no idea of our sacrifices.'

'What?' Theseus slurred, staring at him with bloodshot eyes Helios knew mirrored his own.

'Nothing.'

Even if he'd wanted to confide in his brother, Theseus was clearly in no state to listen. He knew he should ask him what was wrong, but the truth was he was in no state of mind to listen either.

Moody silence followed, both brothers locked in their

own thoughts. The anticipated numbness failed to materialise. All the gin had brought on was the monster of all headaches.

Helios slammed his glass on the table. 'It's time for you to crawl to your own apartment—I'm going to bed.'

Theseus downed his drink without a murmur of protest and got to his unsteady feet. At least his brother was drunk enough to pass out without any problems, he mused darkly.

As Theseus staggered out Helios promised himself that he would leave Amy to sleep. It was long past midnight. Soon the sun would rise. To wake her would be cruel. To go to her at all, tonight of all nights, would be the height of crassness.

Dammit. He'd just become officially engaged. Couldn't he show some decorum for *one* night?

But the memory of Amy's ashen face during the exhibition tour refused to leave him and he knew he had to go to her. He had to see for himself that she was all right.

He walked down the passageway, promising himself that he would leave if there was no answer. When he reached her bedroom door, he rapped on it lightly.

Within seconds he heard the telltale turning of the lock.

When she'd opened the door Amy gazed up at him with an expression he couldn't distinguish. One that combined anguish, desire and need in one big melting pot.

And as he stepped into her welcoming arms he realised that, for all his talk of sacrifice, he didn't yet know how great his biggest sacrifice would be.

With the early-morning sunlight peeking through the curtains, Amy gazed at Helios's sleeping form.

Hours after the post-Gala party had finished he'd come to her. And for the first time since they'd started their relationship all those months ago, nothing physical had happened between them.

Until he'd quietly knocked on her door she'd been trying to sleep, without any luck. She hadn't wanted to stay awake for him. She'd been scared that he wouldn't come to her and equally scared that he would.

Images had tortured her: thoughts of Helios and the Princess dancing together, becoming an official couple, discussing their wedding plans, showing the world how perfect they were for each other. Her stomach had ached so much it had been as if she'd swallowed a jug of battery acid.

With the hours ticking down until morning, she'd assumed the worst. She'd seen the helicopters and limousines taking their honoured guests away from the palace and had been unable to stop herself from wondering which of them carried the Princess.

Then, just as any hope that he would appear had gone, Helios had arrived at her door with bloodshot eyes, exhaustion etched on his face. He'd stripped off his clothes, climbed into her bed, pulled her into his arms and promptly fallen asleep.

How many more nights would he do this? How many more nights would they have together?

The official announcement had set off an alarm clock in her battery-acid-filled stomach and its persistent tick was excruciating.

Careful not to wake him, she sat up, doing nothing but drink him in.

How many more nights could she do this? Simply look at him?

Later that day he would be flying to the US for the start of an official state visit.

In her heart she knew that now, this moment, truly was the beginning of the end for them.

She reached out a hand and gently palmed his cheek. He nuzzled sleepily into her hand and kissed it. Lightly, she began to trace her fingers over the handsome face she loved so much, from his forehead—over which locks of hair had fallen—to his cheekbones, then over the bump on his nose, the bow of his lips, the jawline where thick stubble had broken out, and down his neck. She took his silver chain between her fingers and then touched the mandarin garnet necklace around her own neck.

It had been a birthday present from him, one he'd given her shortly after they'd started sleeping together. Of all the gifts he'd bestowed upon her, it was the one to which she felt the closest. The meaning behind it, the fact Helios had gone out of his way to find an item of jewellery made with her birthstone, meant that she'd swallowed her guilt and taken it out of the padded envelope where the rest of the jewellery he'd given her remained.

Whatever lay in the future, she knew she would never take it off again.

Slowly she explored his naked body, trailing her fingers over his collarbone and shoulder, down his right arm, lacing them through the fine black hair covering his forearm. When she reached his hand and took each finger in turn, gently pressing into them, he gave a light squeeze in response but otherwise remained still.

After repeating her exploration down his left arm, she moved to his chest. Helios's breathing had changed. It no longer had the deep, rhythmic sound of sleep. A heavier, more ragged sound was coming from him.

Over his pecs she traced her hands, encircling his dark brown nipples, catching the dark hair that was spread finely across his chest, pressing her palm down where the beat of his heart was strongest, then moving them across his ribcage and down to his abdomen...

His erection stopped her in her tracks.

Sucking in a breath, she ignored it, outlining the smooth skin on either side and drawing her fingers over his narrow hips. Gently spreading his muscular thighs, she knelt between them and carried her exploration down his left leg, tracing the silvery scar on his calf—the result of being thrown from a horse at the age of nine—and down to his feet. Then she moved to his right leg, this time starting from his toes and making her way up...all the way to the line where his thigh met his groin.

Helios's hand dug into her hair, spearing it, his breaths now erratic. Still only using her fingers, she traced the long stretch of his erection, cupping him, delighting in his tortured groans, before she put him out of his misery and ran her tongue along its length, then took him into her mouth.

For an age she moved him with her hand whilst licking and sucking. His hand cradled her scalp, massaging it, but he let her set the pace. Heat bubbled deep inside her, burning her from her core outwards, enflaming her skin. Giving him pleasure gave her as much joy as when he pleasured her.

When she sensed him getting close to breaking point she pulled away, unable to give him the playful smile she would normally give. She had never felt less playful when making love to him.

Moving up to straddle him, she gazed into his eyes, thrilling to see the heady desire ringing in them. He cupped her neck and pulled her down to meet his mouth. His tongue swept into hers, his kiss full of all the dark, potent neediness flowing through her own veins.

Slowly, with their lips and tongues still entwined, she sank onto him until he was fully sheathed inside her.

Breaking the kiss, she pulled back to sit atop him, needing to look at him.

As his groans became louder he placed one hand flat on her breast, whilst his other hand held tightly to her hip, steadying and supporting her. Then, with her hands resting lightly on his shoulders, she began to move. The feel of him deep inside her, the friction of their movements, it all built on the sensations already whirling inside her.

She could make love to this man every day for the rest of her life and it still wouldn't be enough. She would always want—need—more. Even if they had all the time in the world it wouldn't be enough time for her to look at his face, to touch him, to hear his voice, to witness his smile.

But there was only now, this moment in time when it was just them. There was no palace, no duty...

Just them. One man. One woman.

She wished she could hold on to it for ever.

She tried to hold back the climax growing within her, tried to blunt her responses, but it was all too intoxicating. With a cry that was as much dismay as it was delight, the pulsations swept through her, starting deep in the very heart of her and rippling out to embrace her every atom.

She threw herself down to bury her face in his neck and his arms immediately wrapped around her. A strangled groan escaped his mouth and he gave one last thrust upwards as his own climax tore through him with the same strength as her own. Both of them rode it for as long as they could until there was nothing left but their breaths, burning heavily into each other's necks.

The hotel, arranged by Talia under Helios's instructions, had a charming air to it, an ambience that carried through inside, through the cosy lobby and into the even cosier restaurant.

It was Agon's oldest hotel and a favourite on the tourist trail. It was guaranteed to be busy, whatever the time of year. Thus, two women could meet and dine together during the lunchtime rush without attracting any attention. It was safe for Amy's birth mother here. No one would know who she was. No one would report back to her husband. Ignorance would continue to be bliss for him.

As strange as she knew it to be, Amy would have recognised Neysa even if she hadn't known who she was. Her heart stuttered as she was caught in the gaze of eyes that were identical to her own.

This was the woman who had carried her in her womb for nine months.

This was the woman who had abandoned her.

Neysa Soukis hesitated before asking, 'Amy...?'

'Neysa?' Calling her Mum or Mother was *not* an option.

Grasping the outstretched hand, Amy marvelled at how it was an identical size to her own. It was like seeing a model of herself twenty years from now, although she doubted she would ever be as well groomed. Neysa was expensively dressed and immaculately coiffured.

After ordering drinks and some mezzes Neysa gave a brittle smile, opened her mouth and then closed it again.

Amy filled the silence. 'Why didn't you want to meet me?'

Fingers similar to her own but older, and with buffed nails, drummed on the table. 'You are a stranger to me.' Her English accent was heavy and unpractised.

'You carried me. You gave birth to me.' *You abandoned me.* 'Weren't you curious?'

'I have a life now. Husband. A son.'

Yes... Her son. Leander. The man-child Neysa doted on.

'What made you change your mind?'

She gave a harsh bark of laughter. 'The threat that my husband would learn of you.'

That would be Helios's doing. He was not a man one could say no to. Neysa was here because Helios had effectively blackmailed her, not because she wanted to meet the child she'd given up.

'Leander could tell your husband.'

'Leander would never tell.'

Neysa's confidence in this statement didn't surprise her. Helios had done some more digging into the mother-son relationship and discovered that Leander's father had all but given up on him. Neysa was the one to lavish him with love and the all-important money. He was dependent on her. If she withdrew her funds he would, heaven forbid, have to get a job and keep it.

If her husband was to learn that Neysa had been keeping such a monumental secret from him throughout their twenty-five-year marriage who knew how he would react? Both Neysa and Leander might be thrown off the gravy train they worshipped so much.

A waiter appeared with a tray of drinks.

'Did you ever think of me?' Amy asked when they were alone again.

A flicker of something she couldn't decipher crossed Neysa's face. 'Many times.'

She was lying. Amy didn't know how she could be certain of this, but certain she was. Neysa had forged a new life for herself, with a rich husband two decades her senior. Amy was a dirty little secret she couldn't afford to let anyone find out about. She had no interest in her child. Her only interest was in protecting her secret.

'I knew your father would take good care of you,' Neysa explained earnestly. Too earnestly.

She had known nothing of the sort, and neither had she tried to find out. For all she knew Amy might have been dumped in an orphanage. She'd had no way of knowing that Elaine—the woman who had taken Neysa into her home and trusted her with her young son, the woman Neysa had betrayed in such a heinous way without one word of remorse—had raised Amy as her own.

Amy had spent seventeen years hoping that it had been shame which had kept Neysa away. That she'd acknowledged that what she'd done to the Green family had been so great a sin that she couldn't bring herself to face Elaine and say sorry.

She couldn't have been more wrong.

At least her father had been genuinely remorseful. Her mum had promised her that. *He'd* acknowledged the terrible deed he'd done and had spent twenty-seven years trying to make amends for it. One mad weekend alone, without his wife and with a hot young woman parading herself around the house before him... He'd been too weak not to take advantage and he'd paid the price every day of his life since.

Looking at her birth mother now, Amy couldn't believe her mum had been able to love her the way she did. Amy was the image of Neysa. Every time her mum had looked at Amy's face she must have seen the image of the woman who had betrayed her and the living proof of her husband's infidelity.

How could Amy even be in the same room as this woman? Neysa hadn't cared that she'd almost destroyed Amy's mum—her *real* mum...the woman who had loved her every day of her life from the age of two weeks.

And she'd been scared that her mum secretly wanted to get rid of her? Never. Not her loving, generous mum.

The waiter returned to the table with their food.

Amy waited until he'd laid everything out before getting to her feet and hooking the strap of her handbag over her shoulder.

'You have nothing to fear from me,' she said slowly. 'I want no part of your life. I wanted to see you. And now I have.'

'You are going?'

'I shouldn't have come. Goodbye, Neysa.'

Leaving her birth mother open-mouthed in shock, Amy made her way out of the hotel and into the warm spring street brimming with tourists.

She stood for a moment, breathing in the sweet scent. She hadn't found a single place in Agon where the air didn't smell good. And yet an acrid odour lingered around her from her encounter.

Breathing heavily, Amy raised her eyes to the sky and thanked whatever benevolent being that was up there for allowing Neysa to abandon her.

Who would she be if she'd been raised on Agon under Neysa's narcissistic hand? If she'd grown up with Leander? If she'd lived without Danny and Neil's fierce protection, her mum's loving guidance and her dad's silent but constant presence?

And she thanked Helios too. His interference had allowed her to put to bed one of the biggest questions in her life: who had made her?

That 'who' was someone she had no wish to see again. But at least she knew that now. Thanks to Helios she could move on and stop wondering what if...?

As she thought his name her phone buzzed. It was a brief message from him, checking that everything was okay. Her darling Helios was on a state visit to America and had still found the time to think of her and send her a message.

But how could she be okay? she thought as she replied, saying that she was fine and that she would explain everything to him later, when he called. Which he would. He called her every night when he travelled abroad.

How could everything be okay when very soon she would have to say goodbye to the one person who *did* make everything okay?

CHAPTER ELEVEN

AMY CARRIED ON as best she could over the next few days, never letting her smile drop or her shoulders slouch. She was determined that no one looking at her would have reason to suspect that she was suffering in any way.

The entire island was aflame with gossip following the confirmation of Helios's engagement to the Princess. Naturally this enthusiasm was tripled in the palace itself. Everywhere she went she heard excited chatter. It had got to the stage where, even if she didn't understand what was being said, she imagined it was all about the forthcoming wedding.

The date had been set. In six weeks and one day Helios would marry. It was going to happen sooner than she had thought. She had forgotten about all the work for the wedding that had been going on behind the scenes. Helios had wisely never mentioned it in any of their calls.

Other than in the privacy of her apartment, the only place she found any crumb of solace was amongst the staff in the museum. Whereas the visitors—whose numbers were daily in the thousands—kept up a non-stop commentary about the wedding, the staff took a different approach. They knew Amy had been Helios's lover. *Everyone* had known. So when she was in the same room conversation was kept as far away from matrimony as it was possible to get. But she caught the pitying, often worried glances that were thrown her way.

Her colleagues were a good, kindly, close-knit bunch who supported and looked out for each other. It was in this vein that Claudia, one of the tour guides, approached her in the staff room during Amy's break on the Friday after the Gala.

'I'm sorry to disturb your lunch, but Princess Catalina is here.'

Amy immediately froze, as if a skewer of ice had been thrust into her central nervous system. Somehow she managed to swallow her mouthful of tomato and feta salad, the food clawing its way down her numbed throat.

The tour guide bit her lip. 'She is asking for you.'

'For *me*?' she choked out.

Claudia nodded. 'She wants a tour of the King's exhibition and has asked for you personally.'

It was on the tip of her tongue to ask if Helios was with her, but she stopped herself in time. If Helios was with the Princess they wouldn't need Amy. Helios could do the tour himself.

She didn't even know if he was back from his trip to America. She'd thought he was due back sometime that afternoon.

She'd spent five nights without him.

It had been much harder than any of their other separations. She'd missed him desperately, as a small child missed home.

It was a pain she would have to get used to.

Her main source of comfort had come from Benedict, who had stayed in her apartment during Helios's absence. The lovable black Labrador had seemed to sense Amy's despondency and had kept close to her. Their evenings together had been spent on the sofa, watching films, Benedict's head on her lap.

When she returned to England she would get her own Labrador for company.

Blowing out a long breath of air, Amy closed the lid of her salad box and forced herself to her feet. She couldn't manage another bite.

'Where is she?'

'In the entrance hall.'

'Okay. Give me two minutes to use the bathroom.'

Concentrating on her breathing, Amy took her handbag and locked herself in the staff bathroom. She took stock of her reflection in the mirror and pulled a face. Hastily she loosened her hair from its ponytail, brushed it and then tied it back again. From her handbag she pulled her compressed face powder and a make-up brush and applied a light covering. She would have added eyeliner and lip gloss but her hands were shaking too much.

As a means of buying time for herself, her trip to the bathroom was wasted. The hopes she'd had of making it through the next few months without having to meet the Princess had been blown to pieces.

Why *her*? Why had the Princess asked for her by name? How did she even know who she was?

Terror gripped her, but she forced herself to straighten up and pushed air into her cramped lungs.

The Princess was an honoured guest, she reminded herself. It was natural she would ask for the exhibition's curator to be her guide. *Just be professional,* she told herself as she left her sanctuary.

The Princess awaited her in the entrance hall, flanked by two huge bodyguards.

She was the epitome of glamour, wearing skintight white jeans, an off-the-shoulder rose-pink top, an elegant pale blue silk scarf and blue high heels. Her ebony hair was loose around her shoulders, and an expensive pair of sunglasses sat atop her head.

But there was more to her than mere glamour; a beautiful, almost ethereal aura she carried effortlessly. She was a princess in every sense of the word. If she slept on a hundred mattresses no doubt she would still feel the pea at the bottom.

Swallowing down the dread lodged like bile in her throat, Amy strode towards her with a welcoming smile. 'Your Highness, I am Amy Green,' she said, dropping into a curtsy. 'It is an honour to meet you.'

The Princess smiled graciously. 'Forgive me for disturbing your break, but I wanted a tour of the exhibition. I've been told you're the curator and that you have a wealth of knowledge about my fiancé's family. I couldn't think of a better person to show me around.' All of this was delivered in almost faultless English.

'I am honoured.' And it *was* an honour. A true honour.

They went slowly around the exhibition rooms, with Amy politely discussing the various artefacts and their context in the Kalliakis family's history. She answered the Princess's questions as best she could whilst all too aware of her constantly clammy hands.

Princess Catalina might look as if she would feel the pea through a hundred mattresses, but she was so much more than a princess from the realms of fairy tales.

She was a flesh and blood human.

It wasn't until they entered The Wedding Room, with the bodyguards keeping a close but respectable distance, that the Princess showed any real animation. She was immediately drawn to Queen Rhea's wedding dress, staring at it adoringly for long, excruciating seconds before she turned to Amy.

'Isn't this the most beautiful dress?' she said with her gaze fixed on her, her eyes searching.

Amy nodded, the bile in her throat burning.

'The dressmaker who made this has agreed to come out of retirement to make mine. I'm having my first fitting tomorrow—did Helios tell you I will be staying at the palace for the weekend?'

'I've heard it mentioned,' she whispered. She'd overheard a couple of the tour guides discussing the visit. They'd been wondering whether the Princess would bring her fabulous Vuitton bag with her. She had.

The Princess smiled. Despite her amiability, sadness lurked behind her eyes. It filled Amy with horror.

'There isn't much that happens within the palace that's kept secret, is there?'

Flames licked her cheeks. It took all her willpower for her not to cover them with her hands.

The Princess seemed not to want a response of the verbal kind. Her sad, probing eyes never left Amy's face, but she smiled. 'I thank you for your time.'

'Do you not want to see the other exhibition rooms?' Caught off guard, Amy took the Princess's hand; a major breach of protocol. She had the softest skin imaginable.

The Princess's squeeze of her hand was gentle and... forgiving? The smile thrown at her was enigmatic. 'I have seen what I came to see.'

Nodding at her bodyguards, she glided away, tall, lithe and poised.

Amy stared at the retreating figure and rubbed the nape of her neck, feeling as if all the wind had been knocked out of her.

The Princess knew.

Dear God, the Princess *knew*.

* * *

Her concentration lost, Amy wandered around the exhibition rooms, praying no one would ask her anything that required any thought to answer. Feeling nauseous to the bone, she eventually settled in the entrance hall, trying her hardest to keep herself together.

But all too soon the influx of guests had reduced and reality was given space to taunt her.

The marble sculptures of the four Kings kept drawing her attention, and as much as she knew she shouldn't she went and stood before them.

King Astraeus the Third had been famed for his wisdom. She wished he could transmute some of it to herself. But it was King Astraeus the Second she couldn't tear her eyes away from. His resemblance to Helios was so strong she could fool herself into thinking it *was* him.

One day, decades from now, a statue much like this would be made of him. If she closed her eyes she could see it, could envisage every inch of the ten-foot marble figure. If the sculptor were to show her the block of stone she would be able to tell him where every line and sinew should go.

It came to her then what she'd been doing that night after the Gala—or early morning—when she'd touched every part of him. She'd been committing him to memory. She hadn't been able to face the truth at the time, but it hit her now. She'd imprinted him on her mind because her subconscious had known that it would be their last time.

Their time together was truly over.

The walls of the great exhibition room suddenly loomed large over her, swallowing her. The statues and the other exhibits blurred. She needed air. But to flee outside would mean risking seeing the Princess or, worse, Helios. She couldn't face him with an audience watching. The next time she saw him she had to be alone with him.

Pulling her identity card from around her neck and stuffing it in her pocket, she walked into the main museum, hurrying through the crowds of visitors until she found Claudia.

'I've got a migraine coming,' she said. 'I need to rest—can you give my apologies to Pedro?'

'Sure.' Claudia looked at her with concern Amy knew she didn't deserve. 'Can I get you anything?'

'No, thank you. Please, I just need to get some sleep in a darkened room.'

Not waiting for a response, Amy wove her way through the remaining people to the private staff entrance to the palace, then hurried up the stairs to her apartment, kicked off her shoes and threw herself onto the bed.

She might not really have a migraine, but her head pounded as if a dozen church bells were ringing inside it. Let it pound. Let the bells clang as loudly as they could and the decibels increase.

She deserved nothing less.

Helios stood in the green stateroom, holding discussions with a group of German business people who wanted to invest considerable sums in Agon's infrastructure and, naturally, recoup their investment with considerable profit. With them was Agon's Transport Minister.

Agon had its own senate, and committees which decided on issues such as outside investors, but an endorsement from one of the royal Princes meant this would be as good as a done deal. Helios knew his opinions carried a great deal of weight and did his utmost to use his influence wisely.

When his phone rang he was tempted to ignore it, but

it was his personal phone and only the most important people in his life had been given the number. He frowned when he saw Amy's name on the screen.

He hadn't had a chance to call her and let her know he was back from his trip to the US. In any case he'd assumed she would be busy at the museum... She hardly ever called him and *never* out of the blue.

'Excuse me,' he murmured to the delegation, stepping away from the group with an apologetic smile. He swiped the screen to answer. 'Amy?'

'I'm sorry to disturb you,' she said, her usual soft tones sounding strangely muffled. 'I know you're busy, but I wondered if you're coming to me tonight.'

Not only did she never call him, she never questioned his movements either. A dark sense of foreboding snaked up his spine. 'Is something the matter?'

He heard her hesitation.

'I just need to see you.'

He looked at his watch. 'Where are you?'

'In my apartment.'

'Are you ill?'

'No. Not really. Not ill, ill.'

He wanted to pump her for information but, aware of the delegation, Talia and all the courtiers eyeing him with curiosity, he resisted.

'I'll be with you as soon as I can,' he said, before hanging up.

He'd be with her as soon as he could politely extricate himself. Something was wrong. The cold dread wedged in the marrow of his bones told him that.

It was half an hour before he was able to extract himself from the group, saying he had some personal business to catch up with and that he would see them at the dinner being held in their honour. He then told Talia that she could leave early. Talia didn't argue the matter—in fact he would swear she left so quickly she left a trail of dust in her wake. He didn't blame her. It had been a long few weeks and she must be exhausted.

When he reached his office he cut through to his apartment and slipped through the passageway into Amy's apartment. She answered his knock quickly, with a startled expression on her face.

'I didn't think I would see you until much later,' she said wanly. 'I hope I haven't put you out.'

'You could never put me out.' He studied her carefully. Her face was grey, her eyes were bloodshot and her hair looked unkempt. 'Have you been crying?'

She bit her lip and took a shuddery breath. Closing the door, she rested her hand on the handle. 'The Princess knows.'

'Catalina? What does she know?'

'About us.' She met his gaze. 'She came to the museum. She wanted me, personally, to give her a tour of the exhibition.'

'You're the exhibition's curator,' he pointed out.

She shook her head. 'It was more than that. She knows, Helios. I think… I think she's heard rumours about us. Maybe someone saw me walking Benedict… I think she was looking for confirmation. Whatever I did, I don't know, but I'm sure something confirmed her suspicions.'

He ran a hand through his hair. 'Even assuming you're right, there is nothing for you to worry about. Catalina isn't stupid. She knows there will be other women.'

It was the wrong thing to say. Amy looked as if he'd slapped her.

'I didn't mean it like that,' he added hastily. 'All I meant was that Catalina has no illusions of fidelity. You know there is no love between us.'

There was nothing between them. Not the smallest twinge.

Shaking her head again, Amy sidestepped past him and went through to her kitchen. 'You're a fool if you believe that. She *wants* it to be a love match.'

'No…'

'Yes,' she said through gritted teeth. 'She does. Whatever you think you know about her, you've got it wrong.'

'She does not love me.'

'Not yet.'

Her eyes bored into his as her words hung in the air between them, then she turned sharply and pulled a bottle of white wine out of the fridge.

'Glass?' she asked.

'You're drinking already?' A trace of his bemusement cut through the darkening atmosphere.

'Right now I need it.'

She leant against the work surface and closed her eyes briefly, then poured them both some wine. When she passed his glass to him she snatched her hand away before there was any chance of their fingers brushing.

She went to take a sip from her own, but as she brought it to her mouth her face crumpled.

Stepping quickly to her, Helios took the glass from her shaking hand and placed it with his own on the counter, then wrapped his arms around her.

At first she resisted, but then she gave in to it, almost burying her head in his chest. Within seconds his shirt was wet with her tears.

'Don't cry, *matakia mou,*' he whispered, stroking her hair. 'It will all work out. I promise.'

'How?' she asked between sobs. 'How can it ever work out? We're breaking her heart.'

'No, we're not.'

'We *are*. Maybe she doesn't love you yet, but she wants to. She wants your marriage to work. Have you even seen her since you got back from America?'

'I've been busy.'

Disentangling herself from his hold, Amy grabbed a handful of tissues from a box. The tears kept falling.

'Helios, the Princess is your fiancée. She's come all this way to see you. You should be with her. This time before your marriage should be spent getting to know each other...'

'We do know each other.'

'Do you?' She raised her shoulders. 'Then tell me this— what are her dreams? What are her fears? Can you answer any of that? You're going to be spending the rest of your life with her.'

'Yes,' he agreed tightly. 'The rest of my life. But the rest of my life hasn't started yet.'

'It started the minute you put an engagement ring on her finger.'

The engagement ring. He'd told Catalina to choose her own, with the excuse that she would be the one wearing it and so she should have something that was to her own taste. He hadn't been able to bring himself to do the deed himself.

He knew she coveted his mother's sapphire ring. Growing up, he'd always known that ring would be given to the woman he made his wife. He'd had the ready-made excuse that it was a feature of the exhibition to stop him sliding it onto Catalina's finger yet, but he'd promised that when the exhibition was over it would be hers.

'I can't do this any more,' Amy said, her voice choking on the words. 'What we're doing to the Princess is abhorrent. She's a princess but she's *real*, not a fairy-tale creation. She's human, and the guilt is eating me alive.'

He moved to take her back into his arms but she held up a hand to him and shook her head.

'We can't. *I* can't. I won't be the cause of someone else's misery. How can I when I've seen first-hand the damage it causes?' Wiping away a fresh batch of tears, she swallowed before saying, 'When I came to Agon and I wanted to find my birth mother, it wasn't because I wanted to form a relationship with her. I wanted to know my other family and my roots, yes, and I was *desperate* to see what she looked like. But what I really wanted from her was to know why.'

'Why she abandoned you?' She had told him on the phone about the meeting. How she had left within minutes, abandoning the mother who'd abandoned her.

'Partly. What I really wanted to know was how she could have done what she did to my mum. She was her au pair— Mum had trusted her with her child and welcomed her into her home. My mum is the most loving woman in the world. There is no way she would have treated Neysa with anything but kindness. How could she sneak around behind her back with her husband? What kind of evil selfishness makes a person act like that?'

'Did you ask her that?'

'No. I was so desperate to get away from her that I didn't ask her any of the questions I'd been storing up for seventeen years.' She gave a half-hearted shrug. 'And now I don't want to know. I don't want to hear her excuses because that's all they'll be. I don't think she feels any remorse.'

'Amy, our situation is very different. How Neysa and your father behaved…it's not like for like.'

'You might not be married yet, but the intention and commitment are still there. The agony my mum must have gone through… She never got over it. She forgave my father but she's never forgotten, and she's not been able to trust him properly since.'

More tears fell, harder now, turning her face into a torrent of salt water.

'I can't live with the guilt. I've spent my entire life, through no fault of my own, being a person people point at and whisper about. I've had to work so hard to make myself believe that I didn't deserve it and that I was innocent. But how can I be innocent when *I'm* the one now causing someone's misery? I don't want to be the selfish woman Neysa is. I don't want to hurt anyone. The Princess is a good and lovely person and she doesn't deserve this—no one does. Whatever she's been raised to be, she's still human.'

The depth of Amy's guilt and misery stabbed at him, right in his guts, evoking a wave of shame that came rushing through him, a wave so powerful that he reeled and held on to the small kitchen table for support.

'Listen to me,' he said urgently. 'The very fact you feel such guilt proves you are *nothing* like Neysa, so put such thoughts from your mind. You would never hurt anyone, not on purpose.'

'But that is what I've been doing!' she cried. 'I'm *exactly* like her.'

'No! All you inherited from Neysa was her looks. Everything else came from Elaine and the rest of your English family and the goodness that is *you*. You are a good person—the best I know.'

She didn't look the slightest bit convinced by anything he'd said. Helios's mind worked frantically as he tried to think of a solution whereby Amy's guilt could be obliterated. But nothing came to him. He *had* to marry someone of royal blood to secure the Kalliakis line.

He was hurting her, the last thing he'd ever wanted to do. Not Amy. Not her. Not ever.

His father had done more than hurt his mother physically; the destruction had been emotional too. Helios had always known he would never follow his footsteps on the physical side, but to discover he was guilty of an emotional destruction every bit as great...

Something that felt suspiciously like panic clawed at him, biting and contracting through every part of him, converging in his stomach into a pain so acute he wanted to shout out with the agony of it all.

His relationship with Amy was long past being the light, playful interlude it had begun as. Along the way it had developed into something so deep he feared he would no longer be able to see the light if they went any further.

If he had the slightest ounce of decency he would let Amy go before he destroyed her completely.

CHAPTER TWELVE

FOLDING HIS ARMS across his chest, Helios stared at Amy, wondering how he was going to cope without seeing her beautiful face every day and making love to her every night. She was so much more to him than just his lover. She was his best friend, the first true friend he'd ever had. She'd been brought into his life not through her own wealth or social standing but simply by being Amy.

Amy gazed back at him with the same intensity and attempted a brave smile. 'Do you think there's a parallel world out there, where we can be free to be together and love each other?'

Love?

She must have registered the shock in his eyes at her use of the *L* word for she laughed wanly. 'Oh, I do love you. Very much. More than I ever knew was possible.'

He stepped out of her reach, backing himself against the kitchen door. He didn't know how to answer. He couldn't think.

His private phone buzzed in his pocket. He pulled it out and rejected the call without looking at it.

'Love is not something I have ever required,' he finally said, his brain reeling as much as his body.

'I know that.' Her chin wobbled and she took deep breaths, raising her eyes to the ceiling.

'*Theos*, Amy, you...' He blew out a long breath as his brain scrambled to unravel itself. 'I've always known I must marry for duty. Love isn't something I've ever expected or thought about. It has no place in my life, you must see that?'

'Yes, I do.'

Of course she did. Amy knew his full ancestral history better than she could ever know her own.

'If you love me then how can you leave me?' he asked, still shell-shocked at her declaration but grasping at straws.

'Because I want to be able to look at my reflection every day and not throw darts at it,' she answered with a choked laugh. 'And my leaving isn't just to do with Catalina.'

There. She'd finally uttered the Princess's name aloud.

'I might have been made from a dirty secret but I don't want to live my life as one. You're right that I'm not Neysa, and I will not allow myself to be like her. Even if you wanted it—even if you loved me—you're not in a position to give me the commitment and fidelity I need. I want to be yours. Just yours. Openly yours. With the whole world knowing we belong together. I can't make love with you while you're sleeping in the bed of another, and I can't make love knowing I'm good enough for sex but not good enough for for ever.'

What she didn't say was that Helios had lodged himself so deeply into her heart she doubted there was room left in there for any other man to find an opening. Her heart belonged to him now.

She should have left weeks ago. The physical pain she'd experienced when he'd told her of his intention to marry as soon as possible should have acted as a warning. If she'd gone then she would have left with her pride intact and her heart would still have enough room for someone else.

His face contorted. 'Don't you *ever* say you're not good enough.'

'But that's how I feel,' she said, shrugging her shoulders helplessly. 'I know that's not your intention, and that you don't think or believe that—I *know*—but I've spent most of my life feeling like a dirty secret. For us to carry on, even if it's only until you marry, will *make* me one.'

He didn't say anything, just stared at her as if he were seeing her for the first time.

'Helios, when you marry the Princess be faithful to her. Give your marriage a chance. She deserves that and so do you.'

'You sound like you're planning to leave now...' A strange look flashed in his eyes and suddenly he sprang to life like *Galatea*, the statue created with such love by Pygmalion.

He strode out of the kitchen and into her bedroom, taking in the suitcases on the bed, half-filled with clothing.

His face contorted and he shook his head. 'No.'

'Helios...'

'No.' His hands clenched into fists.

She could see him fighting the urge to throw her cases out of the window.

His phone buzzed again, the third time it had rung in as many minutes.

'Answer it,' she insisted. 'It might be important.'

'This is important.' After a moment's pause he swore and pulled the phone to his ear. 'Yes?'

After a few moments his demeanour changed. As he listened he straightened his neck and rolled his shoulders, breathing deeply. His only contribution to the conversation was a few short words of Greek.

'I need to go,' he said when he'd finished the call. 'My

grandfather's suffering from a mild infection and is fighting with the doctors over his treatment.'

'I hope it's nothing too serious,' she said, immediately concerned.

'Just my grandfather being a stubborn old man.' He rubbed his chin and glared at her with his jaw clenched. 'I'll be back later. Don't even *think* of going anywhere.'

She didn't answer.

'I need to hear it, Amy. Tell me you won't go anywhere or do anything until I get back. Promise me.'

Knowing even as she spoke them that her words were a lie, she said, 'I'll be here.'

His shoulders loosened a little. Pacing over to her, he took her face in his hands and crushed her lips with his mouth, kissing her as if he'd been starved of her kisses for ever. And then he dropped his hold on her and walked out of her bedroom.

She heard the slam of the interconnecting door as he left.

Theos, his grandfather had to be the most stubborn man alive. He was refusing the intravenous drugs his doctors wanted to give him.

What could he do? He couldn't force him. The King wasn't a baby to be coaxed into doing his elders' bidding.

That hadn't stopped Helios from trying to make him see reason. Now he wanted to tear his hair out, to claw at his scalp and draw blood.

'At least he's not in pain,' Talos said quietly.

Their grandfather hadn't resisted painkillers for the pain racking his body. The cancer, kept at bay by months of chemotherapy, was making another, deadlier assault on his body. No one would say it, but time was slipping away from them.

One good thing to come out of the mess this day had turned into was the news from Theseus, who had gone tearing after Jo, the mother of his child, a couple of days ago. The fool had realised when it was almost too late that he truly did love her, and luckily it seemed Jo loved him too and had agreed to marry him.

No coercion, no thoughts of duty. They were marrying for love. Helios had never heard his brother sound so happy.

Both his brothers were marrying.

As Talos—who was marrying his violinist—had chosen someone not of royal blood, any child he had would not be in the line of succession to the throne, but Toby, Theseus's beautiful son, had already secured the throne for the next generation. Until Helios's own children were born.

Helios sighed and got to his feet. 'I need to change for dinner.'

He wished he could pull out of it, but it was a matter of honour amongst his family that personal matters never got in the way of duty. And this dinner was duty.

Nausea fermented in him as he remembered that Catalina would be attending. She was already there in the palace. He still couldn't bring himself to call her.

As much as he wanted to, there wasn't time to make a diversion to Amy's apartment and check that she was okay. Instead he fired off a quick message to her before showering and changing into his dinner jacket. He put his cufflinks on during his walk to the designated dining room for the evening, his courtiers struggling to keep up with his long strides.

Forcing bonhomie, Helios plastered a smile on his face and entered the dining room, where the delegation was waiting for him. Catalina was already there, holding court like a professional. When she saw him she excused herself to join him.

If she really did suspect him and his relationship with Amy, she covered it well.

'I understand your grandfather is unwell?' she said quietly.

'He's been better.' It was all he could bring himself to answer with.

Why couldn't he feel anything for her? Here was a beautiful, compassionate woman of royal blood and all he felt when she touched him was cold.

He tried again, using a milder tone of voice. 'He has an infection.'

She smiled sympathetically. 'I hope he recovers quickly.'

'So do I.'

But he didn't hold out much hope. These past five months had been a battle to keep him alive long enough for him to see the Gala. That was all his grandfather had been focusing on. Now, with the Gala over, his grandsons all paired off and the succession to the throne secured, King Astraeus was preparing to die.

His duty was done. His grandfather wanted to be with the woman he'd loved for his entire adult life.

And Amy had said she loved *him*.

Helios wished he could unhear those words.

What kind of selfish monster was he to tie her to him when he knew doing so was destroying her?

It was possibly the longest meal of his life. For once, the power of speech had deserted him. He couldn't think of a single witty remark or any of the tales that usually had guests enthralled.

Throughout the meal disquiet grew within him, a foreboding which came upon him from an unseen direction.

As soon as the coffee had been cleared away he cleared

his throat. 'My apologies, ladies and gentlemen, but I need to retire for the evening. I know I haven't been very good company this evening—I think exhaustion has crept up on me—but be assured that I am very impressed with every-thing you've told me and will give my recommendation to the committee early next week.'

When he'd finished speaking he glanced at Catalina. She was staring at him with a cool, thoughtful expression.

It took fifteen minutes, time spent saying goodnight to everyone individually, before he was finally able to leave the dining room.

Catalina made no effort to follow him.

The disquiet in his chest grew with every step he took towards his apartment. By the time he reached his door and was able to shake off the courtiers, perspiration had broken out on his brow and his pulse had surged.

He headed straight down the passageway and rapped on Amy's connecting door.

No answer.

He banged again, louder.

No answer.

'Amy?' he shouted, pounding on the door with his fist.

On impulse he tried the handle, even though Amy al-ways kept the door locked...

The door opened.

His heart thundering painfully beneath his ribs, he stepped into her apartment.

'Amy?' he called into the silence.

His heart knew before his head could comprehend it.

On legs weighted down with lead, he stepped into her bedroom.

The room was spotless. And empty.

All that lay on the dressing table, which was usually heaped with cosmetics and bottles of perfume, was a large padded envelope he recognised as the one he'd given to her all those weeks ago, containing the jewellery he'd bought her. Next to it lay a scrap of paper. Written on it were two words.

Forgive me.

'You look troubled, Helios,' his grandfather said, in the wheezing voice Helios hated so much.

They were playing chess, his grandfather's favourite game. The King was in his wheelchair, an oxygen tank to his right, a nurse set back a little to his left.

'I'm just tired.' Helios moved a pawn two spaces forward, unable to stop his stomach curdling with the fear that this might be the last game they played together.

'How are the wedding preparations going?'

'Well.'

Not that he was having anything to do with them. The palace staff were more than capable of handling it without his input. And without Catalina, who seemingly had as much interest in the preparations as he had. None at all.

His grandfather placed the oxygen mask on his face for a minute, before indicating for the nurse to take it off.

'I remember my own wedding day well.' The misty eyes grew mistier. 'Your grandmother looked like an angel sent from heaven.' Then the old eyes sharpened. 'Your mother looked beautiful on her wedding day too. It is my eternal sorrow that your father couldn't see her beauty. Your mother was beautiful, inside and out.'

Helios's spine stiffened. His parents' marriage was a subject they rarely touched upon other than in the most generic terms.

'The biggest regret of my life—and your grandmother's, rest her soul—was that your father couldn't choose his own wife. Would it have made a difference if he'd been able to choose?' He raised a weak, bony shoulder. 'We will never know. Despite our best efforts he was a vain and cruel man. He thrived on power. Your mother didn't stand a chance.'

He moved his castle forward with a quivering, gnarled finger.

'We pushed through the changes in law that would allow you and your heirs to select your own spouses in the hope that your parents' marriage would never be repeated.' His voice weakening with each word he said, the King turned his gaze to Helios again. 'However important duty is, marriage to someone you feel no affection for can only bring misery. And for ever is a long time to be miserable.'

The nurse, attuned to his weakening, placed the oxygen mask back over his face.

Helios waited for him to inhale as much as he needed, all the time his mind was reeling over what it was, exactly, that his grandfather was trying to tell him. Was it a reproach that he wasn't spending enough time with Catalina and that his indifference to her was showing?

But how could he feel anything *but* indifference when his head was still consumed with thoughts of Amy? She'd left the palace a week ago but she was still *everywhere*.

He moved his knight, then opened his mouth to pose the question, only to find his grandfather's head had lolled to one side and he'd dozed off mid-game and mid-conversation.

He looked at the nurse, who raised her shoulders sympathetically. Helios exhaled and gazed at his sleeping grandfather, a huge wave of love washing through him.

Whatever his grandfather had tried to tell him, it could wait.

'I'll put him to bed tonight,' he told the nurse, whose eyes immediately widened in fright.

'It's okay,' he assured her with a wry smile. 'I know what I'm doing. You can supervise if you want.'

Half an hour later the King was in his bed, his medication having been given and the oxygen mask attached to his face. His gentle snores were strangely calming.

Helios placed a kiss to his grandfather's forehead. 'I love you,' he said, before leaving him to sleep.

Movement beside her woke Amy from the light doze she'd fallen into. Since returning to England a week ago she'd slept a lot. She liked sleeping. It was the perfect route to forgetting. It was waking that was the problem.

Her mum handed her a cup of tea and sat in the deck-chair next to her.

When she'd returned to England she'd given the taxi driver directions to her childhood home rather than the flat she shared in central London. Sometimes a girl just needed her mum. Her *real* mum. The woman who'd loved and raised her since she'd barely been able to open her eyes.

And her mum had been overjoyed to see her.

Amy's last lingering doubts had been well and truly banished.

A late-night confession between them had culminated with the admission that her mum had been terrified that Amy would forge a relationship with Neysa.

'Never,' Amy had said with a firm shake of her head. 'You're my mum. Not her.'

'Good.' Ferocity had suddenly flashed in her mum's usually calm eyes. 'Because you're *my* daughter. Not hers.'

'Then why did you encourage me to learn about my roots?' she'd asked, bewildered.

'We all need to know where we come from. And I was scared that if I discouraged it you would do it in secret and one day you'd be gone and I would lose you.'

'You will never lose me.'

The tears had flowed easily that night.

Now they sat in companionable silence in the English sun, the only sound the chirruping of fledgling birds in the garden's thick hedges. It was a quintessentially British beautiful late-spring day.

'Are you ready to talk now?' her mum asked.

A lump forming in her throat, Amy shook her head. For all their late-night talks, she hadn't been able to bring up the subject of Helios.

To even think of him was too painful.

She'd had only one piece of correspondence from him since she'd left—a text message that said: I do.

He forgave her for running away.

Judging by his silence since, he'd accepted it too. She had no right to feel hurt that he'd made no further attempt to contact her.

'What's that you keep fingering around your neck?'

Wordlessly, Amy leaned forward to show her the garnet necklace.

Her mum took it between her fingers and smiled. 'It's lovely.'

Amy couldn't find the words to answer. When her mum let the necklace go Amy clasped it in her own hand and held it close.

'Broken hearts do mend,' her mum said softly.

Amy gave a ragged nod and swallowed, terrified of crying again. 'It hurts,' she choked out.

Her mum took her hand and squeezed it. 'Do you know what to do when life gives you lemons?'

'Make lemonade?'

'No. You throw them back and get yourself an orange.'

Amy spluttered, laughing. 'I haven't the faintest idea what that means.'

'Neither do I! It was something my mother used to say when I was a child.'

Still holding on tightly to each other's hands, they settled back in their deckchairs, sunglasses on, and basked in the sun.

After a while, her mum spoke again. 'I think what my mother was trying to say is that, whatever life throws at you, there are always choices and options other than the obvious ones. When your father first brought you home the obvious solution for me would have been to throw him out, and you with him. That would have been me making lemonade. But when I looked at you all I saw was an innocent, helpless newborn baby—a sister to the child I already had and a sister to the child I carried in my belly. So I chose to get myself an orange instead. I kept you— *you* were my orange. And I have never regretted it. My only regret is that I never carried you in my womb like I did your brothers.'

She took her sunglasses off and smiled the warm, motherly smile Amy loved so much.

'This man who's broken your heart…is he a good man?'

'He's the best,' she whispered.

'Is he worth the pain?'

She jerked a nod.

'Then you have to decide whether you're going to make lemonade or find an orange. Are you going to wallow in your pain or turn it into something constructive?'

'I wouldn't know where to start.'

'You start by accepting the pain for what it is but refusing to let it define you.'

Amy closed her eyes. If anyone knew how to cope with pain it was her mum. She'd handled a mountain of it and had never let it define her.

Compared to her mum she had nothing to complain about. Her mum had been innocent. She, Amy, had brought her misery upon herself.

Helios stood at the door to his grandfather's apartments and braced himself for the medicinal odour that would attack his senses when he stepped over the threshold.

Inside, all was quiet.

Stepping through to what had once been the King's bedroom and now resembled a hospital ward, he found his grandfather sleeping in his adjustable medical bed, with an oxygen mask over his nose and mouth.

At his side sat Helios's brothers. A nurse read unobtrusively in the corner.

'Any change?' he asked quietly. He'd only left the room for an hour, but the speed of his grandfather's deterioration over the past couple of days had been frightening. They all knew it wouldn't be long now.

Talos shook his head.

Taking his place on the other side of the bed from his brothers, Helios rolled his shoulders. Every part of his body felt stiff.

Theseus was holding their grandfather's right hand. Leaning forward, Helios took the left one, assuming the same position his grandfather had taken when his Queen had lain in an identical bed in the adjoining room, the life leaching out of her.

After a few long, long minutes their grandfather's eyes fluttered open. 'Water...' he croaked.

With Helios and Theseus working together from separate sides of the bed to raise him, Talos brought a glass to his mouth and placed the straw between his lips.

When he'd settled back the King looked at his three

grandsons, his stare lingering on each of them in turn, emotion ringing the rapidly dulling eyes.

The pauses between each of his inhalations grew. Then the corners of his lips twitched as if in a smile and his eyes closed for the last time.

CHAPTER THIRTEEN

AMY SAW THE announcement on the morning news.

'A statement from the palace said, "His Majesty King Astraeus the Fourth of Agon passed away peacefully in his sleep last night. His three grandsons were at his side."'

There then followed some speculation by the presenters and royal correspondents about what this meant for the island nation.

Without warning a picture of Helios and Catalina flashed onto the screen. It was an unofficial shot taken at the Gala. And then there was an off-screen voice saying, 'It is believed the heir to the throne will marry the Princess before taking the crown.'

Amy switched off the television, grabbed a pillow and cuddled into it, her head pounding.

Helios's grandfather, the King, had *died*.

She'd known it was coming, but still it hit her like a blow. She'd created his exhibition. During those happy months of curating that tribute to his life and the ancestors closest to him she'd felt as if she'd got to know him. Somehow she'd fooled herself into believing he was immortal. He had been a proud, dutiful man and she'd been privileged to meet him.

And then she thought of his eldest grandson, who had revered him.

Her phone lay on the floor beside her and she stared at it, wishing with all her heart that she could call Helios.

Would he even want to hear her condolences? The condolences of the woman who had sneaked out of the palace while he was dining with potential investors, supporting the island he loved?

She'd told him she would stay.

He'd forgiven her lie, but he had Catalina now. Without Amy's presence there, distracting him, he would turn to the Princess for comfort. Just as he should. Maybe grief would bring them together properly.

And as she prayed for a happy ending for her Prince and his Princess, hot tears spilled out of her eyes. She brought her knees to her chest and cried her broken heart out for the happy ending that would never be hers.

The funeral, a full state affair, was a sombre occasion.

People lined the streets in tens of thousands, all there to bow their heads in silence and pay their respects to the man who had served them with such dedication for fifty years.

The wake was an entirely different matter.

Out on the streets the atmosphere changed markedly. Television coverage showed military re-enactments from throughout the ages, even children dressed in loincloths and armed with plastic tridents. Barbecues lit up Agon's famous beaches, music played on every corner and there was food, drink and dancing everywhere in abundance.

Agon was putting on a show in the only way it knew how.

In the blue stateroom of the palace solemnity had given way to merriness too. The King was with his Queen. His suffering was over. His country and his family had laid him to rest and now they could celebrate his life.

For Helios, the occasion brought no joy. He accepted

that his grandfather had moved on to a better place, but the hole in his heart felt so great he didn't know how it would ever heal.

To know he would never talk to him again, dine with him, play chess… All the things he'd taken for granted were all gone. The man he'd worshipped, a man ten times the man his own father had been, was gone.

Helios watched his brothers, stuck like glue to the sides of their respective fiancées, and smiled for them. Their parents' marriage had been the worst template a child could have asked for. That his brothers were heading into marriages that would be more like their grandparents' gave him much hope. They would be happy.

He was under no illusions that he would follow suit.

Although he had seen little of her since his grandfather's death, Catalina had been at his side throughout the funeral service, a calm presence who had known exactly what to say in all the right moments.

But, however perfect she might be, he knew that fifty years of marriage wouldn't bring them the bond Talos and Theseus shared with their fiancées.

That last smile his grandfather had given them was a white shadow in Helios's mind. It gave him comfort. His grandfather had welcomed death. He'd left the world knowing his grandsons—all of them—would take care of his beloved island, freeing him to move on to his beloved Rhea.

His *three* grandsons.

Three boys raised to be princes.

Catalina came to stand by him. He stared down at her and met her thoughtful gaze.

'*Marriage to someone you feel no affection for can only bring misery.*'

Those were the words his grandfather had said the last time they'd spoken lucidly together. And in that moment he knew those words hadn't been a reproach. They'd been a warning from a man who knew how powerful love could be and had witnessed the destructive nature of his son's contempt for the wife he didn't love.

And in that instant everything became clear.

He couldn't marry Catalina.

If he'd never met Amy everything would be different. *He* would be different.

If he'd never met Amy he would be marrying Catalina with no expectations or knowledge of how things might be. He would be King. She would be Queen. Their only bond would be of duty. He wouldn't know what it felt like to love or be loved.

Love.

The one word he'd never expected to apply to himself other than in an abstract form. Familial love he'd felt and believed in, but romantic love...? That was not something he'd ever been able to hope for, so not something he had ever allowed himself to think about. And, if he was being honest with himself, it was something he'd hidden away from. The scars of his parents' marriage ran so deep that what he'd convinced himself was rational acceptance of his future union was in fact a mask to hide the real truth—that love in all its forms was the most terrifying emotion of all.

But also the most wonderful.

Because, *Theos*, he loved Amy. With everything he had.

Try as he might, he couldn't get used to walking into the museum and not seeing her there. He couldn't get used to being in his apartment and seeing the connecting door, knowing she wasn't at the end of the passageway.

Not a second of his waking day was spent without him wondering where she was and what she was doing.

After his grandfather's death had been announced he'd

kept staring at his phone, willing it to ring. Knowing it wouldn't. Knowing she was right not to call him.

But his intellectual acceptance that she was gone and that it was all for the best wasn't something his heart had any intention of agreeing with.

He'd long trusted Amy with his confidences. Now he understood that he'd also trusted her with his heart, and that a relationship with any other woman was doomed to failure because he belonged to Amy. All of him.

When the day of his own death came the last thing his conscious mind would see would be her face.

Three weeks without her.

The time had dragged like a decade.

How could he think straight without her?

How could he breathe without her when she was as necessary to him as air?

He loved her.

He cast his eyes around the room until he found Theseus, deep in conversation with his fiancée, Jo, and a Swedish politician the three Princes had been at school with. Theseus was settled. He had a child. His marriage would be taking place in a week.

Helios took a deep breath. Before he spoke to his brother there was someone else who needed to be spoken to first.

He looked at her, still by his side, the silence between them stark.

'Catalina…'

'We need to talk, don't we?' she said quietly.

'Yes.'

Weaving their way through the crowd, they walked through a corridor, and then another, and then stepped out into the palace gardens.

'Catalina, I'm sorry but I can't marry you.'

She closed her eyes and breathed deeply.

'I've been grossly unfair to you. I'm not...' It was his turn to take a breath. 'I'm in love with someone else.'

She bowed her head and eventually met his gaze. 'Thank you for finally being honest with me—and with yourself.'

'I never meant to hurt you.'

Her smile was stoical. 'All you have hurt is my pride.'

He opened his mouth to speak further but she raised a hand to stop him.

'It would never have worked between us. I've known it for a while now, but I didn't want to add to the burden you've carried with your grandfather's illness.' She sighed. 'I will get my people to issue a press release in a couple of days, saying I have called the engagement off due to an incompatibility between us.'

It was the least he could let her do. 'Catalina, I am sorry. I never wanted...'

'No. Do not say anything else.' She lifted her chin. 'Let me leave here with *some* dignity.'

For a moment Helios did nothing but stare at the woman he had intended to spend the rest of his life with. Then, taking her shoulders, he pulled her into his embrace. It warmed his heart to feel her arms wrap around his waist.

'You will find a better man than me,' he whispered.

'I doubt that,' she answered drily. 'But perhaps I will find a man whose heart is free to love me.'

'I hope that for you too.'

Pulling apart, they kissed each other on both cheeks and smiled.

The weight he carried on his shoulders lifted a fraction.

'I expect an invitation,' she said as she walked away.

'An invitation to what?'

'To your wedding to your English curator. Your mother's ring will look wonderful on her finger.'

With one final wink she sashayed into the palace, not looking back.

Alone in the gardens Helios did a slow turn, taking in the verdant lawns, the sweet-scented flowers in bloom, the distant maze. It was a paradise of nature and life. Whether he became custodian of it all, as he'd spent his entire life believing he would, or not, the flowers would continue to bloom. That he knew with absolute certainty.

His heart beating loudly, echoing through every chamber of his body, he took his phone out of his pocket and dialled the number he had spent the past three weeks fighting not to call.

It went straight to voicemail.

He tried again.

The same thing happened.

Back in the palace, he entered the stateroom and found the person he was looking for.

'I need to borrow you,' he said to Pedro, interrupting his Head of Museum's conversation with a person he did not recognise.

'Where are we going?' Pedro asked.

'To the museum. I need to get something.'

The museum was closed out of respect for his grandfather and to allow all the staff to pay their respects too.

With long strides they followed the corridors into the museum's private entrance and cut through the large exhibition rooms until they reached the rooms that mattered to Helios at that moment. The Kalliakis Family exhibition rooms.

After he'd explained to Pedro what he wanted, a thought struck him.

'Do you know where Amy's working now?'

'She's back at the British Museum.'

No wonder she'd turned her phone off. She would be working. 'Do you have the number?'

Pedro scrolled through his phone until he found the relevant number and thrust the phone at him.

Helios put it to his ear whilst indicating that Pedro could start on the task he'd set for him. It rang a couple of times, a passage of time that to Helios's ears was longer than for ever, before it was answered.

'Put me through to Amy Green,' he said.

'One moment, please.'

There followed a merry little game in which he was routed to varying offices until a voice said, 'Ancient Greece Department.'

'I wish to speak to Amy Green.'

'I'm sorry, sir, but Amy is on leave. She'll be back on Monday.'

'Do you know where she's gone?'

'As far as I'm aware she's attending a funeral.'

'Thank you.'

Disconnecting the call, his brain reeling, Helios rubbed the nape of his neck.

Now what?

And as he wondered what the hell his next step should be his heart went out to her. To think she too had lost someone important... She would be in need of comfort just as he—

And in the space of a heartbeat he knew whose funeral she'd attended.

Hope filled him, spreading from his toes right to the roots of his hair.

He put a call through to his private secretary. 'Talia,' he said as soon as she answered, 'I need you to find Amy Green for me. She's in the country. Go through to Immigration and take it from there.'

To her credit, Talia took his instructions in her stride. 'The Immigration Minister is here.'

'Good. Speak to him. Now.'

While all this was going on Pedro had completed the task he'd been set and so the pair of them reset the alarms, closed the museum and went back to the wake.

Helios found Talia in a quiet corridor, with her phone pressed to her ear by her shoulder, writing information on her hand. She gave him a thumbs-up and carried on her conversation.

'She's at the airport,' she said without preamble a few minutes later. 'Her flight back to England leaves in forty-five minutes. The passengers for her flight will be boarding any minute.'

'I need to get to the airport.'

A tremor of fear flashed over Talia's face. 'All the roads are blocked. You'll never make it in time.'

'Watch me.'

With that, he headed back into the stateroom and, ignoring everyone who tried to speak to him, found the butler of Theseus's private villa, Philippe, a man who looked as if he should be catching the surf, not running a Prince's household.

He pulled him aside to speak to him privately.

'You have a motorbike, don't you?'

'Yes, Your Highness.'

'Is it here at the palace?'

'It's in the staff courtyard.'

'I need to borrow it.'

'Now?'

'Now.'

'Do you know how to ride?'

'You have the time it takes us to walk there to teach me. Let's go.'

* * *

Amy stared out of the oval window with a heavy heart.

She was glad she'd come.

It had been a snap decision, driven by a sense of certainty that she had to go, to pay her respects to the man for whom she'd devoted almost six months of her life to creating an exhibition of *his* life.

Watching Helios and his brothers walking with military precision in front of the coffin, their gazes aimed forward, knowing how they must be bleeding inside...

The crowds had been so thick there had been no chance of Helios catching sight of her, but even so she hadn't taken any chances, keeping a good distance from the barrier.

What good would it have done for him to see her? The Princess had been there for him, just as Amy had known she would be, travelling in an official car with Theseus's and Talos's fiancées.

A steward made his sweep down the aisle, checking everyone's seat belts were fastened. The plane began to move. Over the speakers came the sombre voice of the captain, welcoming them all to this flight to London.

The ache in her chest told her she'd been wise to get a return flight home straight after the funeral. Any longer and the temptation to call Helios and seek him out would have become too great to resist. One night on Agon was as much as she'd been prepared to risk.

She'd taken her mother's advice to heart, and God knew she was trying to get herself an orange.

She'd taken up her old job at the museum and enrolled in a postgraduate course on the Ancient Romans, which she would start in September. She figured she might as well expand her knowledge so that her life wasn't all about Agon and its people, whether from history or the present. There was a big world out there to explore and learn about.

She'd kept herself busy, working by day and socialising by evening. It was the nights that were unbearable. Despite the mild heatwave sweeping through the UK, her nights were always cold.

Somehow she would find a way to forget him.

The plane had reached the place where it would turn around and face the runway.

The woman sitting beside her gripped the armrests, her knuckles turning white in anticipation of take-off.

But no sooner had the plane started its journey down the runway than it was brought to a stop.

It took a while before the passengers realised something was wrong, and then low murmurs began spreading throughout the plane.

The voice of a stewardesses came over the speaker. 'Could passenger Miss Amy Green please make herself known to a member of the cabin crew?'

Amy barely heard, her attention caught by a motorcyclist, speeding over the tarmac, heading towards them. Behind him was a buggy, with two men in orange high-visibility jackets towing metal steps. There was something about the figure riding the motorbike...

'Amy Green? Miss Amy Green—please make yourself known to a member of the cabin crew.'

With a jolt she realised it was *her* they were asking for. Tearing her gaze away from the window, she raised a hesitant hand.

A stewardess bustled over to her, looking harassed. 'Amy Green?'

Amy nodded, bemused and not a little scared.

'I need you to come with me.'

'Why?'

'We've been asked to escort you off this flight.'

'But *why*? Have I done something wrong?'

The stewardess shook her head. 'I don't know why.'

The couple she was sitting next to had to get out of their seats to let her pass, but it wasn't long before she was trailing the stewardess to the exit, her face burning with mortification, her brain burning with confusion.

What the hell was going on...?

At the rear exit of the plane the crew were all staring at her unabashedly, no doubt wondering if she was some kind of fugitive.

Was she a fugitive? Had she unwittingly committed a crime that necessitated her being escorted off a plane and arrested?

And then the door opened, the metal stairs were hastily bolted on and she stood at the threshold, looking to see if a dozen police officers were waiting at the bottom to take her into custody.

The only person waiting for her was the motorcyclist she'd spotted. He sat astride the bike, his helmet resting under an arm...

CHAPTER FOURTEEN

AMY'S HEART LEAPT so hard it almost jumped out of her mouth.

Behind her came a collective sigh from the crew. One of them squeezed her shoulder. 'Go to him.'

But she couldn't. Her legs had turned to jelly.

She covered her mouth, unable to believe her eyes.

What was he doing here?

His handsome face immobile, he got off his bike, placed the helmet on the seat and climbed the stairs with heavy treads.

It was only when he was at eye level with her and she was able to gaze into the liquid dark brown eyes she loved so much that Amy dared to breathe.

'Helios,' she whispered, raising a hand to brush it against his cheek, to feel for herself that he truly was there and that this wasn't some dream she'd fallen into.

But no. No dream.

His cheek was warm and smooth, his jawline rough, at the stage where stubble was just starting to poke through the skin. His warm, familiar scent played under her nose.

'Sneaking away again?' he asked, in a voice that was meant to be humorous but that cracked on the last syllable.

'What...? What are you doing here?'

His eyes bored into her, emotion seeping out of them.

'I'm taking you home.' Then he took the final step up and lifted her into his arms. 'I'm taking you home,' he repeated.

Another collective 'Ooh…' sounded from behind her, and as Helios carried her down the steps a round of applause broke out. One of the men in high-visibility jackets, who was waiting by the buggy, wolf-whistled.

Amy heard it all, but none of it penetrated. All her senses were focused so intensely on her lover that everything else had become a blur.

At the bottom of the steps Helios placed her carefully on her feet.

Suddenly the biggest, widest grin spread over his face. 'Would Despinis Green like a ride on my bike?'

Laughter bubbled up in her throat and broke through her daze. She flung her arms around him. 'Yes. Please. Take me anywhere.'

Amy kept a tight hold on Helios as he drove them through the streets of Resina. She didn't *have* to hold him tightly— the dense throng of partying people meant he had to ride at a snail's pace—but she needed to. Keeping her cheek pressed into the solidity of his back and her arms around his waist grounded her, helped her accept the reality of what had just happened.

Soon they had passed through the capital and were out in the verdant countryside, with Agon's mountains looming before them. Helios found a road that took them up Mount Ares, the rockiest of Agon's mountains, past goats casually chewing grass by sheer drops, taking them higher and higher until they arrived at a clearing.

He turned the engine off and clicked the stand down to keep the bike upright before helping her off.

She looked at him, laughing as she properly noticed for the first time that he'd ridden with her up a mountain in a pair of handmade black trousers, black brogues, now covered in dust, and a white shirt with the sleeves rolled up that had probably been as crisp as freshly baked pie earlier but was now crumpled and stained.

'Your clothes are ruined.'

He shrugged, his eyes sparkling. 'I couldn't care less.'

Taking her hand, he led her to a flat grassy area and sat down, enfolding her in his arms so her back rested against his chest and her head was tucked beneath his chin.

'When I was a child my brothers and I would race to the top of this mountain. When we'd all reached the summit we would come down to this clearing and eat our picnic. This spot has the best view of the sunset on the whole of Agon.'

The sun was already making its descent, causing a darkly colourful hue to settle over the island.

'How did you know I was here?' she asked eventually.

'Your museum told me you'd gone to a funeral. I guessed.'

'But how did you know what plane I was on?'

'Do you really need me to answer that?' he said with bemusement.

She smiled to herself, tightening her hold on his hands, which were still wrapped around her waist. And then she remembered *why* she had come to Agon today.

'I'm so sorry about your grandfather,' she said softly.

He kissed her head. 'He was ready to go.'

'I wanted to call you.'

'I know you did. And you were right not to.'

She sighed. Now that she had come to her senses, reality was poking at her painfully.

'How did you manage to sneak out without your bodyguards?'

'Simple. I didn't tell them what I was doing. The palace was so busy with the wake it was easy. Talia will have told them by now.'

'She knows you came for me?'

'Yes. So does Pedro.'

'How long do we have? Here, I mean?'

'As long as we want.'

'But you'll be missed,' she said with another sigh, thinking that, however wonderful it was to be sat in his arms again, she would be dragged away from him again soon.

She was here now, though. A short interlude. Two lovers snatching a few minutes together to watch the sunset. One final sweet goodbye.

'I have done my duty by my grandfather today. And, *matakia mou*, he would want me to be here with you.'

'He would?'

'My grandfather was a great believer in two things— duty and love.'

Her heart gave a little skip at his words, a skip she tried frantically to dampen.

'Please, Helios, don't say things like that. It isn't fair.'

He caught her chin and turned her face to look at him. 'How can the truth not be fair? You are my whole world. I love you.'

'Please, stop,' she beseeched, clutching at his shirt. 'Don't speak of love to me when you will be marrying Catalina—'

'I'm not marrying Catalina,' Helios interrupted, castigating himself for being foolish enough to believe Amy was a mind reader who would have known the truth from the minute she'd seen him from her plane window. 'The wedding is off.'

Her eyes widened into huge round orbs. 'It is? Since when?'

'Since about three hours ago, when I realised I couldn't live another day without you. Catalina and I had a talk.' Knowing Amy would be concerned for the Princess, he took pains to reassure her. 'She will be fine. She's as good a woman as you always told me, and I promise you we have her blessing.'

'But...' Nothing else came. Her mouth was opening and closing as if her tongue had forgotten how to form words.

He pressed his lips to hers, inhaling the warm, sweet breath he had believed he would never taste again.

'I love you,' he repeated, looking at her shocked face. 'It's you I want to marry. Just you. Only you.'

'I want that too. More than anything in the world.'

'Then why do you look so sad?'

'Because I know it can never be. You aren't allowed to marry a commoner.'

He took hold of her hand and pressed it to his chest. 'Listen to my heart,' he said quietly. 'I knew I had to find a wife when my grandfather was given his diagnosis, but I put it off and put it off because deep down I knew it would mean losing you. My heart has been beating for you from the very start.'

Her breath gave a tiny hitch.

'You asked me what I would have been if I hadn't been born heir to the throne and I had no good answer for you, because it wasn't something I had ever allowed myself to think about. The throne, my country...they were my life. I didn't expect love. My only hope for marriage was that it would be better than what my parents had. However it panned out I would do my duty and I would respect my wife. That was the most I hoped for. I didn't *want* love. I saw the way my father abused the power of my mother's love and I never wanted to have the power to inflict such hurt on a woman. That's why Catalina seemed so perfect— I thought she was emotionally cold.'

Amy shivered.

Helios tightened his hold and gently kissed her. 'I know

I have the power to hurt you, *matakia mou*, and I swear on everything holy that I will never abuse it. But you need to understand one thing.'

'What's that?' she whispered.

'You have equal power to hurt me.'

'I do?'

'Living without you… It's been like living in an emotional dungeon. Cold and dark and without hope.' He brushed his thumb over her soft cheek. 'If spending the rest of my life with you means I have to relinquish the throne, then that's the price I'll pay and I'll pay it gladly.'

Her hold on his shirt tightening, her eyes wide and fearful, she said, 'But what about the throne? What will happen to it?'

'I don't know.' He laughed ruefully. 'Theseus is next in line. That's one of the things that struck me earlier—my grandparents raised *three* princes. It doesn't have to be me. We're all capable and worthy of taking the throne. Except Talos,' he added as an afterthought. 'Never mind that he's marrying a commoner too. He can be particularly fierce. He'll probably scare more people away from our country than attract them.'

She managed a painful chortle at his attempt at humour. 'But what if Theseus doesn't want it?'

'He probably *won't* want it,' he answered honestly. 'But he understands what it's like to be without the one you love. His fiancée has royal blood in her. It should be enough.'

'And if it isn't?'

'Then we will work something out. Whatever happens, I swear to you that we will be together until we take our dying breaths and that the Agon monarchy will remain intact. Have faith, *matakia mou*. And to prove it…'

Disentangling himself from her arms, he dug into his

pocket and pulled out the object Pedro had set about re-
trieving a few short hours ago.

Dumbstruck, she simply stared at it as he displayed it
to her.

'This, my love, belongs to you.' He took her trembling left
hand, slid the ring onto her engagement finger, then kissed
it. 'One day the eldest of our children will inherit it, and in
turn they will pass it to the eldest of their children—either to
wear themselves upon marriage or for their wives to wear.'

'Our *children*?'

'You do want them, don't you?' he asked, suddenly anxious that he might have made one assumption too many.
'If you don't we can pass the ring to Theseus…'

'No, no—I *do* want your children,' she said. And then,
like a cloud moving away from the sun, the fear left her
eyes and a smile as wide as the sunset before them spread
across her cheeks, lighting up her whole face. 'We're really going to be together?'

'Until death us do part.'

Such was the weight of her joy that when she threw
herself into him he fell back onto the grass, taking her
with him, and her overjoyed kisses as she straddled him
filled him with more happiness than he had ever thought
possible.

She was *his*. He was hers.

And as they lay on the grass, watching the orange sun
make its final descent through the pink sky, he knew in
his heart that the rest of his life would be filled with the
glorious colours of this most beautiful of sunsets.

EPILOGUE

Six months later

THE RED DOME of the Aghia Sophia, the cathedral located in the exact central point between the Agon palace and the capital, Resina, gleamed as if it were burnt liquid gold under the autumn sky.

As Amy was taken through the cheering crowds on a horse-drawn carriage she turned her face upwards, letting the sun's rays warm her face, and sighed with contentment. Unlike many brides on their big day, she had no fear or apprehension whatsoever.

Beside her sat her father, who would be walking her down the aisle, and little Toby, proud as Punch to have been given the important role of ring bearer. In the carriage ahead of them sat her three bridesmaids: her soon-to-be sisters-in-law, Amalie and Jo, and Greta. Ahead of them were seven mounted military guards, in all their ceremonial attire, with the front rider holding the Kalliakis Royal Standard. More guards rode alongside the carriages, and there were a dozen at the rear.

It was pure pageantry at its finest. Triple the number of military guards were scheduled for a fortnight's time, when she and Helios would return to the cathedral to be crowned King and Queen of Agon.

In the sky were dozens of helicopters, sent from news outlets across the world to film the event.

Unbelievably she, Amy Green—a woman abandoned as a two-week-old baby by her birth mother, a woman who had never been quite sure of her place in the world—was going to be Queen of Agon.

Helios would be King. And it was the woman who'd abandoned her who'd made it all possible.

According to Helios, Theseus had turned the colour of puce when he'd sat his two brothers down and explained the situation to them. As Helios had suspected, Theseus had reluctantly agreed he would take the throne but only if all other avenues had first been explored.

Constitutional experts had been put on the case, to no avail, until Talos had come up with the bright idea of changing the constitution, rightly pointing out it had been changed numerous times before.

A meeting with the Agon senate had been arranged, and there the president, who, like all the members of the senate, was sympathetic to the Crown Prince's plight, had murmured about how much easier it would be to bring about the constitutional change if the bride were of Agon blood...

A referendum had taken place. Of the ninety per cent turnout, ninety-three per cent had voted for changing the constitution to allow a person of non-royal blood to marry into the royal family, provided that she was of Agon blood.

And now, as the carriage pulled up at the front of the cathedral, where the cheers from the crowd were deafening, Amy was helped down. She stepped carefully, so as not to trip over the fifteen-foot train of her ivory silk dress, handmade by Queen Rhea's personal designer, Natalia.

How she loved her dress, with its spaghetti straps and the rounded neck that skimmed her cleavage, the flared skirt that was as far from the traditional meringue shape as could be. Simpler in form and design than both Queen Rhea's dress and Helios's mother's dress, it was utterly perfect for her. And it was lucky she had insisted on something simpler considering they'd had to expand the waistline at the last fitting, to take into account the swelling of her stomach...

She and Helios had taken the decision a couple of months ago for Amy to come off the contraceptive pill, both of them figuring that it would take a good few months for the hormones to get out of her system. The hope had been that she would conceive after their coronation.

Whoops.

A month after taking her last pill Amy's breasts had suddenly grown in size. Their baby—the new heir to the throne—was due in six months, something they had decided not to make public until after their coronation. Naturally half the palace knew about it.

Greta had been given Corinna's job at the museum and was thoroughly enjoying bossing Amy about. Amy had gone back to curating King Astraeus's exhibition and then, when the exhibition had closed, she'd taken on the role of museum tour guide. It was a job she would be able to fit around the royal duties she would have to take on when she was crowned Queen.

Helios still thought it appropriate to give bloodthirsty Agon history lessons to children in the dungeons.

In all, everything had worked out perfectly, as if the stars had aligned for them.

Jo stepped forward to adjust Amy's veil, having to stretch to accommodate her own swollen stomach, which was fast resembling a beach ball, and then it was time.

When her arm was held tightly in her father's, the doors of the cathedral were thrown open, the music started and Amy took the first step towards the rest of her life.

The congregation rose as one, every head turning to stare. The first face she saw was that of Princess Catalina, who, as gracious as ever, smiled at Amy with both her lips and her eyes. When the press had bombarded her with questions about Helios and Amy's marriage her statement of support for them had been heartfelt and touching.

Surely somewhere in this packed cathedral stood a prince in need of a beautiful, elegant princess to make his own?

In the back row was the woman who had made all this happen—Neysa Soukis, there with her husband, and their son, Leander. It was amazing how the thought of being Queen Mother had spurred Neysa to recognise Amy as her child with enthusiasm and thus proclaim her a child of Agon blood. No doubt Neysa had imagined this moment many times, had thought she would be sitting in the front row of the congregation.

Alas, Neysa had soon learned that the only place she had in Amy's life was as a name on a piece of paper. Elaine—her mum, the woman who had raised and loved her—would be the officially recognised Queen Mother.

And, thinking of her mum, there she stood in the front row, beautiful in a pea-green skirt suit and an enormous hat, beaming with pride. Next to her stood Amy's *real* brothers, Neil and Danny, with identical grins on their faces. Both of them had been fit to burst with pride when Helios had appointed them as his ushers. Their wives had a dazed, 'someone pinch me to prove this is really happening' look about them.

And best of all, standing at the front, beside the altar, his brothers by his side, stood Helios; her lover and her best friend all rolled into one.

The three Princes were dressed in their military uniforms: the Kalliakis livery complete with sashes. They all looked magnificent, like three benevolent giants.

Helios might not be able to see her face through her veil, but she could see his, and see the full beard he'd grown especially for her. The expression in his eyes made every step she took closer to him feel as if she were bouncing on the moon.

When she reached him Helios took her hand, and together they knelt at the altar to pledge their lives, fidelity and love to each other for ever.

They were pledges neither of them would ever break.

* * * * *

THE BILLIONAIRE'S
SECRET PRINCESS

CAITLIN CREWS

To all the secret princesses cruelly stuck working in
horrible offices: as long as you know the truth,
that's what matters.

CHAPTER ONE

ACHILLES CASILIERIS REQUIRED PERFECTION.

In himself, certainly. He prided himself on it, knowing all too well how easy it was to fall far, far short. And in his employees, absolutely—or they would quickly find themselves on the other side of their noncompete agreements with indelible black marks against their names.

He did not play around. He had built everything he had from nothing, step by painstaking step, and he hadn't succeeded the way he had—building the recession-proof Casilieris Company and making his first million by the age of twenty-five, then expanding both his business and his personal fortune into the billions—by accepting anything less than 100 percent perfection in all things. Always.

Achilles was tough, tyrannical when necessary, and refused to accept what one short-lived personal assistant had foolishly called "human limitations" to his face.

He was a man who knew the monster in himself. He'd seen its face in his own mirror. He did not allow for "human limitations."

Natalie Monette was his current executive assistant and had held the position for a record five years because she had never once asserted that she was human as some kind of excuse. In point of fact, Achilles thought of her as a remarkably efficient robot—the highest praise he could think to bestow on anyone, as it removed the possibility of human error from the equation.

Achilles had no patience for human error.

Which was why his assistant's behavior on this flight today was so alarming.

The day had started out normally enough. When Achilles had risen at his usual early hour, it had been to find Natalie already hard at work in the study of his Belgravia town house. She'd set up a few calls to his associates in France, outlined his schedule for the day and his upcoming meetings in New York. They'd swung by his corporate offices in the City, where Achilles had handled a fire he thought she should have put out before he'd learned of it, but then she'd accompanied him in his car to the private airfield he preferred without appearing the least bit bothered that he'd dressed her down for her failure. And why should she be bothered? She knew he expected perfection and had failed to deliver it. Besides, Natalie was never bothered. She'd acquitted herself with her usual cool competence and attitude-free demeanor, the way she always did or she never would have lasted five minutes with him. Much less five years.

And then she'd gone into the bathroom at the airfield, stayed in there long enough that he'd had to go find her himself, and come out changed.

Achilles couldn't put his finger on *how* she'd changed, only that she had.

She still looked the part of the closest assistant to a man as feared and lauded as Achilles had been for years now. She looked like his public face the way she always did. He appreciated that and always had. It wasn't enough that she was capable of handling the complications of his personal and company business without breaking a sweat, that she never seemed to sleep, that she could protect him from the intrusive paparazzi and hold off his equally demanding board members in the same breath—it was necessary that she also look like the sort of woman who belonged in his exalted orbit for the rare occasions when he needed to escort someone to this or that function and couldn't trouble himself to expend the modicum of charm necessary to squire one of his mistresses. Today she wore one of her usual outfits, a pencil skirt and soft blouse and a feminine sort of sweater that wrapped around her torso and was no different from any other outfit she'd worn a million times before.

Natalie dressed to disappear in plain sight. But for some reason, she caught his eye this odd afternoon. He couldn't quite figure it out. It was as if he had never seen her before. It was as if she'd gone into the bathroom in the airport lounge and come out a completely different person.

Achilles sat back in his remarkably comfortable leather chair on the jet and watched her as she took her seat opposite him. Did he imagine that she hesitated? Was he making up the strange look he'd seen in her eyes before she sat down? Almost as if she was looking for clues instead of taking her seat as she always did?

"What took you so long in that bathroom?" he asked, not bothering to keep his tone particularly polite. "I should not have to chase down my own assistant, surely."

Natalie blinked. He didn't know why the green of her eyes behind the glasses he knew she didn't need for sight seemed…too bright, somehow. Or brighter, anyway, than they'd been before. In fact, now that he thought about it, everything about her was brighter. And he couldn't understand how anyone could walk into a regular lavatory and come out…gleaming.

"I apologize," she said quietly. Simply. And there was something about her voice then. It was almost…musical.

It occurred to Achilles that he had certainly never thought of Natalie's voice as anything approaching *musical* before. It had always been a voice, pure and simple. And she had certainly never *gleamed*.

And that, he thought with impatience, was one of the reasons that he had prized Natalie so much for all these years. Because he had never, ever noticed her as anything but his executive assistant, who was reasonably attractive because it was good business to give his Neanderthal cronies something worth gazing at while they were trying to ignore Achilles's dominance. But there was a difference between noting that a woman was attractive and *being attracted to* that woman. Achilles would not have hired Natalie if he'd been attracted to her. He never had been. Not ever.

But to his utter astonishment that was what seemed to be happening. Right here. Right now. His body was sending him unambiguous signals. He wasn't simply *attracted* to his assistant. What he felt roll in him as she crossed her legs at the ankle and smiled at him was far more than *attraction*.

It was need.

Blinding and impossible and incredibly, astonishingly inconvenient.

Achilles Casilieris did not do inconvenience, and he was violently opposed to *need*. It had been beaten into him as an unwanted child that it was the height of foolishness to want something he couldn't have. That meant he'd dedicated his adult life to never allowing himself to need anything at all when he could buy whatever took his fancy, and he hadn't.

And yet there was no denying that dark thread that wound in him, pulling tight and succeeding in surprising him—something else that happened very, very rarely.

Achilles knew the shadows that lived in him. He had no intention of revisiting them. Ever.

Whatever his assistant was doing, she needed to stop. Now.

"That is all you wish to say?" He sounded edgy. Dangerous. He didn't like that, either.

But Natalie hardly seemed to notice. "If you would like me to expand on my apology, Mr. Casilieris, you need only tell me how."

He thought there was a subtle rebuke in that, no matter how softly she'd said it, and that, too, was new. And unacceptable no matter how prettily she'd voiced it.

Her copper-colored hair gleamed. Her skin glowed as she moved her hands in her lap, which struck him as odd, because Natalie never sat there with her hands folded in her lap like some kind of diffident Catholic schoolgirl. She was always in motion, because she was always working. But tonight, Natalie appeared to be sitting there like some kind of regal Madonna, hands folded in her lap, long, silky legs crossed at the ankles, and an inappropriately serene smile on her face.

If it wasn't impossible, he would have thought that she really was someone else entirely. Because she looked exactly the same save for all that gold that seemed to wrap itself around her and him, too, making him unduly fascinated with the pulse he could see beating at her throat—except he'd never, ever noticed her that way before.

Achilles did not have time for this, whatever it was. There was entirely too much going on with his businesses at the moment, like the hotel deal he'd been trying to put together for the better part of the last year that was by no means assured. He hadn't become one of the most feared and fearsome billionaires in the world because he took time off from running his businesses to pretend to care about the personal lives of his employees.

But Natalie wasn't just any employee. She was the one he'd actually come to rely on. The only person he relied on in the world, to be specific.

"Is there anything you need to tell me?" he asked.

He watched her, perhaps too carefully. It was impossible not to notice the way she flushed slightly at that. That was strange, too. He couldn't remember a single instance Natalie had ever flushed in response to anything he'd done. And the truth was he'd done a lot. He didn't hide his flashes of irritation or spend too much time worrying about anyone else's feelings. Why should he? The Casilieris Company was about profit—and it was about Achilles. Who else's feelings should matter? One of the things he'd long prized about his assistant was that she never, ever reacted to anything that he did or said or shouted. She just did her job.

But today Natalie had spots of red, high on her elegant cheekbones, and she'd been sitting across from him for whole minutes now without doing a single thing that could be construed as her job.

Elegant? demanded an incredulous voice inside him. *Cheekbones?*

Since when had Achilles ever noticed anything of the kind? He didn't pay that much attention to the mistresses he took to his bed—which he deigned to do in the first place only after they passed through all the levels of his application process and signed strict confidentiality agreements. And the women who made it through were in no doubt as to why they were there. It was to please him, not render him disoriented enough to be focusing on their bloody *cheekbones*.

"Like what, for example?" She asked the question and then she smiled at him, that curve of her mouth that was suddenly wired to the hardest part of him, and echoed inside him like heat. Heat he didn't want. "I'll be happy to tell you anything you wish to hear, Mr. Casilieris. That is, after all, my job."

"Is that your job?" He smiled, and he doubted it echoed much of anywhere. Or was anything but edgy and a little but harsh. "I had started to doubt that you remembered you had one."

"Because I kept you waiting? That was unusual, it's true."

"You've never done so before. You've never dared." He tilted his head slightly as he gazed at her, not understanding why everything was different when nothing was. He could see that she was exactly the same as she always was, down to that single freckle centered on her left cheekbone that he wasn't even aware he'd noticed before now. "Again, has some tragedy befallen you? Were you hit over the head?" He did nothing to hide the warning or the menace in his voice. "You do not appear to be yourself."

But if he thought he'd managed to discomfit her, he saw in the next moment that was not to be. The flush faded from her porcelain cheeks, and all she did was smile at him again. With that maddeningly enigmatic curve of her lips.

Lips, he noticed with entirely too much of his body, that were remarkably lush.

This was insupportable.

"I am desolated to disappoint you," she murmured as the plane began to move, bumping gently along the tarmac. "But there was no tragedy." Something glinted in her green gaze, though her smile never dimmed. "Though I must confess in the spirit of full disclosure that I was thinking of quitting."

Achilles only watched her idly, as if she hadn't just said that. Because she couldn't possibly have just said that.

"I beg your pardon," he said after a moment passed and there was still that spike of something dark and furious in his chest. "I must have misheard you. You do not mean that you plan to quit this job. That you wish to leave *me*."

It was not lost on him that he'd phrased that in a way that should have horrified him. Maybe it would at some point. But today what slapped at him was that his assistant spoke of quitting without a single hint of anything like uncertainty on her face.

And he found he couldn't tolerate that.

"I'm considering it," she said. Still smiling. Unaware of her own danger or the dark thing rolling in him, reminding him of how easy it was to wake that monster that slept in him. How disastrously easy.

But Achilles laughed then, understanding finally catching up with him. "If this is an attempt to wrangle more money out of me, Miss Monette, I cannot say that I admire the strategy. You're perfectly well compensated as is. Overcompensated, one might say."

"Might one? Perhaps." She looked unmoved. "Then again, perhaps your rivals have noticed exactly how much you rely on me. Perhaps I've decided that I want more than being at the beck and call of a billionaire. Much less standing in as your favorite bit of target practice."

"It cannot possibly have bothered you that I lost my temper earlier."

Her smile was bland. "If you say it cannot, then I'm sure you must be right."

"I lose my temper all the time. It's never bothered you before. It's part of your job to not be bothered, in point of fact."

"I'm certain that's it." Her enigmatic smile seemed to deepen. "I must be the one who isn't any good at her job."

He had the most insane notion then. It was something about the cool challenge in her gaze, as if they were equals. As if she had every right to call him on whatever she pleased. He had no idea why he wanted to reach across the little space between their chairs and put his hands on her. Test her skin to see if it was as soft as it looked. Taste that lush mouth—

What the hell was happening to him?

Achilles shook his head, as much to clear it as anything else. "If this is your version of a negotiation, you should rethink your approach. You know perfectly well that there's entirely too much going on right now."

"Some might think that this is the perfect time, then, to talk about things like compensation and temper tantrums," Natalie replied, her voice as even and unbothered as ever. There was no reason that should make him grit his teeth. "After all, when one is expected to work twenty-two hours a day and is shouted at for her trouble, one's thoughts automatically turn to what one lacks. It's human nature."

"You lack nothing. You have no time to spend the money I pay you because you're too busy traveling the world—which I also pay for."

"If only I had more than two hours a day to enjoy these piles of money."

"People would kill for the opportunity to spend even five minutes in my presence," he reminded her. "Or have you forgotten who I am?"

"Come now." She shook her head at him, and he had the astonishing sense that she was trying to chastise him. *Him.* "It would not kill you to be more polite, would it?"

Polite.

His own assistant had just lectured him on his manners.

To say that he was reeling hardly began to scratch the surface of Achilles's reaction.

But then she smiled, and that reaction got more complicated. "I got on the plane anyway. I decided not to quit today." Achilles could not possibly have missed her emphasis on that final word. "You're welcome."

And something began to build inside him at that. Something huge, dark, almost overwhelming. He was very much afraid it was rage.

But that, he refused. No matter what. Achilles left his demons behind him a long time ago, and he wasn't going back. He refused.

"If you would like to leave, Miss Monette, I will not stop you," he assured her coldly. "I cannot begin to imagine what has led you to imagine I would try. I do not beg. I could fill your position with a snap of my fingers. I might yet, simply because this conversation is intolerable."

The assistant he'd thought he knew would have swallowed hard at that, then looked away. She would have smoothed her hands over her skirt and apologized as she did it. She had riled him only a few times over the years, and she'd talked her way out of it in exactly that way. He gazed at her expectantly.

But today, Natalie only sat there with distractingly perfect posture and gazed back at him with a certain serene confidence that made him want to...mess her up. Get his hands in that unremarkable ponytail and feel the texture of all that gleaming copper. Or beneath her snowy-white blouse. Or better yet, up beneath that skirt of hers.

He was so furious he wasn't nearly as appalled at himself as he should have been.

"I think we both know perfectly well that while you could snap your fingers and summon crowds of candidates for my position, you'd have a very hard time filling it to your satisfaction," she said with a certainty that...gnawed at him. "Perhaps we could dispense with the threats. You need me."

He would sooner have her leap forward and plunge a knife into his chest.

"I need no one," he rasped out. "And nothing."

His suddenly mysterious assistant only inclined her

head, which he realized was no response at all. As if she was merely patronizing him—a notion that made every muscle in his body clench tight.

"You should worry less about your replacement and more about your job," Achilles gritted out. "I have no idea what makes you think you can speak to me with such disrespect."

"It is not disrespectful to speak frankly, surely," she said. Her expression didn't change, but her green gaze was grave—very much, he thought with dawning incredulity, as if she'd expected better of him.

Achilles could only stare back at her in arrogant astonishment. Was he now to suffer the indignity of being judged by his own assistant? And why was it she seemed wholly uncowed by his amazement?

"Unless you plan to utilize a parachute, it would appear you are stuck right here in your distasteful position for the next few hours," Achilles growled at her when he thought he could speak without shouting. Shouting was too easy. And obscured his actual feelings. "I'd suggest you use the time to rethink your current attitude."

He didn't care for the brilliant smile she aimed at him then, as if she was attempting to encourage him with it. *Him.* He particularly didn't like the way it seemed too bright, as if it was lighting him up from the inside out.

"What a kind offer, Mr. Casilieris," she said in that self-possessed voice of hers that was driving him mad. "I will keep it in mind."

The plane took off then, somersaulting into the London sky. Achilles let gravity press him back against the seat and considered the evidence before him. He had worked with this woman for five years, and she had never spoken to him like that before. Ever. He hardly knew what to make of it.

But then, there was a great deal he didn't know what

to do with, suddenly. The way his heart pounded against his ribs as if he was in a real temper, when he was not the sort of man who lost control. Of his temper or anything else. He expected nothing less than perfection from himself, first and foremost. And temper made him think of those long-ago days of his youth, and his stepfather's hovel of a house, victim to every stray whim and temper and fist until he'd given himself over to all that rage and fury inside him and become little better than an animal himself—

Why was he allowing himself to think of such things? His youth was off-limits, even in his own head. What the hell was *happening*?

Achilles didn't like that Natalie affected him. But what made him suspicious was that she'd never affected him before. He'd approved when she started to wear those glasses and put her hair up, to make herself less of a target for the less scrupulous men he dealt with who thought they could get to him through expressing their interest in her. But he hadn't needed her to downplay her looks because *he* was entranced by her. He hadn't been.

So what had changed today?

What had emboldened her and, worse, allowed her to get under his skin?

He kept circling back to that bathroom in the airport and the fact she'd walked out of it a different person from the one who'd walked in.

Of course, she wasn't a *different person*. Did he imagine the real Natalie had suffered a body snatching? Did he imagine there was some elaborate hoax afoot?

The idea was absurd. But he couldn't seem to get past it. The plane hit its cruising altitude, and he moved from his chair to the leather couch that took pride of place in the center of the cabin that was set up like one of his high-end hotel rooms. He sat back with his laptop and pretended to be looking through his email when he was watching Natalie instead. Looking for clues.

She wasn't moving around the plane with her usual focus and energy. He thought she seemed tentative. Uncertain—and this despite the fact she seemed to walk taller than before. As if she'd changed her very posture in that bathroom. But who did something like that?

A different person would have different posture.

It was crazy. He knew that. And Achilles knew further that he always went a little too intense when he was closing a deal, so it shouldn't have surprised him that he was willing to consider the insane option today. Part of being the sort of unexpected, out-of-the-box thinker he'd always been was allowing his mad little flights of fancy. He never knew where they might lead.

He indulged himself as Natalie sat and started to look through her own bag as if she'd never seen it before. He pulled up the picture of her he kept in his files for security purposes and did an image search on it, because why not.

Achilles was prepared to discover a few photos of random celebrities she resembled, maybe. And then he'd have to face the fact that his favorite assistant might have gone off the deep end. She was right that replacing her would be hard—but it wouldn't be impossible. He hadn't overestimated his appeal—and that of his wildly successful company—to pretty much anyone and everyone. He was swamped with applicants daily, and he didn't even have an open position.

But then none of that mattered because his image search hit gold.

There were pages and pages of pictures. All of his assistant—except it wasn't her. He knew it from the exquisitely bespoke gowns she wore. He knew it from the jewels that flowed around her neck and covered her hands, drawing attention to things like the perfect manicure she had today—when the Natalie he knew almost never had time to care for her nails like that. And every picture he clicked on identified the woman in them not as Natalie Monette, assistant to Achilles Casilieris, but Her Royal Highness, Princess Valentina of Murin.

Achilles didn't have much use for royals, or really anyone with inherited wealth, when he'd had to go to so much trouble to amass his own. He'd never been to the tiny Mediterranean kingdom of Murin, mostly because he didn't have a yacht to dock there during a sparkling summer of endless lounging and, further, didn't need to take advantage of the country's famously friendly approach to taxes. But he recognized King Geoffrey of Murin on sight, and he certainly recognized the Murinese royal family's coat of arms.

It had been splashed all over the private jet he'd seen on the same tarmac as his back in London.

There was madness, Achilles thought then, and then there was a con job that no one would ever suspect—because who could imagine that the person standing in front of them, looking like someone they already knew, was actually someone else?

If he wasn't mistaken—and he knew he wasn't, because there were too many things about his assistant today that didn't make sense, and Achilles was no great believer in coincidence—Princess Valentina of Murin was trying to run a con.

On him.

Which meant a great many things. First, that his actual assistant was very likely pretending to be the princess somewhere, leaving him and her job in the hands of someone she had to know would fail to live up to Achilles's high standards. That suggested that second, she really wasn't all that happy in her position, as this princess had dared to throw in his face in a way he doubted Natalie ever would have. But it also suggested that third, Natalie had effectively given her notice.

Achilles didn't like any of that. At all. But the fourth thing that occurred to him was that clearly, neither this princess nor his missing assistant expected their little switch to be noticed. Natalie, who should have known better, must honestly have believed that he wouldn't notice an imposter in her place. Or she hadn't cared much if he did.

That was enraging, on some level. Insulting.

But Achilles smiled as Valentina settled herself across the coffee table from him, with a certain inbred grace that whispered of palaces and comportment classes and a lifetime of genteel manners.

Because she thought she was tricking him.

Which meant he could trick her instead. A prospect his body responded to with great enthusiasm as he studied her, this woman who looked like an underling whom a man in his position could never have touched out of ethical considerations—but wasn't.

She wasn't his employee. He didn't pay her salary, and she wasn't bound to obey him in anything if she didn't feel like it.

But she had no idea that he knew that.

Achilles almost felt sorry for her. Almost.

"Let's get started," he murmured, as if they'd exchanged no harsh words. He watched confusion move over her face in a blink, then disappear, because she was a royal princess and she was used to concealing her reactions. He planned to have fun with that. The possibilities were endless, and seemed to roll through him like heat. "We have so much work to do, Miss Monette. I hardly know where to begin."

CHAPTER TWO

BY THE TIME they landed in New York, Princess Valentina of Murin was second-guessing her spontaneous, impulsive decision to switch places with the perfect stranger she'd found wearing her face in the airport lounge.

Achilles Casilieris could make anyone second-guess anything, she suspected.

"You do not appear to be paying attention," he said silkily from beside her, as if he knew exactly what she was thinking. And who she was. And every dream she'd ever had since she was a girl—that was how disconcerting this man was, even lounging there beside her in the back of a luxury car doing nothing more alarming than *sitting*.

"I am hanging on your every word," she assured him as calmly as she could, and then she repeated his last three sentences back to him.

But she had no idea what he was talking about. Repeating conversations she wasn't really listening to was a skill she'd learned in the palace a long, long time ago. It came in handy at many a royal gathering. And in many longwinded lectures from her father and his staff.

You have thrown yourself into deep, deep water, she told herself now, as if that wasn't entirely too apparent already. As if it hadn't already occurred to her that she'd better learn how to swim, and fast.

Achilles Casilieris was a problem.

Valentina knew powerful men. Men who ruled countries. Men who came from centuries upon centuries of power and consequence and wielded it with the offhanded superiority of those who had never imagined *not* ruling all they surveyed.

But Achilles was in an entirely different league.

He took over the whole of the backseat of the car that had waited for them on the tarmac in the bright and sunny afternoon, looking roomy and spacious from the outside. He'd insisted she sit next to him on the plush backseat that should have been more than able to fit two people with room to spare. And yet Valentina felt crowded, as if he was pressing up against her when he wasn't. Achilles wasn't touching her, but still, she was entirely too *aware* of him.

He took up all the air. He'd done it on his plane, too.

She had the hectic notion, connected to that knot beneath her breastbone that was preventing her from taking anything like a deep breath, that it wasn't the enclosed space that was the issue. That he would have this same effect anywhere. All that brooding ruthlessness he didn't bother to contain—or maybe he couldn't contain even if he'd wanted to—seemed to hum around him like a kind of force field that both repelled and compelled at once.

If she was honest, the little glimpse she'd had of him in the airport had been the same—she'd just ignored it.

Valentina had been too busy racing into the lounge so she could have a few precious seconds alone. No staff. No guards. No cameras. Just her perched on the top of a closed toilet seat, shut away from the world, breathing. Letting her face do what it liked. Thinking of absolutely nothing. Not her duty. Not her father's expectations.

Certainly not her bloodless engagement to Prince Rodolfo of Tissely, a man she'd tuned out within moments of their first meeting. Or their impending wedding in two months' time, which she could feel bearing down on her like a thick hand around her throat every time she let herself think about it. It wasn't that she didn't *want* to do her duty and marry the Crown Prince of Tissely. She'd been promised in marriage to her father's allies since the day she was born. It was that she'd never given a great deal of thought to what it was she wanted, because *want* had never been an option available to her.

And it had suddenly occurred to her at her latest wedding dress fitting there in London that she was running out of time.

Soon she would be married to a man in what was really more of a corporate merger of two great European brands, the houses of Tissely and Murin. She'd be expected to produce the necessary heirs to continue the line. She would take her place in the great sweep of her family's storied history, unite two ancient kingdoms, and in so doing fulfill her purpose in life. The end.

The end, she'd thought in that bathroom stall, high-end and luxurious but still, a bathroom stall. *My life fulfilled at twenty-seven.*

Valentina was a woman who'd been given everything, including a healthy understanding of how lucky she was. She didn't often indulge herself with thoughts of what was and wasn't fair when there was no doubt she was among the most fortunate people alive.

But the thing was, it still didn't seem fair. No matter how hard she tried not to think about it that way.

She would do what she had to do, of course. She always had and always would, but for that single moment, locked away in a bathroom stall where no one could see her and no one would ever know, she basked in the sheer, dizzying unfairness of it all.

Then she'd pulled herself together, stepped out and had been prepared to march onto her plane and head back to the life that had been plotted out for her since the day she arrived on the planet.

Only to find her twin standing at the sinks.

Her identical twin—though that was, of course, impossible.

"What is this?" the other woman had asked when they'd faced each other, looking something close to scared. Or unnerved, anyway. "How…?"

Valentina had been fascinated. She'd been unable to keep herself from studying this woman who appeared to be wearing her body as well as her face. She was dressed in a sleek pencil skirt and low heels, which showed legs that Valentina recognized all too well, having last seen them in her own mirror. "I'm Valentina."

"Natalie."

She'd repeated that name in her head like it was a magic spell. She didn't know why she felt as if it was.

But then, running into her double in a London bathroom seemed something close enough to magic to count. Right then when she'd been indulging her self-pity about the unchangeable course of her own life, the universe had presented her with a glimpse of what else could be. If she was someone else.

An identical someone else.

They had the same face. The same legs, as she'd already noted. The same coppery hair that her double wore up in a serviceable ponytail and the same nose Valentina could trace directly to her maternal grandmother. What were the chances, she'd wondered then, that they *weren't* related?

And didn't that raise all kinds of interesting questions?

"You're that princess," Natalie had said, a bit haltingly.

But if Valentina was a princess, and if they were related as they surely had to be…

"I suspect you might be, too," she'd said gently.

"We can't possibly be related. I'm a glorified secretary who never really had a home. You're a royal princess. Presumably your lineage dates back to the Roman Conquest."

"Give or take a few centuries." Valentina tried to imagine having a job like that. Or any job. A secretary, glorified or otherwise, who reported to work for someone else and actually *did things* with her time that weren't directly related to being a symbol. She couldn't really wrap her head around it, or being effectively without a home, either, having been a part of Murin since her birth. As much Murin as its beaches and hills, its monuments and its palace. She might as well have been a park. "Depending which branch of the family you mean, of course."

"I was under the impression that people with lineages that could lead to thrones and crown jewels tended to keep better track of their members," Natalie had said, her tone just dry enough to make Valentina decide that given the right circumstances—meaning anywhere that wasn't a toilet—she'd rather like her doppelganger.

And she knew what the other woman had been asking.

"Conspiracy theorists claim my mother was killed and her death hushed up. Senior palace officials have assured me my whole life that no, she merely left to preserve her mental health, and is rumored to be in residence in a hospital devoted to such things somewhere. All I know is that I haven't seen her since shortly after I was born. According to my father, she preferred anonymity to the joys of motherhood."

And she waited for Natalie to give her an explanation in turn. To laugh, perhaps, and then tell her that she'd been raised by two perfectly normal parents in a happily normal somewhere else, filled with golden retrievers and school buses and pumpkin-spiced coffee drinks and whatever else normal people took for granted that Valentina only read about.

But instead, this woman wearing Valentina's face had looked stricken. "I've never met my father," she'd whispered. "My mother's always told me she has no idea who he was. And she bounces from one affair to the next pretty quickly, so I came to terms with the fact it was possible she really, truly didn't know."

And Valentina had laughed, because what else could she do? She'd spent her whole life wishing she'd had more of a family than her chilly father. Oh, she loved him, she did, but he was so excruciatingly proper. So worried about appearances. His version of a hug was a well-meaning critique on her latest public appearance. Love to her father was maintaining and bolstering the family's reputation across the ages. She'd always wanted a sister to share in the bolstering. A brother. A mother. *Someone.*

But she hadn't had anyone. And now she had a stranger who looked just like her.

"My father is many things," she'd told Natalie. It was too soon to say *our father.* And who knew? Maybe they were cousins. Or maybe this was a fluke. No matter that little jolt of recognition inside her, as if she'd been meant to know this woman. As if this was a reunion. "Including His Royal Majesty, King Geoffrey of Murin. What he is not now, nor has ever been, I imagine, is forgettable."

Natalie had shaken her head. "You underestimate my mother's commitment to amnesia. She's made it a life choice instead of a malady. On some level I admire it."

"My mother was the noblewoman Frederica de Burgh, from a very old Murinese family." Valentina watched Natalie closely as she spoke, looking for any hint of…anything, really, in her gaze. "Promised to my father at birth, raised by nuns and kept deliberately sheltered, and then widely held to be unequal to the task of becoming queen. Mentally. But that's the story they would tell, isn't it, to explain why she disappeared? What's your mother's name?"

Natalie sighed and swung her shoulder bag onto the counter. Valentina had the impression that she'd really, truly wanted not to answer. But she had. "She calls herself Erica."

And there it was. Valentina supposed it could be a coincidence that *Erica* was a shortened form of *Frederica*. But how many coincidences were likely when they resulted in two women who'd never met—who never should have met—who happened to be mirror images?

If there was something in her that turned over at the notion that her mother had, in fact, had a maternal impulse after all—just not for Valentina—well, this wasn't the time to think about that. It might never be the time to think about that. She'd spent twenty-seven years trying her best not to think about that.

She changed the subject before she lost her composure completely and started asking questions she knew she shouldn't.

"I saw Achilles Casilieris, out there in the lounge," she'd said instead. The notorious billionaire had been there on her way in, brooding in a corner of the lounge and scowling at the paper he'd been reading. "He looks even more fearsome in person. You can almost *see* all that brash command and dizzying wealth ooze from his pores, can't you?"

"He's my boss," Natalie had said, sounding amused—if rather darkly. "If he was really oozing anything, anywhere, it would be my job to provide first aid until actual medical personnel could come handle it. At which point he would bite my head off for wasting his precious time by not curing him instantly."

Valentina had been flooded with a rash of follow-up questions. Was the biting off of heads normal? Was it fun to work for a man who sounded half-feral? Most important, did Natalie like her life or merely suffer through it?

But then her mobile started buzzing in her clutch. She'd forgotten about ferocious billionaires and thought about things she knew too much about, like the daredevil prince she was bound to marry soon, instead, because their fathers had agreed regardless of whether either one of them liked it. She'd checked the mobile's display to be sure, but wasn't surprised to find she'd guessed correctly. Lucky her, she'd had another meeting with her husband-to-be in Murin that very afternoon. She'd expected it to go the way all their meetings so far had gone. Prince Rodolfo, beloved the world over for his good looks and devil-may-care attitude, would talk. She would listen without really listening. She'd long since concluded that foretold a very happy royal marriage.

"My fiancé," she'd explained, meeting Natalie's gaze again. "Or his chief of staff, to be more precise."

"Congratulations," Natalie murmured.

"Thank you, I'm very lucky." Valentina's mouth curved, though her tone was far more dry than Natalie's had been. "Everyone says so. Prince Rodolfo is objectively attractive. Not all princes can make that claim, but the tabloids have exulted over his abs since he was a teenager. Just as they have salivated over his impressive dating history, which has involved a selection of models and actresses from at least four continents and did not cease in any noticeable way upon our engagement last fall."

"Your Prince Charming sounds…charming," Natalie had said.

Valentina raised one shoulder, then dropped it. "His theory is that he remains free until our marriage, and then will be free once again following the necessary birth of his heir. More discreetly, I can only hope. Meanwhile, I am beside myself with joy that I must take my place at his side in two short months. Of course."

Natalie had laughed, and the sound had made Valentina's stomach flip. Because it sounded like her. It sounded exactly like her.

"It's going to be a terrific couple of months all around, then," her mirror image was saying. "Mr. Casilieris is in rare form. He's putting together a particularly dramatic deal and it's not going his way and he...isn't used to that. So that's me working twenty-two-hour days instead of my usual twenty for the foreseeable future, which is even more fun when he's cranky and snarling."

"It can't possibly be worse than having to smile politely while your future husband lectures you about the absurd expectation of fidelity in what is essentially an arranged marriage for hours on end. The absurdity is that *he* might be expected to curb his impulses for a year or so, in case you wondered. The expectations for *me* apparently involve quietly and chastely finding fulfillment in philanthropic works, like his sainted absentee mother, who everyone knows manufactured a supposed health crisis so she could live out her days in peaceful seclusion. It's easy to be philanthropically fulfilled while living in isolation in Bavaria."

Natalie had smiled. "Try biting your tongue while your famously short-tempered boss rages at you for no reason, for the hundredth time in an hour, because he pays you to stand there and take it without wilting or crying or selling whingeing stories about him to the press."

Valentina had returned that smile. "Or the hours and hours of grim palace-vetted prewedding press interviews in the company of a pack of advisers who will censor everything I say and inevitably make me sound like a bit of animated treacle, as out of touch with reality as the average overly sweet dessert."

"Speaking of treats, I also have to deal with the board of directors Mr. Casilieris treats like irritating schoolchildren, his packs of furious ex-lovers each with her own vendetta, all his terrified employees who need to be coached through meetings with him and treated for PTSD after, and every last member of his staff in every one of his households, who like me to be the one to ask him the questions they know will set him off on one of his scorch-the-earth rages." Natalie had moved closer then, and lowered her voice. "I was thinking of quitting, to be honest. Today."

"I can't quit, I'm afraid," Valentina had said. Regretfully.

But she'd wished she could. She'd wished she could just…walk away and not have to live up to anyone's expectations. And not have to marry a man whom she barely knew. And not have to resign herself to a version of the same life so many of her ancestors had lived. Maybe that was where the idea had come from. Blood was blood, after all. And this woman clearly shared her blood. What if…?

"I have a better idea," she'd said, and then she'd tossed it out there before she could think better of it. "Let's switch places. For a month, say. Six weeks at the most. Just for a little break."

"That's crazy," Natalie said at once, and she was right. Of course she was right.

"Insane," Valentina had agreed. "But you might find royal protocol exciting! And I've always wanted to do the things everyone else in the world does. Like go to a real job."

"People can't *switch places*." Natalie had frowned. "And certainly not with a princess."

"You could think about whether or not you really want to quit," Valentina pointed out, trying to sweeten the deal. "It would be a lovely holiday for you. Where will Achilles Casilieris be in six weeks' time?"

"He's never gone from London for too long," Natalie had said, as if she was considering it.

Valentina had smiled. "Then in six weeks we'll meet in London. We'll text in the meantime with all the necessary details about our lives, and on the appointed day we'll just meet up and switch back and no one will ever be the wiser. Doesn't that sound like *fun*?"

"It would never work," Natalie had replied. Which wasn't exactly a *no*. "No one will ever believe I'm you."

Valentina waved a hand, encompassing the pair of them. "How would anyone know the difference? I can barely tell myself."

"People will take one look at me and know I'm not you. *You* look like a *princess*."

"You, too, can look like a princess," Valentina assured her. Then smiled. "This princess, anyway. You already do."

"You're elegant. Poised. You've had years of training, presumably. How to be a diplomat. How to be polite in every possible situation. Which fork to use at dinner, for God's sake."

"Achilles Casilieris is one of the wealthiest men alive," Valentina had pointed out. "He dines with as many kings as I do. I suspect that as his personal assistant, Natalie, you have, too. And have likely learned how to navigate the cutlery."

"No one will believe it," Natalie had insisted. But she'd sounded a bit as if she was wavering.

Valentina tugged off the ring on her left hand and placed it down on the counter between them. It made an audible *clink* against the marble surface, as well it should, given it was one of the crown jewels of the kingdom of Tissely.

"Try it on. I dare you. It's an heirloom from Prince Rodolfo's extensive treasury of such items, dating back to the dawn of time, more or less." She smiled. "If it doesn't fit we'll never speak of switching places again."

But the ring had fit her double as if it had been made especially for her.

And after that, switching clothes was easy. Valentina found herself in front of the bathroom mirror, dressed like a billionaire's assistant, when Natalie walked out of the stall behind her in her own shift dress and the heels her favorite shoe designer had made just for her. It was like looking in a mirror, but one that walked and looked unsteady on her feet and was wearing her hair differently.

Valentina couldn't tell if she was disconcerted or excited. Both, maybe.

She'd eyed Natalie. "Will your glasses give me a headache, do you suppose?"

But Natalie had pulled them from her face and handed them over. "They're clear glass. I was getting a little too much attention from some of the men Mr. Casilieris works with, and it annoyed him. I didn't want to lose my job, so I started wearing my hair up and these glasses. It worked like a charm."

"I refuse to believe men are so idiotic."

Natalie had grinned as Valentina took the glasses and slid them onto her nose. "The men we're talking about weren't exactly paying me attention because they found me enthralling. It was a diversionary tactic during negotiations, and yes, you'd be surprised how many men fail to see a woman who looks smart."

She'd freed her hair from its utilitarian ponytail and shook it out, then handed the stretchy elastic to Valentina. It took Valentina a moment to re-create the ponytail on her own head, and then it was done.

And it really was like magic.

"This is crazy," Natalie had whispered.

"We have to switch places now," Valentina said softly, hearing the rough patch in her own voice. "I've always wanted to be…someone else. Someone normal. Just for a little while."

And she'd gotten exactly what she'd wanted, hadn't she?

"I am distressed, Miss Monette, that I cannot manage to secure your attention for more than a moment or two," Achilles said then, slamming Valentina back into this car he dominated so easily when all he was doing was sitting there.

Sitting there, filling up the world without even trying.

He was *devastating*. There was no other possible word that could describe him. His black hair was close-cropped to his head, which only served to highlight his strong, intensely masculine features. She'd had hours on the plane to study him as she'd repeatedly failed to do the things he'd expected of her, and she still couldn't really get her head around why it was that he was so…affecting. He shouldn't have been. Dark hair. Dark eyes that tended toward gold when his temper washed over him, which he'd so far made no attempt to hide. A strong nose that reminded her of ancient statues she'd seen in famous museums. That lean, hard body of his that wasn't made of marble or bronze but seemed to suggest both as he used it so effortlessly. A predator packed into a dark suit that seemed molded to him, whispering suggestions of a lethal warrior when all he was doing was taking phone calls with a five-hundred-thousand-dollar watch on one wrist that he didn't flash about, because he was Achilles Casilieris. He didn't need flash.

Achilles was something else.

It was the power that seemed to emanate from him, even when he was doing nothing but sitting quietly. It was the fierce hit of his intelligence, that brooding, unmistakable cleverness that seemed to wrap around him like a cloud. It was something in the way he looked at her, as if he saw too much and too deeply and no matter that Valentina's unreadable game face was the envy of Europe. Besides all that, there was something untamed about him. Fierce.

Something about him left her breathless. Entirely too close to reeling.

"Do you require a gold star every time you make a statement?" she asked, careful not to look at him. It was too hard to look away. She'd discovered that on the plane ride from London—and he was a lot closer now. So close she was sure she could feel the heat of his body from where she sat. "I'll be certain to make a note to celebrate you more often. Sir."

Valentina didn't know what she was doing. In Natalie's job, certainly, but also with this man in general. She'd learned one thing about powerful people—particularly men—and it was that they did not enjoy being challenged. Under any circumstances. What made her think Achilles would go against type and magically handle this well?

But she couldn't seem to stop herself.

And the fact that she had never been one to challenge much of anything before hardly signified. Or maybe that was why she felt so unfettered, she thought. Because this wasn't her life. This wasn't her remote father and his endless expectations for the behavior of his only child. This was a strange little bit of role-playing that allowed her to be someone other than Princess Valentina for a moment. A few weeks, that was all. Why not challenge Achilles while she was at it? *Especially* if no one else ever did?

She could feel his gaze on the side of her face, that brooding dark gold, and she braced herself. Then made sure her expression was nothing but serene as she turned to face him.

It didn't matter. There was no minimizing this man.

She could feel the hit of him—like a fist—deep in her belly. And then lower.

"Are you certain you were not hit in the head?" Achilles asked, his dark voice faintly rough with the hint of his native Greek. "Perhaps in the bathroom at the airport? I fear that such places can often suffer from slippery floors. Deadly traps for the unwary."

"It was only a bathroom," she replied airily. "It wasn't slippery or otherwise notable in any way."

"Are you sure?" And something in his voice and his hard gaze prickled into her then. Making her chest feel tighter.

Valentina did not want to talk about the bathroom, much less anything that had happened there. And there was something in his gaze that worried her—but that was insane. He couldn't have any idea that she'd run into her own twin. How could he? Valentina had been unaware that there was the faintest possibility she might have a twin until today.

Which made her think about her father and his many, many lectures about his only child in a new, unfortunate light. But Valentina thrust that aside. That was something to worry about when she was a princess again. That was a problem she could take up when she was back in Murin Castle.

Here, now, she was a secretary. An executive assistant, no more and no less.

"I beg your pardon, Mr. Casilieris." She let her smile deepen and ignored the little hum of...something deep inside her when his gaze seemed to catch fire. "Are you trying to tell me that you need a bathroom? Should I ask the driver to stop the car right here in the middle of the George Washington Bridge?"

She expected him to get angry again. Surely that was what had been going on before, back in London before the plane had taken off. She'd seen temper all over that fierce, hard face of his and gleaming hot in his gaze. More than that, she'd felt it inside her. As if the things he felt echoed within her, winding her into knots. She felt something a whole lot like a chill inch its way down her spine at that notion.

But Achilles only smiled. And that was far more dangerous than merely devastating.

"Miss Monette," he said and shook his head, as if she amused him, when she could see that the thing that moved over that ruthless face of his was far too intense to be simple *amusement*. "I had no idea that beneath your officious exterior you've been hiding a comedienne all this time. For five years you've worked at my side and never let so much as a hint of this whimsical side of your personality out into the open. Whatever could have changed?"

He knows. The little voice inside her was certain— and terrified.

But it was impossible. Valentina knew it was impossible, so she made herself smile and relax against the leather seat as if she'd never in her life been so at her ease. Very much as if she was not within scant inches of a very large, very powerful, very intense male who was eyeing her the way gigantic lions and tigers and jaguars eyed their food. When they were playing with it.

She'd watched enough documentaries and made enough state visits to African countries to know firsthand.

"Perhaps I've always been this amusing," she suggested, managing to tamp down her hysteria about oversize felines, none of which was particularly helpful at the moment. "Perhaps you've only recently allowed yourself to truly listen to me."

"I greatly enjoy listening to you," Achilles replied. There was a laziness in the way he sat there, sprawled out in the backseat of his car, that dark gold gaze on hers.

A certain laziness, yes—but Valentina didn't believe it for a second. "I particularly enjoy listening to you when you are doing your job perfectly. Because you know how much I admire perfection. I insist on it, in fact. Which is why I cannot understand why you failed to provide it today."

"I don't know what you mean."

But she knew what he meant. She'd been on the plane and she'd been the one to fail repeatedly to do what was clearly her job. She'd hung up on one conference call and failed entirely to connect another. She'd expected him to explode—if she was honest, there was a part of her that wanted him to explode, in the way that anyone might want to poke and poke and poke at some kind of blister to see if it would pop. But he hadn't popped. He hadn't lost his temper at all, despite the fact that it had been very clear to Valentina very quickly that she was a complete and utter disaster at doing whatever it was that Natalie did.

When Achilles had stared at her in amazement, however, she hadn't made any excuses. She'd only gazed right back, serenely, as if she'd meant to do whatever utterly incorrect thing it was. As if it was all some kind of strategy.

She could admit that she hadn't really thought the job part through. She been so busy fantasizing herself into some kind of normal life that it had never occurred to her that, normal or not, a life was still *a whole life*. She had no idea how to live any way but the way she'd been living for almost thirty years. How remarkably condescending, she'd thought up there on Achilles Casilieris's jet, that she'd imagined she could simply step into a job—especially one as demanding as this appeared to be—and do it merely because she'd decided it was her chance at something "normal."

Valentina had found the entire experience humbling, if she was honest, and it had been only a few hours since she'd switched places with Natalie in London. Who knew what else awaited her?

But Achilles was still sprawled there beside her, that unnerving look of his making her skin feel too small for her bones.

"Natalie, Natalie," he murmured, and Valentina told herself it was a good thing he'd used that name. It wasn't her name, and she needed the reminder. This wasn't about her. It wasn't her job to advocate for Natalie when the other woman might not wish for her to do anything like that. She was on a fast track to losing Natalie her job, and then what? Valentina didn't have to worry about her employment prospects, but she had no idea what the market was like for billionaire's assistants.

But maybe there was a part of her that already knew that there was no way Natalie Monette was a stranger to her. Certainly not on the genetic level. And that had implications she wasn't prepared to examine just yet, but she did know that the woman who was in all likelihood her long-lost identical twin did not have to work for Achilles Casilieris unless she wanted to.

How arrogant of you, a voice inside her said quietly. *Her Royal Highness, making unilateral decisions for others' lives without their input.*

The voice sounded a little too much like her father's.

"That is my name," Valentina said to Achilles, in case there had been any doubt. Perhaps with a little too much force.

But she had the strangest notion that he was...*tasting* the name as he said it. As if he'd never said it before. Did he call Natalie by her first name? Valentina rather thought not, given that he'd called her *Miss Monette* when she'd met him—but that was neither here nor there, she told herself. And no matter that she was a woman who happened to know the power of titles. She had many of her own. And her life was marked by those who used the different versions of her titles, not to mention the few who actually called her by her first name.

"I cannot tolerate this behavior," he said, but it wasn't in that same infuriated tone he'd used earlier. If anything, he sounded almost…indulgent. But surely that was impossible. "It borders on open rebellion, and I cannot have that. This is not a democracy, I'm afraid. This is a dictatorship. If I want your opinion, I'll tell you what it is."

There was no reason her heart should have been kicking at her like that, her pulse so loud in her ears she was sure he must be able to hear it himself.

"What an interesting way to foster employee loyalty," she murmured. "Really more of a scorch-the-earth approach. Do you find it gets you the results you want?"

"I do not need to breed employee loyalty," Achilles told her, sounding even lazier than before, those dark eyes of his on hers. "People are loyal to me or they are fired. You seem to have forgotten reality today, Natalie. Allow me to remind you that I pay you so much money that I own your loyalty, just as I own everything else."

"Perhaps," and her voice was a little too rough then. A little too shaky, when what could this possibly have to do with her? She was a visitor. Natalie's loyalty was no concern of hers. "I have no wish to be owned. Does anyone? I think you'll find that they do not."

Achilles shrugged. "Whether you wish it or do not, that is how it is."

"That is why I was considering quitting," she heard herself say. And she was no longer looking at him. That was still far too dangerous, too disconcerting. She found herself staring down at her hands, folded in her lap. She could feel that she was frowning, when she learned a long, long time ago never to show her feelings in public. "It's all very well and good for you, of course. I imagine it's quite pleasant to have minions. But for me, there's more to life than blind loyalty. There's more to life than work." She blinked back a strange heat. "I may not have experienced it myself, but I know there must be."

"And what do you think is out there?" He shifted in the seat beside her, but Valentina still refused to look back at him, no matter how she seemed almost physically compelled to do just that. "What do you think you're missing? Is it worth what you are throwing away here today, with this aggressive attitude and the childish pretense that you don't know your own job?"

"It's only those who are bored of the world, or jaded, who are so certain no one else could possibly wish to see it."

"No one is keeping you from roaming about the planet at will," he told her in a low voice. Too low. So low it danced along her skin and seemed to insinuate itself beneath her flesh. "But you seem to wish to burn down the world you know in order to see the one you don't. That is not what I would call wise. Would you?"

Valentina didn't understand why his words seemed to beat beneath her own skin. But she couldn't seem to catch her breath. And her eyes seemed entirely too full, almost scratchy, with an emotion she couldn't begin to name.

She was aware of too many things. Of the car as it slid through the Manhattan streets. Of Achilles himself, too big and too masculine in the seat beside her, and much too close besides. And most of all, that oddly weighted thing within her, rolling around and around until she couldn't tell the difference between sensation and reaction.

And him right there in the middle of it, confusing her all the more.

CHAPTER THREE

ACHILLES DIDN'T SAY another word, and that was worse. It left Valentina to sit there with her own thoughts in a whirl and nothing to temper them. It left no barrier between that compelling, intent look in his curiously dark eyes and her.

Valentina had no experience with men. Her father had insisted that she grow up as sheltered as possible from public life, so that she could enjoy what little privacy was afforded to a European princess before she turned eighteen. She'd attended carefully selected boarding schools run strictly and deliberately, but that hadn't prevented her classmates from involving themselves in all kinds of dramatic situations. Even then, Valentina had kept herself apart.

Your mother's defection was a stain on the throne, her father always told her. *It is upon us to render it clean and whole again.*

Valentina had been far too terrified of staining Murin any further to risk a scandal. She'd concentrated on her studies and her friends and left the teenage rebellions to others. And once out of school, she'd been thrust unceremoniously into the spotlight. She'd been an ambassador for her kingdom wherever she went, and more than that, she'd always known that she was promised to the Crown

Prince of Tissely. Any scandals she embroiled herself in would haunt two kingdoms.

She'd never seen the point.

And along the way she'd started to take a certain pride in the fact that she was saving herself for her predetermined marriage. It was the one thing that was hers to give on her wedding night that had nothing to do with her father or her kingdom.

Is it pride that's kept you chaste—or is it control? a little voice inside her asked then, and the way it kicked in her, Valentina suspected she wouldn't care for the answer. She ignored it.

But the point was, she had no idea how to handle men. Not on any kind of intimate level. These past few hours, in fact, were the longest she'd ever spent alone in the company of a man. It simply didn't happen when she was herself. There were always attendants and aides swarming around Princess Valentina. Always.

She told herself that was why she was having such trouble catching her breath. It was the novelty—that was all. It certainly wasn't *him*.

Still, it was almost a relief when the car pulled up in front of a quietly elegant building on the Upper West Side of Manhattan, perched there with a commanding view of Central Park, and came to a stop.

The late-afternoon breeze washed over her when she stepped from the car, smelling improbably of flowers in the urban sprawl of New York City. But Valentina decided to take it as a blessing.

Achilles remained silent as he escorted her into the building. He only raised his chin in the barest of responses to the greeting that came his way from the doormen in the shiny, obviously upscale lobby, and then he led her into a private elevator located toward the back and behind another set of security guards. It was a gleaming, shining thing that he operated with a key. And it was blessedly without any mirrors.

Valentina wasn't entirely sure whom she'd see if she looked at her own reflection just then.

There were too many things she didn't understand churning inside her, and she hadn't the slightest idea what she was doing here. What on earth she hoped to gain from this odd little lark across the planet, literally in another woman's shoes.

A break, she reminded herself sternly. A vacation. A little holiday away from all the duties and responsibilities of Princess Valentina, which was more important now than ever. She would give herself over to her single-greatest responsibility in a matter of weeks. She would marry Prince Rodolfo and make both of their fathers and all of their subjects very, very happy.

And a brief escape had sounded like bliss for that split second back there in London—and it still did, when she thought about what waited for her. The terribly appropriate royal marriage. The endlessly public yet circumspect life of a modern queen. The glare of all that attention that she and any children she bore could expect no matter where they went or what they did, yet she could never comment upon lest she seem ungrateful or entitled.

Hers was to wave and smile—that was all. She was marrying a man she hardly knew who would expect the marital version of the same. This was a little breather before the reality of all that. This was a tiny bit of space between her circumscribed life at her father's side and more of the same at her husband's.

She couldn't allow the brooding, unreadable man beside her to ruin it, no matter how unnerving his dark gold gaze was. No matter what fires it kicked up inside her that she hardly dared name.

The elevator doors slid open, delivering them straight

into the sumptuous front hall of an exquisitely decorated penthouse. Valentina followed Achilles as he strode deep inside, not bothering to spare her a glance as he moved. She was glad that he walked ahead of her, which allowed her to look around so she could get her bearings without seeming to do so. Because, of course, Natalie would already know her way around this place.

She took in the high ceilings and abundant windows all around. The sweeping stairs that led up toward at least two more floors. The mix of art deco and a deep coziness that suggested this penthouse was more than just a showcase; Achilles actually *lived* here.

Valentina told herself—sternly—that there was no earthly reason that notion should make her shiver.

She was absurdly grateful when a housekeeper appeared, clucking at Achilles in what it took Valentina longer than it should have to realize was Greek. A language she could converse in, though she would never consider herself anything like fluent. Still, it took her only a very few moments to understand that whatever the danger Achilles exuded and however ruthless the swath he cut through the entire world with a single glance, this woman thought he was wonderful.

She *beamed* at him.

It would not do to let that get to her, Valentina warned herself as something warm seemed to roll its way through her, pooling in the strangest places. She should not draw any conclusions about a man who was renowned for his fierceness in all things and yet let a housekeeper treat him like family.

The woman declared she would feed him no matter if he was hungry or not, lest he get skinny and weak, and bustled back in the direction of what Valentina assumed was the kitchen.

"You're looking around as if you are lost," Achilles

murmured, when Valentina didn't think she'd been looking around at all. "When you have spent more time in this penthouse over the last five years than I have."

Valentina hated the fact that she started a bit when she realized his attention was focused on her again. And that he was speaking in English, which seemed to make him sound that much more knowing.

Or possibly even mocking, unless she was very much mistaken.

"Mr. Casilieris," she said, lacing her voice with gentle reprove, "I work for you. I don't understand why you appear to be quite so interested in what you think is happening inside my head today. Especially when you are so mistaken."

"Am I?"

"Entirely." She raised her brows at him. "If I could suggest that we concentrate more on matters of business than fictional representations of what might or might not be going on inside my mind, I think we might be more productive."

"As productive as we were on the flight over?" His voice was a lazy sort of lash, as amused as it was on target.

Valentina only smiled, hoping she looked enigmatic and strategic rather than at a loss.

"Are *you* lost?" she asked him after a moment, because neither one of them had moved from the great entry that bled into the spacious living room, then soared up two stories, a quiet testament to his wealth and power.

"Careful, Miss Monette," Achilles said with a certain dark precision. "As delightful as I have found today's descent into insubordination, I have a limit. It would be in your best interests not to push me there too quickly."

Valentina had made a study out of humbly accepting all kinds of news she didn't wish to hear over the years. She bent her head, let her lips curve a bit—but not enough to be called a smile, only enough to show she was feeling… something. Then she simply stood there quietly. It was amazing how many unpleasant moments she'd managed to get through that way.

So she had no earthly idea why there was a part of her that wanted nothing more than to look Achilles straight in his dark eyes and ask him, *Or what?*

Somehow, thankfully, she refrained.

Servants came in behind them with luggage—some of which Valentina assumed must be Natalie's and thus hers—but Achilles did not appear to notice them. He kept his attention trained directly on her.

A lesser woman would have been disconcerted, Valentina thought. Someone unused to being the focus of attention, for example. Someone who hadn't spent a part of every day since she turned eighteen having cameras in her face to record every flutter of her eyelashes and rip apart every facet of whatever she happened to be wearing and how she'd done her hair. Every expression that crossed her face was a headline.

What was a cranky billionaire next to that?

"There's no need to repair to our chambers after the flight, I think," he said softly, and Valentina had that odd notion again. That he could see right through her. That he knew things he couldn't possibly know. "We can get right to it."

And there was no reason that that should feel almost… dirty. As if he was suggesting—

But, of course, that was absurd, Valentina told herself staunchly. He was Achilles Casilieris. He was renowned almost as much for his prowess in the sheets as he was for his dominance in the boardroom. In some circles, more.

He tended toward the sort of well-heeled women who

were mainstays on various charity circuits. Not for him the actresses or models whom so many other men of his stature preferred. That, apparently, was not good enough for Achilles Casilieris. Valentina had found herself with some time on the plane to research it herself, after Achilles had finished the final call she'd failed entirely to set up to his liking and had sat a while, a fulminating stare fixed on her. Then he'd taken himself off to one of the jet's finely appointed staterooms, and she'd breathed a bit easier.

A bit.

She'd looked around for a good book to read, preferably a paperback romance because who didn't like hope and happiness with a bit of sex thrown in to make it spicy, but there had been nothing of the sort. Achilles apparently preferred dreary economic magazines that trumpeted out recession and doom from all quarters. Valentina had kicked off her shoes, tucked her legs beneath her on the smooth leather chair she'd claimed for the flight, and indulged herself with a descent into the tabloid and gossip sites she normally avoided. Because she knew how many lies they told about her, so why would she believe anything she read about anyone else?

Still, they were a great way to get a sense of the kind of coverage a man like Achilles suffered, which would surely tell her…something. But the answer was…not much. He was featured in shots from charity events where other celebrities gathered like cows at a trough, but was otherwise not really a tabloid staple. Possibly because he was so sullen and scowling, she thought.

His taste in bedmates, however, was clear even without being splashed across screeching front pages all over the world. Achilles tended toward women who were less celebrated for their faces and more for their actions. Which wasn't to say they weren't all beautiful, of course. That seemed to be a requirement. But they couldn't only be beautiful.

This one was a civil rights attorney of some renown. That one was a journalist who spent most of her time in terrifying war zones. This one had started a charity to benefit a specific cancer that had taken her younger sister. That one was a former Olympic athlete who had dedicated her post-competition life to running a lauded program for at-risk teenagers.

He clearly had a type. Accomplished, beautiful women who did good in the world and who also happened to be wealthy enough all on their own. The uncharitable part of her suspected that last part was because he knew a woman of independent means would not be as interested in his fortune as a woman who had nothing. No gold diggers need apply, clearly.

But the point was, she knew she was mistaken about his potentially suggestive words. Because "assistant to billionaire" was not the kind of profession that would appeal to a man like Achilles. It saved no lives. It bettered nothing.

Valentina found herself glaring at his back as he led her into a lavish office suite on the first level of his expansive penthouse. When she stood in the center of the room, awaiting further instructions, he only crooked a brow. He leaned back against the large desk that stretched across one wall and regarded her with that hot sort of focus that made everything inside her seem to shift hard to the left.

She froze. And then she could have stood there for hours, for all she knew, as surely as if he'd caught her and held her fast in his fists.

"When you are ready, Miss Monette, feel free to take your seat." His voice was razor sharp, cut through with that same rough darkness that she found crept through her limbs. Lighting her up and making her feel something like sluggish. She didn't understand it. "Though I do love being kept waiting."

More chastened than she wanted to admit, Valentina moved to one of the seats set around a table to the right of the desk, at the foot of towering bookshelves stuffed full of serious-looking books, and settled herself in it. When he continued to stare at her as if she was deliberately keeping him waiting, she reached into the bag—Natalie's bag, which she'd liberated from the bathroom when she'd left the airport with Achilles—until she found a tablet.

A few texts with her double had given her the passwords she needed and some advice.

Just write down everything he says. He likes to forget he said certain things, and it's always good to have a record. One of my jobs is to function as his memory.

Valentina had wanted to text back her thoughts on that, but had refrained. Natalie might have wanted to quit this job, but that was up to her, not the woman taking her place for a few weeks.

"Anything else?" Achilles's voice had a dark edge. "Would you like to have a snack? Perhaps a brief nap? Tell me, is there any way that I can make you more comfortable, Miss Monette, such that you might actually take it upon yourself to do a little work today?"

And Valentina didn't know what came over her. Because she wanted to argue. She, who had made a virtue out of remaining quiet and cordial under any circumstances, wanted to fight. She didn't understand it. She knew it was Achilles. That there was something in him that made her want to do or say anything to get some kind of reaction. It didn't matter that it was madness. It was something about that look in his eyes. Something about that hard, amused mouth of his.

It was something about *him*.

But Valentina reminded herself that this was not her life.

This was not her life and this was not her job, and none of this was hers to ruin. She was the steward of Natalie's life for a little while, nothing more. She imagined that Natalie would be doing the same for her. Maybe breathing a little bit of new life into the tired old royal nonsense she'd find waiting for her at Murin Castle, but that was all. Neither one of them was out to wreck what they found.

And she'd never had any trouble whatsoever keeping to the party line. Doing her father's bidding, behaving appropriately, being exactly the princess whom everyone imagined she was. She felt that responsibility—to her people, to her bloodline, to her family's history—deeply. She'd never acted out the way so many of her friends had. She'd never fought against her own responsibilities. It wasn't that she was afraid to do any of those things, but simply that it had never occurred to her to try. Valentina had always known exactly who she was and what her life would hold, from her earliest days.

So she didn't recognize this thing in her that wanted nothing more than to cause a commotion. To stand up and throw the tablet she held at Achilles's remarkably attractive head. To kick over the chair she was sitting in and, while she was at it, that desk of his, too, all brash steel and uncompromising masculinity, just like its owner.

She wanted to do *something*. Anything. She could feel it humming through her veins, bubbling in her blood. As if something about this normal life she'd tried on for size had infected her. Changed her. When it had only been a few hours.

He's a ruthless man, something reckless inside her whispered. *He can take it.*

But this wasn't her life. She had to protect it, not destroy it, no matter what was moving in her, poking at her, tempting her to act out for the first time in her life.

So Valentina smiled up at Achilles, forced herself to remain serene the way she always did, and got to work.

It was late into the New York night when Achilles finally stopped torturing his deceitful princess.

He made her go over byzantine contracts that rendered his attorneys babbling idiots. He questioned her on clauses he only vaguely understood himself, and certainly couldn't expect her to be conversant on. He demanded she prepare memos he had no intention of sending. He questioned her about events he knew she could not possibly know anything about, and the truth was that he enjoyed himself more than he could remember enjoying anything else for quite some time.

When Demetria had bustled in with food, Achilles had waved Valentina's away.

"My assistant does not like to eat while she works," he told his housekeeper, but he'd kept his gaze on Valentina while he'd said it.

"I don't," she'd agreed merrily enough. "I consider it a weakness." She'd smiled at him. "But you go right ahead."

Point to the princess, he'd thought.

The most amazing thing was that Princess Valentina never backed down. Her ability to brazen her way through the things she didn't know, in fact, was nothing short of astounding. Impressive in the extreme. Achilles might have admired it if he hadn't been the one she was trying to fool.

"It is late," he said finally, when he thought her eyes might glaze over at last. Though he would cast himself out his own window to the Manhattan streets below before he'd admit his might, too. "And while there is always more to do, I think it is perhaps wise if we take this as a natural stopping place."

Valentina smiled at him, tucked up in that chair of hers that she had long since claimed as her own in a way he couldn't remember the real Natalie had ever done, her green eyes sparkling.

"I understand if you need a rest," she said sweetly. Too sweetly. "Sir."

Achilles had been standing at the windows, his back to the mad gleam of Manhattan. But at that, he let himself lean back, his body shifting into something...looser. More dangerous.

And much, much hotter than contracts.

"I worry my hearing has failed me. Because it sounded very much as if you were impugning my manhood."

"Only if your manhood is so fragile that you can't imagine it requires a rest," she said, and aimed a sunny smile at him as if that would take away the sting of her words. "But you are Achilles Casilieris. You have made yourself a monument to manhood, clearly. No fragility allowed."

"It is almost as if you think debating me like this is some kind of strategy," he said softly, making no attempt to ratchet back the ruthlessness in his voice. Much less do something about the fire he could feel storming through him everywhere else. "Let me warn you, again, it is only a strategy if your goal is to find yourself without a job and without a recommendation. To say nothing of the black mark I will happily put beside your name."

Valentina waved a hand in the air, airily, dismissing him. And her possible firing, black marks—all of it. Something else he very likely would have found impressive if he'd been watching her do it to someone else.

"So many threats." She shook her head. "I understand that this is how you run your business and you're very successful, but really. It's exhausting. Imagine how many more bees you could get with honey."

He didn't want to think about honey. Not when there were only the two of them here, in this office cushioned by the night outside and the rest of the penthouse. No shared walls on these floors he owned. This late, none of the staff would be up. It was only Achilles and this princess pretending to be his assistant, and the buttery light of the few lamps they'd switched on, making the night feel thick and textured everywhere the light failed to reach.

Like inside him.

"Come here."

Valentina blinked, but her green gaze was unreadable then. She only looked at him for a moment, as if she'd forgotten that she was playing this game. And that in it, she was his subordinate.

"Come here," he said again. "Do not make me repeat myself, I beg you. You will not like my response."

She stood the way she did everything else, with an easy grace. With that offhanded elegance that did things to him he preferred not to examine. And he knew she had no desire to come any closer to him. He could feel it. Her wariness hung between them like some kind of smoke, and it ignited that need inside him. And for a moment he thought she might disobey him. That she might balk—and it was in that moment he thought she'd stay where she was, across the room, that he had understood how very much he wanted her.

In a thousand ways he shouldn't, because Achilles was a man who did not *want*. He took. Wanting was a weakness that led only to darkness—though it didn't feel like a weakness tonight. It felt like the opposite.

But he'd underestimated his princess. Her shoulders straightened almost imperceptibly. And then she glided toward him, head high like some kind of prima ballerina, her face set in the sort of pleasant expression he now knew she could summon and dispatch at will. He admired that, too.

And he'd thrown out that summons because he could. Because he wanted to. And he was experimenting with this new *wanting*, no matter how little he liked it.

Still, there was no denying the way his body responded as he watched her walk toward him. There was no denying the rich, layered tension that seemed to fill the room. And him, making his pulse a living thing as his blood seemed to heat in his veins.

Something gleamed in that green gaze of hers, but she kept coming. She didn't stop until she was directly beside him, so close that if she breathed too heavily he thought her shoulder might brush his. He shifted so that he stood slightly behind her, and jutted his chin toward the city laid out before them.

"What do you see when you look out the window?"

He felt more than saw the glance she darted at him. But then she kept her eyes on the window before them. On the ropes of light stretching out in all hectic directions possible below.

"Is that a trick question? I see Manhattan."

"I grew up in squalor." His voice was harsher than he'd intended, but Achilles did nothing to temper it. "It is common, I realize, for successful men to tell stories of their humble beginnings. Americans in particular find these stories inspiring. It allows them to fantasize that they, too, might better themselves against any odds. But the truth is more of a gray area, is it not? Beginnings are never quite so humble as they sound when rich men claim them. But me?" He felt her gaze on him then, instead of the mess of lights outside. "When I use the word *squalor*, that's an upgrade."

Her swallow was audible. Or perhaps he was paying her too close attention. Either way, he didn't back away.

"I don't know why you're telling me this."

"When you look through this window you see a city. A place filled with people going about their lives, traffic and isolation." He shifted so he could look down at her. "I see hope. I see vindication. I see all the despair and all the pain and all the loss that went into creating the man you see before you tonight. Creating this." And he moved his chin to indicate the penthouse. And the Casilieris Company while he was at it. "And there is nothing that I wouldn't do to protect it."

And he didn't know what had happened to him while he was speaking. He'd been playing a game, and then suddenly it seemed as if the game had started to play him—and it wasn't finished. Something clutched at him, as if he was caught in the grip of some massive fist.

It was almost as if he wanted this princess, this woman who believed she was tricking him—deceiving him—to understand him.

This, too, was unbearable.

But he couldn't seem to stop.

"Do you think people become driven by accident, Miss Monette?" he asked, and he couldn't have said why that thing gripping him seemed to clench harder. Making him sound far more intense than he thought he should have felt. Risking the truth about himself he carried inside and shared with no one. But he still didn't stop. "Ambition, desire, focus and drive—do you think these things grow on trees? But then, perhaps I'm asking the wrong person. Have you not told me a thousand times that you are not personally ambitious?"

It was one of the reasons he'd kept Natalie with him for so long, when other assistants to men like him used positions like hers as springboards into their own glorious careers. But this woman was not Natalie. If he hadn't known it before, he'd have known it now, when it was a full-scale struggle to keep his damned hands to himself.

"Ambition, it seems to me, is for those who have the freedom to pursue it. And for those who do not—" and Valentina's eyes seemed to gleam at that, making Achilles wonder exactly what her ambitions were "—it is nothing more than dissatisfaction. Which is far less worthy and infinitely more destructive, I think we can agree."

He didn't know when he'd turned to face her fully. He didn't know when he'd stopped looking at the city and was looking only at her instead. But he was, and he compounded that error by reaching out his hand and tugging on the very end of her silky, coppery ponytail where it kissed her shoulder every time she moved her head.

Her lips parted, as if on a soundless breath, and Achilles felt that as if she'd caressed him. As if her hands were on his body the way he wished they were, instead of at her sides.

"Are you dissatisfied?" It was amazing how difficult it was not to use her real name then. How challenging it was to stay in this game he suddenly didn't particularly want to play. "Is that what this is?"

Her green eyes, which had been so unreadable, suddenly looked slick. Dark and glassy with some or other emotion. He couldn't tell what it was, and still, he could feel it in him like smoke, stealing through his chest and making it harder than it should have been to breathe.

"There's nothing wrong with dissatisfaction in and of itself," she told him after a moment, then another, that seemed too large for him to contain. Too dark and much too edgy to survive intact, and yet here they both were. "You see it as disloyalty, but it's not."

"How can it be anything else?"

"It is possible to be both loyal and open to the possibility that there is a life outside the one you've committed yourself to." Her green eyes searched his. "Surely there must be."

"I think you will find that there is no such possibility." His voice was harsh. He could feel it inside him, like a stain. Like need. "We must all decide who we are, every moment of every day. You either keep a vow or you do not. There is no between."

She stiffened at that, then tried to force her shoulders back down to an easier, less telling angle. Achilles watched her do it. He watched something like distress cross her lovely face, but she hid that, too. It was only the darkness in her gaze that told him he'd scored a direct hit, and he was a man who took great pride in the strikes he leveled against anyone who tried to move against him. Yet what he felt when he looked at Valentina was not pride. Not pride at all.

"Some vows are not your own," she said fiercely, her gaze locked to his. "Some are inherited. It's easy to say that you'll keep them because that's what's expected of you, but it's a great deal harder to actually *do* it."

He knew the vows she'd made. That pointless prince. Her upcoming royal wedding. He assumed that was the least of the vows she'd inherited from her father. And he still thought it was so much smoke and mirrors to hide the fact that she, like so many of her peers, was a spoiled and pampered creature who didn't like to be told what to do. Wasn't that the reason *poor little rich girl* was a saying in the first place?

He had no sympathy for the travails of a rich, pampered princess. But he couldn't seem to unwind that little silken bit of copper from around his finger, either. Much less step back and put the space between them that he should have left there from the start.

Achilles shook his head. "There is no gray area. Surely

you know this. You are either who you say you are or you are not."

There was something like misery in those eyes of hers then. And this was what he'd wanted. This was why he'd been goading her. And yet now that he seemed to have succeeded, he felt the strangest thing deep in his gut. It was an unpleasant and unfamiliar sensation, and at first Achilles couldn't identify it. It was a low heat, trickling through him, making him restless. Making him as close to uncertain as he'd ever been.

In someone else, he imagined, it might be shame. But shame was not something Achilles allowed in himself. Ever.

This was a night full of things he did not allow, apparently. Because he wanted her. He wanted to punctuate this oddly emotional discussion with his mouth. His hands. The whole of his too-tight, too-interested body pressed deep into hers. He wanted to taste those sweetly lush lips of hers. He wanted to take her elegant face in his hands, tip her head back and sate himself at last. It seemed to him an age or two since he'd boarded his plane and realized his assistant was not who she was supposed to be. An agony of waiting and all that *want*, and he was not a man who agonized. Or waited. Or wanted anything, it seemed, but this princess who thought she could fool him.

What was the matter with him that some part of him wanted to let her?

He did none of the things he longed to do.

Achilles made himself do the hard thing, no matter how complicated it was. Or how complicated it felt, anyway. When really it was so simple. He let her go. He let her silky hair fall from between his fingers, and he stepped back, putting inches between them.

But that did nothing to ease the temptation.

"I think what you need is a good night's sleep," he told

her, like some kind of absurd nurturer. Something he had certainly never tried to be for anyone else in the whole of his life. He would have doubted it was possible—and he refused to analyze that. "Perhaps it will clear your head and remind you of who you are. Jet lag can make that so very confusing, I know."

He thought she might have scuttled from the room at that, filled with her own shame if there was any decency in the world, but he was learning that this princess was not at all who he expected her to be. She swallowed, hard. And he could still see that darkness in her eyes. But she didn't look away from him. And she certainly didn't scuttle anywhere.

"I know exactly who I am, Mr. Casilieris," she said, very directly, and the lenses in her glasses made her eyes seem that much greener. "As I'm certain you do, too. Jet lag makes a person tired. It doesn't make them someone else entirely."

And when she turned to walk from the room then, it was with her head held high, graceful and self-contained, with no apparent second thoughts. Or anything the least bit like shame. All he could read on her as she went was that same distracting elegance that was already too far under his skin.

Achilles couldn't seem to do a thing but watch her go.

And when the sound of her footsteps had faded away, deep into the far reaches of the penthouse, he turned back to the wild gleam of Manhattan on the other side of his windows. Frenetic and frenzied. Light in all directions, as if there was nothing more to the world tonight than this utterly mad tangle of life and traffic and people and energy and it hardly mattered what he felt so high above it. It hardly mattered at all that he'd betrayed himself. That this woman who should have been nothing to him made him act like someone he barely recognized.

And her words stayed with him. *I know exactly who I am.* They echoed around and around in his head until it sounded a whole lot more like an accusation.

As if she was the one playing this game, and winning it, after all.

CHAPTER FOUR

AS THE DAYS PASSED, Valentina thought that she was getting the hang of this assistant thing—especially if she endeavored to keep a minimum distance between herself and Achilles when the night got a little too dark and close. And at all other times, for that matter.

She'd chalked up those odd, breathless moments in his office that first night to the strangeness of inhabiting someone else's life. Because it couldn't be anything else. Since then, she hadn't felt the need to say too much. She hadn't defended herself—or her version of Natalie. She'd simply tried to do the job that Natalie, apparently, did so well she was seen by other employees of the Casilieris Company as superhuman.

With every day she became more accustomed to the demands of the job. She felt less as if she really ought to have taken Achilles up on his offer of a parachute and more as if this was something she could handle. Maybe not well or like superhuman Natalie, but she could handle it all the same in her own somewhat rudimentary fashion.

What she didn't understand was why Achilles hadn't fired her already. Because it was perfectly clear to Valentina that her version of handling things in no way lived up to Achilles's standards.

And if she'd been any doubt about that, he was the first to tell her otherwise.

His corporate offices in Manhattan took up several floors at one of Midtown's most esteemed addresses. There was an office suite set aside for him, naturally enough, that sprawled across the top floor and looked out over Manhattan as if to underscore the notion that Achilles Casilieris was in every way on top of the world. Valentina was settled in the immediate outer office, guarded by two separate lines of receptionist and secretarial defense should anyone make it through security. It wasn't to protect Achilles, but to further illuminate his importance. And Natalie's, Valentina realized quickly.

Because Natalie controlled access to Achilles. She controlled his schedule. She answered his phone and his email, and was generally held to have that all-important insight into his moods.

"What kind of day is it?" the senior vice presidents would ask her as they came in for their meetings, and the fact they smiled as they said it didn't make them any less anxious to hear her answer.

Valentina quickly discovered that Natalie controlled a whole lot more than simple access. There was a steady line of people at her desk, coming to her to ask how best to approach Achilles with any number of issues, or plot how to avoid approaching him with the things they knew he'd hate. Over the course of her first week in New York City, Valentina found that almost everyone who worked for Achilles tried to run things past her first, or used her to gauge his reactions. Natalie was less the man's personal assistant, she realized, and more the hub around which his businesses revolved. More than that, she thought he knew it.

"Take that up with Natalie," he would say in the middle of a meeting, without even bothering to look over at her. Usually while cutting someone off, because even he appeared not to want to hear certain things until Natalie had assessed them first.

"Come up with those numbers and run them past Natalie," he would tell his managers, and sometimes he'd even sound irritated while he said such things.

"Why are you acting as if you have never worked a day in my company?" he'd demanded of one of his brand managers once. "I am not the audience for your uncertain first drafts, George. How can you not know this?"

Valentina had smiled at the man in the meeting, and then had been forced to sit through a brainstorming/therapy session with him afterward, all the while hoping that the noncommittal things she'd murmured were, at the very least, not the *opposite* of the sort of things Natalie might have said.

Not that she texted Natalie to find out. Because that might have led to a conversation Valentina didn't really want to have with her double about strange, tense moments in the darkness with her employer.

She didn't know what she was more afraid of. That Natalie had never had any kind of tension with Achilles and Valentina was messing up her entire life…or that she did. That *tension* was just what Achilles did.

Valentina concentrated on her first attempt at a normal life, complete with a normal job, instead. And whether Achilles was aware of it or not, Natalie had her fingers in everything.

Including his romantic life.

The first time Valentina had answered his phone to find an emotional woman on the other end, she'd been appalled.

"There's a crying woman on the phone," she'd told Achilles. It had taken her a day or so to realize that she wasn't only allowed to walk in and out of his office when necessary, but encouraged to do so. That particular afternoon Achilles had been sitting on the sofa in his office, his feet up on his coffee table as he'd scowled down at his laptop. He shifted that scowl to her instead, in a way that made Valentina imagine that whatever he was looking at had something to do with her—

But that was ridiculous. There was no *her* in this scenario. There was only Natalie, and Valentina very much doubted Achilles spent his time looking up his assistant on the internet.

"Why are you telling me this?" he'd asked her shortly. "If I wanted to know who called me, I would answer my phones myself."

"She's crying about you," Valentina had said. "I assume she's calling to share her emotions with you, the person who caused them."

"And I repeat—why are you telling me this." This time it wasn't a question, and his scowl deepened. "You are my assistant. You are responsible for fielding these calls. I'm shocked you're even mentioning another crying female. I thought you stopped bringing them to my attention years ago."

Valentina had blinked at that. "Aren't you at all interested in why this woman is upset?"

"No."

"Not at all. Not the slightest bit interested." She studied his fierce face as if he was an alien. In moments like this, she thought he must have been. "You don't even know which woman I'm referring to, do you?"

"Miss Monette." He bit out that name as if the taste of it irritated him, and Valentina couldn't have said why it put her back up when it wasn't even her name. "I have a number of mistresses, none of whom call that line to manufacture emotional upsets. You are already aware of this." And he'd set his laptop aside, as if he needed to concentrate fully on Valentina before him. It had made her spine prickle, from her neck to her bottom and back up again. "Please let me know exactly what agenda it is we are pursuing today, that you expect to interrupt me in order to have a discussion about nuisance calls. When I assure you, the subject does not interest me at all. Just as it did not interest me five years ago, when you vowed to stop bothering me about them."

There was a warning in that. Valentina had heard it, plain as day. But she hadn't been able to heed it. Much less stop herself.

"To be clear, what you're telling me is that tears do not interest you," she'd said instead of beating a retreat to her desk the way she should have. She'd kept her tone even and easy, but she doubted that had fooled either one of them.

"Tears interest me least of all." She'd been sure that there was a curve in that hard mouth of his then, however small.

And what was the matter with her that she'd clung to that as if it was some kind of lifeline? As if she needed such a thing?

As if what she really wanted was his approval, when she hadn't switched places with Natalie for him. He'd had nothing to do with it. Why couldn't she seem to remember that?

"If this is a common occurrence for you, perhaps you need to have a think about your behavior," she'd pointed out. "And your aversion to tears."

There had definitely been a curve in his mouth then, and yet somehow that hadn't made Valentina any easier.

"This conversation is over," he'd said quietly. Though not gently. "Something I suggest you tell the enterprising actress on the phone."

She'd thought him hideously cold, of course. Heartless, even. But the calls kept coming. And Valentina had quickly realized what she should perhaps have known from the start—that it would be impossible for Achilles to actually be out there causing harm to so many anonymous women when he never left the office. She knew this because she spent almost every hour of every day in his company. The man literally had no time to go out there smashing hearts left and right, the way she'd be tempted to believe he did if she paid attention only to the phone calls she received, laden with accusations.

"Tell him I'm falling apart," yet another woman on the phone said on this latest morning, her voice ragged.

"Sorry, but what's your name again?" Valentina asked, as brightly as possible. "It's only that he's been working rather hard, you see. As he tends to do. Which would, of course, make it extremely difficult for him to be tearing anyone apart in any real sense."

The woman had sputtered. But Valentina had dutifully taken her name into Achilles when he next asked for his messages.

"I somewhat doubted the veracity of her claim," Valentina murmured. "Given that you were working until well after two last night."

Something she knew very well since that had meant she'd been working even longer than that.

Achilles laughed. He was at his desk today, which meant he was framed by the vertical thrust of Manhattan behind him. And still, that look in his dark gold gaze made the city disappear. "As well you should. I have no idea who this woman is. Or any of them." He shrugged. "My attorneys are knee-deep in paternity suits, and I win every one of them."

Valentino was astonished by that. Perhaps that was naive. She'd certainly had her share of admirers in her day, strange men who claimed an acquaintance or who sent rather disturbing letters to the palace—some from distant prisons in foreign countries. But she certainly never had men call up and try to pretend they had relationships with her *to* her.

Then again, would anyone have told her if they had? That sat on her a bit uneasily, though she couldn't have said why. She only knew that his gaze was like a touch, and that, too, seemed to settle on her like a weight.

"It's amazing how many unhinged women seem to think that if they claim they're dating you, you might go along with it," she said before she could think better of it.

That dark gold gaze of his lit with a gleam she couldn't name then. And it sparked something deep inside her, making her fight to draw in a breath. Making her feel unsteady in the serviceable low heels that Natalie favored. Making her wish she'd worn something more substantial than a nice jacket over another pencil skirt. Like a suit of armor. Or her very own brick wall.

"There are always unhinged women hanging about," Achilles said in that quietly devastating way of his. "Trying to convince me that they have relationships with me that they adamantly do not. Why do you imagine that is, Miss Monette?"

She told herself he couldn't possibly know that she was one of those women, no matter how his gaze seemed to pin her where she stood. No matter the edge in his voice, or the sharp emphasis he'd put on *Miss Monette*.

Even if he suspected something was different with his assistant, he couldn't know. Because no one could know. Because Valentina herself hadn't known Natalie existed until she'd walked into that bathroom. And that meant all sorts of things, such as the fact that everything she'd been told about her childhood and her birth was a lie. Not to mention her mother.

But there was no way Achilles could know any of that.

"Perhaps it's you," she murmured in response. She smiled when his brows rose in that expression of sheer arrogance that never failed to make her feel the slightest bit dizzy. "I only mean that you're a public figure and people imagine you a certain way based on the kind of press coverage you allow. Unless you plan to actively get out there and reclaim your public narrative, I don't think there's any likelihood that it will change."

"I am not a public figure. I have never courted the public in any way."

Valentina checked a sigh. "You're a very wealthy man. Whether you like it or not, the public is fascinated by you."

Achilles studied her until she was forced to order herself not to fidget beneath the weight of that heavy, intense stare.

"I'm intrigued that you think the very existence of public fascination must create an obligation in me to cater to it," he said quietly. "It does not. In fact, it has the opposite effect. In me. But how interesting that you imagine you owe something to the faceless masses who admire you."

Valentina's lips felt numb. "No masses, faceless or otherwise, admire me, Mr. Casilieris. They have no idea I exist. I'm an assistant, nothing more."

His hard mouth didn't shift into one of those hard curves, but his dark gold eyes gleamed, and somehow that made the floor beneath her seem to tilt, then roll.

"Of course you are," he said, his voice a quiet menace that echoed in her like a warning. Like something far more dangerous than a simple warning. "My mistake."

Later that night, still feeling as off balance as if the floor really wasn't steady beneath her feet, Valentina found herself alone with Achilles long after everyone else in the office had gone home.

It had been an extraordinarily long couple of days,

something Valentina might have thought was business as usual for the Casilieris Company if so many of the other employees hadn't muttered about how grueling it was. Beneath their breath and when they thought she couldn't hear them, that was. The deal that Achilles was so determined to push through had turned out to have more tangles and turns than anyone had expected—especially, it seemed, Achilles. What that meant was long hour after long hour well into the tiny hours of the night, hunched over tables and conference rooms, arguing with fleets of attorneys and representatives from the other side over take-out food from fine New York restaurants and stale coffee.

Valentina was deep into one of the contracts Achilles had slid her way, demanding a fresh set of eyes on a clause that annoyed him, when she noticed that they were the only ones there. The Casilieris Company had a significant presence all over the planet, so there were usually people coming and going at all conceivable hours to be available to different workdays in distant places. Something Valentina had witnessed herself after spending so much time in these offices since she'd arrived in New York.

But when she looked up from the dense and confusing contract language for a moment to give her ever-impending headache a break, she could see from the long conference room table where she sat straight through the glass walls that allowed her to see all the way across the office floor. And there was no one there. No bustling secretaries, no ambitious VPs putting in ostentatiously late hours where the boss could see their vigilance and commitment. No overzealous interns making busy work for themselves in the cubicles. No late-night cleaning crews, who did their jobs in the dark so as not to bother the workers by day. There wasn't a soul. Anywhere.

Something caught in her chest as she realized that it was only the two of them. Just Valentina and the man across the table from her, whom she was trying very hard not to look at too closely.

It was an extraordinarily unimportant thing to notice, she chastised herself, frowning back down at the contract. They were always alone, really. In his car, on his plane, in his penthouse. Valentina had spent more time with this man, she thought, than with any other save her father.

Her gaze rose from the contract of its own accord. Achilles sat across from her in the quiet of the otherwise empty office, his laptop cracked open before him and a pile of contracts next to the sleek machine. He looked the way he always did at the end of these long days. *Entirely too good*, something in her whispered—though she shoved that aside as best she could. It did no good to concentrate on things like that, she'd decided during her tenure with him. The man's appearance was a fact, and it was something she needed to come to terms with, but she certainly didn't have to ogle him.

But she couldn't seem to look away. She remembered that moment in his penthouse a little too clearly, the first night they'd been in New York. She remembered how close they'd stood in that window, and the things he'd told her, that dark gold gaze of his boring into her. As if he had every intention of looking directly to her soul. More than that, she remembered him reaching out and taking hold of the end of the ponytail she'd worn, that he'd looked at as if he had no idea how it had come to be attached to her.

But she'd dreamed about it almost every time she'd slept, either way.

Tonight Achilles was lounging in a pushed-back chair, his hands on top of his head as if, had he had longer hair, he'd be raking his hands through it. His jaw was dotted with stubble after a long day in the office, and it lent him the look of some kind of pirate.

Valentina told herself—sternly—that there was no

need for such fanciful language when he already made her pulse heat inside her simply by being in the same room. She tried to sink down a bit farther behind the piles and piles of documents surrounding her, which she was viewing as the armor she wished she was wearing. The remains of the dinner she'd ordered them many hours before were scattered across the center of the table, and she took perhaps too much pride in the fact she'd completed so simple a task. Normal people, she was certain, ordered from take-out menus all the time, but Valentina never had before she'd taken over Natalie's life. Valentina was a princess. She'd discussed many a menu and sent requests to any number of kitchens, but she'd never ordered her own meal in her life, much less from stereotypical New Yorkers with accents and attitudes.

She felt as if she was in a movie.

Valentina decided she would take her victories where she found them. Even if they were as small and ultimately pointless as sending out for a takeaway meal.

"It's late," Achilles said, reminding her that they were all alone here. And there was something in his voice then. Or the way his gaze slammed into hers when she looked up again.

Or maybe it was in her—that catch. That little kick of something a little too much like excitement that wound around and around inside her. Making her feel…restless. Undone. Desperate for something she couldn't even name.

"And here I thought you planned to carry straight through until dawn," she said, as brightly as possible, hoping against hope he couldn't see anything on her face. Or hear it in her voice.

Achilles lowered his hand to the arms of his chair. But he didn't shift that gaze of his from hers. And she kept catching him looking at her like this. Exactly like this. Simmering. Dark and dangerous, and spun through with gold. In the cars they took together. Every morning when he walked out of his bedchamber and found her sitting in the office suite, already starting on the day's work as best she could. Across boardroom tables just like this one, no matter if they were filled with other people.

It was worse now. Here in the quiet of his empty office. So late at night it felt to Valentina as if the darkness was a part of her.

And Valentina didn't have any experience with men, but oh, the books she'd read. Love stories and romances and happy-ever-afters, and almost all of them started just like this. With a taut feeling in the belly and fire everywhere else.

Do not be absurd, she snapped at herself.

Because she was Princess Valentina of Murin. She was promised to another and had been since her birth. There wasn't space in her life for anything but that. Not even here, in this faraway place that had nothing at all to do with her real life. Not even with this man, whom she never should have met, and never would have had she not seized that moment in the London bathroom.

You can take a holiday from your life, apparently, she reminded herself. *But you still take you along with you wherever you go.*

She might have been playing Natalie Monette, but she was still *herself.* She was still the same person she'd always been. Dutiful. Mindful of what her seemingly inconsequential behavior might mean to her father, to the kingdom, to her future husband's kingdom, too. Whatever else she was—and she wasn't sure she knew anymore, not here in the presence of a man who made her head spin without seeming to try very hard—Valentina was a person who had always, always kept her vows.

Even when it was her father who had made them, not her.

"If you keep staring at me like that," Achilles said softly, a kind of ferociousness beneath his rough words that made her stomach knot, then seemed to kindle a different, deeper fire lower down, "I am not certain I'll be able to contain myself."

Valentina's mouth was dry. "I don't know what you mean."

"I think you do."

Achilles didn't move, she could see that he wasn't moving, and yet everything changed at that. He filled every room he entered—she was used to that by now—but this was something different. It was as if lightning flashed. It was if he was some kind of rolling thunder all his own. It was as if he'd called in a storm, then let it loose to fill all of the room. The office.

And Valentina, too.

"No," she whispered, her voice scratchy against all that light and rumble.

But she could feel the tumult inside her. It was fire and it was light and it threatened to burst free of the paltry cage of her skin. Surely she would burst. Surely no person could survive this. She felt it shake all through her, as if underlining her fear.

"I don't know what you mean, and I don't like what you're implying. I think perhaps we've been in this office too long. You seem to have mistaken me for one of your mistresses. Or worse, one of those desperate women who call in, hoping to convince you they ought to be one of them."

"On the contrary, Miss Monette."

And there was a starkness to Achilles's expression then. No curve on his stern mouth. No gleaming thing in the seductive gold of his dark eyes. But somehow, that only made it worse.

"You're the one who manages my mistresses. And

those who pretend to that title. How could I possibly confuse you for them?" He cocked his head slightly to one side, and something yawned open inside her, as if in response. "Or perhaps you're auditioning for the role?"

"No." Her voice was no less scratchy this time, but there was more power in it. *Or more fear,* something inside her whispered. "I am most certainly not auditioning for anything like that. Or anything at all. I already have a job."

"But you told me you meant to quit." She had the strangest notion then that he was enjoying himself. "Perhaps you meant you were looking to make a lateral move. From my boardroom to my bed?"

Valentina tried to summon her outrage. She tried to tell herself that she was deeply offended on Natalie's behalf, because of course this was about her, not Valentina herself... She tried to tell herself a whole lot of things.

But she couldn't quite get there. Instead, she was awash with unhelpful little visions, red hot and wild. Images of what a "lateral move" might look like. Of what his bed might feel like. Of him.

She imagined that lean, solidly muscled form stretched over hers, the way she'd read in so many books so many times. Something almost too hot to bear melted through her then, pulling deep in her belly, and making her breath go shallow before it shivered everywhere else.

As if it was already happening.

"I know that this might come as a tremendous shock," Valentina said, trying to make herself sound something like fierce—or unmoved, anyway. Anything other than thrown and yearning. "But I have no interest in your bed. Less than no interest."

"You are correct." And something gleamed bright and hot and unholy gold in that dark gaze of his. "I am in shock."

"The next time an aspiring mistress calls the office," Valentina continued coolly, and no matter that it cost her, "I'll be certain to put her through to you for a change. You can discuss lateral moves all day long."

"What if a random caller does not appeal to me?" he asked lazily, as if this was all a game to him. She told herself it was. She told herself the fact that it was a game made it safe, but she didn't believe it. Not when all the things that moved around inside her made it hard to breathe, and made her feel anything at all but *safe*. "What if it is I who wish to alter our working relationship after all these years?"

Valentina told herself that this was clearly a test. If, as this conversation seemed to suggest, Natalie's relationship with her boss had always been strictly professional, why would he want to change that now? She'd seen how distant he kept his romantic entanglements from his work. His work was his life. His women were afterthoughts. There was no way the driven, focused man she'd come to know a bit after the close proximity of these last days would want to muddy the water in his office, with the assistant who not only knew where all the bodies were buried, but oversaw the funeral rites herself.

This had to be a test.

"I don't wish to alter a thing," she told him, very distinctly, as if there was nothing in her head but thorny contract language. And certainly nothing involving that remarkably ridged torso of his. "If you do, I think we should revisit the compensation package on offer for my resignation."

Achilles smiled as if she delighted him. But in an entirely too wicked and too hot sort of way.

"There is no package, Miss Monette," he murmured. "And there will be no resignation. When will you understand? You are here to do as I wish. Nothing more and nothing less than that. And perhaps my wishes concerning your role here have changed."

He wants you to fall apart, Valentina snapped at herself. *He wants to see if this will break you. He's poking at* Natalie *about her change in performance, not at you. He doesn't know* you *exist.*

Because there could be no other explanation. And it didn't matter that the look in his eyes made her shudder, down deep inside.

"Your wishes concerning my role now involve me on my back?" It cost her to keep her voice that flat. She could feel it.

"You say that as if the very idea disgusts you." And that crook in the corner of his lethal mouth deepened, even as that look in his eyes went lethal. "Surely not."

Valentina forced herself to smile. Blandly. As if her heart wasn't trying to claw its way out of her chest.

"I'm very flattered by your offer, of course," she said.

A little too sweetly to be mistaken for sincerity.

Achilles laughed then. It was an unsettling sound, too rough and too bold. It told her too much. That he knew— everything. That he knew all the things that were moving inside her, white hot and molten and too much for her to handle or tamp down or control. There was a growing, impossible fire raging in places she hardly understood, rendering her a stranger to herself.

As if he was the one in control of her body, even sitting across the table, lounging in his seat as if none of this was a matter of any concern at all.

While she felt as if she was both losing pieces of herself—and seeing her true colors for the very first time.

"Are you letting me down easy?" Achilles asked.

There was still laughter in his voice, his gaze and, somehow, dancing in the air between them despite all that fire still licking at her. She felt it roll through her, as if those big hands of his were on her skin.

And then she was suddenly incapable of thinking about anything at all but that. His hands all over her body. Touching places only she had ever seen. She had to swallow hard. Then again. And still there was that ringing in her ears.

"Do think it will work?" he asked, laughter still making his words sound a little too much like the rough, male version of honey.

"I imagine it will work beautifully, yes." She held on to that smile of hers as if her life depended on it. She rather thought it did. It was that or tip over into all that fire, and she had no idea what would become of her if she let that happen. She had no idea what would be left. "Or, of course, I could involve Human Resources in this discussion."

Achilles laughed again, and this time it was rougher. Darker and somehow hotter at the same time. Valentina felt it slide all over her, making her breasts feel heavy and her hips restless. While deep between her legs, a slick ache bloomed.

"I admire the feigned naïveté," Achilles said, and he looked like a pirate again, all dark jaw and that gleam in his gaze. It lit her up. Everywhere. "I have obviously failed to appreciate your acting talent sufficiently. I think we both know what Human Resources will tell you. To suck it up or find another position."

"That does not sound at all like something Human Resources would say," Valentina replied crisply, rather than spending even a split second thinking about *sucking*. "It sounds as if you're laboring under the delusion that this is a cult of personality, not a business."

If she expected him to look at all abashed, his grin disabused her of it. "Do you doubt it?"

"I'm not sure that is something I would brag about, Mr. Casilieris."

His gaze was hot, and she didn't think he was talking about her job or his company any longer. Had he ever been?

"Is it bragging if it's true?" he asked.

Valentina stood then, because it was the last thing she wanted to do. She could have sat there all night. She could have rung in a new dawn, fencing words with this man and dancing closer and closer to that precipice she could feel looming between them, even if she couldn't quite see it.

She could have pretended she didn't feel every moment of this deep inside her, in places she shouldn't. And then pretend further she didn't know what it meant just because she'd never experienced any of it before outside the pages of a book.

But she did know. And this wasn't her life to ruin. And so she stood, smoothing her hands down her skirt and wishing she hadn't been quite so impetuous in that London bathroom.

If you hadn't been, you wouldn't be here, something in her replied. *Is that what you want?*

And she knew that she didn't. Valentina had a whole life left to live with a man she would call husband who would never know her, not really. She had duty to look forward to, and a lifetime of charity and good works, all of which would be vetted by committees and commented on by the press. She had public adulation and a marriage that would involve the mechanical creation of babies before petering off into a nice friendship, if she was lucky.

Maybe the making of the babies would be fun with her prince. What did she know? All she knew so far was that he didn't do…this. He didn't affect her the way Achilles did, lounging there like hard-packed danger across a conference table, his gaze too dark and the gold in it making her pulse kick at her.

She'd never felt anything like this before. She doubted she'd ever feel it again.

Valentina couldn't quite bring herself to regret it.

But she couldn't stay here tonight and blow up the rest of Natalie's life, either. That would be treating this little gift that she'd been given with nothing but contempt.

"Have I given you leave to go?" Achilles asked, with what she knew was entirely feigned astonishment. "I am clearly confused in some way. I keep thinking you work for me."

She didn't know how he could do that. How he could seem to loom over her when she was the one standing up and looking down at him.

"And because I'd like to continue working for you," Valentina forced herself to say in as measured a tone as she could manage, "I'm going to leave now. We can pick this up in the morning." She tapped the table with one finger. "Pick *this* up, I mean. These contracts and the deal. Not this descent into madness, which I think we can chalk up to exhaustion."

Achilles only watched her for a moment. Those hands that she could picture too easily against her own flesh curled over the armrests of his chair, and her curse was that she imagined she *was* that chair. His legs were thrust out before him, long and lean. His usual suit was slightly rumpled, his tie having been tugged off and tossed aside hours earlier, so she could see the olive skin at his neck and a hint of crisp, black hair. He looked simultaneously sleepy and breathlessly, impossibly lethal—with an intensity that made that hot ache between her legs seem to swallow her whole.

And the look in his eyes made everything inside her draw tight, then pulse harder.

"Do you have a problem with that?" she asked, and she meant to sound impatient. Challenging. But she thought both of them were entirely too aware that what came out instead was rather more plaintive than planned.

As if she was really asking him if he was okay with everything that had happened here tonight. She was clearly too dazed to function.

She needed to get away from him while she still had access to what little of her brain remained in all this smoke and flame.

"Do you require my permission?" Achilles lifted his chin, and his dark eyes glittered. Valentina held her breath. "So far tonight it seems you are laboring under the impression that you give the permission, not me. You make the rules, not me. It is as if I am here for no other purpose than to serve you."

And there was no reason at all that his words, spoken in that soft, if dangerous way, should make her skin prickle. But they did. As if a man like Achilles did not have to issue threats, he was the threat. Why pile a threat on top of the threat? When the look on his face would do.

"I will see you in the morning," Valentina said, resolutely. "When I'll be happy to accept your apology."

Achilles lounged farther down in his chair, and she had the strangest notion that he was holding himself back. Keeping himself in place. Goose bumps shivered to life over her shoulders and down her arms.

His gaze never left hers.

"Go," he said, and there was no pretending it wasn't an order. "But I would not lie awake tonight anticipating the contours of my apology. It will never come."

She wanted to reply to that, but her mouth was too dry and she couldn't seem to move. Not so much as a muscle.

And as if he knew it, Achilles kept going in that same intensely quiet way.

"Tonight when you can't sleep, when you toss and turn and stare up at yet another ceiling I own, I want you to think of all the other reasons you could be wide awake in the small hours of the night. All the things that I could do to you. Or have you do to me. All the thousands of ways I will be imagining us together, just like that, under the same roof."

"That is completely inappropriate, Mr. Casilieris, and I think you know it."

But she knew full well she didn't sound nearly as outraged as she should. And only partially because her voice was a mere whisper.

"Have you never wondered how we would fit? Have you not tortured herself with images of my possession?" Achilles's hard mouth curved then, a wicked crook in one corner that she knew, somehow, would haunt her. She could feel it deep inside her like its own bright fire. "Tonight, I think, you will."

And Valentina stopped pretending there was any way out of this conversation besides the precise images he'd just mentioned, acted out all over this office. She walked stiffly around the table and gave him a wide, wide berth as she passed.

When she made it to the door of the conference room, she didn't look behind her to see if he was watching. She knew he was. She could feel it.

Fire and lightning, thunder and need.

She ran.

And heard his laughter follow behind her like the leading edge of a storm she had no hope of outwitting, no matter how fast she moved.

CHAPTER FIVE

ACHILLES ORDINARILY ENJOYED his victory parties. Reveled in them, in fact. Not for him any nod toward false humility or any pretense that he didn't deeply enjoy these games of high finance with international stakes. But tonight he couldn't seem to get his head into it, and no matter that he'd been fighting to buy out this particular iconic Manhattan hotel—which he planned to make over in his own image, the blend of European elegance and Greek timelessness that was his calling card in the few hotels scattered across the globe that he'd deemed worthy of the Casilieris name—for nearly eighteen months.

He should have been jubilant. It irritated him—deeply—that he couldn't quite get there.

His group had taken over a New York steak house renowned for its high-end clientele and specialty drinks to match to celebrate the deal he'd finally put through today after all this irritating wrangling. Ordinarily he would allow himself a few drinks to blur out his edges for a change. He would even smile and pretend he was a normal man, like all the rest, made of flesh and blood instead of dollar signs and naked ambition—an improvement by far over the monster he kept locked up tight beneath. Nights like this were his opportunity to pretend to be like anyone else, and Achilles usually indulged that impulse.

He might not have been a normal man—he'd never been a normal man—but it amused him to pretend otherwise every now and again. He was renowned for his surliness as much as his high expectations, but if that was all there was to it—to him—he never would have gotten anywhere in business. It took a little charm to truly manipulate his enemies and his opponents and even his acolytes the way he liked to do. It required that he be as easy telling a joke as he was taking over a company or using his fiercest attorneys to hammer out a deal that served him, and only him, best.

But tonight he was charmless all the way through.

He stood at the bar, nursing a drink he would have much preferred to toss back and follow with a few more of the same, his attention entirely consumed by his princess as she worked the room. As ordered.

"Make yourself useful, please," he'd told her when they'd arrived. "Try to charm these men. If you can."

He'd been deliberately insulting. He'd wanted her to imagine he had some doubt that she could pull such a thing off. He'd wanted her to feel the way he did—grouchy and irritable and outside his own skin.

She made him feel like an adolescent.

But Valentina had not seemed the least bit cowed. Much less insulted—which had only made him feel that much more raw.

"As you wish," she'd murmured in that overly obsequious voice she used when, he thought, she most wanted to get her claws into him. She'd even flashed that bland smile of hers at him, which had its usual effect—making his blood seem too hot for his own veins. "Your slightest desire is my command, of course."

And the truth was, Achilles should have known better. The kind of men he liked to manipulate best, especially when it came to high-stakes deals like the one he'd closed tonight, were not the sort of men he wanted anywhere near his princess. If the real Natalie had been here, she would have disappeared. She would have dispensed her usual round of cool greetings and even cooler congratulations, none of which encouraged anyone to cozy up to her. Then she would have sat in this corner or that, her expression blank and her attention focused entirely on one of her devices. She would have done that remarkable thing she did, that he had never thought to admire as much as perhaps he should have, which was her ability to be both in the room and invisible at the same time.

Princess Valentina, by contrast, couldn't have stayed invisible if her life depended on it. She was the furthest thing from *invisible* that Achilles had ever seen. It was as if the world was cast into darkness and she was its only light, that bright and that impossibly silvery and smooth, like her own brand of moonlight.

She moved from one group to the next, all gracious smiles. And not that bland sort of smile she used entirely too pointedly and too well, which invariably worked his last nerve, but one he'd seen in too many photographs he'd looked at much too late at night. Hunched over his laptop like some kind of obsessed troll while she slept beneath the same roof, unaware, which only made him that much more infuriated.

With her, certainly. But with himself even more.

Tonight she was the consummate hostess, as if this was her victory celebration instead of his. He could hear her airy laugh from across the room, far more potent than another woman's touch. And worse, he could see her. Slender and graceful, inhabiting a pencil skirt and well-cut jacket as if they'd been crafted specifically for her. When he knew perfectly well that those were his assistant's clothes, and they certainly weren't bespoke.

But that was Valentina's power. She made everything in her orbit seem to be only hers. Crafted specifically and especially for her.

Including him, Achilles thought—and he hated it. He was not a man a woman could put on a leash. He'd never given a woman any kind of power over him in his life, and he didn't understand how this creature who was engaged in a full-scale deception—who was running a con on him *even now*—somehow seemed to have the upper hand in a battle he was terribly afraid only he knew they were fighting.

It was unconscionable. It made him want to tear down this building—hell, the whole city—with his bare hands.

Or better yet, put them on her.

All the men around her lapped it up, of course. They stood too close. They put their hands on her elbow, or her shoulder, to emphasize a point that Achilles did not have to hear to know did not require emphasis. And certainly did not require touch.

She was moonlight over this grim, focused life of his, and he had no idea how he was going to make it through a world cast in darkness without her.

If he was appalled by that sentiment—and he was, deeply and wholly—it didn't seem to matter. He couldn't seem to turn it off.

It was far easier to critique her behavior instead.

So Achilles watched. And seethed. He catalogued every single touch, every single laugh, every single time she tilted back her pretty face and let her sleek copper hair fall behind her, catching all the light in the room. He brooded over the men who surrounded her, knowing full well that each and every one of them was imagining her naked. Hell, so was he.

But he was the only person in this room who knew what he was looking at. They thought she was Natalie

Monette, his dependable assistant. He was the only one who knew who she really was.

By the time Valentina finished a full circuit of the room, Achilles was in a high, foul temper.

"Are you finished?" he asked when she came to stand by his side again, his tone a dark slap he did nothing at all to temper. "Or will you actually whore yourself out in lieu of dessert?"

He meant that to hurt. He didn't care if he was an ass. He wanted to knock her back a few steps.

But of course Valentina only shot him an arch, amused look, as if she was biting back laughter.

"That isn't very nice," she said simply.

That was all.

And yet Achilles felt that bloom of unfortunate heat inside him all over again, and this time he knew exactly what it was. He didn't like it any better than he had before, and yet there it sat, eating at him from the inside out.

It didn't matter if he told himself he didn't wish to feel shame. All Valentina had to do was look at him as if he was a misbehaving child, tell him he *wasn't being nice* when he'd built an entire life out of being the very opposite of nice and hailing that as the source of his vast power and influence—and there it was. Heavy in him, like a length of hard, cold chain.

How had he given this woman so much power over him? How had he failed to see that was what was happening while he'd imagined he was giving her the rope with which to hang herself?

This could not go on. He could not allow this to go on.

The truth was, Achilles couldn't seem to get a handle on this situation the way he'd planned to when he'd realized who she was on the plane. He'd imagined it would be an amusing sort of game to humble a high and mighty spoiled-rotten princess who had never worked a day in her life and imagined she could deceive *the* Achilles Casilieris so boldly. He'd imagined it would be entertaining—and over swiftly. He supposed he'd imagined he'd be shipping her back to her palace and her princessy life and her proper royal fiancé by the end of the first day.

But Valentina wasn't at all who he'd thought she'd be. If she was spoiled—and she had to be spoiled, by definition, he was certain of it—she hid it. No matter what he threw at her, no matter what he demanded, she simply did it. Not always well, but she did it. She didn't complain. She didn't try to weasel out of any tasks she didn't like. She didn't even make faces or let out those long-suffering sighs that so many of his support staff did when they thought he couldn't hear them.

In fact, Valentina was significantly more cheerful than any other assistant he'd ever had—including Natalie.

She was nothing like perfect, but that made it worse. If she was perfect, maybe he could have dismissed her or ignored her, despite the game she was playing. But he couldn't seem to get her out of his head.

It was that part he couldn't accept. Achilles lived a highly compartmentalized life by design, and he liked it that way. He kept his women in the smallest, most easily controlled and thus ignored space. It had been many, many years since he'd allowed sex to control his thoughts, much less his life. It was only sex, after all. And what was sex to a man who could buy the world if he so chose? It was a release, yes. Enjoyable, even.

But Achilles couldn't remember the last time he'd woken in the night, his heart pounding, the hardest part of him awake and aware. With nothing in his head but her. Yet it was a nightly occurrence since Valentina had walked onto his plane.

It was bordering on obsession.

And Achilles did not get obsessed. He did not *want*.

He did not *need*. He took what interested him and then he forgot about it when the next thing came along.

And he couldn't think of a single good reason why he shouldn't do the same with her.

"Do you have something you wish to say to me?" Valentina asked, her soft, smooth voice snapping him back to this party that bored him. This victory that should have excited him, but that he only found boring now.

"I believe I said it."

"You misunderstand me," she replied, smiling. From a distance it would look as if they were discussing something as light and airy as that curve to her mouth, he thought. Achilles would have been impressed had he not been close enough to see that cool gleam in her green gaze. "I meant your apology. Are you ready to give it?"

He felt his own mouth curve then, in nothing so airy. Or light.

"Do I strike you as a man who apologizes, Miss Monette?" he asked her, making no attempt to ease the steel in his voice. "Have I ever done so in all the time you've known me?"

"A man who cannot apologize is not quite a man, is he, Mr. Casilieris?" This time he thought her smile was meant to take away the sting of her words. To hide the insult a little. Yet it only seemed to make it worse. "I speak philosophically, of course. But surely the only people who can't bring themselves to apologize are those who fear that any admission of guilt or wrongdoing diminishes them. I think we can both agree that's the very opposite of strength."

"You must tell me if I appear diminished, then," he growled at her, and he had the satisfaction of watching that pulse in her neck go wild. "Or weak in some way."

He wasn't surprised when she excused herself and went back to working the crowd. But he was surprised he let her.

Not here, he cautioned that wild thing inside him that he'd never had to contend with before, not over a woman. And never so raw and bold. *Not now.*

Later that night, they sat in his car as it slid through the streets of Manhattan in the midst of a summer thunderstorm, and Achilles cautioned himself not to act rashly.

Again.

But Valentina sat there beside him, staring out the window with a faint smile on her face. She'd settled beside him on the wide, plush seat without a word, as if it hardly mattered to her if he spoke or not. If he berated her, if he ignored her. As if she was all alone in this car or, worse, as if her mind was far away on more interesting topics.

And he couldn't tolerate it.

Achilles could think of nothing but her, she was eating him alive like some kind of impossible acid, yet *her* mind was miles away. She didn't seem to notice or care what she did to him when he was the one who was allowing her grand deception to continue—instead of outing her the way he should have the moment he'd understood who she was.

His hands moved before he knew what he meant to do, as if they had a mind of their own.

He didn't ask. He didn't push or prod at her or fence more words, forcing some sort of temper or explosion that would lead them where he wanted her to go. He didn't stack that deck.

He simply reached across the backseat, wrapped his hand around the back of her neck and hauled her closer to him.

She came easily, as if she really was made of nothing but light. He pulled her until she was sprawled across his lap, one hand braced on his thigh and another at his side. Her body was as lithe and sweetly rounded as he'd imagined it would be, but better. Much, much better.

She smelled like a dream, something soft and something sweet, and all of it warm and female and *her*. Valentina.

But all he cared about was the fact that that maddening mouth of hers was close to his.

Finally.

"What are you doing?" she breathed.

"I should think that was obvious," he growled. "And overdue."

And then, at last, he kissed her.

He wasn't gentle. He wasn't anything like tentative. He was neither soft nor kind, because it was too late for that.

He claimed her. Took her. He reminded her who he was with every slick, intense slide of his tongue. Or maybe he was reminding himself.

And he couldn't stop himself once the taste of her exploded inside him, making him reel. He wanted more. He wanted everything.

But she was still fighting him, that stubbornness of hers that made his whole body tight and needy. Not with her body, which was wrapped around him, supple and sweet, in a way that made him feel drunk. Not with her arms, which she'd sneaked around his shoulders as if she needed to hold on to him to keep herself upright.

It was that mouth of hers that had been driving him wild since the start.

He pulled his lips from hers. Then he slid his hands up to take her elegant cheekbones between his palms. He tilted her face where he wanted it, making the angle that much slicker. That much sweeter.

"Kiss me back," he demanded, pulling back farther to scowl at her, all this unaccustomed need making him impatient. And testy.

She looked stunned. And entirely too beautiful. Her green eyes were wide and dazed behind those clear glasses she wore. Her lips were parted, distractingly soft and faintly swollen already.

Achilles was hard and he was greedy and he wanted nothing more than to bury himself inside her here and now, and finally get rid of this obsession that was eating him alive.

Or indulge in it awhile.

"In case you are confused," he told her, his voice still a growl, "that was an order."

She angled herself back, just slightly. As if she was trying to sit up straighter against him. He didn't allow it. He liked her like this. Off balance and under his control, and he didn't much care if that made him a savage. He'd only ever pretended to be anything else, and only occasionally, at that.

"I *am* kissing you back," she said, and there was a certain haughtiness in her voice that delighted him. It made him grin, imagining all the many ways he could make her pay for that high-born, inbred superiority that he wanted to lap up like cream.

"Not well enough," he told her.

Her cheeks looked crisp and red, but she didn't shrink away from him. She didn't so much as blink.

"Maybe we don't have any chemistry," she theorized in that same voice, making it sound as if that was a foregone conclusion. "Not every woman in the world finds you attractive, Mr. Casilieris. Did you ever think of that?"

Achilles pulled her even more off balance, holding her over his lap and in his arms, right where he wanted her.

"No," he said starkly, and he didn't care if his greed and longing was all over his face, revealing more to her than he had ever shared with anyone. Ever. "I don't think either of those things is a problem."

Then he set his mouth to hers, and proved it.

* * *

Valentina thought she'd died and gone to a heaven she'd never dreamed of before. Wicked and wild and *better*. So very much better than anything she could have come up with in her most brilliant and dark-edged fantasies.

She had never been truly kissed before—if that was even the word to describe something so dominant and so powerful and so deeply, erotically thrilling—but she had no intention of sharing her level of inexperience with Achilles. Not when he seemed so close to some kind of edge and so hell-bent on taking her with him, toppling over the side into all of this sensation and need.

So she simply mimicked him. When he tilted his head, she did the same. She balled up her hands in his exquisitely soft shirt, up there against the hard planes of his chest tucked beneath his dark suit coat. She was aware of his hard hands on her face. She exulted in his arms like steel, holding her and caging her against him. She lost herself in that desperately cruel mouth as it moved over hers, the touch of his rough jaw, the impossible heat.

God help her, the heat.

And she was aware of that hard ridge beneath her, suddenly. She couldn't seem to keep from wriggling against it. Once, daringly. Then again when she heard that deep, wild and somehow savagely beautiful male noise he made in response.

And Valentina forgot about her vows, old and forthcoming. She forgot about faraway kingdoms and palaces and the life she'd lived there. She forgot about the promises she'd made and the ones that had been made in her name, because all of that seemed insubstantial next to the sheer, overwhelming wonder of Achilles Casilieris kissing her like a man possessed in the back of his town car.

This was her holiday. Her little escape. This was nothing but a dream, and he was, too. A fantasy of the life she might have lived had she been anyone else. Had she ever been anything like normal.

She forgot where they were. She forgot the role she was supposed to be playing. There was nothing in all the world but Achilles and the wildness he summoned up with every drag of his mouth against hers.

The car moved beneath them, but all Valentina could focus on was him. That hot possession of his mouth. The fire inside her.

And the lightning that she knew was his, the thunder storming through her, teaching her that she knew less about her body than he did. Much, much less. When he shifted so he could rub his chest against hers, she understood that he knew her nipples had pebbled into hard little points. When he laughed slightly as he rearranged her arms around his shoulders, she understood that he knew all her limbs were weighted down with the force of that greedy longing coursing through her veins.

The more he kissed her, over and over again as if time had no meaning and he could do this forever, she understood that he knew everything.

When he pulled his mouth from hers again, Valentina heard a soft, whimpering sound of protest. It took her one shuddering beat of her heart, then another, to realize she'd made it.

She couldn't process that. It was so abandoned, so thoughtless and wild—how could that be her?

"If we do not get out of this car right now," Achilles told her, his gaze a dark and breathtaking gold that slammed into her and lit her insides on fire, "we will not get out of it for some time. Not until I've had my fill of you. Is that how you want our first time to go, *glikia mou*? In the backseat of a car?"

For a moment Valentina didn't know what he meant.

One hastily sucked-in breath later, she realized the car

had come to a stop outside Achilles's building. Her cheeks flushed with a bright heat, but worse, she knew that he could see it. He saw everything—hadn't she just realized the truth of that? He watched her as she flushed, and he liked it. That deeply male curve in the corner of his mouth made that plain.

Valentina struggled to free herself from his hold then, to climb off his lap and sit back on the seat herself, and she was all too aware that he let her.

She didn't focus on that. She couldn't. That offhanded show of his innate strength made her feel...slippery, inside and outside and high between her legs. She tossed herself off his lap, her gaze tangling with his in a way that made the whole world seem to spin a little, and then she threw herself out the door. She summoned a smile from somewhere and aimed it at the doormen.

Breathe, she ordered herself. *Just breathe.*

Because she couldn't do this. This wasn't who she was. She hadn't held on to her virginity all this time to toss it aside at the very first temptation...had she?

This couldn't be who she was. It couldn't.

She'd spent her whole life practicing how to appear unruffled and serene under any and all circumstances, though she couldn't recall ever putting it to this kind of test before. She made herself breathe. She made herself smile. She sank into the familiarity of her public persona, wielding it like that armor she'd wanted, because it occurred to her it was the toughest and most resilient armor she had.

Achilles followed her into that bright and shiny elevator in the back of the gleaming lobby, using his key to close the doors behind them. He did not appear to notice or care that she was newly armored, especially while he seemed perfectly content to look so...disreputable.

His suit jacket hung open, and she was sure it had to be

obvious to even the most casual observer that she'd had her hands all over his chest and his shirt. And she found it was difficult to think of that hard mouth of his as cruel now that she knew how it tasted. More, how it felt on hers, demanding and intense and—

Stop, she ordered herself. *Now.*

He leaned back against the wall as the elevator started to move, his dark gold eyes hooded and intent when they met hers. He didn't say a word. Maybe he didn't have to. Her heart was pounding so loud that Valentina was certain it would have drowned him out if he'd shouted.

But Achilles did not shout.

On the contrary, when the elevator doors shut behind them, securing them in his penthouse, he only continued to watch her in that same intense way. She moved into the great living room, aware that he followed her, silent and faintly lazy.

It made her nervous. That was what she told herself that fluttery feeling was, lodged there beneath her ribs. And lower, if she was honest. Much lower.

"I'm going to bed," she said. And then instantly wished she'd phrased that differently when she heard it echo there between them, seeming to fill up the cavernous space, beating as madly within her as her own frenzied heart. "Alone."

Achilles gave the impression of smiling without actually doing so. He thrust his hands into the pockets of his dark suit and regarded her solemnly, save for that glittering thing in his dark gaze.

"If that is what you wish, *glikia mou*."

And that was the thing. It wasn't what she wished. It wasn't what she wanted, and especially not when he called her that Greek name that she thought meant *my sweet*. It made her want to taste that word on that mouth of his. It made her want to find out exactly how sweet he thought she was.

It made her want to really, truly be someone else so she could do all the things that trampled through her head, making her chest feel tight while the rest of her... yearned.

Her whole life had been an exercise in virtue and duty, and she'd thought that meant something. She'd thought that *said* something about who she was. Valentina had been convinced that she'd held on to her chastity all this time, long after everyone she'd known had rid themselves of theirs, as a gift to her future.

But the night all around her told her something different. It had stripped away all the lies she'd told herself—or Achilles had. All the places she'd run and hid across all these years. Because the truth was that she'd never been tested. Was it truly virtue if she'd never been the least bit tempted to give it away? Or was it only coincidence that she'd never encountered anything that had felt the least bit compelling in that regard? Was it really holding on to something if she'd never felt the least bit like getting rid of it?

Because everything tonight was different. Valentina was different—or, worse, she thought as she stared at Achilles across the little bit of space that separated them, she had never been who she'd imagined she was. She had never understood that it was possible that a body could drown out what the mind knew to be prudent.

Until now.

She had judged passion all her life and told herself it was a story that weak people told themselves and others to make their sins seem more interesting. More complicated and unavoidable. But the truth was, Valentina had never experienced passion in her life.

Not until Achilles.

"I am your assistant," she told him. Or perhaps she was telling herself. "This must never happen again. If it does, I can't work for you."

"I have already told you that I am more than happy to accommodate—"

"There will be no lateral moves," she threw at him, appalled to hear her voice shaking. "You might lie awake at night imagining what that means and what it would look like, but I don't. I won't."

"Liar."

If he had hauled off and hit her, Valentina didn't think she could have been any more surprised. Shocked. No one had ever called her a liar before, not in all her life.

Then again, chimed in a small voice deep inside, *you never used to lie, did you? Not to others and not to yourself.*

"I have no doubt that you enjoy doing as you please," she spat at him, horrified that any of this was happening and, worse, that she'd let it—when Valentina knew who she was and what she'd be going back to in a few short weeks. "No matter the consequences. But not everyone is as reckless as you."

Achilles didn't quite smirk. "And that is why one of us is a billionaire and the other is his assistant."

"And if we were having a discussion about how to make money," Valentina said from between her teeth, no sign of her trademark serenity, "I would take your advice— but this is my life."

Guilt swamped her as she said that. Because, of course, it wasn't her life. It was Natalie's. And she had the sick feeling that she had already complicated it beyond the point of return. It didn't matter that Natalie had texted her to say that she'd kissed Prince Rodolfo, far away in Murin and neck-deep in Valentina's real life, however little Valentina had thought about it since she'd left it behind.

Valentina was going to marry Rodolfo. That her double had kissed him, the way Valentina probably should have, wasn't completely out of line.

But this… This thing she was doing… It was unacceptable on every level. She knew that.

Maybe Natalie has this same kind of chemistry with Rodolfo, something in her suggested. *Maybe he was engaged to the wrong twin.*

Which meant, she knew—because she was that self-serving—that maybe the wrong twin had been working for Achilles all this time and all of this was inevitable.

She wasn't sure she believed that. But she couldn't seem to stop herself. Or worse, convince herself that she should.

Achilles was still watching her too closely. Once again, she had the strangest notion that he knew too much. That he could see too far inside her.

Don't be silly, she snapped at herself then. *Of course he can't. You're just looking for more ways to feel guilty.*

Because whatever else happened, there was no way Achilles Casilieris would allow the sort of deception Valentina was neck-deep in to take place under his nose if he knew about it. She was certain of that, if nothing else.

"This is what I know about life," Achilles said, his voice a silken thread in the quiet of the penthouse, and Valentina had to repress a little shiver that threatened to shake her spine apart. "You must live it. If all you do is wall yourself off, hide yourself away, what do you have at the end but wasted time?"

Her throat was dry and much too tight. "I would take your advice more seriously if I didn't know you had an ulterior motive."

"I don't believe in wasting time or in ulterior motives," he growled back at her. "And not because I want a taste of you, though I do. And I intend to have it, *glikia mou*, make no mistake. But because you have put yourself on hold. Do you think I can't see it?"

She thought she had to be reeling then. Nothing was solid. She couldn't help but put her hand out, steadying herself on the back of the nearest chair—though it didn't seem to help.

And Achilles was watching her much too closely, with far too much of that disconcerting awareness making his dark gaze shine. "Or is it that you don't know yourself?"

When she was Princess Valentina of Murin, known to the world before her birth. Her life plotted out in its every detail. Her name literally etched in stone into the foundations of the castle where her family had ruled for generations. She had never had the opportunity to lose herself. Not in a dramatic adolescence. Not in her early twenties. She had never been beside herself at some crossroads, desperate to figure out the right path—because there had only ever been one path and she had always known exactly how to walk it, every step of the way.

"You don't know me at all," she told him, trying to sound less thrown and more outraged at the very suggestion that she was any kind of mystery to herself. She'd never had that option. "You're my employer, not my confidant. You know what I choose to show you and nothing more."

"But what you choose to show, and how you choose to show it, tells me exactly who you are." Achilles shook his head, and it seemed to Valentina that he moved closer to her when she could see he didn't. That he was exactly where he'd always been—it was just that he seemed to take over the whole world. She wasn't sure he even tried; he just did. "Or did you imagine I achieved all that I've achieved without managing to read people? Surely you cannot be so foolish."

"I was about to do something deeply foolish," she said

tightly. And not exactly smartly. "But I've since come to my senses."

"No one is keeping you here." His hands were thrust deep into his pockets, and he stood where he'd stopped, a few steps into the living room from those elevator doors. His gaze was all over her, but nothing else was touching her. He wasn't even blocking her escape route back to the guest room on this floor.

And she understood then. He was giving her choice. He was putting it on her. He wasn't simply sweeping her off into all that wild sensation—when he must have known he could have. He easily could have. If he hadn't stopped in the car, what would they be doing now?

But Valentina already knew the answer to that. She could feel her surrender inside her like heat.

And she thought she hated him for it.

Or should.

"I'm going to sleep," she said. She wanted her voice to be fierce. Some kind of condemnation. But she thought she sounded more determined than resolved. "I will see you in the morning. Sir."

Achilles smiled. "I think we both know you will see me long before that. And in your dreams, *glikia mou*, I doubt I will be so chivalrous."

Valentina pressed her lips tight together and did not allow herself to respond to him. Especially because she wanted to so very, very badly—and she knew, somehow, that it would lead nowhere good. It couldn't.

Instead, she turned and headed for her room. It was an unremarkable guest room appropriate for staff, but the best thing about it was the lock on the door. Not that she thought he would try to get in.

She was far more concerned that she was the one who would try to get out.

"One of these days," he said from behind her, his voice

low and intense, "you will stop running. It is a foregone conclusion, I am afraid. And then what?"

Valentina didn't say a word. But she didn't have to.

When she finally made it to her room and threw the dead bolt behind her, the sound of it echoed through the whole of the penthouse like a gong, answering Achilles eloquently without her having to open her mouth.

Telling him exactly how much of a coward she was, in case he hadn't already guessed.

CHAPTER SIX

IN THE DAYS that followed that strange night and Achilles's world-altering kiss that had left her raw and aching and wondering if she'd ever feel like herself again, Valentina found she couldn't bear the notion that she was twenty-seven years old and somehow a stranger to herself.

Her future was set in stone. She'd always known that. And she'd never fought against all that inevitability because what was the point? She could fight as much as she wanted and she'd still be Princess Valentina of Murin, only with a stain next to her name. That had always seemed to her like the very definition of futility.

But in the days that followed that kiss, it occurred to her that perhaps it wasn't the future she needed to worry about, but her past. She hadn't really allowed herself to think too closely about what it meant that Natalie had been raised by the woman who was very likely Valentina's own mother. Because, of course, there was no other explanation for the fact she and Natalie looked so much alike. Identical twins couldn't just randomly occur, and certainly not when one of them was a royal. There were too many people watching royal births too closely. Valentina had accepted the story that her mother had abandoned her, because it had always been couched in terms of Frederica's mental illness. Valentina had imagined her mother living out her days in some or other institution somewhere, protected from harm.

But the existence of Natalie suggested that Frederica was instead a completely different person from the one Valentina had imagined all this time. The woman who now called herself Erica had clearly not wasted away in a mental institution, all soothing pastels and injections and no ability to contact her own child. On the contrary, this Erica had lived a complicated life after her time in the palace that had nothing to do with any hospital—and though she'd clearly had two daughters, she'd taken only one with her when she'd gone.

Valentina didn't entirely understand how she could be quite so hurt by a betrayal that had happened so long ago and that she hadn't known about until recently. She didn't understand why it mattered so much to her. But the more she tried to tell herself that it was silly to be so bothered, the more bothered she got.

It was only when she had gone round and round and round on that almost too many times to count that Valentina accepted the fact she was going to have to do something about it.

And all these years, she'd never known how to go about looking for her mother even if she'd wanted to. She would have had to ask her father directly, the very idea of which made her shudder—even now, across an ocean or two from his throne and his great reserve and his obvious reluctance to discuss Frederica at all. Barring that, she would have had to speak to one of the high-level palace aides whose role was to serve her father in every possible way and who therefore had access to most of the family secrets. She doubted somehow that they would have told her all the things that she wanted to know—or even a few of them. And they certainly would have run any questions she had past her father first, which would have defeated the purpose of asking them.

Valentina tried to tell herself that was why she'd never asked.

But now she was tucked up in a lethally dangerous billionaire's penthouse in New York City, away from all the palace intrigue and protocol, and far too aware of the things a man like Achilles could do with only a kiss. To say nothing of his businesses. What was an old family secret to a man like Achilles?

And even though in many ways she had fewer resources at her fingertips and fewer people to ask for ancient stories and explanations, in the end, it was very simple. Because Valentina had Natalie's mobile, which had to mean she had direct access to her own story. If she dared look for it.

The Valentina who had seen her own mirror image in a bathroom in London might not have dared. But the Valentina who had lost herself in the raw fire of Achilles's kiss, on the other hand, dared all manner of things.

It was that Valentina who opened up Natalie's list of contacts, sitting there in her locked bedroom in Achilles's penthouse. She scrolled down, looking for an entry that read *Mom*. Or *Mum*. Or any variation of *Mother* she could think of.

But there was nothing.

That stymied her, but she was aware enough to realize that the sensation deep in her belly was not regret. It was relief. As if, in the end, she preferred these mysteries to what was likely to be a vicious little slap of truth.

You are such a coward, she told herself.

Because it wasn't as if her father—or Valentina herself, for that matter—had ever been in hiding. The truth was that her mother could have located her at any point over these last twenty-seven years. That she hadn't done so told Valentina all she needed to know about Frederica's maternal feelings, surely.

Well. What she *needed* to know perhaps, but there was a great deal more she *wanted* to know, and that was the trouble.

She kept scrolling until she found an entry marked *Erica*. She thought that told her a great deal about Natalie's relationship with this woman who was likely mother to them both. It spoke of a kind of distance that Valentina had certainly never contemplated when she'd thought about her own mother from time to time over the past nearly thirty years. In her head, of course, any reunion with the woman she'd imagined had been locked away in a pleasantly secure institution would be filled with love. Regret. Soft, sweet arms wrapped around her, and a thousand apologies for somehow managing to abandon and then never find her way back to a baby who lived at one of the most famous addresses in the world.

She wasn't entirely sure why the simple fact of the woman's first name in a list of contacts made it so clear that all of that was a lie. Not just a harmless fantasy to make a motherless child feel better about her fate, but something infinitely more dangerous, somehow.

Valentina wanted to shut down the mobile phone. She wanted to throw it across the small room and pretend that she'd never started down this road in the first place.

But it occurred to her that possibly, she was trying to talk herself out of doing this thing she was certain she needed to do.

Because Achilles might have imagined that he could see these mysteries in her, but what scared Valentina was that she could, too. That he'd identified a terrible weakness in her, and that meant anyone could.

Perhaps she wasn't who she thought she was. Perhaps

she never had been. Perhaps, all this time, she'd imagined she'd been walking down a set path when she hadn't.

If she was honest, the very idea made her want to cry.

It had been important, she thought then, sitting cross-legged on the bed with the summer light streaming in from the windows—crucially important, even—to carry on the morning after that kiss as if nothing had changed. Because she had to pretend that nothing had. That she didn't know too much now. That she didn't think of that kiss every time she looked at Achilles. She'd gone to work, and she'd done her job, and she'd stayed as much in his presence as she ever did—and she thought that she deserved some kind of award for the acting she'd done. So cool, so composed.

So utterly unbothered by the fact she now knew how he tasted.

And she tried to convince herself that only she knew that she was absolutely full of it.

But one day bled into the next, and she'd found that her act became harder and harder to pull off, instead of easier. She couldn't understand it. It wasn't as if Achilles was doing anything, necessarily. He was Achilles, of course. There was always that look in his eyes, as if he was but waiting for her to give him a sign.

Any sign.

As if, were she to do so, he would drop everything he was doing—no matter where they were and what was happening around them—and sweep them right back into that storm of sensation that she found simmered inside her, waiting. Just waiting.

Just as he was.

It was the notion that she was the one who held the power—who could make all of that happen with a simple word or glance—that she found kept her up at night. It made her shake. It polluted her dreams and made her drift off entirely too many times while she was awake, only to be slapped back down to earth when Achilles's voice turned silken, as if he knew.

Somehow, this all made her determined to seek out the one part of her life that had never made sense, and had never fit in neatly into the tidy narrative she'd believed all her life and knew back and forth.

Today was a rare afternoon when Achilles had announced that he had no need of her assistance while he tended to his fitness in his personal gym because, he'd gritted at her, he needed to clear his head. Valentina had repaired to her bedroom to work out a few snarls in his schedule and return several calls from the usual people wanting advice on how to approach him with various bits of news he was expected to dislike intensely. She'd changed out of Natalie's usual work uniform and had gratefully pulled on a pair of jeans and a T-shirt, feeling wildly rebellious as she did so. And then a little bit embarrassed that her life was clearly so staid and old-fashioned that she found denim a personal revolution.

Many modern princesses dressed casually at times, she was well aware. Just as she was even more aware that none of them were related to her father, with his antiquated notions of propriety. And therefore none of them would have to suffer his disapproval should she find herself photographed looking "common" despite her ancient bloodline.

But she wasn't Princess Valentina here in New York, where no one cared what she wore. And maybe that was why Valentina pulled the trigger. She didn't cold-call the number that she'd found on her sister's phone—and there was something hard and painful in her chest even thinking that word, *sister*. She fed the number into a little piece of software that one of Achilles's companies had been working on, and she let it present her with information that she supposed she should have had some sort of scruple about using. But she didn't.

Valentina imagined that said something about her, too, but she couldn't quite bring herself to care about that the way she thought she ought to have.

In a push of a button, she had a billing address. Though the phone number itself was tied to the area code of a far-off city, the billing address was right here in Manhattan.

It was difficult not see that as some kind of sign.

Valentina slipped out of the penthouse then, without giving herself time to second-guess what she was about to do. She smiled her way through the lobby the way she always did, and then she set out into New York City by herself.

All by herself.

No guards. No security. Not even Achilles's brooding presence at her side. She simply walked. She made her way through the green, bright stretch of Central Park, headed toward the east side and the address Achilles's software had provided. No one spoke to her. No one called her name. No cameras snapped at her, recording her every move.

After a while, Valentina stopped paying attention to the expression on her face. She stopped worrying about her posture and whether or not her hair looked unkempt as the faint breeze teased at it. She simply...walked.

Her shoulders seemed to slip down an extra inch or two from her ears. She found herself breathing deeper, taking in the people she passed without analyzing them—without assuming they wanted something from her or were look-ing to photograph her supposedly "at large" in the world.

About halfway across the park it occurred to her that she'd never felt this way in her life. Alone. Free. Better yet, anonymous. She could have been anybody on the streets. There were locals all over the paths in the park, walking and talking and taking in the summer afternoon as if that was a perfectly normal pastime. To be out on their own, no one the wiser, doing exactly as they pleased.

Valentina realized that whatever happened next, this was the normal she'd spent her life looking for and dreaming about. This exact moment, walking across Central Park while summer made its cheerful noises all around her, completely and entirely on her own.

Freedom, it turned out, made her heart beat a little too fast and too hard inside her chest.

Once she made it to the east side, she headed a little bit uptown, then farther east until she found the address that had been on that billing statement. It looked like all the other buildings on the same block, not exactly dripping in luxury, but certainly no hovel. It was difficult for Valentina to determine the difference between kinds of dwellings in a place like this. Apartment buildings, huge blocks of too many people living on top of each other by choice, seemed strange to her on the face of it. But who was she to determine the difference between prosperous New Yorkers and regular ones? She had lived in a palace all her life. And she suspected that Achilles's sprawling penthouse wasn't a far cry from a palace itself, come to that.

But once she'd located the building she wanted and its dark green awning marked with white scrollwork, she didn't know what to do. Except wait there. As if she was some kind of daring sleuth, just like in the books she'd read as a little girl, when she was just...that same old motherless child, looking for a better story to tell herself.

She chided herself for that instantly. It felt defeating. Despairing. She was anonymous and free and unremarkable, standing on a city street. Nobody in the entire world knew where she was. Nobody would know where to look and nobody was likely to find her if they tried. Valentina couldn't decide if that notion made her feel small and fragile, or vast and powerful. Maybe both at the same time.

She didn't know how long she stood there. She ignored the first few calls that buzzed at her from Natalie's mobile tucked in her pocket, but then realized that standing about speaking on her phone gave her far more of a reason to be out there in the street. Instead of simply standing there doing nothing, looking like she was doing exactly what she was doing, which was looming around as she waited for somebody to turn up.

So she did her job, out there on the street. Or Natalie's job, anyway. She fielded the usual phone calls from the office and, if she was honest, liked the fact that she had somewhere to put all her nervous energy. She was half-afraid that Achilles would call and demand that she return to his side immediately, but she suspected that she was less afraid of that happening than she was hoping that it would, so she didn't have to follow this through.

Because even now, there was a part of her that simply wanted to retreat back into what she already knew. What she'd spent her life believing.

Afternoon was bleeding into evening, and Valentina was beginning to think that she'd completely outstayed her welcome. That Erica was in one of the other places she sometimes stayed, like the one in the Caribbean Natalie had mentioned in a text. That at any moment now it was likely that one of the doormen in the surrounding buildings would call the police to make her move along at last. That they hadn't so far she regarded as some kind of miracle. She finished up the last of the calls she'd been fielding, and told herself that it had been foolish to imagine that she could simply turn up one afternoon, stand around and solve the mysteries of her childhood so easily.

But that was when she saw her.

And Valentina didn't know exactly what it was that had

caught her eye. The hair was wrong, not long and coppery like her daughters' but short. Dark. And it wasn't as if Valentina had any memories of this woman, but still. There was something in the way she moved. The way she came down the block, walking quickly, a plastic bag hanging from one wrist and the other hand holding a phone to her ear.

But Valentina knew her. She knew that walk. She knew the gait and the way the woman cocked her head toward the hand holding her phone. She knew the way this woman carried herself.

She recognized her, in other words, when she shouldn't have. When, she realized, despite the fact she'd spent a whole summer afternoon waiting for this moment—she really didn't want to recognize her.

And she'd been nursing fantasies this whole time, little as she wanted to admit that, even to herself. She'd told herself all the things that she would do if this woman appeared. She'd worked out scenarios in her head.

Do you know who I am? she would ask, or demand, and this woman she had always thought of as Federica, but who went by a completely different name—the better to hide, Valentina assumed—would... Cry? Flail about? Offer excuses? She hadn't been able to decide which version she would prefer no matter how many times she'd played it out in her head.

And as this woman who was almost certainly her mother walked toward her, not looking closely enough to see that there was anyone standing down the block a ways in front of her, much less someone who she should have assumed was the daughter she knew as Natalie, Valentina realized what she should have known already. Or maybe, deep down, she had known it—she just hadn't really wanted to admit it.

There was nothing this woman could do to fix anything

or change anything or even make it better. She couldn't go back in time. She couldn't change the past. She couldn't choose Valentina instead of Natalie, if that had been the choice she'd made. Valentina wasn't even certain that was something she'd want, if she could go back in time herself, but the fact of the matter was that there was nothing to be done about it now.

And her heart beat at her and beat at her, until she thought it might beat its way straight out through her ribs, and even as it did, Valentina couldn't pretend that she didn't know that what she was feeling was grief.

Grief, thick and choking. Dark and muddy and deep.

For the childhood she'd never had, and hadn't known she'd missed until now. For the life she might have known had this woman been different. Had Valentina been different. Had her father, perhaps, not been King Geoffrey of Murin. It was all speculation, of course. It was that tearing thing in her belly and that weight on her chest, and that thick, deep mud she worried she might never find her way out of again.

And when Erica drew close to her building's green awning, coming closer to Valentina than she'd been in twenty-seven years, Valentina…said nothing. She let her hair fall forward to cover her face where she leaned against the brick wall. She pretended she was on a serious phone call while the woman who was definitely her mother—of course she was her mother; how had Valentina been tricking herself into pretending she could be anything but that?—turned into the building that Valentina had been staking out all afternoon, and was swallowed up into her own lobby.

For long moments, Valentina couldn't breathe. She wasn't sure she could think.

It was as if she didn't know who she was.

She found herself walking. She lost herself in the tumult of this sprawling mess of a bright and brash city, the noise of car horns in the street, and the blasts of conversation and laughter from the groups of strangers she passed. She made her way back to the park and wandered there as the summer afternoon took on that glassy blue that meant the hour was growing late.

She didn't cry. She hardly saw in front of her. She simply walked.

And dusk was beginning to steal in at last, making the long blocks cold in the long shadows, when she finally made it back to Achilles's building.

One of the doormen brought her up in the elevator, smiling at her as she stepped off. It made her think that perhaps she had smiled in return, though she couldn't tell. It was as if her body was not her own and her face was no longer under her control. She walked into Achilles's grand living room, and stood there. It was as if she still didn't know where she was. As if she still couldn't see. And the huge windows that let Manhattan in all around her only seemed to make her sense of dislocation worse.

"Where the hell have you been?"

That low growl came from above her. Valentina didn't have to turn and look to know that it was Achilles from on high, standing at the top of the stairs that led to his sprawling master suite.

She looked up anyway. Because somehow, the most dangerous man she'd ever met felt like an anchor.

He looked as if he'd just showered. He wore a T-shirt she could tell was soft from down two flights, stretched over his remarkable chest as if it was as enamored of him as she feared she was. Loose black trousers were slung low on his hips, and she had the giddy sense that if he did something like stretch, or breathe too heavily, she would be able to see a swathe of olive skin between the waistband and the hem of his T-shirt.

And suddenly, she wanted nothing more than to see exactly that. More than she could remember wanting anything else. Ever.

"Careful, *glikia mou*, or I will take you up on that invitation written all over your face," Achilles growled as if he was irritated...but she knew better.

Because he knew. He always knew. He could read her when no one else ever had. The masks she wore like they were second nature and the things she pretended for the whole of the rest of the world fooled everybody, but never him.

Never, ever him.

As if there was a real Valentina buried beneath the exterior she'd thought for years was the totality of who she was, and Achilles was the only one who had ever met her. Ever seen her. Ever suspected she existed and then found her, again and again, no matter how hard Valentina worked to keep her hidden away.

Her throat was dry. Her tongue felt as if it no longer fit in her own mouth.

But she couldn't bring herself to look away from him.

She thought about her mother and she thought about her childhood. She thought about the pride she'd taken in that virtue of hers that she'd clung to so fiercely all these years. Or perhaps not so fiercely, as it had been so untested. Was that virtue at all, she wondered?

Or was this virtue?

She had spent all of this time trying to differentiate herself from a woman she thought she knew, but who it turned out she didn't know at all. And for what? She was already trapped in the same life that her mother had abandoned.

Valentina was the one who hadn't left her father. She was the one who had prided herself on being perfect. She was the one who was decidedly not mentally ill, never too overwrought to do the job required of her by her blood and her father's expectations, nothing but a credit to her father in all ways. And she'd reveled in it.

More than reveled in it. It had become the cornerstone of her own self-definition.

And all of it was built on lies. The ones she told herself, and more than that, the lies that had been told to her for her entire life. By everyone.

All Valentina could think as she gazed up the stairs to the man she was only pretending was her employer was that she was done with lies. She wanted something honest. Even—especially—if it was raw.

And she didn't much care if there were consequences to that.

"You say that is if it is a threat," she said quietly. Distinctly. "Perhaps you should rethink your own version of an invitation before it gets you in trouble." She raised her brows in challenge, and knew it. Reveled in it, too. "Sir."

And when Achilles smiled then, it was with sheer masculine triumph, and everything changed.

He had thought she'd left him.

When Achilles had come out of the hard, brutal workout he'd subjected himself to that had done absolutely nothing to make his vicious need for her settle, Achilles had found her gone.

And he'd assumed that was it. The princess had finally had enough. She'd finished playing this down-market game of hers and gone back to her palaces and her ball gowns and her resplendent little prince who waited for her across the seas.

He'd told himself it was for the best.

He was a man who took things for a living and made an empire out of his conquests, and he had no business whatsoever putting his commoner's hands all over a woman of her pedigree. No business doing it, and worse, he shouldn't want to.

And maybe that was why he found himself on his treadmill again while he was still sucking air from his first workout, running as if every demon he'd vanquished in his time was chasing him all over again, and gaining. Maybe that was why he'd run until he'd thought his lungs might burst, his head might explode or his knees might give out beneath him.

Then he'd run more. And even when he'd exhausted himself all over again, even when he was standing in his own shower with his head bent toward the wall as if she'd bested him personally, it hadn't helped.

The fact of the matter was that he had a taste of Valentina, and nothing else would do.

And what enraged him the most, he'd found—aside from the fact he hadn't had her the way he'd wanted her—was that he'd let her think she'd tricked him all this time. That she would go back behind her fancy gates and her moats and whatever the hell else she had in that palace of hers that he'd looked up online and thought looked exactly like the sort of fairy tale he disdained, and she would believe that she'd played him for a fool.

Achilles thought that might actually eat him alive.

And now here she stood when he thought he'd lost her. At the bottom of his stairs, looking up at him, her eyes dark with some emotion he couldn't begin to define.

But he didn't want to define it. He didn't want to talk about her feelings, and he'd die before he admitted his own, and what did any of that matter anyway? She was here and he was here, and a summer night was creeping in outside.

And the only thing he wanted to think about was sating himself on her at last.

At last and for as long as he could.

Achilles was hardly aware of moving down the stairs even as he did it.

One moment he was at the top, staring down at Valentina's upturned face with her direct challenge ringing in him like a bell, and the next he was upon her. And she was so beautiful. So exquisitely, ruinously beautiful. He couldn't seem to get past that. It was as if it wound around him and through him, changing him, making him new each time he beheld her.

He told himself he hated it, but he didn't look away.

"There is no going back," he told her sternly. "There will be no pretending this didn't happen."

Her smile was entirely too graceful and the look in her green eyes too merry by far. "Do you get that often?"

Achilles felt like a savage. An animal. Too much like that monster he kept down deep inside. And yet he didn't have it in him to mind. He reached out and indulged himself at last while his blood hammered through his veins, running his fingers over that elegant cheekbone of hers, and that single freckle that marred the perfection of her face—and somehow made her all the more beautiful.

"So many jokes," he murmured, not sure how much of the gruffness in his voice was need and how much was that thing like temper that held him fast and fierce. "Everything is so hilarious, suddenly. How much longer do you think you will be laughing, *glikia mou*?"

"I think that is up to you," Valentina replied smoothly, and she was still smiling at him in that same way, graceful and knowing. "Is that why you require so much legal documentation before you take a woman to bed? Do you make them all laugh so much that you fear your reputation as a grumpy icon would take a hit if it got out?"

It was a mark of how far gone he was that he found that amusing. If anyone else had dreamed of saying such a thing to him, he would have lost his sense of humor completely.

He felt his mouth curve. "There is only one way to find out."

And Achilles had no idea what she might do next. He wondered if that was what it was about her, if that was why this thirst for her never seemed to ebb. She was so very different from all the women he'd known before. She was completely unpredictable. He hardly knew, from one moment to the next, what she might do next.

It should have irritated him, he thought. But instead it only made him want her more.

Everything, it seemed, made him want her more. He hadn't realized until now how pale and insubstantial his desires had been before. How little he'd wanted anything.

"There is something I must tell you." She pulled her bottom lip between her teeth after she said that, a little breathlessly, and everything in him stilled.

This was it, he thought. And Achilles didn't know if he was proud of her or sad, somehow, that this great charade was at an end. For surely that was what she planned to tell him. Surely she planned to come clean about who she really was.

And while there was a part of him that wanted to deny that what swirled between them was anything more than sex, simple and elemental, there was a far greater part of him that roared its approval that she should think it was right to identify herself before they went any further.

"You can tell me anything," he told her, perhaps more fiercely than he should. "But I don't know why you imagine I don't already know."

He was fascinated when her cheeks bloomed with that crisp, bright red that he liked a little too much. More each time he saw it, because he liked his princess a little flustered. A little off balance.

But something in him turned over, some foreboding perhaps. Because he couldn't quite imagine why it was that she should be *embarrassed* by the deception she'd practiced on him. He could think of many things he'd like her to feel for attempting to pull something like that over on him, and he had quite a few ideas about how she should pay for that, but embarrassment wasn't quite it.

"I thought you might know," she whispered. "I hope it doesn't matter."

"Everything matters or nothing does, *glikia mou*."

He shifted so he was closer to her. He wanted to care about whatever it was she was about to tell him, but he found the demands of his body were far too loud and too imperative to ignore. He put his hands on her, curling his fingers over her delicate shoulders and then losing himself in their suppleness. And in the delicate line of her arms. And in the sweet feel of her bare skin beneath his palms as he ran them down from her shoulders to her wrists, then back again.

And he found he didn't really care what she planned to confess to him. How could it matter when he was touching her like this?

"I do not require your confession," he told her roughly. "I am not your priest."

If anything, her cheeks flared brighter.

"I'm a virgin," she blurted out, as if she had to force herself to say it.

For a moment, it was as if she'd struck him. As if she'd picked up one of the sculptures his interior designer had littered about his living room and clobbered him with it.

"I beg your pardon?"

But she was steadier then. "You heard me. I'm a virgin. I thought you knew." She swallowed, visibly, but she didn't look away from him. "Especially when I didn't know how to kiss you."

Achilles didn't know what to do with that.

Or rather, he knew exactly what to do with it, but was

afraid that if he tossed his head back and let himself go the way he wanted to—roaring out his primitive take on her completely unexpected confession to the rafters—it might terrify her.

And the last thing in the world he wanted to do was terrify her.

He knew he should care that this wasn't quite the confession he'd expected. That as far as he could tell, Valentina had no intention of telling him who she was. Ever. He knew that it should bother him, and perhaps on some level it did, but the only thing he could seem to focus on was the fact that she was untouched.

Untouched.

He was the only man in all the world who had ever tasted her. Touched her. Made her shiver, and catch her breath, and moan. That archaic word seemed to beat in place of his heart.

Virgin. Virgin. Virgin.

Until it was as if he knew nothing but that. As if her innocence shimmered between them, beckoning and sweet, and she was his for the taking.

And, oh, how Achilles liked to take the things he wanted.

"Are you sure you wish to waste such a precious gift on the likes of me?" he asked, and he heard the stark greed beneath the laziness he forced into his tone. He heard exactly how much he wanted her. He was surprised it didn't seem to scare her the way he thought it should. "After all, there is nothing particularly special about me. I have money, that's all. And as you have reminded me, I am your boss. The ethical considerations are legion."

He didn't know why he said that. Any of that. Was it to encourage her to confess her real identity to him? Was it to remind her of the role she'd chosen to play—although not today, perhaps?

Or was it to remind him?

Either way, she only lifted her chin. "You don't have to take it," she said, as if it was of no import to her one way or the other. "Certainly not if you have some objection."

She lifted one shoulder, then dropped it, and the gesture was so quintessentially royal that it should have set Achilles's teeth on edge. But instead he found it so completely her, so entirely Princess Valentina, that it only made him harder. Hotter. More determined to find his way inside her.

And soon.

"I have no objection," he assured her, and there was no pretending his tone wasn't gritty. Harsh. "Are we finished talking?"

And the nerves he'd been unable to detect before were suddenly all over her face. He doubted she knew it. But she was braver than she ought to have been, his deceitful little princess, and all she did was gaze back at him. Clear and sure, as if he couldn't see the soft, vulnerable cast to her mouth.

Or maybe, he thought, she had no idea how transparent she was.

"Yes," Valentina said softly. "I'm ready to stop talking."

And this time, as he drew her to him, he knew it wouldn't end in a kiss. He knew they weren't going to stop until he'd had her at last.

He knew that she was not only going to be his tonight, but she was going to be only his. That no one had ever touched her before, and if he did it right, no one else ever would.

Because Achilles had every intention of ruining his princess for all other men.

CHAPTER SEVEN

VALENTINA COULDN'T BELIEVE this was happening.

At last.

Achilles took her mouth, and there was a lazy quality to his kiss that made her knees feel weak. He set his mouth to hers, and then he took his time. As if he knew that inside she was a jangle of nerves and longing, anticipation and greed. As if he knew she hardly recognized herself or all the needy things that washed around inside her, making her new.

Making her his.

He kissed her for a long while, it seemed to her. He slid his arms around her, he pulled her against his chest, and then he took her mouth with a thoroughness that made a dangerous languor steal all over her. All through her. Until she wasn't sure that she would be able to stand on her own, were he to let go of her.

But he didn't let go.

Valentina thought she might have fallen off the edge of the world anyway, because everything seemed to whirl and cartwheel around, but then she realized that what he'd done was stoop down to bend a little and then pick her up. As if she was as weightless as she felt. He held her in his arms, high against his chest, and she felt her shoes fall off her feet like some kind of punctuation. And when he gazed down into her face, she thought he looked like some kind of conquering warrior of old, though she chided herself for being so fanciful.

There was nothing fanciful about Achilles.

Quite the opposite. He was fierce and masculine and ruthless beyond measure, and still, Valentina couldn't think of anywhere she would rather be—or anyone she would rather be with like this. It all felt inevitable, as if she'd been waiting her whole life for this thing she hardly understood to sweep her away, just like this.

And it had come into focus only when she'd met Achilles.

Because he was her only temptation. She had never wanted anyone else. She couldn't imagine she ever would.

"I don't know what to do," she whispered, aware on some level that he was moving. That he was carrying her up those penthouse stairs as if she weighed nothing at all. But she couldn't bring herself to look away from his dark gold gaze. And the truth was, she didn't care. He could take her anywhere. "I don't want to disappoint you."

"And how would you do that?" His voice was so deep. So lazy and, unless she was mistaken, amused, even as that gaze of his made her quiver, deep inside.

"Well," she stammered out. "Well, I don't—"

"Exactly," he said, interrupting her with that easy male confidence that she found she liked a little too much. "You don't know, but I do. So perhaps, *glikia mou*, you will allow me to demonstrate the breadth and depth of my knowledge."

And when she shuddered, he only laughed.

Achilles carried her across the top floor, all of which was part of his great master bedroom. It took up the entire top level of his penthouse, bordered on all sides by the wide patio that was also accessible from a separate staircase below. The better to maintain and protect his privacy, she thought now, which she felt personally invested in at the moment. He strode across the hardwood floor with bold-colored rugs tossed here and there, and she took in the exposed brick walls and the bright, modern works of art that hung on them. This floor was all space and silence, and in between there were more of those breathtaking windows that brightened the room with the lights from the city outside.

Achilles didn't turn on any additional light. He simply took Valentina over to the huge bed that was propped up on a sleek modern platform crafted out of a bright, hard steel, and laid her out across it as if she was something precious to him. Which made her heart clutch at her, as if she wanted to be.

And then he stood there beside the bed, his hands on his lean hips, and did nothing but gaze down at her.

Valentina pushed herself up onto her elbows. She could feel her breath moving in and out of her, and it was as if it was wired somehow to all that sensation she could feel lighting her up inside. It made her breasts feel heavier. It made her arms and legs feel somehow restless and sleepy at once.

With every breath, she could feel that bright, hot ache between her legs intensify. And this time, she knew without a shred of doubt that he was aware of every last part of it.

"Do you have anything else to confess?" he asked her, and she wondered if she imagined the dark current in his voice then. But it didn't matter. She had never wanted anyone, but she wanted him. Desperately.

She would confess anything at all if it meant she could have him.

And it wasn't until his eyes blazed, and that remarkable mouth of his kicked up in one corner, that she realized she'd spoken out loud.

"I will keep that in mind," he told her, his voice a rasp into the quiet of the room. Then he inclined his head. "Take off your clothes."

It was as if he'd plugged her into an electrical outlet. She felt zapped. Blistered, perhaps, by the sudden jolt of power. It felt as if there were something bright and hot, wrapped tight around her ribs, pressing down. And down farther.

And she couldn't bring herself to mind.

"But—by myself?" she asked, feeling a little bit light-headed at the very idea. She'd found putting on these jeans a little bit revolutionary. She couldn't imagine stripping them off in front of a man.

And not just any man. Achilles Casilieris.

Who didn't relent at all. "You heard me."

Valentina had to struggle then. She had to somehow shove her way out of all that wild electrical madness that was jangling through her body, at least enough so she could think through it. A little bit, anyway. She had to struggle to sit up all the way, and then to pull the T-shirt off her body. Her hands went to her jeans next, and she wrestled with the buttons, trying to pull the fly open. It was all made harder by the fact that her hands shook and her fingers felt entirely too thick.

And the more she struggled, the louder her breathing sounded. Until she was sure it was filling up the whole room, and more embarrassing by far, there was no possible way that Achilles couldn't hear it. Or see the flush that she could feel all over her, electric and wild. She wrestled the stiff, unyielding denim down over her hips, that bright heat that churned inside her seeming to bleed out everywhere as she did. She was sure it stained her, marking her bright hot and obvious.

She sneaked a look toward Achilles, and she didn't

know what she expected to see. But she froze when her eyes met his.

That dark gold gaze of his was as hot and demanding as ever. That curve in his mouth was even deeper. And there was something in the way that he was looking at her that soothed her. As if his hands were on her already, when they were not. It was as if he was helping her undress when she suspected that it was very deliberate on his part that he was not.

Because of course it was deliberate, she realized in the next breath. He was giving her another choice. He was putting it in her hands, again. And even while part of her found that inordinately frustrating, because she wanted to be swept away by him—or more swept away, anyway—there was still a part of her that relished this. That took pride in the fact that she was choosing to give in to this particular temptation.

That she was choosing to truly offer this particular man the virtue she had always considered such a gift.

It wasn't accidental. She wasn't drunk the way many of her friends had been, nor out of her mind in some other way, or even outside herself in the storm of an explosive temper or wild sensation that had boiled over.

He wanted her to be very clear that she was choosing him.

And Valentina wanted that, too. She wanted to choose Achilles. She wanted this.

She had never wanted anything else, she was sure of it. Not with this fervor that inhabited her body and made her light up from the inside out. Not with this deep certainty.

And so what could it possibly matter that she had never undressed for a man before? She was a princess. She had dressed and undressed in rooms full of attendants her whole life. Achilles was different from her collection of royal aides, clearly. But there was no need for her to be embarrassed, she told herself then. There was no need to go red in the face and start fumbling about, as if she didn't know how to remove a pair of jeans from her own body.

Remember who you are, she chided herself.

She was Princess Valentina of Murin. It didn't matter that seeing her mother might have shaken her. It didn't change a thing. That had nothing to do with who she was, it only meant that she'd become who she was in spite of the choices her mother had made. She could choose to do with that what she liked. And she was choosing to gift her innocence, the virginity she'd clung to as a badge of honor as if that differentiated her from the mother who'd left her, to Achilles Casilieris.

Here. Now.

And there was absolutely nothing to be ashamed about.

Valentina was sure that she saw something like approval in his dark gaze as she finished stripping her jeans from the length of her legs. And then she was sitting there in nothing but her bra and panties. She shifted up and onto her knees. Her hair fell down over her shoulders as she knelt on the bed, swirling across her bared skin and making her entirely too aware of how exposed she was.

But this time it felt sensuous. A sweet, warm sort of reminder of how much she wanted this. Him.

"Go on," he told her, a gruff command.

"That sounded a great deal like an order," Valentina murmured, even as she moved her hands around to her back to work the clasp of her bra. And it wasn't even a struggle to make her voice so airy.

"It was most definitely an order," Achilles agreed, his voice still gruff. "And I would suggest you obey me with significantly more alacrity."

"Or what?" she taunted him gently.

She eased open the silken clasp and then moved her hands around to the bra cups, holding them to her breasts when the bra would have fallen open. "Will you hold it against me in my next performance review? Oh, the horror."

"Are you defying me?"

But Achilles sounded amused, despite his gruffness. And there was something else in his voice then, she thought. A certain tension that she felt move inside her even before she understood what it was. Maybe she didn't have to understand. Her body already knew.

Between her legs, that aching thing grew fiercer. Brighter. And so did she.

"I think you can take it," she whispered.

And then she let the bra fall.

She felt the rush of cooler air over the flesh of her breasts. Her nipples puckered and stung a little as they pulled tight. But what she was concentrating on was that taut, arrested look on Achilles's face. That savage gleam in his dark gold eyes. And the way his fierce, ruthless mouth went flat.

He muttered something in guttural Greek, using words she had never heard before, in her blue-blooded academies and rarefied circles. But she knew, somehow, exactly what he meant.

She could feel it, part of that same ache.

He reached down to grip the hem of his T-shirt, then tugged it up and over his head in a single shrug of one muscled arm. She watched him do it, not certain she was breathing any longer and not able to make herself care about that at all, and then he was moving toward the bed.

Another second and he was upon her.

He swept her up in his arms again, moving her into the center of the bed, and then he bore her down to the mattress beneath them. And Valentina found that they fit together beautifully. That she knew instinctively what to do.

She widened her legs, he fit himself between them, and

she cushioned him there—that long, solid, hard-packed form of his—as if they'd been made to fit together just like this. His bare chest was a wonder. She couldn't seem to keep herself from exploring it, running her palms and her fingers over every ridge and every plane, losing herself in his hot, extraordinary male flesh. She could feel that remarkable ridge of his arousal again, pressed against her right where she ached the most, and it was almost too much.

Or maybe it really was too much, but she wanted it all the same.

She wanted him.

He set his mouth to hers again, and she could taste a kind of desperation on his wickedly clever mouth.

That wild sensation stormed through her, making her limp and wild and desperate for things she'd only ever read about before. He tangled his hands in her hair to hold her mouth to his, then he dropped his chest down against hers, bearing her down into the mattress beneath them. Making her feel glorious and alive and insane with that ache that started between her legs and bloomed out in all directions.

And then he taught her everything.

He tasted her. He moved his mouth from her lips, down the long line of her neck, learning the contours of her clavicle. Then he went lower, sending fire spinning all over her as he made his way down to one of her breasts, only to send lightning flashing all through her when he sucked her nipple deep into his mouth.

He tested the weight of her breasts in his faintly calloused palm, while he played with the nipple of the other, gently torturing her with his teeth, his tongue, his cruel lips. When she thought she couldn't take any more, he switched.

And then he went back and forth, over and over again,

until her head was thrashing against the mattress, and some desperate soul was crying out his name. Over and over again, as if she might break apart at any moment.

Valentina knew, distantly, that she was the one making those sounds. But she was too far gone to care.

Achilles moved his way down her body, taking his sweet time, and Valentina sighed with every inch he explored. She shifted. She rolled. She found herself lifting her hips toward him without his having to ask.

"Good girl," he murmured, and it was astonishing how much pleasure two little words could give her.

He peeled her panties down off her hips, tugged them down the length of her legs and then threw them aside. And when he was finished with that, he slid his hands beneath her bottom as he came back over her, lifted her hips up into the air and didn't so much as glance up at her before he set his mouth to the place where she needed him most.

Maybe she screamed. Maybe she fainted. Maybe both at once.

Everything seemed to flash bright, then smooth out into a long, lethal roll of sensation that turned Valentina red hot.

Everywhere.

He licked his way into her. He teased her and he learned her and he tasted her, making even that most private part of her his. She felt herself go molten and wild, and he made a low, rough sound of pleasure, deeply masculine and deliciously savage, and that was too much.

"Oh, no," she heard herself moan. "No—"

Valentina felt more than heard him laugh against the most tender part of her, and then everything went up in flames.

She exploded. She cried out and she shook, the pleasure so intense she didn't understand how anyone could live through it, but still she shook some more. She shook until she thought she'd been made new. She shook until she didn't care either way.

And when she knew her own name again, Achilles was crawling his way over her. He no longer wore those loose black trousers of his, and there was a look of unmistakably savage male triumph stamped deep on his face.

"Beautiful," he murmured. He was on his elbows over her, pressing himself against her. His wall of a chest. That fascinatingly hard part of him below. He studied her flushed face as if he'd never seen her before. "Am I the only man who has ever tasted you?"

Valentina couldn't speak. She could only nod, mute and still shaking.

She wondered if she might shake like this forever, and she couldn't seem to work herself up into minding if she did.

"Only mine," he said with a certain quiet ferocity that only made that shaking inside her worse. Or better. "You are only and ever mine."

And that was when she felt him. That broad smooth head of his hardest part, nudging against the place where she was nothing but soft, wet heat and longing.

She sucked in a breath, and Achilles took her face in his hands.

"Mine," he said again, in the same intense way.

It sounded a great deal like a vow.

Valentina's head was spinning.

"Yours," she whispered, and he grinned then, too fierce and too elemental.

He shifted his hips and moved a little farther against her, pressing himself against that entrance again, and Valentina found her hands in fists against his chest.

"Will it hurt?" she asked before she knew she meant

to speak. "Or is that just something they say in books, to make it seem more…"

But she couldn't quite finish that sentence. And Achilles's gaze was too dark and too bright at once, so intense she couldn't seem to stop shaking or spinning. And she couldn't bring herself to look away.

"It might hurt." He kept his attention on her, fierce and focused. "It might not. But either way, it will be over in a moment."

"Oh." Valentina blinked, and tried to wrap her head around that. "I suppose quick is good."

Achilles let out a bark of laughter, and she wasn't sure if she was startled or something like delighted to hear it. Both, perhaps.

And it made a knot she hadn't known was hardening inside her chest ease.

"I cannot tell if you are good for me or you will kill me," he told her then. He moved one hand, smoothing her hair back from her temple. "It will only hurt, or feel awkward, for a moment. I promise. As for the rest…"

And the smile he aimed at her then was, Valentina thought, the best thing she'd ever seen. It poured into her and through her, as bright and thick as honey, changing everything. Even the way she shook for him. Even the way she breathed.

"The rest will not be quick," Achilles told her, still braced there above her. "It will not be rushed, it will be thorough. Extremely thorough, as you know I am in all things."

She felt her breath stutter. But he was still going.

"And when I am done, *glikia mou*, we will do it again. And again. Until we get it right. Because I am nothing if not dedicated to my craft. Do you understand me?"

"I understand," Valentina said faintly, because it was

hard to keep her voice even when the world was lost somewhere in his commanding gaze. "I guess that's—"

But that was when he thrust his way inside her. It was a quick, hard thrust, slick and hot and overwhelming, until he was lodged deep inside her.

Inside her.

It was too much. It didn't hurt, necessarily, but it didn't feel good, either. It felt...like everything. Too much of everything.

Too hard. Too long. Too thick and too deep and too—

"Breathe," Achilles ordered her.

But Valentina didn't see how that was possible. How could she breathe when there was a person *inside* her? Even if that person was Achilles.

Especially when that person was Achilles.

Still, she did as he bade her, because he was *inside* her and she was beneath him and splayed open and there was nothing else to do. She breathed in.

She let it out, and then she breathed in again. And then again.

And with each breath, she felt less overwhelmed and more...

Something else.

Achilles didn't seem particularly worried. He held himself over her, one hand tangled in her hair as the other made its way down the front of her body. Lazily. Easily. He played with her breasts. He set his mouth against the crook of her neck where it met her shoulder, teasing her with his tongue and his teeth.

And still she breathed the way he'd told her to do. In. Out.

Over and over, until she couldn't remember that she'd balked at his smooth, intense entry. That she'd ever had a problem at all with *hard* and *thick* and *long* and *deep*.

Until all she could feel was fire.

Experimentally, she moved her hips, trying to get a better feel for how wide he was. How deep. How far inside her own body. Sensation soared through her every time she moved, so she did it again. And again.

She took a little more of him in, then rocked around a little bit, playing. Testing. Seeing how much of him she could take and if it would continue to send licks of fire coursing through her every time she shifted position, no matter how minutely.

It did.

And when she started to shift against him, restlessly, as if she couldn't help herself, Achilles lifted his head and grinned down her, something wild and dark and wholly untamed in his eyes.

It thrilled her.

"Please…" Valentina whispered.

And he knew. He always knew. Exactly what she needed, right when she needed it.

Because that was when he began to move.

He taught her about pace. He taught her depth and rhythm. She'd thought she was playing with fire, but Achilles taught her that she had no idea what real fire was.

And he kept his word.

He was very, very thorough.

When she began to thrash, he dropped down to get closer. He gathered her in his arms, holding her as he thrust inside her, again and again. He made her his with every deep, possessive stroke. He made her want. He made her need.

He made her cry out his name, again and again, until it sounded to Valentina like some kind of song.

This time, when the fire took her, she thought it might have torn her into far too many pieces for her to ever recover. He lost his rhythm then, hammering into her hard and wild, as if he was as wrecked as she was—

And she held him to her as he tumbled off that edge behind her, and straight on into bliss.

Achilles had made a terrible mistake, and he was not a man who made mistakes. He didn't believe in them. He believed in opportunities—it was how he'd built this life of his. Something that had always made him proud.

But this was a mistake. She was a mistake. He couldn't kid himself. He had never wanted somebody the way that he wanted Valentina. It had made him sloppy. He had concentrated entirely too much on her. Her pleasure. Her innocence, as he relieved her of it.

He hadn't thought to guard himself against her.

He never had to guard himself against anyone. Not since he'd been a child. He'd rather fallen out of the habit—and that notion galled him.

Achilles rolled to the side of the bed and sat there, running a hand over the top of his head. He could hear Valentina behind him, breathing. And he knew what he'd see if he looked. She slept hard, his princess. After he'd finished with her the last time, he'd thought she might have fallen asleep before he'd even pulled out of her. He'd held the weight of her, sprawled there on top of him, her breath heavy and her eyes shut tight so he had no choice but to marvel at the length of her eyelashes.

And it had taken him much longer than it should have to shift her off him, lay her beside him and cover her with the sheets. Carefully.

It was that unexpected urge to protect her—from himself, he supposed, or perhaps from the uncertain elements of his ruthlessly climate-controlled bedroom—that had made him go cold. Something a little too close to the sort of panic he did not permit himself to feel, ever, had pressed down on him then. And no amount of controlling his breath or ordering himself to stop the madness seemed to help.

He rubbed a palm over his chest now, because his heart was beating much too fast, the damned traitor.

He had wanted her too much, and this was the price. This treacherous place he found himself in now, that he hardly recognized. It hadn't occurred to him to guard himself against a virgin no matter her pedigree, and this was the result.

He felt things.

He felt things—and Achilles Casilieris did not *feel*. He refused to *feel*. The intensity of sex was physical, nothing more. Never more than that, no matter the woman and no matter the situation and no matter how she might beg or plead—

Not that Valentina had done anything of the sort.

He stood from the bed then, because he didn't want to. He wanted to roll back toward her, pull her close again. He bit off a filthy Greek curse, beneath his breath, then moved restlessly across the floor toward the windows.

Manhattan mocked him. It lay there before him, glittering and sparkling madly, and the reason he had a penthouse in this most brash and American of cities was because he liked to stand high above the sprawl of it as if he was some kind of king. Every time he came here he was reminded how far he'd come from his painful childhood. And every time he stayed in this very room, he looked out over all the wealth and opportunity and untethered American dreams that made this city what it was and knew that he had succeeded.

Beyond even the wildest dreams the younger version of Achilles could have conjured up for himself.

But tonight, all he could think about was a copperhaired innocent who had yet to tell him her real name, who had given him all of herself with that sweet enthusiasm that had nearly killed him, and left him...yearning.

And Achilles did not yearn.

He did not yearn and he did not let himself want things he could not have, and he absolutely, positively did not indulge in pointless nostalgia for things he did not miss. But as he stood at his huge windows overlooking Manhattan, the city that seemed to laugh at his predicament tonight instead of welcoming him the way it usually did, he found himself tossed back to the part of his past he only ever used as a weapon.

Against himself.

He hardly remembered his mother. Or perhaps he had beaten that sentimentality out of himself years ago. Either way, he knew that he had been seven or so when she had died, but it wasn't as if her presence earlier had done anything to save her children from the brute of a man whom she had married. Demetrius had been a thick, coarse sort of man, who had worked with his hands down on the docks and had thought that gave him the right to use those hands however he wished. Achilles didn't think there was anything the man had not beaten. His drinking buddies. His wife. The family dog. Achilles and his three young stepsiblings, over and over again. The fact that Achilles had not been Demetrius's own son, but the son of his mother's previous husband who had gone off to war and never returned, had perhaps made the beatings Demetrius doled out harsher—but it wasn't as if he spared his own flesh and blood from his fists.

After Achilles's mother had died under suspicious circumstances no one had ever bothered to investigate in a part of town where nothing good ever happened anyway, things went from bad to worse. Demetrius's temper worsened. He'd taken it out on the little ones, alternately kicking them around and then leaving them for seven-year-old Achilles to raise.

This had always been destined to end in failure, if not outright despair. Achilles understood that now, as an adult looking back. He understood it analytically and theoretically and, if asked, would have said exactly that. He'd been a child himself, etcetera. But where it counted, deep in those terrible feelings he'd turned off when he had still been a boy, Achilles would never understand. He carried the weight of those lives with him, wherever he went. No matter what he built, no matter what he owned, no matter how many times he won this or that corporate battle— none of that paid the ransom he owed on three lives he could never bring back.

They had been his responsibility, and he had failed. That beat in him like a tattoo. It marked him. It was the truth of him.

When it was all over—after Achilles had failed to notice a gas leak and had woken up only when Demetrius had returned from one of his drinking binges three days later to find the little ones dead and Achilles listless and nearly unresponsive himself—everything had changed. That was the cut-and-dried version of events, and it was accurate enough. What it didn't cover was the guilt, the shame that had eaten Achilles alive. Or what it had been like to watch his siblings' tiny bodies carried out by police, or how it had felt to stand at their graves and know that he could have prevented this if he'd been stronger. Bigger. *Better.*

Achilles had been sent to live with a distant aunt who had never bothered to pretend that she planned to give him anything but a roof over his head, and nothing more. In retrospect, that, too, had been a gift. He hadn't had to bother with any healing. He hadn't had to examine what had happened and try to come to terms with it. No one had cared about him or his grief at all.

And so Achilles had waited. He had plotted. He had taken everything that resembled a feeling, shoved it down as deep inside him as it would go, and made it over into hate. It had taken him ten years to get strong enough. To hunt Demetrius down in a sketchy bar in the same bad neighborhood where he'd brutalized Achilles's mother, beaten his own children and left Achilles responsible for what had happened to them.

And that whole long decade, Achilles had told himself that it was an extermination. That he could walk up to this man who had loomed so large over the whole of his childhood and simply rid the world of his unsavory presence. Demetrius did not deserve to live. There was no doubt about that, no shred of uncertainty anywhere in Achilles's soul. Not while Achilles's mother and his stepsiblings were dead.

He'd staked out his stepfather's favorite dive bar, and this one in the sense that it was repellant, not attractive to rich hipsters from affluent neighborhoods. He'd watched a ramshackle, much grayer and more frail version of the stepfather roaring in his head stumble out into the street. And he'd been ready.

He'd gone up to Demetrius out in the dark, cold night, there in a part of the city where no one would ever dream of interfering in a scuffle on the street lest they find themselves shanked. He'd let the rage wash over him, let the sweet taint of revenge ignite in his veins. He'd expected to feel triumph and satisfaction after all these years and all he'd done to make himself strong enough to take this man down—but what he hadn't reckoned with was that the drunken old man wouldn't recognize him.

Demetrius hadn't known who he was.

And that meant that Achilles had been out there in the

street, ready to beat down a defenseless old drunk who smelled of watered-down whiskey and a wasted life.

He hadn't done it. It wasn't worth it. He might have happily taken down the violent, abusive behemoth who'd terrorized him at seven, but he'd been too big himself at seventeen to find any honor in felling someone so vastly inferior to him in every way.

Especially since Demetrius hadn't the slightest idea who he'd been.

And Achilles had vowed to himself then and there that the night he stood in the street in his old neighborhood, afraid of nothing save the darkness inside him, would be the absolutely last time he let feelings rule him.

Because he had wasted years. Years that could have been spent far more wisely than planning out the extermination of an old, broken man who didn't deserve to have Achilles as an enemy. He'd walked away from Demetrius and his own squalid past and he'd never gone back.

His philosophy had served him well since. It had led him across the years, always cold and forever calculating his next, best move. Achilles was never swayed by emotion any longer, for good or ill. He never allowed it any power over him whatsoever. It had made him great, he'd often thought. It had made him who he was.

And yet Princess Valentina had somehow reached deep inside him, deep into a place that should have been black and cold and nothing but ice, and lit him on fire all over again.

"Are you brooding?" a soft voice asked from behind him, scratchy with sleep. Or with not enough sleep. "I knew I would do something wrong."

But she didn't sound insecure. Not in the least. She sounded warm, well sated. She sounded like his. She sounded like exactly who she was: the only daughter of one of Europe's last remaining powerhouse kings and the only woman Achilles had ever met who could turn him inside out.

And maybe that was what did it. The suddenly unbearable fact that she was still lying to him. He had this burning thing eating him alive from the inside out, he was cracking apart at the foundations, and she was still lying to him.

She was in his bed, teasing him in that way of hers that no one else would ever dare, and yet she lied to him. Every moment was a lie, even and especially this one. Every single moment she didn't tell him the truth about who she was and what she was doing here was more than a lie. More than a simple deception.

He was beginning to feel it as a betrayal.

"I do not brood," he said, and he could hear the gruffness in his own voice.

He heard her shift on the bed, and then he heard the sound of her feet against his floor. And he should have turned before she reached him, he knew that. He should have faced her and kept her away from him, especially when it was so dark outside and there was still so much left of the night—and he had clearly let it get to him.

But he didn't.

And in a moment she was at his back, and then she was sliding her arms around his waist with a familiarity that suggested she'd done it a thousand times before and knew how perfectly she would fit there. Then she pressed her face against the hollow of his spine.

And for a long moment she simply stood there like that, and Achilles felt his heart careen and clatter at his ribs. He was surprised that she couldn't hear it—hell, he was surprised that the whole of Manhattan wasn't alerted.

But all she did was stand there with her mouth pressed against his skin, as if she was holding him up, and through him the whole of the world.

Achilles knew that there was any number of ways to deal with this situation immediately. Effectively. No matter what name she called herself. He could call her out. He could ignore it altogether and simply send her away. He could let the darkness in him edge over into cruelty, so she would be the one to walk away.

But the simple truth was that he didn't want to do any of them.

"I have some land," he told her instead, and he couldn't tell if he was appalled at himself or simply surprised. "Out in the West, where there's nothing to see for acres and acres in all directions except the sky."

"That sounds beautiful," she murmured.

And every syllable was an exquisite pain, because he could feel her shape her words. He could feel her mouth as she spoke, right there against the flesh of his back. And he could have understood if it was a sexual thing. If that was what raged in him then. If it took him over and made him want to do nothing more than throw her down and claim her all over again. Sex, he understood. Sex, he could handle.

But it was much worse than that.

Because it didn't feel like fire, it felt…sweet. The kind of sweetness that wrapped around him, crawling into every nook and cranny inside him he'd long ago thought he'd turned to ice. And then stayed there, blooming into something like heat, as if she could melt him that easily.

He was more than a little worried that she could.

That she already had.

"Sometimes a man wants to be able to walk for miles in any direction and see no one," he heard himself say out loud, as if his mouth was no longer connected to the rest of him. "Not even himself."

"Or perhaps especially not himself," she said softly, her mouth against his skin having the same result as before.

Then he could feel her breathe, there behind him. There was a surprising amount of strength in the arms she still wrapped tight around his midsection. Her scent seemed to fill his head, a hint of lavender and something far softer that he knew was hers alone.

And the truth was that he wasn't done. He had never been a casual man in the modern sense, preferring mistresses who understood his needs and could cater to them over longer periods of time to one-night stands and such flashes in the pan that brought him nothing but momentary satisfaction.

He had never been casual, but this... This was nothing but trouble.

He needed to send her away. He had to fire Natalie, make sure that Valentina left, and leave no possible opening for either one of them to ever come back. This needed to be over before it really started. Before he forgot that he was who he was for a very good reason.

Demetrius had been a drunk. He'd cried and apologized when he was sober, however rarely that occurred. But Achilles was the monster. He'd gone to that bar to kill his stepfather, and he'd planned the whole thing out in every detail, coldly and dispassionately. He still didn't regret what he'd intended to do that night—but he knew perfectly well what that made him. And it was not a good man.

And that was all well and good as long as he kept the monster in him on ice, where it belonged. As long as he locked himself away, set apart.

It had never been an issue before.

He needed to get Valentina away from him, before he forgot himself completely.

"Pack your things," he told her shortly.

He shifted so he could look down at her again, drawing her around to his front and taking in the kick of those wide green eyes and that mouth he had sampled again and again and again.

And he couldn't do it.

He wanted her to know him, and even though that was the most treacherous thing of all, once it was in his head he couldn't seem to let it go. He wanted her to know him, and that meant he needed her to trust him enough to tell who she was. And that would never happen if he sent her away right now the way he should have.

And he was so used to thinking of himself as a monster. Some part of him—a large part of him—took a kind of pride in that, if he was honest. He'd worked so hard on making that monster into an impenetrable wall of wealth and judgment, taste and power.

But it turned out that all it took was a deceitful princess to make him into a man.

"I'm taking you to Montana," he told her gruffly, because he couldn't seem to stop himself.

And doomed them both.

CHAPTER EIGHT

ONE WEEK PASSED, and then another, and the six weeks Valentina had agreed to take stretched out into seven, out on Achilles's Montana ranch where the only thing on the horizon was the hint of the nearest mountain range.

His ranch was like a daydream, Valentina thought. Achilles was a rancher only in a distant sense, having hired qualified people to take care of the daily running of the place and turn its profit. Those things took place far away on some or other of his thousands of acres tucked up at the feet of the Rocky Mountains. They stayed in the sprawling ranch house, a sprawling nod toward log cabins and rustic ski lodges, the better to overlook the unspoiled land in all directions.

It was far away from everything and felt even farther than that. It was an hour drive to the nearest town, stout and quintessentially Western, as matter-of-fact as it was practical. They'd come at the height of Montana's short summer, hot during the day and cool at night, with endless blue skies stretching on up toward forever and nothing to do but soak in the quiet. The stunning silence, broken only by the wind. The sun. The exuberant moon and all those improbable, impossible stars, so many they cluttered up the sky and made it feel as if, were she to take a big enough step, Valentina could toss herself straight off the planet and into eternity.

And Valentina knew she was running out of time. Her wedding was the following week, she wasn't who she was pretending she was, and these stolen days in this faraway place of blue and gold were her last with this man. This stolen life had only ever been hers on loan.

But she would have to face that soon enough.

In Montana, as in New York, her days were filled with Achilles. He was too precise and demanding to abandon his businesses entirely, but there was something about the ranch that rendered him less overbearing. He and Valentina would put out what fires there might be in the mornings, but then, barring catastrophe, he let his employees earn their salaries the rest of the day.

While he and Valentina explored what this dreamy ranch life, so far removed from everything, had to offer. He had a huge library that she imagined would be particularly inviting in winter—not, she was forced to remind herself, that she would ever see it in a different season. A guest could sink into one of the deep leather chairs in front of the huge fireplace and read away a snowy evening or two up here in the mountains. He had an indoor pool that let the sky in through its glass ceiling, perfect for swimming in all kinds of weather. There was the hot tub, propped up on its own terrace with a sweeping view, which cried out for those cool evenings. It was a short drive or a long, pretty walk to the lake a little ways up into the mountains, so crisp and clear and cold it almost hurt.

But it was the kind of hurt that made her want more and more, no matter how it made her gasp and think she might lose herself forever in the cut of it.

Achilles was the same. Only worse.

Valentina had always thought of sex—or her virginity, anyway—as a single, solitary thing. Someday she would have sex, she'd always told herself. Someday she would get rid of her virginity. She had never really imagined that it wasn't a single, finite event.

She'd thought virginity, and therefore sex, was the actual breaching of what she still sometimes thought of as her maidenhead, as if she was an eighteenth-century heroine—and nothing more. She'd never really imagined much beyond that.

Achilles taught her otherwise.

Sex with him was threaded into life, a rich undercurrent that became as much a part of it as walking, breathing, eating. It wasn't a specific act. It was everything.

It was the touch of his hand across the dinner table, when he simply threaded their fingers together, the memory of what they'd already done together and the promise of more braided there between them. It was a sudden hot, dark look in the middle of a conversation about something innocuous or work-related, reminding her that she knew him now in so many different dimensions. It was the way his laughter seemed to rearrange her, pouring through her and making her new, every time she heard it.

It was when she stopped counting each new time he wrenched her to pieces as a separate, astonishing event. When she began to accept that he would always do that. Time passed and days rolled on, and all of these things that swirled between them only deepened. He became only more able to wreck her more easily the better he got to know her. And the better she got to know him.

As if their bodies were like the stars above them, infinite and adaptable, a great mess of joy and wonder that time only intensified.

But she knew it was running out.

And the more Achilles called her Natalie—which she thought he did more here, or perhaps she was far more sensitive to it now that she shared his bed—the more her terrible deception seemed to form into a heavy ball in the pit of her stomach, like some kind of cancerous thing that she very much thought might consume her whole.

Some part of her wished it would.

Meanwhile, the real Natalie kept calling her. Again and again, or leaving texts, but Valentina couldn't bring herself to respond to them. What would she say? How could she possibly explain what she'd done?

Much less the fact that she was still doing it and, worse, that she didn't want it to end no matter how quickly her royal wedding was approaching.

Even if she imagined that Natalie was off in Murin doing exactly the same thing with Rodolfo that Valentina was doing here, with all this wild and impossible hunger, what did that matter? They could still switch back, none the wiser. Nothing would change for Valentina. She would go on to marry the prince as she had always been meant to do, and it was highly likely that even Rodolfo himself wouldn't notice the change.

But Natalie had not been sleeping with Achilles before she'd switched places with Valentina. That meant there was no possible way that she could easily step back into the life that Valentina had gone ahead and ruined.

And was still ruining, day by day.

Still, no matter how self-righteously she railed at herself for that, she knew it wasn't what was really bothering her. It wasn't what would happen to Natalie that ate her up inside.

It was what would happen to her. And what could happen with Achilles. She found that she was markedly less sanguine about Achilles failing to notice the difference between Valentina and Natalie when they switched back again. In fact, the very notion made her feel sick.

But how could she tell him the truth? If she couldn't tell Natalie what she'd done, how could she possibly tell the man whom she'd been lying to directly all this time?

He thought he was having an affair with his assistant. A woman he had vetted and worked closely with for half a decade.

What was she supposed to say, *Oh, by the way, I'm actually a princess?*

The truth was that she was still a coward. Because she didn't know if what was really holding her back was that she couldn't imagine what she would say—or if she could imagine all too well what Achilles would do. And she knew that made her the worst sort of person. Because when she worried about what he would do, she was worried about herself. Not about how she might hurt him. Not about what it would do to him to learn that she had lied to him all this time. But the fact that it was entirely likely that she would tell him, and that would be the last she'd see of him. Ever.

And Valentina couldn't quite bear for this to be over.

This was her vacation. Her holiday. Her escape—and how had it never occurred to her that if that was true, it meant she had to go back? She'd known that in a general sense, of course, but she hadn't really thought it through. She certainly hadn't thought about what it would feel like to leave Achilles and then walk back to the stifling life she'd called her own for all these years.

It was one thing to be trapped. Particularly when it was all she'd ever known. But it was something else again to see exactly how trapped she was, to leave it behind for a while, and then knowingly walk straight back into that trap, closing the cage door behind her.

Forever.

Sometimes when she lay awake at night listening to Achilles breathe in the great bed next to her, his arms thrown over her as if they were slowly becoming one person, she couldn't imagine how she was ever going to make herself do it.

But time didn't care if she felt trapped. Or torn. It marched on whether she wanted it to or not.

"Are you brooding?" a low male voice asked from behind her, jolting her out of her unpleasant thoughts. "I thought that was my job, not yours."

Valentina turned from the rail of the balcony that ambled along the side of the master suite, where she was taking in the view and wondering how she could ever fold herself up tight and slot herself back into the life she'd left behind in Murin.

But the view behind her was even better. Achilles lounged against the open sliding glass door, naked save for a towel wrapped around his hips. He had taken her in a fury earlier, pounding into her from behind until she screamed out his name into the pillows, and he'd roared his own pleasure into the crook of her neck. Then he'd left her there on the bed, limp and still humming with all that passion, while he'd gone out for one of his long, brutal runs he always claimed cleared his head.

It had been weeks now, and he still took her breath. Now that she knew every inch of him, she found herself more in awe of him. All that sculpted perfection of his chest, the dark hair that narrowed at his lean hips, dipping down below the towel where she knew the boldest part of him waited.

She'd tasted him there, too. She'd knelt before the fireplace in that gorgeous library, her hands on his thighs as he'd sat back in one of those great leather chairs. He'd played with her hair, sifting strands of it through his fingers as she'd reached into the battered jeans he wore here on the ranch and had pulled him free.

He'd tasted of salt and man, and he'd let her play with him as she liked. He let her lick him everywhere until she learned his shape. He let her suck him in, then figure out how to make him as wild as he did when he tasted her in this same way. And she'd taken it as a personal triumph when he'd started to grip the chair. And when he'd lost himself inside her mouth, he'd groaned out that name he called her. *Glikia mou.*

Even thinking about it now made that same sweet, hot restlessness move through her all over again.

But time was her enemy. She knew that. And looking at him as he stood there in the doorway and watched her with that dark gold gaze that she could feel in every part of her, still convinced that he could see into parts of her she didn't know how to name, Valentina still didn't know what to do.

If she told him who she was, she would lose what few days with him she had left. This was Achilles Casilieris. He would never forgive her deception. Never. Her other option was never to tell him at all. She would go back to London with him in a few days as planned, slip away the way she'd always intended to do if a week or so later than agreed, and let the real Natalie pick up the pieces.

And that way, she could remember this the way she wanted to do. She could remember loving him, not losing him.

Because that was what she'd done. She understood that in the same way she finally comprehended intimacy. She'd gone and fallen in love with this man who didn't know her real name. This man she could never, ever keep.

Was it so wrong that if she couldn't keep him, she wanted to keep these sun-soaked memories intact?

"You certainly look like you're brooding." There was that lazy note to his voice that never failed to make her blood heat. It was no different now. It was that quick. It was that inevitable. "How can that be? There's nothing here but silence and sunshine. No call to brood about anything. Unless of course, it is your soul that is heavy." And she could have sworn there was something in his gaze then that dared her to come clean. Right then and there. As if, as ever, he knew what she was thinking. "Tell me, Natalie, what is it that haunts you?"

And it was moments like these that haunted her, but she couldn't tell him that. Moments like this, when she was certain that he knew. That he must know. That he was asking her to tell him the truth at last.

That he was calling her the wrong name deliberately, to see if that would goad her into coming clean.

But the mountains were too quiet and there was too much summer in the air. The Montana sky was a blue she'd never seen before, and that was what she felt in her soul. And if there was a heaviness, or a darkness, she had no doubt it would haunt her later.

Valentina wanted to live here. Now. With him. She wanted to *live*.

She had so little time left to truly *live*.

So once again, she didn't tell him. She smiled instead, wide enough to hide the fissures in her heart, and she went to him.

Because there was so little time left that she could do that. So few days left to reach out and touch him the way she did now, sliding her palms against the mouthwatering planes of his chest as if she was memorizing the heat of his skin.

As if she was memorizing everything.

"I don't know what you're talking about," she told him quietly, her attention on his skin beneath her hands. "I never do."

"I am not the mystery here," he replied, and though his voice was still so lazy, so very lazy, she didn't quite believe it. "There are enough mysteries to go around, I think."

"Solve this one, then," she dared him, going up on her toes to press her mouth to his.

Because she might not have truth and she might not have time, but she had this.

For a little while longer, she had this.

Montana was another mistake, because apparently, that was all he did now.

They spent weeks on his ranch, and Achilles made it all worse by the day. Every day he touched her, every day lost himself in her, every day he failed to get her to come clean with him. Every single day was another nail in his coffin.

And then, worse by far to his mind, it was time to leave.

Weeks in Montana, secluded from the rest of the world, and he'd gained nothing but a far deeper and more disastrous appreciation of Valentina's appeal. He hadn't exactly forced her to the light. He hadn't done anything but lose his own footing.

In all those weeks and all that sweet summer sunshine out in the American West, it had never occurred to him that she simply wouldn't tell him. He'd been so sure that he would get to her somehow. That if he had all these feelings churning around inside him, whatever was happening inside her must be far more extreme.

It had never occurred to him that he could lose that bet.

That Princess Valentina had him beat when it came to keeping herself locked up tight, no matter what.

They landed in London in a bleak drizzle that matched his mood precisely.

"You're expected at the bank in an hour," Valentina told him when they reached his Belgravia town house, standing there in his foyer looking as guileless and innocent as she ever had. Even now, when he had tasted every inch of her. Even now, when she was tearing him apart with that serene, untouchable look on her face. "And the board of directors is adamant—"

"I don't care about the bank," he muttered. "Or old men who think they can tell me what to do."

And just like that, he'd had enough.

He couldn't outright demand that Valentina tell him who she really was, because that wouldn't be her telling him of her own volition. It wouldn't be her trusting him.

It's almost as if she knows who you really are, that old familiar voice inside hissed at him. It had been years since he'd heard it, inside him or otherwise. But even though Demetrius had not been able to identify him on the streets when he'd had the chance, Achilles always knew the old man when he spoke. *Maybe she knows exactly what kind of monster you are.*

And a harsh truth slammed into him then, making him feel very nearly unsteady on his feet. He didn't know why it hadn't occurred to him before. Or maybe it had, but he'd shoved it aside out there in all that Montana sky and sunshine. Because he was Achilles Casilieris. He was one of the most sought-after bachelors in all the world. Legions of women chased after him daily, trying anything from trickery to bribery to outright lies about paternity claims to make him notice them. He was at the top of everyone's *most wanted* list.

But to Princess Valentina of Marin, he was nothing but a bit of rough.

She was slumming.

That was why she hadn't bothered to identify herself. She didn't see the point. He might as well have been the pool boy.

And he couldn't take it. He couldn't process it. There was nothing in him but fire and that raw, unquenchable need, and she was so cool. Too cool.

He needed to mess her up. He needed to do something to make all this…wildfire and feeling dissipate before it ate him alive and left nothing behind. Nothing at all.

"What are you doing?" she asked, and he took a little too much satisfaction in that appropriately uncertain note in her voice.

It was only when he saw her move that he realized he was stalking toward her, backing her up out of the gleaming foyer and into one of the town house's elegant sitting rooms. Not that the beauty of a room could do anything but fade next to Valentina.

The world did the same damned thing.

She didn't ask him a silly question like that again. And perhaps she didn't need to. He backed her up to the nearest settee, and took entirely too much pleasure in the pulse that beat out the truth of her need right there in her neck.

"Achilles..." she said hoarsely, but he wanted no more words. No more lies of omission.

No more *slumming*.

"Quiet," he ordered her.

He sank his hands into her gleaming copper hair, then dragged her mouth to his. Then he toppled her down to antique settee and followed her. She was slender and lithe and wild beneath him, rising to meet him with too much need, too much longing.

As if, in the end, this was the only place they were honest with each other.

And Achilles was furious. Furious, or something like it—something close enough that it burned in him as brightly. As lethally. He shoved her skirt up over her hips and she wrapped her legs around his waist, and she was panting already. She was gasping against his mouth. Or maybe he was breathing just as hard.

"Achilles," she said again, and there was something in her gaze then. Something darker than need.

But this was no time for sweetness. Or anything deeper. This was a claiming.

"Later," he told her, and then he took her mouth with

his, tasting the words he was certain, abruptly, he didn't want to hear.

He might be nothing to her but a walk on the wild side she would look back on while she rotted away in some palatial prison, but he would make sure that she remembered him.

He had every intention of leaving his mark.

Achilles tore off his trousers, freeing himself. Then he reached down and found the gusset of her panties, ripping them off and shoving the scraps aside to fit himself to her at last.

And then he stopped thinking about marks and memories, because she was molten hot and wet. She was his. He sank into her, groaning as she encased his length like a hot, tight glove.

It was so good. It was too good.

She always was.

He moved then, and she did, too, that slick, deep slide. And they knew each other so well now. Their bodies were too attuned to each other, too hot and too certain of where this was going, and it was never, ever enough.

He reached between them and pressed his fingers in the place where she needed him most, and felt her explode into a frenzy beneath him. She raised her hips to meet each thrust. She dug her fingers into his shoulders as if she was already shaking apart.

He felt it build in her, and in him, too. Wild and mad, the way it always was.

As if they could tear apart the world this way. As if they already had.

"No one will ever make you feel the way that I do," he told her then, a dark muttering near her ear as she panted and writhed. "No one."

And he didn't know if that was some kind of endearment, or a dire warning.

But it didn't matter, because she was clenching around him then. She gasped out his name, while her body gripped him, then shook.

And he pumped himself into her, wanting nothing more than to roar her damned name. To claim her in every possible way. To show her—

But he did none of that.

And when it was over, when the storm had passed, he pulled himself away from her and climbed to his feet again. And he felt something sharp and heavy move through him as he looked down at her, still lying there half on and half off the antique settee they'd moved a few feet across the floor, because he had done exactly as he set out to do.

He'd messed her up. She looked disheveled and shaky and absolutely, delightfully ravished.

But all he could think was that he still didn't have her. That she was still going to leave him when she was done here. That she'd never had any intention of staying in the first place. It ripped at him. It made him feel something like crazy.

The last time he'd ever felt anything like it, he'd been an angry seventeen-year-old in a foul-smelling street with an old drunk who didn't know who he was. It was a kind of anguish.

It was a grief, and he refused to indulge it. He refused to admit it was ravaging him, even as he pulled his clothes back where they belonged.

And then she made it even worse. She smiled.

She sat up slowly, pushing her skirt back into place and tucking the torn shreds of her panties into one pocket. Then she gazed up at him.

Achilles was caught by that look in her soft green eyes, as surely as if she'd reached out and wrapped her delicate hands around his throat. On some level, he felt as if she had.

"I love you," she said.

They were such small words, he thought through that thing that pounded in him like fear. Like a gong. Such small, silly words that could tear a man down without any warning at all.

And there were too many things he wanted to say then. For example, how could she tell him that she loved him when she wouldn't even tell him her name?

But he shoved that aside.

"That was sex, *glikia mou*," he grated at her. "Love is something different from a whole lot of thrashing around, half-clothed."

He expected her to flinch at that, but he should have known better. This was his princess. If she was cowed at all, she didn't show it.

Instead, she only smiled wider.

"You're the expert on love as in all things, of course," she murmured, because even here, even now, she was the only person alive who had ever dared to tease him. "My mistake."

She was still smiling when she stood up, then walked around him. As if she didn't notice that he was frozen there in some kind of astonishment. Or as if she was happy enough to leave him to it as she headed toward the foyer and, presumably, the work he'd always adored that seemed to loom over him these days, demanding more time than he wanted to give.

He'd never had a life that interested him more than his empire, until Valentina.

And he didn't have Valentina.

She'd left Achilles standing there with her declaration heavy in his ears. She'd left him half fire and a heart that long ago should have turned to ice. He'd been so certain it had when he was seven and had lost everything, including his sense of himself as anything like good.

He should have known then.

But it wasn't until much later that day—after he'd quizzed his security detail and household staff to discover she'd walked out with nothing but her shoulder bag and disappeared into the gray of the London afternoon—that he'd realized that had been the way his deceitful princess said goodbye.

CHAPTER NINE

VALENTINA COULDN'T KEEP her mind on her duties now that she was back in Murin. She couldn't keep her mind focused at all, come to that. Not on her duties, not on the goings-on of the palace, not on any of the many changes that had occurred since she'd come back home.

She should have been jubilant. Or some facsimile thereof, surely. She had walked back into her well-known, well-worn trap, expecting the same old cage, only to find that the trap wasn't at all what she had imagined it was— and the cage door had been tossed wide open.

When she'd left London that day, her body had still been shivering from Achilles's touch. She hadn't wanted to go. Not with her heart too full and a little bit broken at her own temerity in telling him how she felt when she'd known she had to leave. But it was time for her to go home, and there had been no getting around that. Her wedding to Prince Rodolfo was imminent. As in, the glittering heads of Europe's ancient houses were assembling to cheer on one of their own, and she needed to be there.

The phone calls and texts that she'd been ignoring that whole time, leaving Natalie to deal with it all on her own, had grown frantic. And she couldn't blame her sister, because the wedding was a mere day away. *Your twin sister*, she'd thought, those terms still feeling too unwieldy. She'd made her way to Heathrow Airport and bought herself a ticket on a commercial plane—the first time she'd ever done anything of the sort. One more normal thing to tuck away and remember later.

"Later" meaning after tomorrow, when she would be wed to a man she hardly knew.

It had taken Valentina a bit too long to do the right thing. To do the only possible thing and tear herself away from Achilles the way she should have done a long time ago. She should never have gone with him to Montana. She should certainly never have allowed them to stay there all that time, living out a daydream that could end only one way.

She'd known that going in, and she'd done it anyway. What did that make her, exactly?

Now I am awake, she thought as she boarded the plane. *Now I am awake and that will have to be as good as* alive, *because it's all I have left.*

She hadn't known what to expect from a regular flight into the commercial airport on the island of Murin. Some part of her imagined that she would be recognized. Her face was on the cover of the Murin Air magazines in every seat back, after all. She'd had a bit of a start when she'd sat down in the remarkably uncomfortable seat, pressed up against a snoring matron on one side and a very gray-faced businessman on the other.

But no one had noticed her shocking resemblance to the princess in the picture. No one had really looked at her at all. She flashed Natalie's passport, walked on the plane without any issues and walked off again in Murin without anyone looking at her twice—even though she was quite literally the spitting image of the princess so many were flocking to Murin to see marry her Prince Charming at last.

Once at the palace, she didn't bother trying to sneak

in because she knew she'd be discovered instantly—and that would hardly allow Natalie to switch back and escape, would it? So instead she'd walked up to the guard station around the back at the private family entrance, gazed politely at the guard who waited there and waited.

"But the…the princess is within," the guard had stammered. Maybe he was thrown by the fact Valentina was dressed like any other woman her age on the street. Maybe he was taken back because he'd never spoken to her directly before.

Or maybe it was because, if she was standing here in front of him, she wasn't where the royal guard thought she was. Which he'd likely assumed meant she'd sneaked out, undetected.

All things considered, she was happy to let that mystery stand.

Valentina had aimed a conspiratorial smile at the guard. "The princess can't possibly be within, given that I'm standing right here. But it can be our little secret that there was some confusion, if you like."

And then, feeling heavier than she ever had before and scarred somehow by what she'd gone through with Achilles, she'd walked back in the life she'd left so spontaneously and much too quickly in that London airport.

She'd expected to find Natalie as desperate to leave as she supposed, in retrospect, she had been. Or why else would she have suggested this switch in the first place?

But instead, she'd found a woman very much in love. With Crown Prince Rodolfo of Tissely. The man whom Valentina was supposed to marry the following day.

More than that, Natalie was pregnant.

"I don't know how it happened," Natalie had said, after Valentina had slipped into her bedroom and woken her up—by sitting on the end of the bed and pulling at Natalie's foot until she'd opened her eyes and found her double sitting there.

"Don't you?" Valentina had asked. "I was a virgin, but I had the distinct impression that you had not saved yourself for marriage all these years. Because why would you?"

Natalie had flushed a bit, but then her eyes had narrowed. "*Was* a virgin? Is that the past tense?" She'd blinked. "Not Mr. Casilieris."

But it wasn't the time then for sisterly confessions. Mostly because Valentina hadn't the slightest idea what she could say about Achilles that wasn't…too much. Too much and too unformed and unbearable, somehow, now that it was over. Now that none of it mattered, and never could.

"I don't think that you have a job with him anymore," Valentina had said instead, keeping her voice even. "Because I don't think you want a job with him anymore. You said you were late, didn't you? You're having a prince's baby."

And when Natalie had demurred, claiming that she didn't know one way or the other and it was likely just the stress of inhabiting someone else's life, Valentina had sprung into action.

She'd made it her business to find out, one way or another. She'd assured Natalie that it was simply to put her mind at ease. But the truth was a little more complicated, she admitted to herself as she made her way through the palace.

The fact was, she was relieved. That was what had washed through her when Natalie had confessed not only her love for Rodolfo, but her suspicions that she might be carrying his child. She'd pushed it off as she'd convinced one of her most loyal maids to run out into the city and buy her a few pregnancy tests, just to be certain. She'd shoved it to the side as she'd smuggled the tests back into her rooms, and then had handed them over to Natalie so she could find out for certain.

But there was no denying it. When Natalie had emerged from the bathroom with a dazed look on her face and a positive test in one hand, Valentina finally admitted the sheer relief that coursed through her veins. It was like champagne. Fizzy and a little bit sharp, washing through her and making her feel almost silly in response.

Because if Natalie was having Rodolfo's baby, there was no possible way that Valentina could marry him. The choice—though it had always been more of an expected duty than a choice—was taken out of her hands.

"You will marry him," Valentina had said quietly. "It is what must happen."

Natalie had looked pale. "But you… And I'm not… And you don't understand, he…"

"All of that will work out," Valentina had said with a deep certainty she very badly wanted to feel. Because it had to work out. "The important thing is that you will marry him in the morning. You will have his baby and you will be his queen when he ascends the throne. Everything else is spin and scandal, and none of that matters. Not really."

And so it was.

Once King Geoffrey had been brought into the loop and had been faced with the irrefutable evidence that his daughter had been stolen from him all those years ago—that Erica had taken Natalie and, not only that, had told Geoffrey that Valentina's twin had died at birth— he was more than on board with switching the brides at the wedding.

He'd announced to the gathered crowd that a most blessed miracle had occurred some months before. A daughter long thought dead had returned to him to take her rightful place in the kingdom, and they'd all kept it a secret to preserve everyone's privacy as they'd gotten to know each other.

Including Rodolfo, who had always been meant to be part of the family, the king had reminded the assembled crowd and the whole of the world, no matter how. And feelings had developed between Natalie and Rodolfo, where there had only ever been duty and honor between Valentina and her intended.

Valentina had seen this and stepped aside of her own volition, King Geoffrey had told the world. There had been no scandal, no sneaking around, no betrayals. Only one sister looking out for another.

The crowds ate it up. The world followed suit. It was just scandalous enough to be both believable and newsworthy. Valentina was branded as something of a Miss Lonely Hearts, it was true, but that was neither here nor there. The idea that she would sacrifice her fairy-tale wedding—and her very own Prince Charming—for her long-lost sister captured the public's imagination. She was more popular than ever, especially at home in Murin.

And this was a good thing, because now that her father had two heirs, he could marry one of his daughters off to fulfill his promises to the kingdom of Tissely, and he could prepare the other to take over Murin and keep its throne in the family.

And just like that, Valentina went from a lifetime preparing to be a princess who would marry well and support the king of a different country, to a new world in which she was meant to rule as queen in her own right.

If it was another trap, another cage, it was a far more spacious and comfortable one than any she had known before.

She knew that. There was no reason at all she should have been so unhappy.

"Your attention continues to drift, daughter," King Geoffrey said then.

Valentina snapped herself out of those thoughts in her head that did her no good and into the car where she sat with her father, en route to some or other glittering gala down at the water palace on the harbor. She couldn't even remember which charity it was this week. There was always another.

The motorcade wound down from the castle, winding its way along the hills of the beautiful capital city toward the gleaming Mediterranean Sea. Valentina normally enjoyed the view. It was pretty, first and foremost. It was home. It reminded her of so many things, of her honor and her duty and her love of her country. It renewed her commitment to her kingdom, and made her think about all the good she hoped she could do as its sovereign.

And yet these days, she wasn't thinking about Murin. All she could seem to think about was Achilles.

"I am preparing myself for the evening ahead," Valentina replied calmly enough. She aimed a perfectly composed smile at her father. "I live in fear of greeting a diplomat with the wrong name and causing an international incident."

Her father's gaze warmed, something that happened more often lately than it ever had before. Valentina chalked that up to the rediscovery of Natalie and, with it, some sense of family that had been missing before. Or too caught up in the past, perhaps.

"I have never seen you forget a name in all your life," Geoffrey said. "It's one among many reasons I expect you will make a far better queen than I have been a king. And I am aware I gave you no other choice, but I cannot regret that your education and talents will be Murin's gain, not Tissely's."

"I will confess," Valentina said then, "that stepping

aside so that Natalie could marry Rodolfo is not quite the sacrifice some have made it out to be."

Her father's gaze then was so canny that it reminded her that whatever else he was, King Geoffrey of Marin was a force to be reckoned with.

"I suspected not," he said quietly. "But there is no reason not to let them think so. It only makes you more sympathetic."

His attention was caught by something on his phone then. And as he frowned down at it, Valentina looked away. Back out the window to watch the sun drip down over the red-tipped rooftops that sloped all the way to the crystal blue waters below.

She let her hand move, slowly so that her father wouldn't notice, and held it over that faint roundness low in her belly she'd started to notice only a few weeks ago.

If her father thought she was a sympathetic figure now, she thought darkly, he would be delighted when she announced to him and the rest of the world that she was going to be a mother.

A single mother. A princess destined for his throne, with child.

Her thoughts went around and around, keeping her up at night and distracting her by day. And there were never any answers or, rather, there were never any good answers. There were never any answers she liked. Shame and scandal were sure to follow anything she did, or didn't do for that matter. There was no possible way out.

And even if she somehow summoned the courage to tell her father, then tell the kingdom, and then, far more intimidating, tell Achilles—what did she think might happen then? As a princess with no path to the throne, she had been expected to marry the Crown Prince of Tissely. As the queen of Murin, by contrast, she would be expected to marry someone of equally impeccable lineage. There were only so many such men alive, Valentina had met all of them, and none of them were Achilles.

No one was Achilles. And that shouldn't have mattered to her. There were so many other things she needed to worry about, like this baby she was going to be able to hide for only so long.

But he was the only thing she could seem to think about, even so.

The gala was as expected. These things never varied much, which was both their charm and their curse. There was an endless receiving line. There were music and speeches, and extremely well-dressed people milling about complimenting each other on the same old things. A self-congratulatory trill of laughter here, a fake smile there, and so it went. Dignitaries and socialites rubbing shoulders and making money for this or that cause the way they always did.

Valentina danced with her father, as tradition dictated. She was pleased to see Rodolfo and Natalie, freshly back from their honeymoon and exuding exactly the sort of happy charm that made everyone root for them, Valentina included.

Valentina especially, she thought.

She excused herself from the crush as soon as she could, making her way out onto one of the great balconies in this water palace that took its cues from far-off Venice and overlooked the sea. Valentina stood there for a long while, helplessly reliving all the things she'd been so sure she could lock away once she came back home. Over and over—

And she thought that her memory had gotten particularly sharp—and cruel. Because when she heard a foot against the stones behind her and turned, her smile already in place the way it always was, she saw him.

But it couldn't be him, of course. She assumed it was

her hormones mixing with her memory and making her conjure him up out of the night air.

"Princess Valentina," Achilles said, and his voice was low, a banked fury simmering there in every syllable. "I do not believe we have been introduced properly. You are apparently of royal blood you sought to conceal and I am the man you thought you could fool. How pleasant to finally make your acquaintance."

It occurred to her that she wasn't fantasizing at the same moment it really hit her that he was standing before her. Her heart punched at her. Her stomach sank.

And in the place she was molten for him, instantly, she ached. Oh, how she ached.

"Achilles…"

But her throat was so dry. It was in marked contrast to all that emotion that flooded her eyes at the sight of him that she couldn't seem to control.

"Are those tears, Princess?" And he laughed then. It was a dark, angry sort of sound. It was not the kind of laughter that made the world shimmer and change. And still, it was the best sound Valentina had heard in weeks. "Surely those are not tears. I cannot think of a single thing you have to cry about, Valentina. Not one. Whereas I have a number of complaints."

"Complaints?"

All she could seem to do was echo him. That and gaze at him as if she was hungry, and the truth was that she was. She couldn't believe he was here. She didn't care that he was scowling at her—her heart was kicking at her, and she thought she'd never seen anything more beautiful than Achilles Casilieris in a temper, right here in Murin.

"We can start with the fact that you lied to me about who you are," he told her. "There are numerous things to cover after that, culminating in your extremely bad decision to walk out. *Walk out*." He repeated it with three times the fury. "On *me*."

"Achilles." She swallowed, hard. "I don't think—"

"Let me be clear," he bit out, his dark gold gaze blazing as he interrupted her. "I am not here to beg or plead. I am Achilles Casilieris, a fact you seem to have forgotten. I do not beg. I do not plead. But I feel certain, princess, that you will do both."

He had waited weeks.

Weeks.

Having never been walked out on before—ever—Achilles had first assumed that she would return. Were not virgins forever making emotional connections with the men who divested them of their innocence? That was the reason men of great experience generally avoided virgins whenever possible. Or so he thought, at any rate. The truth was that he could hardly remember anything before Valentina.

Still, he waited. When the royal wedding happened the day after she'd left, and King Geoffrey made his announcement about his lost daughter—who, he'd realized, was his actual assistant and also, it turned out, a royal princess—Achilles had been certain it was only a matter of time before Valentina returned to London.

But she never came.

And he did not know when it had dawned on him that this was something he was going to have to do himself. The very idea enraged him, of course. That she had walked out on him at all was unthinkable. But what he couldn't seem to get his head around was the fact that she didn't seem to have seen the error of her ways, no matter how much time he gave her to open her damned eyes.

She was too beautiful and it was worse now, he thought

darkly, here in her kingdom, where she was no longer pretending anything.

Tonight she was dressed like the queen she would become one day, all of that copper hair piled high on the top of her head, jewels flashing here and there. Instead of the pencil skirts he'd grown accustomed to, she wore a deep blue gown that clung to her body in a way that was both decorous and alluring at once. And if he was not mistaken, made her curves seem more voluptuous than he recalled.

She was much too beautiful for Achilles's peace of mind, and worse, she did not break down and begin the begging or the pleading, as he would have preferred. He could see that her eyes were damp, though the tears that had threatened seemed to have receded. She smoothed her hand over her belly, as if the dress had wrinkles when it was very clear that it did not, and when she looked up from that wholly unnecessary task her green eyes were as guarded as her smile was serene.

As if he was a stranger. As if he had never been so deep inside her she'd told him she couldn't breathe.

"What are you doing here?" she asked.

"That is the wrong question."

She didn't so much as blink, and that smile only deepened. "I had no idea that obscure European charities were of such interest to men of your stature, and I am certain it was not on your schedule."

"Are you questioning how I managed to score an invite?" he asked, making no particular move to keep the arrogant astonishment from his voice. "Perhaps I must introduce myself again. There is no guest list that is not improved by my presence, princess. Even yours."

Her gaze became no less guarded. Her expression did not change. But still, Achilles thought something in her steeled. And her shoulders straightened almost imperceptibly.

"I must apologize to you," she said, very distinctly.

And this was what Achilles had wanted. It was why he'd come here. He had imagined it playing out almost exactly this way.

Except there was something in her tone that rubbed him the wrong way, now that it was happening. It was that guarded look in her eyes perhaps. It was the fact that she didn't close the distance between them, but stayed where she was, one hand on the balcony railing and the other at her side. As distant as if she was on some magazine cover somewhere instead of standing there in front of him.

He didn't like this at all.

"You will have to be more specific, I am afraid," he said coolly. "I can think of a great many apologies you owe me."

Her mouth curved, though he would not call it a smile, precisely.

"I walked into a bathroom in an airport in London and saw a woman I had never met before, who could only be my twin. I could not resist switching places with her." Valentina glanced toward the open doors and the gala inside, as if it called to her more than he did, and Achilles hated that, too. Then she looked back at him, and her gaze seemed darker. "Do not mistake me. This is a good life. It is just that it's a very specific, very planned sort of life and it involves a great many spotlights. I wanted a normal one, for a change. Just for a little while. It never occurred to me that that decision could affect anyone but me. I would never have done it if I ever thought that you—"

But Achilles couldn't hear this. Because it sounded entirely too much like a postmortem. When he had traveled across Europe to find her because he couldn't bear the thought that it had already ended, or that he hadn't picked up on the fact that she was leaving him until she'd already gone.

"Do you need me to tell you that I love you, Valentina?" he demanded, his voice low and furious. "Is that what this is? Tell me what you need to hear. Tell me what it will take."

She jolted as if he'd slapped her. And he hated that, so he took the single step that closed the distance between them, and then there was no holding himself back. Not when she was so close again—at last—after all these weeks. He reached over and wrapped his hands around her shoulders, holding her there at arm's length, like some kind of test of his self-control. He thought that showed great restraint, when all he wanted was to haul her toward him and get his mouth on her.

"I don't need anything," she threw at him in a harsh sort of whisper. "And I'm sorry you had to find out who I was after I left. I couldn't figure out how to tell you while I was still with you. I didn't want to ruin—"

She shook her head, as if distressed.

Achilles laughed. "I knew from almost the first moment you stepped on the plane in London. Did you imagine I would truly believe you were Natalie for long? When you could not perform the most basic of tasks she did daily? I knew who you were within moments after the plane reached its cruising altitude."

Her green eyes went wide with shock. Her lips parted. Even her face paled.

"You knew?"

"You have never fooled me," he told her, his voice getting a little too low. A little too hot. "Except perhaps when you claimed you loved me, then left."

Her eyes overflowed then, sending tears spilling down her perfect, elegant cheeks. And he was such a bastard that some part of him rejoiced.

Because if she cried for him, she wasn't indifferent to him. She was certainly not immune to him.

It meant that it was possible he hadn't ruined this, after all, the way he did everything else. It meant it was possible this was salvageable.

He didn't like to think about what it might mean if it wasn't.

"Achilles," she said again, more distinctly this time. "I never saw you coming—it never occurred to me that I could ever be anything but honorable, because I had never been tempted by anything in my life. Only you. The only thing I lied to you about was my name. Everything else was true. Is true." She shook her head. "But it's hopeless."

"Nothing is hopeless," he growled at her. "I have no intention of losing you. I don't lose."

"I'm not talking about a loss," she whispered fiercely, and he could feel a tremor go through her. "This isn't a game. You are a man who is used to doing everything in his own way. You are not made for protocol and diplomacy and the tedious necessities of excruciating propriety. That's not who you are." Her chin tilted up slightly. "But I'm afraid it is exactly who I am."

"I'm not a good man, *glikia mou*," he told her then, not certain what was gripping him. He only knew he couldn't let her go. "But you know this. I have always known who I am. A monster in fine clothes, rubbing shoulders with the elites who would spit on me if they could. If they did not need my money and my power."

Achilles expected a reaction. He expected her to see him at last as she had failed to see him before. The scales would fall from her eyes, perhaps. She would recoil, certainly. He had always known that it would take so very little for people to see the truth about him, lurking right there beneath his skin. Not hidden away at all.

But Valentina did not seem to realize what had happened. She continued to look at him the way she always did. There wasn't the faintest flicker of anything like revulsion, or bleak recognition, in her gaze.

If anything, her gaze seemed warmer than before, for all it was wet. And that made him all the more determined to show her what she seemed too blind to see.

"You are not hearing me, Valentina. I'm not speaking in metaphors. Do you have any idea what I have done? The lives that I have ruined?"

She smiled at that, through her tears. "I know exactly who you are," she said, with a bedrock certainty that shook him. "I worked for you. You did not wine me or dine me. You did not take me on a fancy date or try to impress me in any way. You treated me like an assistant, an underling, and believe me, there is nothing more revealing. Are you impatient? Are you demanding and often harsh? Of course." She shrugged, as if this was all so obvious it was hardly worth talking about. "You are a very powerful man. But you are not a monster."

If she'd reached over and wrenched his mangled little heart from between his ribs with her elegant hands and then held it there in front of him, it could not possibly have floored him more.

"And you will not convince me otherwise," she added, as if she could see that he was about to say something. "There's something I have to tell you. And it's entirely possible that you are not going to like it at all."

Achilles blinked. "How ominous."

She blew out a breath. "You must understand that there are no good solutions. I've had no idea how to tell you this, but our… What happened between us had consequences."

"Do you think that I don't know that?" he belted out at her, and he didn't care who heard him. He didn't care if the whole of her pretty little kingdom poured out of the party behind them to watch and listen. "Do you think that I would be here if I was unaware of the consequences?"

"I'm not talking about feelings—"

"I am," he snapped. "I have not felt anything in years. I have not wanted to feel. And thanks to you all I do now is feel. Too damned much, Valentina." She hadn't actually ripped his heart out, he reminded himself. It only felt as if she had. He forced himself to loosen his grip on her before he hurt her. "And it doesn't go anywhere. Weeks pass, and if anything grows worse."

"Achilles, please," she whispered, and the tears were falling freely again. "I never wanted to hurt you."

"I wish you had hurt me," he told her, something dark and bitter, and yet neither of those things threaded through him. "Hurt things heal. This is far worse."

She sucked in a breath as if he'd punched her. He forged on, throwing all the doom and tumult inside him down between them.

"I have never loved anything in my life, Princess. I have wanted things and I've taken them, but love has always been for other men. Men who are not monsters by any definition. Men who have never ruined anything—not lives, not companies and certainly not perfect, virginal princesses who had no idea what they were signing up for." He shook his head. "But there is nothing either one of us can do about it now. I'm afraid the worst has already happened."

"The worst?" she echoed. "Then you know...?"

"I love you, *glikia mou*," he told her. "There can be no other explanation, and I feel sorry for you, I really do. Because I don't think there's any going back."

"Achilles..." she whispered, and that was not a look of transported joy on her face. It wasn't close. "I'm so sorry. Everything is different now. I'm pregnant."

CHAPTER TEN

ACHILLES WENT SILENT. Stunned, if Valentina had to guess. If that frozen astonishment in his dark gold gaze was any guide.

"And I am to be queen," she told him, pointedly. His hands were still clenched on her shoulders, and what was wrong with her that she should love that so much? That she should love any touch of his. That it should make her feel so warm and safe and wild with desire. All at once. "My father thought that he would not have an heir of his own blood, because he thought he had only one daughter. But now he has two, and Natalie has married Rodolfo. That leaves me to take the throne."

"I'm not following you," Achilles said, his voice stark. Something like frozen. "I can think of no reason that you have told me in one breath that I am to be a father and in the next you feel you must fill me in on archaic lines of succession."

"There is very strict protocol," she told him, and her voice cracked. She slid her hands over her belly. "My father will never accept—"

"You keep forgetting who I am," Achilles growled, and she didn't know if he'd heard a word she'd said. "If you are having my child, Valentina, this conversation is over. We will be married. That's an end to it."

"It's not that simple."

"On the contrary, there is nothing simpler."

She needed him to understand. This could never be. They could never happen. She was trapped just as surely as she'd ever been. Why couldn't he see that? "I am no longer just a princess. I'm the Crown Princess of Murin—"

"Princess, princess." Achilles shook his head. "Tell me something. Did you mean it when you told me that you loved me? Or did you only dare to tell me in the first place because you knew you were leaving?"

That walloped Valentina. She thought that if he hadn't been holding on to her, she would have staggered and her knees might well have given out from beneath her.

"Don't be ridiculous." But her voice was barely a whisper.

"Here's the difference between you and me, princess. I have no idea what love is. All I know is that you came into my life and you altered something in me." He let go of her shoulder and moved his hand to cover his heart, and broke hers that easily. "Here. It's changed now, and I can't change it back. And I didn't tell you these things and then leave. I accepted these things, and then came to find you."

She felt blinded. Panicked. As if all she could do was cower inside her cage—and worse, as if that was what she wanted.

"You have no idea what you're talking about," she told him instead. "You might be a successful businessman, but you know nothing about the realities of a kingdom like Murin."

"I know you better than you think. I know how desperate you are for a normal life. Isn't that why you switched places with Natalie?" His dark gaze was almost kind.

"But don't you understand? Normal is the one thing you can never be, *glikia mou*."

"You have no idea what you're talking about," she said again, and this time her voice was even softer. Fainter.

"You will never be normal, Valentina," Achilles said quietly. His fingers tightened on her shoulder. "I am not so normal myself. But together, you and I? We will be extraordinary."

"You don't know how much I wish that could happen." She didn't bother to wipe at her tears. She let them fall. "This is a cage, Achilles. I'm trapped in it, but you're not. And you shouldn't be."

He let out a breath that was too much like a sigh, and Valentina felt it shudder through her, too. Like foreboding.

"You can live in fear, or you can live the life you want, Valentina," he told her. "You cannot do both."

His dark gaze bored into her, and then he dropped his other hand, so he was no longer touching her.

And then he made it worse and stepped back.

She felt her hands move, when she hadn't meant to move at all. Reaching out for him, whether she wanted to or not.

"If you don't want to be trapped, don't be trapped," Achilles said, as if it was simple. And with that edge in his voice that made her feel something a little more pointed than simply restless. "I don't know how to love, but I will learn. I have no idea how to be a father, but I will dedicate myself to being a good one. I never thought that I'd be a husband to anyone, but I will be the husband you need. You can sit on your throne. You can rule your kingdom as you wish. I have no need to be a king. But I will be one for you." He held out his hand. "All you have to do is be brave, princess. That's all. Just be a little brave."

"It's a cage, Achilles," she told him again, her voice ragged. "It's a beautiful, beautiful cage, this life. And there's no changing it. It's been the same for untold centuries."

"Love me," he said then, like a bomb to her heart. What was left of it. "I dare you."

And the music poured out from the party within. Inside, her father ruled the way he always did, and her brand-new sister danced with the man Valentina had always imagined she would marry. Natalie had come out of nowhere and taken her rightful place in the kingdom, and the world hadn't ended when brides had been switched at a royal wedding. If anything, life had vastly improved for everyone involved. Why wasn't that the message Valentina was concentrating on?

She realized that all this time, she'd been focused on what she couldn't do. Or what she had to do. She'd been consumed with duty, honor—but none of it her choice. All of it thrust upon her by an accident of birth. If Erica had taken Valentina instead of Natalie, she would have met Achilles some time ago. They wouldn't be standing here, on this graceful balcony, overlooking the soothing Mediterranean and her father's kingdom.

Her whole life seemed to tumble around before her, year after year cracking open before her like so many fragile eggs against the stones beneath her feet. All the things she never questioned. All the certainties she simply accepted, because what was the alternative? She'd prided herself on her serenity in the face of anything that had come her way. On her ability to do what was asked of her, always. What was expected of her, no matter how unfair.

And she'd never really asked herself what she wanted to do with her life. Because it had never been a factor. Her life had been meticulously planned from the start.

But now Achilles stood before her, and she carried their baby inside her. And she knew that as much as she wanted to deny it, what he said was true. She was a coward. She'd used her duty to hide behind. She could have stayed in London, could have called off her wedding. But she hadn't.

And had she really imagined she could walk down that aisle to Rodolfo, having just left Achilles in London? Had she really intended to do that?

It was unimaginable. And yet she knew she'd meant to do exactly that.

She'd been saved from that vast mistake, and yet here she was, standing in front of the man she loved, coming up with new reasons why she couldn't have the one thing in her life she ever truly wanted.

All this time she'd been convinced that her life was the cage. That her royal blood trapped her.

But the truth was, she was the one who did that.

She was her own cage, and she always would be if she didn't do something to stop it right now. If she didn't throw open the door, step through the opening and allow herself to reach out for the man she already knew she loved.

Be brave, he'd told her, as if he knew she could do it. As if he had no doubt at all.

"I love you," she whispered helplessly. Lost somewhere in that gaze of his, and the simple fact that he was here. Right here in front of her, his hand stretched toward her, waiting for her with a patience she would have said Achilles Casilieris did not possess.

"Marry me, *glikia mou*. And you can love me forever." His mouth crept up in one corner, and all the scars Valentina had dug into her own heart when she'd left him seemed to glow a little bit. Then knit themselves into something more like art. "I'm told that's how it goes. But you know me. I always like to push the boundaries a little bit farther."

"Farther than forever?"

And she smiled at him then, not caring if she was still crying. Or laughing. Or whatever was happening inside her that was starting to take her over.

Maybe that was what it was to be brave. Doing whatever it was not because she felt it was right, but because it didn't matter what she felt. It was right, so she had to do it.

"Three forevers," Achilles said, as if he was promising them to her, here and now. "To start."

And he was still holding out his hand.

"Breathe," he murmured, as if he could see all the tumult inside her.

Valentina took a deep breath. She remembered lying in that bed of his with all of New York gleaming around them. He'd told her to breathe then, too.

In. Out.

Until she felt a little less full, or a little more able to handle what was happening. Until she had stopped feeling overwhelmed, and had started feeling desperate with need.

And this was no different.

Valentina breathed in, then out. Then she stepped forward and slid her hand into his, as easily as if they'd been made to fit together just like that, then let him pull her close.

He shifted to take her face in his hands, tilting her head back so he could fit his mouth to hers. Though he didn't. Not yet.

"Forever starts now," Valentina whispered. "The first one, anyway."

"Indeed." Achilles's mouth was so deliriously hard, and directly over hers. "Kiss me, Valentina. It's been too long."

And Valentina did more than kiss him. She poured herself into him, pushing herself up on her toes and winding her arms around his neck, and that was just the start.

Because there was forever after forever stacked up in front of them, just waiting for them to fill it. One after the next.

Together.

And he knew that Valentina remembered. The first vows they'd taken, though neither of them had called it that, in his New York penthouse so long ago.

The smile she gave him then was brighter than the sun, and warmed him all the same. Their son wriggled in his arms, as if he felt it, too. His mother's brightness that had lit up a monster lost in his own darkness, and convinced him he was a man.

Not just a man, but a good one. For her.

Anything for her.

"Yours," she agreed softly.

And Achilles reckoned that three forevers would not be nearly enough with Valentina.

But he was Achilles Casilieris. Perfection was his passion.

If they needed more forever they'd have it, one way or another.

He had absolutely no doubt.

* * * * *

MILLS & BOON

THE HEART OF ROMANCE

A ROMANCE FOR EVERY READER

MODERN

Prepare to be swept off your feet by sophisticated, sexy and seductive heroes, in some of the world's most glamourous and romantic locations, where power and passion collide.

HISTORICAL

Escape with historical heroes from time gone by. Whether your passion is for wicked Regency Rakes, muscled Vikings or rugged Highlanders, awaken the romance of the past.

MEDICAL

Set your pulse racing with dedicated, delectable doctors in the high-pressure world of medicine, where emotions run high and passion, comfort and love are the best medicine.

True Love

Celebrate true love with tender stories of heartfelt romance, from the rush of falling in love to the joy a new baby can bring, and a focus on the emotional heart of a relationship.

Desire

Indulge in secrets and scandal, intense drama and sizzling hot action with heroes who have it all: wealth, status, good looks…everything but the right woman.

HEROES

The excitement of a gripping thriller, with intense romance at its heart. Resourceful, true-to-life women and strong, fearless men face danger and desire - a killer combination!

To see which titles are coming soon, please visit

millsandboon.co.uk/nextmonth